ROOTS
UNEARTHED

Also By Anne Elizabeth

The Roots Trilogy
A World Within Roots

THE ROOTS TRILOGY
BOOK TWO

ROOTS UNEARTHED

ANNE ELIZABETH

Emily, Hannah, and Sydney,
Thank you for listening to me time and time again as I worked through plot details, figured out where I wanted this story to go, and who I wanted the characters to be. Thank you for the questions you asked and the ideas you gave.
I love you all.

Chapter One

Sweat coated my skin. Releasing my clenched fists, I ripped the sheet off and sat up. Cold air swirled over my body as I leaned forward, cradling my head in my hands. Goosebumps raced across my skin, but I didn't mind. The chill was a welcome balm against the terrors of the night.

As my breathing slowed, I looked up. The torch still burned bright from a sconce set into the wall. Something glinted out of the corner of my eye. A small oil lantern sat on the table. *Kono.* It hadn't been there the night before. I closed my eyes. The torch helped keep the dark at bay. Or was it my fears? No, it was all of it.

Does it even matter?

I slid off the mattress, the rocky floor cool against my bare feet. I opened the door, which creaked as it revealed the darkness beyond. Hesitating, I stepped back and slid my boots on before taking an unused candle and lighting it from the torch on the wall. The flame burst forth, full of energy and life, so unlike the dull glow of the other one. But as soon as I turned on my heel, the flame died.

I stared at it for a moment. *Even a flame dies out eventually.*

Taking the lantern instead, I left the room. The light danced on the walls as I crept along, silent as a wraith. I blended in with the quiet hallways and caverns of the mountain refuge. Not even the cooks were up and about. No comforting scents of breakfast wafted through the corridors.

I stopped when I found myself standing in the awning to the women's sleeping and working quarters. *I used to stay here.* My eyes sought the alcove against the far wall, where I'd slept until two nights prior. *Until Tristan decided I should have privacy.* I leaned my back against the rocky wall and inspected the noisy cavern. Here, it was loud. Here, quiet did not reign, not when the dull thrumming of snores reverberated around the natural amphitheater. I knew Tristan had meant well. But he wouldn't take no for an answer, and I didn't want to tell him the truth. He wanted to show the people how much he cared for me, and this was one small way he could.

But now I'm alone. My breath caught in my throat. *Always alone now.* Adnan was gone. Even Saya had all but disappeared since the day we'd returned from the village. It hurt. I'd slept here with the other women before, but I guess I'd always been alone, in a way.

I glanced over my shoulder the way I'd come, down the twisting passage I knew led to my new little room. It was shut away—shut away from the others, shut away from the comforts of being with the living, and yet it was as lonely as it had been here.

At least here, I knew there were others with me. I sighed. *The dreams hadn't been quite as bad here.* I yawned and rubbed my eyes with the back of my free hand. Exhaustion pulled at the corners of my mind.

Somewhere in the distance, a *plop, plop* of water on stone echoed. I turned away from it and slipped back down the tunnel toward my room, and soon it faded and silence surrounded me. That, and the oppressive blackness pushing against my small, warm light.

My foot caught a rocky protrusion in the floor, and I gasped as I fell forward. The lantern flew out of my hand as I reached out to catch myself. It clanged somewhere in the surrounding darkness. Hard rock met the soft skin of my palms, and I bit my lip from the burning pain. The light was gone. Grimacing, I reached out, but there was nothing. The lantern had fallen to who-knows-where.

Rising to my feet, I stumbled along, one hand feeling along the wall until I felt the wood of my door. Inside the small room, I fumbled for the matches before using one to light my last candle. Lowering the small box to the table, I watched as wax began to pool under the flame. I sat down on the edge of the mattress and lowered myself onto my back. Shadows wavered on the low ceiling, contrasting the rough, uneven patchwork of hewn stone and earth.

A light thud echoed through the small room. I stirred. Again, it came. A quick hiss heralded the door opening. Kono's small, familiar figure stood there, a ready smile on her rosy lips and in her bright eyes. *My maid ... of sorts.* Tristan had assigned her to take care of my needs, something I still wasn't used to, though it was nice to have her company.

"Morning!" she exclaimed, stepping into the small room, her silky hair falling over one shoulder.

"Morning," I mumbled, my heart falling in my chest. I tried pushing away the deadening exhaustion as I sat up.

Her nose wrinkled. "You'd best hurry up and get dressed. Someone arrived during the night, a friend of yours, I believe." Her pale face almost glowed with excitement, reminding me of her niece, Honoka.

A glimmer of hope awoke within me as I leaned forward. "Who is it?"

Kono smiled and winked. "Someone handsome."

"The Unknown is here? He's back?"

"Benkei?" She laughed as she bent over to place some clean clothes on the small table.

I scrambled to my feet, trying to loosen the sheet that had become tangled about my legs. Adnan hadn't even been gone for two weeks, but so much had happened during that time. Tristan had sent him out. Another mission. Another secret. But now ... excitement bubbled within me. *He's back?*

"Yes, Benkei." I fought to keep my voice controlled.

Kono straightened. "Ah, so you know of whom I speak. Yes, he has returned, and if you hurry, you might catch him at breakfast. I saw him headed that way moments ago. Here." Kono handed me the clothes from the table. "This is a new set that Lord Tristan ordered made. They are in the same style as the clothes you wear, but are a little lighter and have a little more stretch to the material. He thought they may be easier for training. And"—she paused and showed me the other set of clothes on the table—"this is for nicer occasions. It is a dress, but has more fabric to allow for movement and is shorter than we usually make them, but it should be comfortable."

I laid a finger on the material and stroked the soft material. "It's green."

"Yes." Kono shrugged and reached out to touch the dress. "Deep green is Lord Tristan's favorite color, and he thought you would look well in it. He's right. It'll bring out the blue of your eyes." Her shoulders rose enthusiastically. "I love how much he cares." Wistfulness strung along her voice.

"Do you have someone?" I asked as I finished dressing and splashed cold water on my face.

Kono shook her head. "No, which is why ..." She searched the rocky walls surrounding us as though she would find the right word there. "Never mind." She smiled, but it never reached her eyes.

I nodded and turned to leave, but she called after me.

"Wait! You look a little—" She hesitated. "Tired."

I glanced in the small mirror over the table. Dark circles surrounded my eyes, and my skin had a pale cast to it. I looked away. "I'm fine."

Kono laid a hand on my arm. "Let me at least do something with your hair. It looks like a rat's nest."

I let her hustle me onto the room's single chair. "I don't care what my hair looks like."

"Lord Tristan might."

I winced as she tore through a tough tangle. *Tristan.* He had been courting me since I'd returned from Mari and Haniel's village. His strong, broad shoulders with his blond hair and blue eyes filled my vision.

"Benkei is a good *friend* of yours?" Kono's white teeth shone as her lips parted. "Serious-looking, but mighty handsome in a rugged sort of way. He seems mysterious."

I frowned. "Yes, he is a good friend."

Kono pulled at my hair again. "There is nothing between you?"

"No!" I blurted out.

She let out a relieved chuckle. "I know you and Lord Tristan are an item, but you were just so excited ..."

"He's just a friend," I assured her. *I like Tristan.* Adnan, with his rugged looks, slipped in and replaced Tristan, but I shook my head. Adnan? No. There was nothing there between us.

"Is he seeing anyone?"

"What?" The word bounced around the small room with a little too much force.

"Does he have a sweetheart?"

My frown deepened.

"I hope I'm not being presumptuous." She inclined her head apologetically.

"I—no," I blubbered, struggling to find the words. "I mean, yes—no, I don't know."

"Perhaps you could introduce me sometime." Kono's cheeks reddened.

I stared at her through the mirror, struggling to find words. "I—"

"There!" She nudged me onto my feet and shooed me out of the room. "Now hurry. Wait, where is your lantern? Never mind, here, take mine."

Nodding my thanks, I left the door open behind me, not bothering to shut it as my feet carried me down the corridor. My boots echoed in the narrow rock confines.

"Otherworlder," a man said, bowing as I passed.

I hardly acknowledged him, my feet swift and sure as they carried me through the tunnel. Tendrils of hair began to fall from the loose bun Kono had secured. I paused to tuck my hair back up as best I could before continuing down a corridor. The smell of food grew stronger as I approached the dining cavern. My heartbeat thrummed within my chest, half from my quick pace and half from my excitement. When I reached the entrance, I stopped just inside. Voices rose and fell in conversation as people ate. Laughter rang through the air. I smiled. It was almost peaceful. No one had taken notice of me. I surveyed the room, searching for a well-known, tall figure.

My heart fell. *He's not here. Is he with Tristan now?* I debated whether to go there next or if I should wait for him to find me. *Would Tristan be upset if I interrupted?*

I tapped the tip of my right boot on the ground.

"Rather unnecessary, yes?"

I whirled around. "Adnan!"

His deep green eyes bore down at me. His lips curved into a smile.

"It's good to see you," I whispered, bowing my head respectfully.

He bobbed his own, and as he looked over me, the smile on his face disappeared. He took a slow step toward me.

"There you both are."

I jumped at the sound of Tristan's voice.

"Good morning," Tristan murmured before brushing his smooth lips against my cheek. He tilted his head as he took in Adnan. "I knew you were back. I waited for you."

"I thought I would get some food first," Adnan replied, his tone holding the slightest hint of ice.

I leaned back from Tristan a little and studied the two men. Adnan had grown distant and emotionless once more. My heartbeat quickened even as my tongue stuck to the roof of my mouth, thick and unresponsive. Anything I could've said receded into the furthest reaches of my mind as I stood there, frozen between the two men.

"Benkei, why not join us for breakfast?" Tristan said, as if nothing had happened. "I am sure you and Juliet have a lot to catch up on."

I looked away from Adnan to the floor, but even there I saw his worn leather boots. Every scuff mark, every scratch etched into the brown leather—

"I will," Adnan grunted.

Tristan led the way to our usual table; his steady stream of conversation was but a muted garble to my ears as we walked along. The voices and sounds of people eating also faded into the background. But I could feel Adnan's lithe form near me as he followed.

In a dreamy blur, I made it to the table, sat, and watched as food was laid in front of me. The smells wafted upward, but I didn't feel hungry. There was no silence, not with Tristan still talking away. Feeling observed, I glanced up to see Adnan sitting across the low table from me, unreadable. But the light in his eyes had gone. My hands fidgeted in my lap as I played with my napkin, folding it repeatedly until the cloth became crinkled and stretched.

Ages seemed to have passed before Tristan rose. He rolled his neck and yawned. "I must return to my work. Later, Juliet, Benkei." He gave my shoulder a gentle squeeze and I swallowed, my throat dry.

I reached for a glass, needing water, needing to quench the aching at the back of my throat, the pressure building within me—

"You haven't been sleeping." Adnan's voice was quiet, confident, no question in his tone. He leaned back against the wall, his hand resting on a drawn-up knee.

"I ... no. Not really."

"But it's more than lack of sleep, isn't it?"

It's everything, I wanted to say. The words danced around my head. *It's the dreams, the faces, the memories ...* I blinked.

"The circles under your eyes, the paleness of your face—those aren't just from a lack of sleep."

"Thanks," I muttered dryly. "So sweet of you to say so."

"What's going on?"

My smile disappeared and I glanced up at the ceiling, my eyes tracing the small hallows in the stone.

Adnan didn't move a muscle as he spoke. "It's Tristan."

I stared at Adnan. "No, it's not him." *Yes, we're courting now ...* But I didn't tell him that.

Adnan raised an eyebrow, and a muscle in his jaw pulsed.

"It's not. It's—"

Something, nothing, everything— What could I say? What should I say?

"It's what?" His voice broke into my reverie.

I sighed. The gleam on his face and his raised eyebrows told me more than words ever could. He saw what I had managed to hide from so many.

Eight days ago. I took a deep breath and pushed the tendrils of hair out of my face. "Did Tristan fill you in on what happened a week ago?"

He shook his head.

Mari.

I blinked, focusing in on Adnan's face, on the stubble growing on his chin and the comforting depths of his—

"Juliet?"

Part of me wanted to tell him. *Why him?* I took him in as he sat there, patient and present. Somehow I knew he would understand, that he would listen. *Let it go ... let it out.* I tapped a finger on my thigh. *I bottle everything up.* My mouth opened and closed.

"Juliet?" Adnan asked again.

I shifted and swallowed. *He's persistent. Like Cam. It's almost been eleven years ... I have to learn to open up.* I licked my lips and pushed past the invisible barrier trying to keep me from speaking. *I'll just tell him the gist of what happened, at least.*

"Did you know Mari?" I asked.

He shrugged.

"She took me under her wing, so to speak. Not the sweetest or most open …" I chuckled. "But direct, and kind in her own way. She left because her niece was soon to give birth, and then we received word of raiders having come down from the north—" I hesitated, taking a deep breath as I drew my thoughts together. "They were heading back north, but their path would go right through the village Mari had gone to." My fingers drummed against the table. "I convinced Tristan to let Haniel, Saya, and I go …" I trailed off as the memories swam to the surface again.

Adnan leaned forward but said nothing as he waited for me to continue. A muscle in his neck pulsed.

I toed the ground with my boot. "When we arrived, it was so silent. I knew something was wrong." The images ran through my mind as though it had been yesterday. "A little boy, no older than ten—he lay in the dirt, staring up at me, his body still and silent. Haniel's parents were next, lying next to one another in their blood, and after that, Mari. But not just her. Her niece, nephew … and the baby." My voice cracked. "They killed the baby. Just a newborn." I stopped. For the first time since that day, tears threatened to come, and my eyes stung. The lump in my throat grew, and I felt like air was hard to come by.

My throat ached. *Don't cry, don't cry, you're stronger than this.* But everything around me began to fade away.

"Come on." Adnan hauled me to my feet. He didn't let go as he hustled me out of the dining room and pulled me down the first empty corridor we came to, down into the darkness until the light dimmed and the shadows enveloped us.

The tears came then, unbidden but persistent, sliding down my cheeks. I shifted, wanting to run away as much as I wanted to stay. "I'm sorry," I mumbled, reaching up to brush away the tears. New ones took their place and fell quickly. *Not now. Why now?* Turning away from Adnan, I took deep breaths, trying to fight it.

Light hands grasped my shoulders and drew me around before arms encircled me, enfolding me in their strength. My face pressed against Adnan's rough jerkin as his chin came down to rest on my head. As I lost myself to grief, sobs wracking my body, Adnan pulled me closer.

The pain grew until it burned with a fever, pouring out from the depths of my numb soul as it started to feel again. Relief took place within my heart and soul as I began to let go.

Adnan rocked me gently, running a hand down the back of my head over and over as he twirled his fingers through my hair. He was warm against me, and soon the sobs slowed. The tears ceased. Nothing occupied my mind in my exhaustion, my energy spent. Peace. I felt more peaceful than I had in a long time.

Drained. It's as though all that had been pent up within me has been released. I sniffed, shifting my head away from the wet spot on Adnan's jerkin, but he didn't relinquish his hold. He was my lifeline, and I clutched him as though he now helped to share the weight I'd been carrying.

They'd been right. Tristan was right. It didn't help to hide my pain. It had only made it worse. *I didn't listen to those who had just tried to help.* I sniffed again, wishing I had a tissue. The warmth of Adnan's arms encompassed me.

Why him? Confusion knotted in my mind, and my body felt hotter as my mind raced. *Why couldn't I tell Tristan? Or Saya?* The knot grew. Saya didn't trust him. But I just opened myself up to him and told him everything. Why him? The question pounded inside my head, but the answer seemed to stay just out of reach. I relaxed my grip on his back and breathed in, the familiar, musty scent of rain a comfort. We remained like that, neither of us feeling like breaking the silence.

After a few minutes, Adnan murmured against my ear, "Have you talked to Tristan?"

"No."

He stiffened against me. "Why?"

"He has enough to deal with, and—and for some reason, the words would never come."

The muscles in Adnan's arms locked. I leaned back, but he tightened his grasp around me, keeping me from looking up into his face. *What does he not want me to see?*

"What is it?" I whispered.

In the briefest of moments, his body relaxed. "And Saya?"

"I haven't seen her since that day."

"She's staying away because that's how she's dealing with it all."

"But I needed her, and she wouldn't come!" I protested. "Telling you … I feel lighter and more at peace now. The memories are still there, but they don't feel as heavy as before."

"Saya is here." He tapped a single, slender finger over my heart. "You both have a bond forged by all you've seen and done together. That is not easy to break."

I frowned and looked up at him. "But—"

"You're bitter," Adnan acknowledged. "Don't let that also weigh on you. And don't keep your emotions locked in as you have done this past week."

"I have to be strong. Everyone here has something they're dealing with."

"It doesn't mean that it is easier to hide yourself away and lock everything in."

A wry grin crossed my face, and I leaned back again. This time, he let me go. I stared up at him. "Are you going to get on my case?"

Adnan stepped away, his arms hanging at his sides. "For what?"

"For going off when I promised you I wouldn't?"

"Should I?"

"I don't know. I almost wish I'd never persisted, that Tristan hadn't let me go. It was … I don't know. I don't even remember giving much thought to the decision."

Adnan took my hand. "It was instinctual. You weren't thinking of yourself, per usual. He shouldn't have let you go."

"It wasn't his decision to make. It was mine," I shot back, squaring my shoulders.

"Do you regret it?"

I stared into his green eyes, which darkened with emotion, and shifted on my feet. Sighing, I felt my muscles relax. "I don't know. Maybe."

"Don't dwell on it."

My eyebrows drew together. "On what?"

"On regret. You have to go on living, no matter what your decisions in the past led to. Think of them, learn from them, but move on."

A nervous chuckle escaped my lips. "It's hard."

"Yes, but you're strong, stronger than you realize."

A warmth simmered in my core, driving away the last of the tightness that had gripped my throat. "How long are you staying this time?"

"I leave tonight."

I blinked, instantly tense. "Already? But you just got back."

"Juliet, we're fighting a war." Adnan ran a hand through his shaggy hair. "You know that now more than ever. Think of the choices you've made because of it."

I bit my lip. *He's right. I've been wallowing in my own pain, hurt ... I'm not incapable. I can help. I can't be passive anymore.* "Please be safe," I pleaded, placing the distractions from my mind aside. "Don't do anything rash."

"Me?" His lips split into a smirk. "Would I ever?"

I pushed against his chest and couldn't help the laugh bubbling out of my throat. "I suppose we both make decisions that prove to be rash. Me more than you." *And I'm probably about to make more.* The flame that had grown within me after Mari's death had been stoked again. It was time to try to change things.

Adnan laid a hand on my shoulder and squeezed it. "Remember what I said. I know more than most what it's like to live with the consequences of decisions that didn't turn out the way I wanted them to, and even worse, for the ones I made knowing what the consequences would be. You have a good heart. You're loyal. No one is perfect. And I think we both know the decision you made in going was the right one."

I sighed and folded my arms across my chest. He'd said I wasn't thinking of myself. Yet I couldn't shake the feeling that all I'd done the past week since the village massacre was think of myself.

"I have to go." Adnan leaned one shoulder against the wall. "I don't know how much you know, but the Uprising is struggling. If we don't gain ground—and quickly—it'll soon be over, and we won't be coming out on the other side."

"I know a little, but not much," I admitted. "Tristan doesn't tell me a whole lot." A note of bitterness underlined the admission. *Then again, neither do you.* I folded my arms across my chest. "But why you?"

"Why any of us?" he asked, studying the tip of his boot. With a sigh, he continued, "I'll say this much. The things Tristan has me doing require a certain level of expertise, and I'm the best suited—"

"For the job," I finished for him. "I know."

"And," Adnan added with a frown, "I don't want to share the details with you, but I do want you to know that he has me spying most of the time. I'm not sure what the next mission will be. Tristan wants to debrief me still and discuss the plans, so I may not see you again before I leave."

"So this is goodbye, then." The goodbyes felt like they'd never end. Except with Mari, they had. *I'll never forget you,* I thought. *But your death won't be in vain.* I craned my head to gaze up at Adnan.

"Juliet, I—" He stopped and drew in a ragged breath before straightening and taking a step back. "Until the next time. Take care of yourself." A stiff bow and he was gone, his silhouette fading into the shadow of the tunnel beyond.

Chapter Two

The guard straightened as I neared. He nodded to me. "My lady. He's alone, but I think he would welcome your presence. Go on in."

"Thank you," I murmured as I passed him. A click alerted me to the guard shutting the door behind me.

Tristan stood, unaware of my presence, his eyebrows furrowed as he glared down at the papers and scrolls scattered across a round table.

I opened my lips to speak but stopped as I watched him rub a hand over his jaw. The bright light from the torches ringing the room accentuated the creases in the corners of his eyes and their dark circles.

I cleared my throat. Tristan's head shot up. His frown eased away, and his lips tilted upward as his usual jovial face returned. "Juliet, I did not hear you come in."

I joined him at the table. "The guard let me in."

Tristan squeezed my hand briefly and rolled his neck.

I peered down at the papers scattered across the table. A word caught my eye, written in tight script at the bottom of a document. I craned to see more. *Natsirt La*—Tristan shuffled the papers into a neat pile, hiding the rest of the phrase.

"What is *Natsirt*?" I asked, struggling to form the strange word.

Tristan shrugged and finished placing the papers in a neat pile. "Nothing much. Just a place that I wanted to note." He sighed and sat down on a cushion.

I sat down next to him. "What's wrong? You look more exhausted than usual."

He smiled, the lines around his eyes deepening. "Nothing to trouble you with."

"Talk to me, please. Maybe I can help."

Tristan chuckled. "Do you not already have enough to concern yourself with? It has been barely a week since ... I will not burden you with more concerns that are not yours."

"Haven't they become mine, though?"

Tristan raised an eyebrow.

"I've been in the middle of this war ever since I decided to pursue the raiders and rescue the townspeople. Everything was set in motion even before Saya, the Unknown, and I rescued the people from Umi no Machi. The two men who took me were acting on the king's orders, then your men, and now my agreeing to help the Uprising even though initially I had no choice—" I paused and gathered my thoughts. "I'm here to help."

Tristan's eyes flashed with a pain I knew he held, but I had never seen it so clearly. His jaw locked. "It is everything," he whispered, his voice husky. "Everything! Winter is approaching, food is scarce, and the king has upped the stakes with how many patrols are out." His tone grew more forceful. "There is a rumor that he is drafting village boys into his army. Boys, Juliet. Nine, ten, eleven years of age."

I recoiled. "What?"

"His army indeed grows larger, but the young are being taken from their families, fed lies, and forced into a life of conscription." He stood up and began to pace. "You have no idea what they are going through. And it is not just them. My kingdom is suffering."

Silence reigned for a long moment.

"No," I began, "you're right. I don't know, because I've not experienced that, but it doesn't mean I don't care. Where did the rumor come from?" I stood and followed him to the table. Tristan looked down at a map unfurled over the surface. A map I hadn't noticed because of the papers that had been covering it.

Tristan hesitated before turning his blue eyes back on me. "I have spies embedded in his court. This was in the latest report, not two hours ago."

Two hours ago. "You have spies in his court?"

"Not many, but yes. It is not enough, though. We cannot seem to get the edge over him. I cannot. We are fighting a losing war."

I leaned forward. "Tristan, what was in the report?"

A thundercloud formed over his features. "There was—" He stopped.

"Go on," I probed, curious.

"One of the spies, she made a mistake. Her body was discovered a week ago. News travels fast, and by the end of the day, everyone knew. Killing her was a show of force, a reminder of who is pulling the strings."

"The king killed her? He knew?"

Tristan's silence was answer enough.

"Are you sure it's true?" I pressed, looking for a reason for it not to be, for there to be some mistake. "Do you trust your spies?"

"Juliet." Tristan's voice was gentle. "They would not be there if I did not trust them. The information is solid."

"Did—the Unknown bring you the report?"

"Yes."

My mind whirled. "How has he been doing it? Is he in danger?"

Tristan raised his eyebrows. "You—never mind." He shook his head.

"What?"

"It is nothing."

I folded my arms over my chest. "If it was nothing, Tristan, you wouldn't have begun to say it, and you certainly wouldn't be trying to backtrack now. What do I not know?" Even as the words left my lips, I knew the answer. *A lot. There is a lot I don't know, that I don't understand.*

Tristan groaned and ran a hand through his blond hair. "It is not my place to tell you, Juliet." He stepped forward, but I backed away.

Adnan. Adnan always has secrets, and now Tristan. He's always known something I don't. My shoulders tensed. "What do you mean? What do you know about him?"

Tristan stepped away from me, his green tunic straining across his chest as his back straightened.

"Tristan? What aren't you telling me? What do you know of him? You're the one who calls him Benkei, and—and ..."

"Oniwaka?" Tristan supplied harshly after hesitating. "I also know him now by Adnan, his true name. Which I think you already know."

He knows. What did I say? When did I slip up? Fear filled me. *What will Adnan say?* I blinked. There was so much surrounding Adnan that I didn't know, and yet Tristan seemed to know more than me since the moment we met him. And the legends ... the legends surrounding Adnan, or Oniwaka— *Saya knows them. Saya fears them.*

"Tristan, what do you know about the legends?" I crossed my arms. "Saya mentioned legends surrounding Benkei and, more specifically, Oniwaka, if I remember correctly."

"They are legends," Tristan dismissed.

"I have a feeling they're more than that," I muttered under my breath, not breaking eye contact with him.

Tristan poured himself a cup of tea and sat down again. "Very well," he said with a resigned tone. Adjusting his broad frame, he took a sip of tea before continuing, "I will tell you about the legends, but not right this moment. First, I will answer a little about Adnan in general, and why he is useful."

My throat dry, I took a cup of tea and joined him on the floor cushions.

"He is instrumental in this entire rebellion," Tristan spoke, breaking into my thoughts as he gestured. "The moment he walked into my presence, he became a prominent piece in the uprising. He is renowned, and I do not just mean in this kingdom. Be glad he has chosen to be on our side."

"Chosen?" I echoed. "What do you mean, chosen? This is the right side; he wouldn't consider working for the king."

Tristan set his cup aside. "Are you sure you want to hear more?"

My hands trembled. "I don't understand. What has Adnan done? Who was he before I met him?"

"Who *is* he, do you mean? That is not for me to tell. Juliet, I meant it when I said it was not my place." He pressed his forefinger against my lips. "All I know are rumors, shadows of truths, and I myself do not know what is factual and what is fable."

"What are you saying?"

Tristan sighed. "I am saying that you should be careful. Guard yourself around him. You do not know him. He is a dangerous man."

"What do you know of the legends?" My voice cracked a little on the last word.

A lock of Tristan's hair fell across his cheek, but he didn't move. His breathing quickened. "Where did you first hear of them?"

"Saya."

His fists unclenched. "And what did she tell you?"

"Not much. Enough, though. The legends scare her."

"They scare anyone who knows of them, and we have all grown up with them."

I shifted on my cushion. "I didn't."

"No, no, you did not."

"He wasn't alive then, so the legends can't be about him."

Tristan rubbed his eyes with one hand. "No, the legends did not begin with him. But they encompass him now. He has become them."

I frowned. "I don't understand."

Another sigh hissed through Tristan's parted lips. "No, I know you do not. I ask again, what did Saya tell you?"

I searched my memory. It seemed so long ago since I'd had that conversation with Saya. "She said that darkness surrounds the Unknown because his name has been linked with the legend. And that the stories about Oniwaka are terrible."

"Which are?" Tristan prompted, tilting his head a little.

"I don't fully remember, but something about a man from a temple, and a blacksmith's daughter being raped ... Others say Oniwaka could be the son of a god."

Tristan cleared his throat. "Anything else?"

I stared at him. "That he's killed hundreds."

"Hundreds," Tristan repeated. "I do not know if Adnan has killed that many, but I am sure the number is still high, along with his other feats," he added under a low voice. "Every myth, every legend, begins with a grain of truth. Some contain more and some contain less. But in this case, I think that Adnan, or Oniwaka, as many know him by, has embraced the role he has been given."

"What do you mean?"

"He is becoming—has become—*Oniwaka*. It is who he is. And Juliet, there is nothing you, nor I, nor anyone else can do to change that. He is good for one purpose and one purpose only." His blue eyes were like ice.

To carry out whatever Tristan wants him to. I didn't need Tristan to finish. The answer hung in the air, unspoken. *Adnan has so many secrets. His emotions are almost always locked away.* Time seemed to pause around me. *He won't speak of his past. He won't even deny what is said about him.* I licked my lips. "Why tell me this?"

"Because I care about you," Tristan replied. His jaw locked before he took a breath and opened his mouth. "And because I see you care about him—as a friend—and I think you need to know more about who he really is."

"Is that all?" The question was out before I could stop myself. *Why did I just ask that? What am I looking for?*

Tristan poured himself a glass of water. He offered me some, but I shook my head. "Benkei has his uses," Tristan said. "He's been instrumental in our cause, to getting the dirty things done. He follows my orders. He is reliable in what he does." Tristan's voice deepened as he grew more serious. "Do not take my warnings lightly."

I drummed my fingers on my thigh. "Won't you explain, then? Who is Adnan?"

"Juliet, it is not for me to tell. Oniwaka is a keeper of secrets. He has one foot in the light and one foot in the dark, and sometimes the two mingle more than I would like. But we could not win this without him. I have no man like him."

My head spun. "Tristan—"

"Come, let us speak no more on this. The Unknown, as you call him, is gone. You shall have to wait for your answers. He will not be back for several days. In the meantime, we have work to do." He led me to the door. "I will see you tomorrow, Juliet. Sleep well." He bowed over my hand, kissed it, and the door closed in my face. The guard averted his eyes, but I had seen the question shining in them. There was nothing to do but leave. I knew Tristan wouldn't let me back in. The conversation was over ... for now.

The patter of my boots echoed off the rocky walls. Inky blackness surrounded me, and the small glow from my candle seemed to amplify the conversation we'd just had. *Secrets. Always, I am surrounded by secrets.* The drip of water on stone provided a soothing monotony in the background. *Raping a girl ... killing hundreds ... the offspring of a god ... What kind of man does Adnan have to be to be named after these legends?* I took a deep breath. *Have I been so deceived by him?* I stopped walking. *Adnan has secrets, but don't we all?* I listened to the white noise the water nearby provided. *Tristan knows more about Adnan than I do ... So why do I find it hard to believe him?* And yet, part of me couldn't deny the facts.

"Stupid, stupid, stupid," I hissed. "Who has Adnan tried to deceive?" I gritted my teeth. *He hasn't once tried to lie. Instead, he's avoided or refused to give answers. That isn't deceiving.* My soul felt as heavy as my thoughts. *But then again,* I mused, *is it right? Even if he wasn't deceiving me, he has still kept his secrets, and now he's bearing the cost.* The more Tristan's words slipped through my mind, the more I found myself believing him.

I stepped forward, watching the small glow of the candle. The silence was oppressive. The walls were oppressive. Freedom felt so far away. I longed to be out of this mountain, out in the clean, crisp air, where I could feel the warmth of the sun. Then again, fall was fast disappearing as winter set her claws into the land. Listening to the silence, I was glad for once that there was no one around to disturb my peaceful imagination. There was no one to call upon me, to disturb me with questions or needs, or worse, with statements that led to more inner turmoil.

Chapter Three

"Otherworlder?"

I stirred and looked up from my hot cup of tea, blinking as my eyes focused on a man and woman standing before me. The dining cavern had gone quiet. I sniffed and straightened. Leftover scents of fried eggs and salty seaweed wafted through the air. My stomach growled. I peered around the couple and saw that we were alone, other than a few kitchen staff. I had been so lost in thought over my conversation with Tristan the day before that I hadn't noticed the room was empty. *Must have been sitting here awhile,* I realized.

The woman shifted, glancing at her companion. "Otherworlder?" she asked again.

"Juliet."

"What?"

"Juliet. My name's Juliet." I smiled in what I hoped was an encouraging way.

"Oh." The woman hesitated, and the man stepped forward.

"We wanted to ask you," he began, "is it true you were one of the ones who went and buried those the king massacred at the village?"

"It was bandits from the north, not the king's men," I corrected, standing.

"So it was you!" the woman exclaimed, ignoring my statement. "I'm Gin, and this is my husband, Gen." They both bowed so low that I was afraid they would fall over.

I opened my mouth. "Please, don't—"

"Gen," the man repeated, pointing to himself. "And Gin." He gestured to his wife. "We would like to extend our heartfelt thanks to you for the honor you bestowed on those fallen."

Gin pulled something out that she had been hiding behind her.

My eyes widened as she gave me a shawl-like piece of cloth. "No, please." I held up a hand. "I appreciate your thanks, but you don't need to give me anything."

"But we want to," Gen insisted, nodding to his wife. Gin thrust the cloth into my hands. It was so soft. The lightness of it almost took my breath away.

"Thank you," they said in unison and backed away.

I inclined my own head and watched them depart. The staff continued cleaning in the background, the clink of dishes and sound of laughter echoing about the cavernous room. I wished I'd eaten earlier. I took another sip of tea. As the couple reached the entrance, I saw them bow and let Tristan pass. Haniel followed a few paces behind him. I watched as Tristan made his way over to my table in the corner.

"What are you doing here?" he asked, tracing my cheek with his finger before sitting next to me.

"Just thinking. Did you see what happened?"

He shook his head.

"Gen and Gin gave me this." I held out the material and watched as Tristan felt it.

His eyes widened. "This is beautiful."

I sighed.

"What? Are you disappointed with it?"

"No! It's gorgeous, but they gave it to me out of thanks for what I did at the village."

"Ah." Tristan nodded to Haniel, who backed off and took a seat. I wondered if he could still hear us, but it was hard to tell with his back turned.

Tristan smiled as he regarded me.

"It's not funny. This isn't the first thanks I've received nor the first gift I've been given."

Tristan's grin grew wider. "Oh, Juliet, this is a compliment to you."

"They're wrong, Tristan. I didn't do anything to deserve this. I don't want this."

"Who does not want to be honored?" Tristan asked with a ready smile. "You are too humble, Juliet. You have done amazing things, and you are brave. You may not see that, but everyone who has eyes can. That is part of what attracts everyone to you." He surveyed the empty cavern.

"Are Haniel and Saya being given gifts?"

Tristan continued without answering my question. "They need a symbol, Juliet. You are from another world; you are someone they feel like they can look up to and fight with."

"I am no fighter," I protested. "And you're the one they're supposed to be looking up to."

Tristan sighed. "Juliet, they *did*. Now, they need something—someone—more. They need you."

"I didn't ask for any of this, Tristan."

"Exactly. 'Otherworlder' does have a nice ring to it," Tristan noted with a chuckle.

I poked him hard in the side. "It's Juliet. I haven't done anything noteworthy. I'm just a girl from another earth."

"Exactly—and to these people, that is everything."

I frowned.

His features hardened. "On a more serious note, I have received word, which is why I came to find you." His face darkened, and he raked a hand through his hair.

Dread rose in my chest. The air was stifling, and whereas the scents of leftover eggs, burnt bread, and smoked meat hadn't bothered me before, it now bordered on nauseating.

"What happened?" I whispered.

"It is not bad," he began, but it was clear he chose his words with care. "That is, there is no cause for serious alarm ... yet. I have had word that Adnan was seen in Cruelon's court."

"What? Is that not where you sent him?"

"No, I did not." Tristan spoke slowly, as though needing to make sure I heard each word.

I leaned forward. "Has he been captured?"

Tristan shook his head. "No, he has not been captured, Juliet. By the account, he was there of his own free will, walking about as though he owned the place. My source tells me he seems to be in Cruelon's inner circle."

I wavered, and Tristan gripped my forearm as though to steady me. "No, no!" I wrenched myself out of his grasp. "That's not possible." *Why would he be there of his own accord?*

"It could be wrong, Juliet. But the description matched completely."

"How reliable is your source?"

"Very," Tristan affirmed, watching me.

Dishes continued to clink in the background. My temples throbbed. "I'm sure there's an explanation."

"Juliet, he was supposed to be in the opposite direction, nowhere near Cruelon."

Nowhere near him. What is he up to? "Where is he now?"

"At one of Cruelon's strongholds, a few days' ride away from here. But perhaps he is working on some lead ..." Tristan trailed off. "As you said, there could be a reason why he was there, how he came to be walking around freely. I know there could be—must be."

I closed my eyes, struggling not to panic against the onslaught of unfinished thoughts flying through my brain, all of them clamoring to be heard at once. *Why is he there?* My mind raced for a plausible explanation. There had to be one. My eyes flew open. "When is he supposed to be back?"

"Not for another week." Tristan's gaze searched mine, his own dark and sad.

It had been five days since he left. "He said he would come back," I whispered. He had promised.

"And he probably will," Tristan replied. "He has no idea that we know. He does not know who my sources are, or that I even have some in Cruelon's court. Perhaps he will tell us himself that our plan went awry somehow."

I shook my head at the futile way in which Tristan strove to reassure me. His tone wasn't persuasive. "It doesn't make sense! He's smart. He wouldn't take risks like this, not if he is truly with Cruelon and pretending to be on your side." *Or unless he's—* I shook my head. The rest of the thought remained unfinished.

"I do not know. I cannot think of how he came to be there." Tristan leaned forward, pressing his fingers to his temples. "I cannot think of why he would disobey my orders, how he would get into Cruelon's court, and all without a word of warning. Perhaps you are right. But I cannot afford to be that optimistic, not with all that is at stake here."

Unless ... I hesitated. "Unless he's a double agent." At the look on Tristan's face, I almost wished I hadn't spoken out loud. He didn't need to tell me he had already been thinking along those lines.

"Juliet, I cannot lie. This is serious. But I do not intend to pass judgment until I hear it from his own lips."

My vision blurred. *He has secrets. But this, this is more than that.* I took a deep breath, trying to calm my nerves. "And Saya?"

"I have not told her yet. But I did send word to Drielle, so she probably knows by now."

"Have they seen anything?" My attention was broken as I watched the kitchen staff leave. Now the room was empty but for Tristan, Haniel, and I.

"If they had," Tristan noted, "they would have told me, but now they may look a little more diligently when it comes to *Oniwaka*."

The secrets, the legend ... If a man could kill hundreds, how easy would it be to betray one? I pushed the thoughts away, but the fear remained. "Can I see Saya?"

"If she does not seek you out, then I will send Haniel to escort you there later today." His expression softened. "I have to go now. There is much to be done. Juliet, take it easy and try not to think about all of this. There is nothing you can do about it right now."

"There is an explanation, Tristan. There has to be." But the spark of hope within me dulled as I watched something flicker across his face. *He doesn't agree.*

He left without saying another word. He didn't need to. I stayed standing there, listless and unsure of what to do next. Inhaling, I forced my limbs to move. I walked down the corridors in a daze, making it to my room by sheer muscle memory.

Inside, I paced back and forth, sat down, stood, lay down, and closed my eyes. But I couldn't sleep. I was afraid of what would come.

"Sleep will do you no good," a voice murmured through the open door.

I sat bolt upright. "Haniel."

He folded his arms, cinching the fabric of his robes. "Sleep is where demons come out of hiding." He tilted his head up to look at the ceiling. "And it is no good praying to the gods either. They do not listen. Not anymore." His voice was monotone, as though he cared for nothing.

"That's almost heresy for you to say."

"Is it?" He shrugged. "Depends on who you say it to."

"When did you stop believing?" Even as the question left my lips, I knew the answer. *The village.* Tears threatened to fall.

Haniel stared at me but did not answer.

I stood up. "This is my room, Haniel. What are you doing here?"

Haniel's short, broad frame filled the doorway as he faced me. "Tristan sent me to make sure no one bothers you."

And what about you? I kept the thought locked within. "What about Saya?" I asked instead.

Haniel's small eyes narrowed. "Not yet. Tristan said that she and the seer are busy until later today."

I made to stride past him, but he didn't move. "I'm going on a walk."

Haniel pulled a torch out of the bracket on the wall before moving to the side.

"He will explain when he returns," I stated as I passed Haniel. "There is an explanation."

"Do you plan on wandering aimlessly?" Haniel asked, following me. The light from his handheld torch filled the tunnel and sent my shadow scurrying in front of me. "Don't you do enough of that in your mind?"

I whirled on him. "What do you know? You don't know me at all." My words echoed back at me from the darkness surrounding us.

Haniel regarded me, his face blank. "Don't I?"

"Leave me alone. Please," I added, continuing onward.

When several seconds of silence had passed, I peered over my shoulder to see Haniel still there. His soft footsteps had given no sign of him still following.

He held out his torch. "Do you want it? I can do without. I have spent enough time here, enough time in the darkness ..."

I nodded, taking it from him and watching as he faded into the hall with heavy footsteps. The warmth from the torch created a wave of goosebumps over my skin. I breathed in, smelling the dank coldness of the air. Striding forward, I welcomed the heat spreading across my body from the movement, pushing away the cold pervading the mountain. *In what world is Haniel sent to watch over me?* Even as I pitied him, I also could not shake the unsettled feeling that stole across me anytime he was near.

CHAPTER FOUR

Dipping the cloth into a shallow basin of water, I pressed it against my side, where Boden had slid his knife across my skin weeks before. I gasped as the pain emanated in waves.

A dull thrum of light knuckles on wood pierced the air.

"Kono?" I called. The door opened, but it wasn't Kono. Saya strode through and shut the door behind her. She surveyed me before crossing her thin arms over her chest.

"It's been a while," I greeted.

Saya's petite shoulders rose in an almost imperceptible shrug. Her eyes flicked down to my side. "How is it?"

"Better than before, though the pain has been worse since—" I broke off and swallowed. *Since that day I helped bury dozens of people.*

Saya frowned, and she shook her head. "Have you seen a healer?"

"No, I'm sure it's fine. There is no pus, and it's closed. It's just an angry red line now. I haven't even been bandaging it lately."

Saya stepped forward. "Can I see?"

I lifted the damp cloth away as Saya approached.

Her cool fingers pressed against my right side. "It's healing. Your ribs, on the other hand, still have some bruising. Do they hurt?"

"Yes."

She stepped back and handed me my tunic. "The break is not fully healed. You need to be careful."

Some of my anger dissipated as I heard the concern lacing her words.

I regarded her as she sat on the mat. "You heard?"

"Drielle told me."

"I don't believe it. I can't." *That's not the truth.* I bit my lip.

"You can't ignore the possibility."

"But Saya, after all we've been through? Why betray us now?" *Still, I play the defender. What do I truly think?*

She shrugged.

"You think he's a traitor."

"I'm not saying that for sure." She hesitated, and her brown eyes flashed with pent-up emotion. "But what do we really know of him? Seems like the more we know, the more questions we have."

"He's from your town."

"Yes and no. He lives there, remember? But he is not one of us. Just as you are not."

"You agree with Tristan," I replied, unable to keep a note of bitterness from creeping into my voice.

"Juliet! It's not a matter of sides. Did Tristan say Shizukana is a traitor?"

"Not in so many words," I admitted. "He said there could be an explanation."

"So it's more your own doubts, then," Saya noted, her voice quieter now.

My lips parted. *My own? Are they just mine?* My mind raced. "Not just mine. You know Tristan has his, just as you have yours. It was obvious he had them. He even said as much when he said it was suspicious."

"I think he's right to not put his faith in someone like Shizukana, given his reputation," Saya replied. "And especially when so many lives depend on it."

"It doesn't matter," I exclaimed. "You think there is a ring of truth to it, and Tristan thinks so as well."

"So do you." She watched as I rose and poured myself a glass of water with the pitcher on the table. "Your name for him fits him more than any of us quite realized, especially now."

"What?" I asked, my hands trembling as I picked the glass up.

"The Unknown. We know nothing about him. No one really does, it seems."

"And that makes him guilty?"

Saya blinked. "That's not what I'm saying. Do you think I want this?" Her jaw clenched, the challenge unmistakable. "You used to speak more." The challenge in her tone had waned.

I shrugged. "Did I?"

Saya's eyes softened. "You never seemed at a loss for words. Now, you are much quieter."

Each word felt like a barb. "How would you know?" I blurted out. "You're never around."

Saya whispered, "Perhaps we're both a little different now."

I strode forward and crossed my arms over my chest, staring down at her. "I'm still me."

Saya stood up. "People change, Juliet. I can see the changes in you, even if you don't." She walked to the door, hesitated, and swiveled to face me. Her eyes had darkened, and for the first time I noticed the dark patches underneath and the lines at the corners. "It's how we change that matters, and who we become in the process." She stopped at the door. Raising a clenched fist, she turned and breathed in and out until she stood, small and vulnerable, before me. "I'm sorry."

"Me too," I admitted. "Do you want to sit?"

She nodded and sat down again. "You were right, you know." She let the words hang in the still air. "I haven't been around. I'm sorry for that, I really am." Her gaze rose to meet mine.

"I assumed you were here because of Tristan."

"No. It wasn't him."

I raised an eyebrow.

"It was Adnan."

I reeled back. "What?"

"He pressured me into coming. And he was right. I haven't been a good friend to you, and I'm sorry for that. It's been easier to dive into my work, to distract myself with all I've been doing with the seer, instead of doing the hard thing and being a friend to you." Saya hesitated. "And not just that, but letting you be my friend in return. Will you forgive me?"

Adnan. He told her to come. It conflicted with everything Tristan had said. *Adnan cares.* Even though I still didn't know what to believe, I felt a small bubble of warmth at the thought of what he had done.

"Juliet?"

I looked at Saya. "Yes, I do forgive you." And I meant it. All the anger, the hurt, the pain washed away, and was replaced with joy. I had a friend again.

Someone who reminded me in so many ways of my childhood friend, Cam, but who wasn't her all at the same time. It had been so long since I'd seen her. I cleared my throat. "How is training going? Have you had any visions?"

Saya's eyes began to shine. "Yes."

"It didn't seem like you wanted to answer that question. Are they about me?" I joked.

Saya didn't answer.

The smile disappeared from my face. "Saya?"

"I have had a vision about you. Two, actually."

"Were you not going to tell me about them?"

"That can be dangerous. You of all people know how a vision can look one way and mean something else entirely."

I remembered the vision she spoke of. She'd seen us returning to Umi no Machi without the townspeople, assuming we'd failed. But we had succeeded, and through unforeseen circumstances, were returning separately. The vision had been true to what she had seen, yet the interpretation was wrong.

"I remember, Saya. What did you see?"

"Don't tell anyone what I'm about to tell you," Saya said. "I mean it, Juliet. No one."

I nodded.

"The first one, you were in the mountains, with bare cherry blossom trees surrounding you."

When I realized Saya wasn't going to say anything further, I asked, "That's it?"

"You looked sad. Sadder than I've ever seen you. And thinner."

I inhaled. "Okay." I didn't know how to respond to that. "And the second vision?"

"I saw you with two people—I think they were your parents," she whispered.

I reeled back, my jaw dropping. "What?"

"You watched them from somewhere they couldn't see you, as if you didn't want them to see you. You were heartbroken. It was almost like there was no place for you there anymore."

A dry chuckle escaped me. "That doesn't make sense. Of course there is a place for me. I'm their daughter. What else did you see?"

"That's it." Saya trembled. Drawing up her knees and laying her chin on them, she said, "I don't know where you were in the first vision, and in the second, I just got the feeling of so much sadness and of you realizing you didn't belong."

"They're just visions," I blurted out, but deep down, I wondered how much was true. "We don't even know when they'll come to pass, if they do."

Saya nodded, but the truth hung in the air between us. The visions would come to pass. And it wouldn't be long before they did.

She stood up. "Juliet—"

"Can we talk a little later?" I asked, fighting to keep my emotions in check. "I think I need a little time."

"Of course," Saya whispered. "I'll come back later." Her footsteps faded, leaving me alone.

I sat down on the mattress, feeling unsure and exposed. Blackness filled the open doorway. *So dark. It's always so dark here.* I lay back. I knew sleep would not come, but at least the same fear that usually lurked behind my eyelids was absent. The ever-pressing dread, my heart drumming quick and fast, and the eerie calm stealing over my body in waves, as that of the quiet before the raging storm—all of it was gone. In its place was an overwhelming cloud of anxiety, yet a lack of thoughts. As though the two went hand in hand, when often they did not.

I rolled over, watching the shadows on the wall flicker from the candle behind me. Turning, I stared. Even the flame threatened to go out as it burned lower, and yet it continued on, small and strong. I tried not to think of how many more hours would pass before the new day dawned.

Saya's visions were confusing, the second more so. *Why would I not belong?* I faced the wall again, tracing the crevices with a finger.

Someone cleared their throat.

I rolled over and sat up.

"I'm sorry, my lady, it's just me—Kono."

"Kono, what is it?"

"I know it's late, but I thought I would check on you, and I saw the door was open. Is everything all right?"

"Yes."

She rocked on the balls of her feet. "Are you sure?"

I forced myself to smile. "Yes, I'm tired, is all."

"You haven't been sleeping much," she noted. "Your eyes, they look tired, and it shows in how you carry yourself too."

I blinked and straightened my shoulders and back. "You should get some sleep yourself. I'll see you in the morning."

"And so should you." She clapped a hand over her mouth. "I'm sorry, my lady—"

I pushed my hair out of my face. "It's all right, Kono." I sighed. "Sometimes sleep won't come no matter how much you wish for it. But for me, I don't want it. Because when sleep comes, so do the nightmares. And I'd rather deal with the lack of sleep than face those."

"Does any of this have to do with Benkei leaving?"

I turned my head to look at her.

She took a step into the room. "You seem sadder than usual, more weighed down. I thought you cared for Tristan?" Her words pierced me like a dagger.

"Too many questions, Kono." I closed my eyes, listening to the echo of water dripping somewhere down the corridor. When I heard the click of the door closing, I knew she'd gone.

❧ ⚘ ❧

I couldn't tell if I'd slept or not when the knock came. Weariness filled my limbs, and my eyes felt heavy and sleep-deprived. How long had it been since Kono left?

Heaving myself to my feet, I went to the door and opened it. I blinked against the brightness of the torch and took in Tristan standing there, with Haniel close behind him, also holding a torch.

"Tristan." I started, reaching up to run a hand through my hair. *I must look awful.* "What are you doing here?"

"I need to talk to you."

Freezing in the act of straightening my tunic, I asked, "What's happened?"

A troubled smile crossed his face, and he raised an eyebrow. "Why do I feel like every time you see me you have grown to assume something is wrong?"

"Because lately it has. Is it different this time?"

"No." He sighed. "Come with me."

I grabbed my belt, cinching it around my waist as I followed him. Haniel fell in a few feet behind me. "It's been a long time since we've gone this way," I murmured, recognizing the route. *The mountainside viewpoint. It's been so long.*

"You have not been without me?"

I shook my head. "No."

Tristan glanced at me. "I thought you would have."

I shrugged, and silence fell between us. Part of me wanted to ask him why he thought I would've gone. The heavier tread of Tristan's and Haniel's boots clanked against the stone beneath our feet. Tristan looked at me again out of the corner of his eyes.

"What is it?" I asked.

"Just wait. We are almost there."

I tried to ignore the knot growing in the pit of my stomach. Dim light appeared in the distance, signaling the end of the tunnel as we neared the opening. Dawn bathed the ledge in her shallow light. I breathed in the fresh, crisp air, shivering as a biting wind cut into my skin.

"Looks like rain," Tristan noted. "We will not stay out here long, but I figured it might be best if we came here, given the circumstances. Is it too cold? I should have had you bring your cloak."

I shook my head. "I just want to know what's going on."

Tristan stood near the edge of the ledge and placed his hands on his hips. "I wanted Saya to be here, but she could not make it. I will talk to her later," he added, almost as an afterthought.

I stared at his back before following his gaze. In the distance, a thin sheen of rain lent a dull haze to the landscape. The lake beyond looked gray and cold. Snow covered the sides of the mountain around us and up above.

"Juliet."

My head lowered as my eyes rose to find his.

"You have come into the middle of all of this," Tristan began, ignoring the cold wind beating against us. His voice rose. "In a way, I suppose you have had it easier than many of us, not having to deal with the hardships and lessons we faced in the beginning. They were too awful for words." He rolled his shoulders back. "It has escalated even more since then, but we have become stronger. Our numbers have grown, our supporters have grown, yet our supplies have dwindled. If we do not strike soon, we will not have another chance. This is our last stronghold, and the more who flock to our banner, the larger the chance of us being found." Tristan's voice deepened. "Now, with the possibility of Adnan being a traitor, things grow more ... unpredictable."

The knot in my stomach grew larger. My hands clenched into fists at my side.

Tristan stepped forward and grasped my shoulders. "It is time, Juliet. We can wait no longer. It becomes more dangerous with each day that passes. We have a few spies embedded in the court, and we will use them."

"Are you still sure you trust them?" I asked.

Tristan blinked. "What?"

I glanced over his shoulder at the approaching rain. "Do you trust them? If they're willing to turn on their king, why wouldn't they turn on you?"

"In war, there are no sureties. Chances must be taken, loyalties tested."

"I thought you didn't want an all-out war." I inhaled, trying to keep the fear from rising within me. "Is that what you're planning?"

Tristan moved his thumb in small circles on my arm. "No, we would not survive the day. The raids will begin tomorrow, in the cities, in the towns, and on the supply trains. They will be hit hard. For the nobles, panic; for the people, hope. We will do whatever we have to, but sacrifices will be made." Tristan let go of my shoulders and strode to the edge of the balcony, his back to me. "Juliet, Mari was not the first, and she will not be the last, especially the longer this goes on." He turned, a wildfire burning in his eyes.

"Is it all worth it?" I asked, leaning my head back as I thought. Above us, stormy clouds billowed across the vanishing blue sky. They whirled, faster and faster, as the wind picked up. "All the lives, the bloodshed, the heartache?"

"For freedom? Yes," Tristan affirmed. "I want my kingdom back!" The fire within him flared brighter. "For my people, I must have it back. I am Tristan Gorvenal, of the house of Gorvenal. My family has held the throne for generations, and I will not stop until it is mine."

I blinked, and a light drop of water landed on my nose. *Held the throne for generations ... I will not stop until it's mine.* Tristan's words repeated in my mind. *Will not stop. Tristan Gorvenal. Gorvenal. Something is missing here. Something about that name. But what?* I fought to remember. There was some memory just there, at the tip of my fingers, but I couldn't place it. My head began to ache as I strove to remember.

"I will conquer them and take back what is mine."

Startled, I pushed away the confusing thoughts.

His voice dripped with disdain. "The gods shall not help them, no matter how hard they pray."

"Do you not believe as the others here do?"

Tristan laughed. "No, for they do not listen to our prayers. I gave up on them long ago. Do I shock you?"

I shrugged, unable to look at the darkness marring his face. "No, I don't pray, much less to multiple gods. I don't believe in the gods your people do."

"In what do you believe, then, Juliet Barrows?"

The scent of musty dirt entered my nostrils as I breathed in. "I don't know."

"Everyone believes in something."

"I believe in loyalty, honor, trust ..." I trailed off at the amused look on his face.

"They can deceive you," Tristan explained with a half-smile. "People can, and always will, deceive you."

"Are you saying you don't trust others?"

He shook his head once. "No, but I am saying I do not let them in easily, nor do I give my trust easily. I have been deceived by too many. And so many lives rely on me."

A soft flake landed on my nose. I squinted at the sky. The light rain had turned into snow drifting down. *Snow.*

I shivered and wrapped my arms around myself for some semblance of warmth. "What, or who, do you believe in, then?"

Tristan's eyes went blank.

Had he not expected me to ask that? Has he ever been asked?

"We should go. You are shivering."

"Tristan—"

He strode to the entrance back into the mountain and turned sideways to let me pass. I hesitated a moment before entering the tunnel.

"Let me know what I can do to help," I whispered as I passed by him. Haniel, waiting inside, lit Tristan's torch with his own and handed it to him.

"Haniel, please escort Juliet back to her quarters."

"Tristan, wait." My lips felt puffy with cold. "What of Adnan? What are you planning?"

"He was—is—key to everything."

"So you still have hope it isn't what it looks like?"

His broad shoulders rose in a shrug. "I hope to ..." He paused. "I hope to the *gods* it is not true." A sardonic smile twisted his lips. "We need him." Tristan began walking down the hallway.

My teeth chattered as I followed. "Give him time to get back here and explain, please."

"I will. *If* he returns. Go with Haniel. You are shivering."

"Six more days," I breathed.

Tristan's response was as harsh as the rock encompassing us. "Six days."

CHAPTER FIVE

My eyes fluttered open. Musty air filled my lungs as I sat up and leaned back against the wall. Memories of the nightmares that had plagued me throughout the night still danced on the fringe of my mind. Adnan was an enigma. Tristan was persuasive. Saya was … Saya. I wanted to listen to each one. But in my dreams, I felt I had to make a decision. And not just about Adnan, but about what I was meant to do in this rebellion. I groaned with frustration. *Why can't this all be easier?* Focusing on taking deep breaths to calm my racing heart, I realized that this time, the nightmares hadn't been about the village—about Mari.

Feeling eyes on me, I looked up to see Kono peeking her head around the door.

"Kono," I said, glad to see another person.

She entered the room, a bright smile on her face. "Oh, you are awake. I didn't knock because I wasn't sure if you were awake yet."

I yawned and swung my feet over onto the floor. "What time is it?"

"Very early. The sun is not up yet, but it will be soon, and the birds will be singing."

I cocked an eyebrow at her and grinned. "How would you know? You can't see or hear them."

"I just know," she answered with a ready smile. "When you are ready, Lord Tristan has sent for you."

Tense, I reached for my boots. "Do you know what it's about?" I asked as I pulled them on. My hands trembled.

Kono knelt in front of me and began lacing the boots up. "Haniel said it is urgent," she replied carefully. "That is all I know."

I stared down at her head full of brown, almost black hair. It took everything I had not to jump up before she was done.

She sat back on her heels and watched me with round eyes. "There is no rush."

"Yes, there is," I snapped. *The last time Tristan summoned me like this, I had to go bury Mari.* I bit my lip and left the room, ignoring the hurt look on Kono's face.

The candle threatened to go out as I strode along the familiar passageway. *What could have happened?* Dread clutched at me with clinging fingers as my mind whirred with possibilities. *It must be about Adnan.* But it hadn't been a week yet, so he wasn't due back. *Did he return early?*

There. My pace didn't change as I neared Tristan's makeshift council room. The guard at the door had enough time to nod before I flung it open. Tristan's head shot up, and my heart quickened as I took in the dark circles underneath his eyes. His clothes were wrinkled, and his hair stood in disarray. His councilors stood about him and stared at me, their expressions hidden as usual.

I clutched at the hem of my tunic. "Kono said you wanted to talk?"

A vein pulsed in Tristan's neck. I waited as his councilors filed out and the door closed behind them. Tristan looked down at the table and gestured questioningly at the tea there.

"No thanks." I had no appetite, nor did I feel thirsty. I just wanted to know what was going on. Approaching him, I waited with my nerves on high alert for him to begin speaking. But nothing came. "Did you sleep at all?" I asked, staring at the weariness filling Tristan's face and body.

He shook his head.

"What happened?"

With a sigh, he gestured to a cushion. "Will you sit down?"

"I think I'd prefer to stand."

"All right." He looked at me then, really looked, for the first time since I'd entered the small, cold room.

My heart raced in my chest, a wild drumming beat. It was so quiet. Too quiet. "Tristan," I whispered. "What *happened*?" I blinked and swallowed. *Is it Adnan? Is it him?*

"It is you."

His words hit me like a crack of thunder.

"*What*?" I couldn't make sense of them. *What about me? What have I done?*

Tristan sighed again and raised his arm. "Are you sure you do not want to sit?"

I nodded and followed suit as he sat on a cushion.

"Juliet," he began, "you know that I thought you would be instrumental to the Uprising—"

"I thought that was Adnan." I took a deep breath and brushed my hair out of my face. "Sorry."

Ignoring my outburst, Tristan continued, "I know I did not give you an option when I had you brought here, or at least, not much of an option. But I think you feel differently about our cause, at least in the past couple of weeks." He paused, and I knew he was trying to avoid mentioning the village and Mari. Running his fingers through his hair, he left his blond locks standing every which way. "I think you are the key, Juliet. At one point, I would have felt differently about all of this than I do now." A hoarse chuckle escaped his lips. "But I believe it is the way it must be. Fate is a hard thing to fight. And I have to accept that—this."

I want to help. I want to do something. But how am I the key? Bewildered, I folded my hands together in my lap. "What are you talking about? I don't understand."

Tristan's complexion darkened. "If you were to be captured by Cruelon, you would be close to him." His voice was slow, careful. "He has made it no secret that he seeks you. He sees you as a prize." Tristan looked me in the eye, then. "It would be the perfect way for you to spy for us, for you to find a way to bring about his downfall."

I blinked. A numbness stole over me as silence fell. *Downfall. Cruelon. Close to the king. A prize.* As Tristan's words sunk in, I inhaled. "What?"

A pang of hurt streaked through Tristan's gaze. He licked his lips. "Cruelon would keep you as he does a pet. You will see everything, hear everything, be anywhere you wish. You will be close enough to see the chinks in his armor, to see the weaknesses we cannot. You will be the one to destroy him."

My lips opened and closed, but no words came out. *You will see, will be, will be …* His words echoed in my mind. *He's already decided that I'm going.* The room blurred.

"Juliet?"

I blinked. "Do I even have a choice?" I couldn't ignore the other little voice on my shoulder. *Be the hero the people see in you.*

"Yes!" Tristan exclaimed. "Of course you do."

"Then why are you speaking as though it's already decided, as though I *am* going to do this?"

"I am sorry," Tristan apologized, anger sparking in his tone and the set of his jaw. "I should not have spoken like that."

"Yeah, you shouldn't have," I replied. But part of me knew I was being harsher than I should.

"Just listen?" Tristan asked, calmer now.

"Cruelon will kill me." He'd wanted me alive when Boden and the other man had taken me, but for what reason? Maybe they wouldn't kill me ...

"No, I do not think he will," Tristan reassured. "Remember, he captured you, not fatally harmed, remember? Those two men he sent were not to harm you—"

"But they did," I interrupted.

"Yes, but I do not think they were supposed to. If Cruelon was going to kill you, why did he not just send assassins? He wants you. We can use that to our advantage."

We can use you. The unspoken words hung in the air between us.

No, no, no. This can't be happening. I laughed. "This is crazy."

"Maybe," Tristan admitted. "You do not have to go. You do not have to do this."

"Really?" I raised an eyebrow.

"Yes!" Tristan exclaimed, leaning forward. "I—" He hesitated. "I do not want you to go."

I shook my head, sending my hair flying. "Then why ask me?"

Tristan looked down at his lap.

"Tristan, I'm confused." I laughed incredulously. "First, you seem like you want me to go and have already planned it all out, and then you switch to being reluctant and not sure about the whole thing. Which is it?"

Tristan ran his hands through his hair again. "I thought this would go better, differently, I do not know. Juliet, this could work."

He ignored my question. What is his game here? "Why do you need me if Adnan is already in Cruelon's inner circle?" *And why is he in Cruelon's inner circle? He hates Cruelon.*

Tristan's voice broke my train of thought. "Because I do not know if he is to be trusted. I trust you. And besides, it was against my orders."

Part of my frustration slipped away. Pieces began to fall into place. *He cares about me. But he also cares about the Uprising. He's torn.* I felt myself softening even more.

"If Adnan is there and he is a traitor, wouldn't he figure out what we're up to? Why send me before you even know whether he is to be trusted?"

"I doubt he will still be at Cruelon's court. He is due back here soon." Tristan cocked his head to the side. "Maybe I am wrong, but I think if he is working for both sides, he is not going to stay there longer than necessary. Besides, time is short. Cruelon knows Benkei's worth, and he is too valuable to keep near rather than sending him out." Tristan took a deep breath. "Much like I have been doing."

I swallowed, my throat tight with the tension filling the air. "What are you going to do when he returns?"

Tristan regarded me cautiously, as if debating how much to tell me. "I am not sure," he admitted.

"Will you tell me when you do?"

He hesitated. "Yes," he agreed, his shoulders slumping a little with a resigned air.

I nodded and played with the end of my hair. "What about me?"

Tristan exhaled, and his voice took on a grave tone. "I trust you. You are perceptive, and while I do not think you always put the pieces together—"

My lips parted to protest, but Tristan held up a hand.

"You do notice details. You have a good memory, and you are strong. Juliet, just think about it. Give it some time. It is hard, but it is a possibility."

Anger rose in me at the thought of becoming a spy and purposefully letting Cruelon capture me. "I can't believe you would ask this of me. Was this your plan all along? To work your way into my affections and then ask me to be a sacrifice to your—your blasted cause?" The words flew out of my mouth.

"You are beautiful when you are on fire." He smiled, but it didn't reach past his lips.

"You are a—a—argh!" I rose and paced the floor.

"That was bad timing," he admitted, talking a little louder as my boots clicked against the floor. He rose and strode up to me, hands spread placatingly. He grabbed my elbows in his grip, but I jerked away. *Stop touching me!* I wanted to scream it out, but the words wouldn't come.

I stilled in front of him. "You realize what you ask of me? To willingly give myself up to someone with no scruples, to be a captive to one whom I have been running away from for months? It doesn't make sense. What could I learn that those disguised as servants have not? Unless ..." My mind raced with Tristan's earlier words. *"You could get close enough to get to the chinks in his armor, to see the weakness he hides ..."*

"You want me to kill him."

A gleam entered Tristan's eyes.

My breath caught in my throat. *I was right. That is what he wants.* Ignoring the shaking of my hands, I clenched them at my sides. *He wants Cruelon off the throne. Of course he does; I already knew that, but not by me.*

"You could make it possible." His voice barely rose above a whisper. "You could make all this possible without more bloodshed."

Without more bloodshed. What if I can do something? What if I can keep more people from dying? I couldn't do anything to save Mari—or Eddie. My eyes grew damp with emotion, but I quickly blinked it away.

Tristan continued, "The person I have left in Cruelon's court, she is reliable. I would trust her with my life. If you go, she will know you are there. She will look out for you and be the point person between you and me."

His words slipped in through one ear, but I couldn't get my mind off the idea Tristan had planted inside of me. "*I* kill him?" I repeated, frozen.

Tristan groaned. "Yes? Maybe? I do not know for sure yet. Our hope is that you could get us close enough that we—I—can do it. I want him to fall by my hand, but yours could be the one that brings that about."

"What do you mean, *our*?" I folded my arms.

"The councilors and Drielle."

"So this isn't just you?"

He shook his head. "It was not even my idea. But I cannot argue against the reasons behind their thought process."

My mind jumped to Saya. *Does she know something?* "What does Drielle have to do with this?" The councilors, I understood, but Drielle?

"She had a vision."

My eyes widened.

"Saya did as well," he added before I could interrupt. "Drielle believes that her vision and Saya's vision show that your going should happen. She is confident that this will work."

"This is her idea."

"Initially, yes." Tristan gripped my elbows, and this time I let him. "I cannot ignore the seers. Visions are not something to ignore."

"And Saya?"

Tristan's hands were gentle, and he applied a little pressure. "Would it help to talk to them?"

I nodded.

"I'll arrange it. And soon."

"I'm no spy," I whispered. "Your sources would be better for this than me."

"They die before they can get close enough."

I laughed, the bitterness ringing through the enclosed room. "Am I to be just another pawn, then?"

"No!" Tristan exclaimed, letting go of me. "No, but what would you have me do? I am stuck, Juliet! I have nothing else up my sleeve. We are losing this battle and we have hardly begun. Cruelon has more guards around him than ever before; terror grows in the land as he leaves it bereft of what little protection there had been. Adnan is no longer here ..." Tristan's gaze slid past me to study the wall, and his foot began tapping a quiet rhythm on the floor.

There is more. I crossed my arms. "What haven't you told me? What was in the visions?"

"Saya's vision was fleeting glimpses, but she and Drielle are certain. You went to Cruelon's court, and soon. She saw your journey, saw the snow still draped over the ground, the skies still gray and stormy from winter. She saw you, dressed in fine silk dresses and mingling with Cruelon's courtiers."

Saya. She told Tristan, but not me. My mind didn't register Tristan's slow approach. *Secrets are everywhere.*

"Her vision could change everything, Juliet." Tristan's voice was soft now. "I cannot, and will not, force you to go."

"What about Drielle's vision?"

"Hers was similar. She saw you with the king, she saw you with my spy, and she saw what she thinks is a possibility of a world with Cruelon gone."

"Thinks?" I couldn't keep the incredulity out of my voice.

"*Believes,*" Tristan amended.

I stamped my feet, trying to stop the shivering and the goosebumps rising on my skin. "This is crazy." I crossed my arms and stared up at him. "Think of what you ask."

His brows furrowed. "I know. This is the last thing I want, believe me." The pain etched into his face was unbearable to see.

He's put this all on me. Tears sprang to my eyes. "And if I don't go?"

"Then we will keep trying. There will be many deaths on both sides, and I do not know what the outcome will be, but we will not give up."

The idea of making a difference burned a slow hole through me. "Rumor has it Cruelon hardly lets anyone get close to him." I stared at the floor as I thought. "His guards are some of the best fighters in the kingdom. The plan sounds almost too easy, too perfect."

Tristan stepped forward, his movements slow and careful, but he didn't say anything.

"How come you hadn't told me sooner?" An ache grew in the pit of my stomach. *Why hasn't Saya?*

"The other visions, they were different. Just snatches, nothing concrete, nothing we felt like we could act on. I was not going to put your life in danger over a whim."

I hesitated. "Why didn't Saya tell me herself?"

Tristan sat on the edge of the table. "She is afraid of influencing your decision one way or another."

"That's her reason?" I spat.

Tristan hesitated. "I ordered her not to say a word to you," he confessed. "But—"

"Why?"

"Because I wanted to be the one to speak to you. This was for me to say, not her. But I am going to have them both speak with you."

I grasped at an invisible tether, needing something to hold me back, to hold the anger filling me back.

"It is a plan that I think may work, Juliet. I pray this will be the king's downfall, that it will end this Uprising."

"All of these are only suspicions, though," I began. "You say I will be in the king's inner circle, but what if he locks me away, never to be seen again? You can never be sure of a person's actions."

"It is possible," Tristan allowed. "It is as I told you: risks must be taken. Everything is a risk, whether you go or whether you stay. If you choose not to go, I do not blame you." He hesitated and licked his lips. "If you wish to leave, try to return to your home, I will let you go."

"And give up everything you have accomplished? Give me up?"

"Yes, Juliet. I don't think of this as giving you up. And I planned all this out with Drielle and with my councilors. I planned it out *because* I love you."

What? Love? I struggled against the lump in my throat. A dry chuckle escaped my lips, dying away before it had even started. *He loves me?*

"If you decide to go, we can talk about the details. Or if you would prefer to know them in order to make a decision, I will tell you. Juliet." Tristan stepped closer. "I thought through the details. I did not just rush blindly into this, and I am not asking you to go without a plan. I know you do not love me yet."

I had to strain to hear Tristan's voice.

"You care, but you do not love. Perhaps you will someday. I know we cannot think of a future together while under Cruelon, not a happy future. Drielle believes this is the way forward. She believes you will survive this."

I couldn't move, couldn't speak. *He's talking for me. Does he know my heart better than I do?* So many emotions tore through me. The air felt stifling, and it grew harder to breathe.

"I hope for a better future," Tristan voiced with longing. "I cannot bear the thought of asking you to do this, but I have to, for my people, for us."

The room felt even smaller than it had been before.

Tristan approached and stopped in front of me. His finger traced my cheek. "Take your time. Think about this. Later today, we can talk with Drielle and Saya." He fell silent, waiting.

I stared at the floor. *I can't talk to Adnan. What would he say? Does it even matter right now?* A faint noise from somewhere in the corridor seeped through the door into the room. It faded as quickly as it had come.

"Adnan is still with Cruelon?" I asked again, as though hoping for a different answer. "Have you had more news?"

"Last I heard, yes." Tristan shrugged his broad shoulders. "Juliet, there are still two days before he is to return."

I studied the wrinkles in his tunic. *This might be my chance. The people look up to me. Tristan trusts me. Can I live up to my desire to help?* A war raged within my heart and mind. *I can do something about this.* I remembered Saya's vision of me dressed in finery, surrounded by cherry blossoms. What if that vision was another sign? The ember burned hotter and brighter.

"I'll do it." The words came out before I could think. *What have I done?* My hands trembled.

"You will?" Tristan repeated. The question seemed to echo in the room.

I couldn't speak, couldn't open my eyes, couldn't do anything. My brain wasn't working, wasn't sending the right signals to my body. My mouth opened and closed, but no sound came out.

"You can do this, Juliet." Tristan wrapped his arms around me and pulled me close. "I believe in you."

He was warm, but I felt rigid in his clasp.

What have I done?

CHAPTER SIX

I stood outside of the door to Tristan's small council chamber. I knew Tristan, Saya, and Drielle waited inside. It had been a few hours since I'd agreed to infiltrate Cruelon's court, but my hands still trembled and my heart raced. I had trained with Sensei since then to fight off the pent-up nerves, but now the door seemed to stare through me. The soft hum of voices inside pressed against me.

The guard nearby cleared his throat, breaking my focus. "Is everything all right?" he asked, giving me a small, uncertain smile.

"Yes." I breathed in and out. *Calm down.* I reached out a hand but never touched the handle. *You can do this. Remember Mari, remember Eddie, remember the cruelty ...*

"Otherworlder?" The guard stepped in front of me and laid his own hand on the handle. "May I?"

I nodded and squared my shoulders. Stepping through, I felt the walls of the council room close in around me, suffocating, leaving me with nothing. The babble of voices quieted in an instant. A half dozen faces turned to stare at me. The click of the door closing behind me was the only sound in the silence. It wasn't just Tristan and the seers; his two advisors and Haniel were also in attendance.

I licked my lips and rocked a little on the balls of my feet.

Tristan put down the paper he was holding and smiled. "Juliet." He approached and took my arm, leading me to the table. The advisors shuffled aside to make room. Saya met my gaze and Drielle inclined her head to me, their faces inscrutable.

Is that a seer for you? I wondered, still feeling as though I saw everything through a blurred haze. *No, the advisors too. Everyone is staring at me. I can't tell what they're thinking.*

"Juliet."

I jumped a little as Tristan spoke my name.

"I filled everyone in on your decision." He hesitated, and I realized he was trying to judge whether I'd changed my mind in the hours that had passed.

I nodded, feeling a little more relaxed as I listened to his melodic voice.

"Drielle and Saya are going to fill you in on what they have interpreted. They can also answer any questions you have."

I nodded again and flicked my gaze toward the two seers. Drielle's face softened the slightest as she looked at me.

Tristan let go of my hand and turned. "Come, let us sit," he instructed, sitting on a cushion. "We all have a lot to discuss."

Long robes rustled as everyone sat in a rough circle on the floor. Even through the cushion, I felt the cold of the rock floor seep up. I took the warm cup of tea Saya offered with a murmur of thanks.

Tristan's shoulder brushed mine as he shifted. "Juliet, first off, after talking, the councilors and I think you should leave in three days."

I blinked. *Three days.* Those words hit me like a hammer. That wasn't much time.

"I know that is not much time," Tristan continued as though he'd read my mind. "But we think all preparations can be made in that time, and there is no point in waiting too long."

"What about the Unknown?" I asked, looking at each person there in turn. Only Saya's eyes flickered with surprise.

"He's due back in two days," one of the councilors, a short man with a gravelly voice, answered. "It gives him a little time to return and for us to learn more about his activities, but not so long that we waste this opportunity."

"I don't understand," I admitted. "Why does waiting waste time?"

Tristan cleared his throat. "It is not that it wastes time," he clarified. "First, Benkei has never been late. He always arrives right on time, so if he does not show up in two days, something has happened." He held up a hand as I opened my lips to speak. "It does not prove anything. It just means that something has happened, and we cannot afford to wait indefinitely." Tristan squeezed my shoulder. "I meant it when I said the Uprising is desperate."

"May I?" asked the other councilor. "Otherworlder, I am Shoto, and that is Kuro. I don't know how much Tristan has told you, but he is right. We *are* in dire straits. We don't have as many men as the king, nor are they trained as well. The black guard, while small compared to the king's army, is deadly. We lost a few back in the underground caves, and we've had some who have not returned from fetching supplies over the past couple of weeks. Not only that, but the king's men grow ever closer in trying to find our hideout, and he has blocked much of our supply train. As of now, we do not have enough food to feed everyone this winter, and we don't have a way of getting more."

I turned to face Tristan. "It's that bad?"

Weariness settled over his shoulders as they slumped. "Yes, that, and now we only have one contact in Cruelon's court. If she is found out ..." He shrugged. "The councilors and Drielle think now is the time. We cannot wait any longer."

I blew out the breath I'd been holding. "All right then. What's the plan?" I hoped my tone sounded brighter and more confident than I felt. I avoided looking at Saya and Tristan, knowing if anyone was going to see past my façade, it would be them.

Kuro's gravelly voice answered, "There is a patrol that has been sighted a few leagues from here. We've been keeping an eye on them, so it would be easy for them to be the ones to 'find' you. Our thought is to send Haniel and two others with you until you are close to the patrol, upon which our men will watch to make sure the patrol takes you with them." Kuro's eyes narrowed. "We don't believe there is any danger for you in this part of the plan, given that we know the king wants you alive."

"Haniel and the two men we send will follow you to make sure you arrive safely at Cruelon's mountain fortress," Tristan interjected.

A small bubble of warmth blossomed within me, gentler than the smoldering fire in the pit of my stomach. *He's trying to watch after me.* Another sliver of doubt dissipated. "What about when I get there?" My words hung in the air. I looked between Tristan and his councilors.

"That is where things get a little complicated," Tristan admitted with a frown, the lines on his face deepening.

I glanced down at my untouched cup of tea. It was cold now. I set it down on the floor.

"In my vision," Drielle began, her voice filling the room, "you were at Cruelon's court quite a while. Long enough that the snows blanketing the ground soon melted away, and the cherry blossom trees bloomed."

"Which is when?" I asked, turning to Tristan.

He ran a hand through his hair. "Early blooms would be February."

I almost knocked over my cup. "*February*?"

"Juliet," Saya said in her soft way. She placed a hand on my arm, forcing me to look at her. "It is a long time, but Drielle and I both have seen enough that we believe you are meant to do something. We don't know what that is, but we think you're meant to go. You're the prize he seeks after, the prize he wants above all others, finally in his grasp." She laughed, but it was bitter. "This is going to be difficult, harder than anything you've faced yet. You must know what you're getting into and want to get through it for yourself and for us. If you don't, you won't be strong enough. You *have* to be strong enough."

"Which leads us to the next point," Tristan interjected. He clasped his hands in front of him as he thought. "It is going to be difficult. I do not think anyone here can tell you otherwise. There are things that can happen that the seers cannot foresee."

I stared at each face in turn: Tristan, serious and somber; Haniel, studying; Kuro, unreadable; Shoto, hopeful; Drielle, matter of fact; and Saya, gentle and encouraging. I listened to the soft breaths filling the air from the six people watching me. *Do they think I will change my mind? Should I?* I fingered the soft pants encasing my legs, stared down at the tunic I wore, and traced a finger along the belt. *These were made by women who have dedicated themselves to the Uprising. These were made for me. Am I strong enough for what's coming?* I knew I would go. It didn't feel like a choice anymore. I had made my decision.

Feeling a soft touch, I peered up at Saya, who leaned forward, her dark hair falling around her pale face. "Am I strong enough?" I whispered, knowing the others could hear, but the question was for Saya alone.

"I believe you're strong enough to overcome what will come your way. I'm not saying it won't be easy. The gods know I wish I could go with you. We've done so much, you and I. We've been through so much. We have a bond, one forged through traveling together for weeks, rescuing friends and neighbors—that's not so easily broken, no matter what is thrown in our path." She paused.

Adnan said the same thing. He knew we had a bond. But this time, I would be alone. Adnan had left. Saya would stay behind.

"I believe in my visions, Juliet." Her voice rang with the strength of her conviction. "I believe that even though we can't see all that will happen, the gods are with us, and they will be with you."

Drielle cleared her throat, bringing everyone's attention to her. "We are the Ryujin," she reminded us all. "We are the people of the sea. It has been a long time since that has been true." She looked at each one of us with her soulful brown eyes. "With the king's downfall, it will be true again. We will again live up to our ancestor's heritage. We will again be Ryujin, more than just a name."

Tristan respectfully inclined his head to Drielle before returning his attention to me. "Juliet, you are going to have to think a lot on your feet. The person we have embedded in the court, she is trustworthy, but it is difficult even for her to get word to me. She will be the one you will send messages through, as well as receive them, but I cannot tell you for sure how often that can or will be. And I am not sure how easy it will be for you to talk with her. I already sent word so she expects you, so you do not have to worry about seeking her out."

My head began to hurt. "What's her name?"

"Kin," Kuro answered. "She is one of the servants. Any information you learn that is pertinent to the king's weaknesses and our rebellion, you will pass to her. Kin will get it to us one way or another." He steepled his fingers together. "You will have to be creative, Otherworlder. You will need to insert yourself in situations you may not want to."

I swallowed, my throat dry.

"You can do this," Saya encouraged. "I saw you in my visions. You looked like one of them. You wore fine dresses, you *fit in*—you got close to Cruelon." She rose to her knees as her excitement grew.

"All of this is fine and good, but we still need to discuss what the Otherworlder's true purpose is," Shoto murmured. Silence fell. Saya sat back on her heels with a jolt.

Tristan waved a hand for him to continue.

"Otherworlder, there is one plan, and it is simple. Your goal is to bring about Cruelon's downfall. Along the way, you will communicate anything of interest to Kin, who will find a way to report back to us." Shoto stared into my eyes. "But you must find a way to kill Cruelon."

I gasped. My heart hammered in my chest. *It's not just Tristan. It's not just a hope.* The plan was for me to kill the king. It felt like there was no time to think. A surreal bubble enveloped me as though I watched through a lens, seeing only what the lens let me, hearing only what filtered through, distant and unapproachable. No one spoke, but they didn't have to. The room echoed with Shoto's words, loud and clear in my own mind. *Kill Cruelon. Kill the king.* The voice whispered over and over. My voice.

"Juliet," Tristan began, leaning forward with a beseeching tilt to his face, "it is easy to see your doubts, but even if I could not, I would know because I would feel the same." His hand balled into a fist. "You are sacrificing yourself for a cause in a world that you were not born into. You are an alien passing through, someone not of this world but a passerby here for a time, whether short or long. These people are not your people, and our causes are not yours. But the choice is yours. It has always been yours, and you committed yourself. You agreed to risk all for the sake of my people, for Benkei's sake, for Saya's ..." He took a deep breath. "You do not have to accept the customs of my world, of my country, nor do I force you to do anything against your will. I cannot lie and say I do not wish for you to do this, as you are the one person Cruelon will not kill the instant he sees you—but I also cannot be certain of what will happen while you are there. Cruelon must die for those he has murdered, for Mari, for her family, for all the heartache he has caused them, and all the countless others he has hurt in some way. You are a part of that, Juliet. You are a piece in a puzzle you cannot begin to comprehend. You have more strength and resilience in you than you will ever know. I can see it, and so can others, but you must begin to see it for yourself if you will ever survive in the world you have entered." He hesitated a moment before taking my hand and rubbing his thumb across my skin.

"How am I supposed to do this?" My voice cracked. I picked up the cup of cold tea from the floor and swallowed it down.

"At first we thought poison," Kuro answered with a shrug. "But then we realized that it would be very difficult for you to have access to his food." He glanced at Saya and Drielle. "Now the plan is for you to kill him with a dagger."

I gulped, my mind frantic. Afraid I would break the cup, I set it down and clasped my hands together in my lap. "Where would I get a dagger?"

Tristan stroked the scruff on his chin and cheeks. "We are not sure," he admitted. "You will have to figure out how to get the actual weapon. But we think this has the best chance of working, and we know, based off of the visions Drielle and Saya have had, that you will get close enough to Cruelon to have the opportunity." His tone quieted. "How do you feel about all of this?"

How do I feel? I knew I may have killed before. I didn't know if Ribahn had survived. I'd seen the blood on my hands. *But to assassinate?* A cold fear threatened to stifle the fire that had been smoldering within me. I closed my eyes. Mari's body, and those of her family, seeped into view, as clear as the day I'd helped bury them. Cruelon was responsible. My fingers twisted the hem of my tunic into a wrinkled mess. The villagers from Umi no Machi, the northern raiders rampaging through the country, and the deaths of Tristan's family—

He must pay. The fire burned, fighting against the fear. My eyes fluttered open. "I'll do what's necessary."

Tristan smiled, but it never reached his eyes. "Good."

⚜ ⚜

The flurry of activity and endless meetings, plans, preparations, and arguments bowled me to the ground over the next couple of days. There was hardly time to think. When I wasn't in yet another meeting, I was training, and when I wasn't training, I was eating or trying to sleep. Kuro and Shoto were obsessive. They were like a pair of vultures vying to be heard with their piece of advice, thoughts, and opinions, driving one another away in their ecstasy and excitement.

When they became too overwhelming, Tristan would wave a hand and Haniel would maneuver them away to give me a brief respite before they were back within minutes. Their arms flapped as they approached for the kill. It was sickening. And it reminded me all too much of what I was expected to do, what I had to do to bring peace to the land.

On the third day, dawn came and went, but there was no sign of it, not this deep within the caverns. I sat on my mattress, my cloak wrapped around me, my tea held between my hands, too hot to drink.

I yawned, and my vision blurred as I realized Adnan hadn't returned. He was a day late. And today was the day when I would leave. Thoughts of Adnan danced on the fringes of my mind, teasing me, prodding me, scolding me for this decision ... and then I'd see his rare smile, shedding the years from his face. But it always disappeared. And now he looked cold, calculating, and unreachable.

"Juliet."

I blinked and focused on Saya, who stood in front of me. A sheen shone in her eyes. She flung herself forward and gave me a hug, her arms wrapping around me. "May the gods be with you," she whispered. "I know they are watching. And thank you." She turned as though to leave.

"Wait, Saya," I blurted out. "Please."

She stopped and stared at me, eyebrows raised.

"You think this will work?"

"Yes." Her voice shook. "I do."

I needed to hear it again, just one more time. My throat constricted as I watched her slip away. When she reached the door, she looked back over her shoulder and smiled, but sadness twinged it, and I saw a tear glisten on her cheek.

"I will see you again, my friend." She bowed low.

I waved a hand, my throat too constricted for words. I closed my eyes and leaned against the wall, the cold rock digging into my back. But I didn't shy away. The pain was an anchor that held me back from being lost.

Feeling someone's gaze on me, I turned around. Tristan stood in front of me, watching, brows furrowed. But he pulled himself together and gave me a weary smile. "It is time."

I raised my chin. "Another adventure."

He gestured for me to join him and led the way into the corridor outside.

"Any word?" I asked, protected next to his broad frame.

Tristan glanced over at me. "No, nothing from him. Be prepared, in case you do see him at Cruelon's court. Remember, we do not know whether we can trust him or not." He rolled his neck. "He has been seen with the king's private guard, out in the countryside."

"But he hasn't sent word."

Tristan shook his head.

"My lady! My lord!" Kono exclaimed, bounding toward us. "Everything is ready." She tried hiding her concern for me behind a bright smile, but she failed. Her eyes also glistened with tears. Everyone's eyes seemed to glisten with tears today. She didn't know the details of what I was about to do, but she knew it was dangerous and that I would be gone for a long time.

"Are you ready?" Tristan asked me as we followed Kono back down the way she'd come.

"Yes."

"Do not do anything rash, Juliet, or anything that could remotely put you in more danger than you will already be in. Be smart and keep your head."

A wry grin crossed my lips. "I definitely plan on keeping my head."

Tristan blinked and nudged me. "This is no joking matter."

"Right, sorry," I muttered as the laughter inside me died. I heard the neigh of horses before we rounded the corner and I saw them.

Tristan pulled me to a halt. "Juliet, wait. I love you. Just ... be careful. Take care of yourself. You do not know how much this means to me."

"I'm not doing this for you." I crossed my arms over my chest, pulling my cloak in closer. "I'm doing this because I know it's what I need to do and because I don't see any other way around it. And you're right. I am here now, not in my world. What if I can't ever return? So I'll fight for the life I want here."

"You may not ever return home, but return to me," Tristan murmured. He bowed, and I saw his men watching us over his head.

"They're waiting," I whispered.

Tristan straightened, taking my hand and leading me over to my mount. I didn't say a word as he helped boost me into the saddle. The rustle of leather and the sharp clack of hooves on rock came with our departure. As we left the mountain stronghold, I glanced over my shoulder to see Tristan still standing there, watching. His figure was shorter, broader than Adnan's. His eyes were clearer, his look more wistful, and yet ... *I miss Adnan.* I tried burying the pang in my heart deep down. *How can I miss someone who may be betraying us all?*

I took a deep breath and turned to face the path ahead. Angry clouds hung heavy in the sky, and a biting breeze rustled across the treeless plain. Fall had long since left his mark, and now the harsh and brittle winter fought for control. Her white blanket stretched over the path, masking the sound of the horses' hooves. I inhaled the cold, crisp air and blinked against the surge of dread filling me. *It's time. There's no going back now.*

⚜ ⚜

We saw one another at the same time. *The king's men.* After a moment's hesitation, they spurred their mounts forward. The ground thundered beneath the hooves of their horses as they approached. Clouds of dirt burst up in their wake. I froze, taking in their black clothing and the curved swords hanging by their sides. *The king's guard.* I had heard the stories. *Did Tristan know the patrol would be them?*

A surge of panic overtook me. My heart raced, and fear drove me into a sprint. My bag slapped against my back with each stride. It didn't matter how fast I could run. They had horses; I didn't. Once they'd spotted the patrol, Haniel and the two men who had accompanied me this far had taken my horse and left to watch from a small knoll at a distance. I didn't have to pretend to be frightened. *This is the plan,* I reminded myself as I ran. Sweat beaded on my skin.

The riders clamored around me, horses dancing, men shouting, saddles creaking, and scabbards clanking. The dank smell of sweat, dirt, and horse filled my nostrils. Unknown faces leered at me.

"Identify yourself!" a man shouted.

I took a deep breath. *Now. Say it.* My mouth felt dry. "My name is Juliet Barrows. I am the Otherworlder."

Eyebrows shot up and jaws dropped. Murmurs encircled me, some fearful, others full of curiosity and wariness.

"Keep a tight formation!" the man spoke again. "*You*—take her."

Within seconds, I was herded onto a horse behind one of the men.

I gritted my teeth against the ache in my side as they set a grueling pace. *Perhaps I should ask for a reward,* I thought. *I am, after all, the one who turned myself in.* I tried to relax with the gait of the horse. *Step one, complete.* I didn't look back. I knew I wouldn't see Haniel and the men hiding, but I knew they'd be following, and for now, at least, I would have someone watching over me. In a few days, I would meet the king. *Help me,* I prayed, hoping someone would hear my plea.

Chapter Seven

On the morning of my fourth day in captivity, as the first scarlet rays of dawn spread over the horizon, the fortress came into view. Against a backdrop of rocky mountains, the tops already thick with a blanket of snow, the fortress rose high over tall stone walls. My jaw dropped. The sharp angles were reminiscent of medieval architecture I'd seen in Japan. The mountains contrasted a near-black background to the almost slate-hued foundation of the fortress. Gray and white walls rose high above, forming two buildings, one larger than the other. Here and there, splashes of red marked the sharp archways and peaks forming the roof.

It was not like the ancient castles I was used to seeing in books or in documentaries. We obviously didn't have them back home in Washington either. No, these belonged to other, older parts of the world. I peered at the fortress, feeling as though I had seen something similar in a Japanese film before. *This is ... grand.* Behind the fortress, a lake spread, its waters a clear blue. I tightened my grip around the man in front of me as the pace picked up. Dust kicked up under hooves as we thundered across the plains. Cherry blossom trees dotted the outside the fortress walls, branches bare and brown.

As the day brightened, so did the gray stone the fortress sat upon. The walls and buildings loomed over us as we approached, and my eyes widened as I took in the aged cracks spreading across the walls. I tilted my head back, looking up at the men manning the battlements. In front of us, the gates creaked open and a dozen guards stood in two lines, watching us pass with careful scrutiny. With a clink of chains and a soft thud, the tall gate closed behind us. Bolts slid across.

And so it begins. I am shut in.

Now that we were here, adrenaline surged through me anew. I looked about me, my heart pounding. The wide courtyard split off at both sides, one side leading to another adjacent building, also tall, but shorter than the main keep. The other led to several smaller buildings. The scent of hay, dirt, ale, and stale sweat filled my nostrils.

"This castle has stood as the stronghold of the kingdom for centuries," the guard in front of me whispered as we rode in a slow file toward the main keep. Those we passed stopped their work. Servants watched with bowed heads, their eyes averted, and more black-clad men with familiar curved swords seemed to watch over everything.

How different compared to last time. I craned my head to see over the man's shoulder. *I'm being treated far better.*

"The palace is in another part of the country," the guard continued. "If you ever see that, you'll be in for a treat."

Maybe someday, but not with Cruelon on the throne.

I felt the man stiffen as he pulled the horse to a halt. He slid off and waited, his face now stoic and serious again.

Breathe. Just breathe. I inhaled and swung my leg over the horse, mindful of those watching. Gritting my teeth, I jumped down, letting my knees relax as my feet hit the ground.

A small, pudgy man walked up to us. His jowls rippled as he shook his head, peering up at me as I shifted on my feet. "What do we have here?" His voice was high and reedy.

No one answered.

"I asked a *question*," he tutted, folding his arms over his stomach.

"It's the Otherworlder, sir."

The little man took a tottering step back. "What?"

"The Otherworlder, Master Hiito."

Master Hiito jerked his head in a quick nod, his double chin widening as he gaped.

Someone's hand came down on my shoulder and shoved me to the ground. My knees jarred as I hit the hard dirt, and pain flared through my still-healing ribcage. Hiito took a step forward and peered into my eyes. He laughed, a high, squeaky sound that reverberated through my head. A throbbing began behind my temples.

"Well, well, well. You certainly don't look like much, do you? Taisa?"

The man, whom I had come to know as the leader of the patrol who had captured me, jumped. "Sir?"

"Why do you think *she*"—a finger jabbed toward my chin—"is the Otherworlder?" Hiito tapped his foot, folding his arms as he waited.

"She—she said so, sir." The taisa's face hardened, and a muscle pulsed in his neck.

"She did, did she?" Hiito pointed a finger in my direction. "Who are you?" His eyes bulged even larger and rounder.

"Juliet Barrows, the one *you* know as the Otherworlder." My tongue flicked out to moisten my dry lips. "I'm the one your king has been searching for weeks, the one who your men failed to bring back."

Hiito's smile fell, then grew brighter, and a greedy light entered his eyes. "You must be her," he whispered. "For who would dare identify herself as such? Who would dare come here like this?" He tapped a pudgy finger against his double chin. "Taisa! Escort her inside. The rest of you"—he fluttered his hand in the air at the patrol—"dismissed!"

The taisa approached, and his hand closed around my forearm in a vice. While stern and a little rough, I was just glad he wasn't the same taisa who had captured me a few weeks before, when I had made my escape from Ribahn. *No, as long as I followed orders, these men were gentler.*

He hauled me to my feet. Blood rushed to my head, and my vision began to swim again. The stench of horse dung and unwashed bodies grew muted as a blurred filter settled over my senses. The jingle of harnesses, the clanking of weapons, and the rough shouts of men faded away as we trudged up the well-worn steps into the darkened keep.

The double doors closed behind us with a thud, shutting out the morning light. I blinked as my vision adjusted to the dim interior, my feet walking without thought as the taisa's hand propelled me forward, down a wide, windowless corridor.

Farther into the dark depths, I thought.

Master Hiito continued to drone as we walked, but his high-pitched voice made little sense to my tired brain. We entered an even smaller corridor, as though it was one that went in between the rooms held within the inner keep. I stumbled as we went up a stairwell to the second floor of the keep, my feet struggling to keep my balance. Hiito glanced back every so often as though afraid that I would disappear, but I never did. His excitement grew with my fear.

My arm ached where the taisa's fingers gripped me like iron. Light streamed through a square archway. My feet tripped over one another as the taisa jerked me toward the entrance. Dark wood panels highlighted the opening. I blinked as my vision cleared. *Why am I dizzy?* The question was but a whisper in my head. I swallowed, my throat dry. As we passed into the well-lit room, adrenaline coursed through my veins, driving away the lightheadedness. Narrow tables lined the room, displaying beautiful vases and urns with detailed paintings. Hiito and the taisa passed them as though the pieces of art weren't even there. Our footsteps echoed on the wood floor, reminiscent of something ancient and old.

We walked through another archway into another hall, then turned right sharply. A patch of sunlight streamed through the plain window, highlighting the dust particles swirling through the air. It was but a small feeling of warmth in the barren, cold corridor. Goosebumps raced across my skin, and the fine hairs stood up straight on my arms.

"Let us in!" Hiito called to a guard as we approached a set of double doors. "Quickly!"

"Sir." The man gave a short bow before stepping aside to allow us entrance. We crossed the low threshold into a room grander in appearance than I'd expected. My eyes widened as I took in the thick tapestries covering the walls, trying to imagine how vibrant the colors would have been when it was made. Another vase decorated a side table.

The pudgy man crossed to yet another set of doors. "Wait here," he ordered without turning.

The taisa shoved me onto a rich, brocaded chair. A cloud of dust swirled up from the material. I waved a hand in front of my face, fighting the urge to sneeze. I shifted, my tired limbs aching as the rigid material forced me into a stiff posture. *What an awful chair. No wonder everyone here sits on cushions.*

I stared about the room, realizing that for all the stone the fortress sat upon, the majority of the interior was built with wood of varying hues and grains. I stared at the dark, imposing wooden doors. *It's time. And this time, I cannot run.* At any moment they would open, and I would begin playing the part that could end my life. I clasped my hands in my lap, struggling to keep them from trembling. How had it come to this?

One of the doors opened a crack. Blood drained from my face and my heart pounded, but I was beyond the reach of control. I jumped as Hiito poked his head through.

"Taisa," he snapped. "You're free to go."

"But, sir—"

"Now."

"Sir," the taisa murmured as he bowed and left the room.

"Come." Hiito grinned, his lips gleaming with something wet. "This way. Come, come."

One foot in front of the other, I walked across the room, my boots clicking against the gleaming floor. The room smelled old and musty, like the smell of an old library. It was as if I had stepped back through centuries. History surrounded me. If some adventurous, sad, and lonely music had been playing, one that pulled at the heartstrings, stirring up deep threads of longing inside its avid listeners, it couldn't have been in better timing. My eyes saw nothing but the open square doorway, the man's toothy smile, his eyes narrowing into slits as I neared.

Then I was through.

The door slid shut behind me with a loud bang. I jumped and peered around. It wasn't a large room, but it was dark, cold, and the light that shone through its two large windows was dim. To my right, a low table lay surrounded by cushions. Papers, an inkwell, quill, and what looked like tea sat upon it. I looked to where Hiito approached the empty, black chair on a dais between the windows, my breath catching at the tall figure standing in front of one of the windows. His long, luxurious robes hung with deep red folds, like that of blood.

He turned, his hands clasped behind his back. And his face—it was not an imposing face that now stared at me but a gaunt face, far older than his years, the sharp lines highlighting the straight eyebrows and his thin lips. His face was pale, something in between the coloring of the Ryujin people and that of Tristan's northern ancestry. *A man who doesn't see much sunlight.* My gaze traveled up. His hair, too—brown, but not dark like those here, and not blond either.

"So," he began, his voice icy.

A man used to giving orders and having them followed. My back straightened, and I squared my shoulders. *The voice of a man who brooks no argument.*

"You claim to be the Otherworlder. Interesting."

I remained silent.

"My patrol caught you traveling south, I believe?" His burnt umber eyes, distant and cold, did not leave my own. He didn't blink, but when I didn't answer, his jaw tightened, and a slight flush of anger stained his cheeks.

My heartbeat quickened. *His eyes look like a snake's.* "Yes," I whispered.

Hiito looked back and forth between us. "My lord—"

"Silence!" the king hissed. He took a deep breath and walked to his chair. Sitting down, he steepled his fingers in front of him.

I shifted on my feet.

"Otherworlder," the king murmured, the words rolling around in his mouth. "Am I to believe you? I want to—what a prize, and in the nick of time. It seems too good to be true." His voice was scarcely louder than a whisper, and I found myself leaning forward to hear him. "You do not look like any from our land." His eyes raked my figure, and he stood. Stepping down off the dais, he approached and circled me. "Quite exotic, and not unpleasant to the eyes."

My heart pounded.

"Ah," he purred. "You have some control, or perhaps you like my epithets." He brushed the tips of his long fingers across my cheek. "How do I know that what you say is the truth? Are you truly the one they call Otherworlder?"

My heart pounded in my chest. I wondered how pale my face had become.

"My lord!" squeaked Master Hiito. "What has she to gain by lying?"

"Exactly, Master Hiito. What would she have to gain? But everyone has something to gain. So what is it?"

The room was too quiet.

"Well, Otherworlder? What do you have to gain?"

I licked my lips, hoping my voice wouldn't crack. "Your men were the ones who captured me. Why would I choose to have my freedoms taken away?" As I took a breath, I squared my shoulders and straightened my back.

The king smiled and tapped a long finger on his temple. "Now that, Master Hiito," he said as he turned, "is a good answer. Why would she want to be captured?"

Hiito looked between us with a beady scrutiny.

"Well?" Cruelon snapped.

Hiito jumped and wrung his hands together. "She wouldn't, my lord."

"Exactly." Cruelon strode to his chair and sat down. "Was there anything she brought with her?" the king bit out, breaking the silence.

"Only a pack, my lord."

"Bring it to me."

"Yes, my lord." Master Hiito stepped out and I stood stock-still, watching Cruelon.

He waved a hand in the air. "For your sake, Otherworlder, I hope you speak the truth." He smiled again, but it never reached his eyes. "You have courage. I will give you that. I like a girl with some backbone. They are more amusing that way." He laughed. "You do not hide your emotions very well. Your rebellion and anger shine through your eyes like a beacon." He shook with delight. "It is rather invigorating, but it will not last long."

Shivers raced down my spine.

"Here, here, my lord!" Master Hiito's voice snapped me out of the frozen state I'd fallen into. He held forth the pack I'd had when the patrol had taken me.

"Well?" Cruelon asked. "Open it." He slammed his fist down on the table. I jumped, my heart leaping in my chest. Out of the corner of my eye, I noticed Hiito bouncing on the balls of his feet.

He pulled items out of the pack, mumbling the names of each as he dropped them on the floor, his hands shaking. "Clothes, clothes, water," he babbled. "Nothing else."

Cruelon steepled his fingers together and regarded me.

I wished for a draft of fresh air to alleviate the stillness in the room. Walls surrounded me.

"So," Cruelon asked, breaking my train of thought. "Otherworlder, what is your name?"

"Juliet Barrows." My voice trembled.

"Juliet Barrows." Cruelon swished my name around his mouth as one would wine. With a swift movement, he slid out of the chair and walked toward me with smooth, gliding steps. His red robes swept the floor. He reached up and slid his fingers through my hair. My breath caught in my throat as I forced myself to remain still, my gaze centered on his chest as he stood in front of me.

A dangerous gleam entered the king's eyes, heightening a sort of reddish haze over the whites. "Tell me who you are."

"I am the Otherworlder," I whispered.

"Again."

"I am the Otherworlder." I licked my lips. *What does he want?* I felt like there was something I was missing, something I was supposed to say.

Cruelon stared at me and let his hand fall away. "Your hair shines as golden as a field of wheat. Your eyes are like the ocean amid a roiling storm. Only those from the north look like you." He grasped my shoulders and, with a quick, violent movement, shoved me until my back hit the stone wall.

I gasped as black filled my vision. "Stop!" I shouted, my breath catching.

"What did you say?" Cruelon crooned. "Do you give the orders? I think not. Even if you are not the Otherworlder, it does not matter. You will be of use to me."

It was then I noticed the small red lines running through the white of his eyes. They were redder than normal, as though he hadn't slept in days. I squinted, noticing what looked like a fine powder under his eyes. What was it covering? More sleeplessness?

Cruelon slapped his hand hard against the side of my head. A searing pain spread across my face and neck from the force of his blow. I groaned and reached up to cup my face.

"Master Hiito?" Cruelon asked, reticent.

"Yes, my lord?"

"Bring some food and water for Lady Juliet."

Lady Juliet? I wanted to ask why the title but remained silent.

"Sir?" Hiito squeaked.

"Now!" the king barked.

"Yes, my lord!" Hiito scrambled to fulfill his master's orders.

Cruelon let me go. I slumped against the wall, my lungs starved for air. I watched as Hiito slid one of the two doors open and called to the guard for food and drink to be brought. He toddled back into the room.

"Master Hiito," Cruelon said with a note of amusement. "How long have I been searching for Lady Juliet?"

"Oh, a very long time now." Hiito stared at me. "She evaded your grasp twice—"

"I do not need to know the number," Cruelon reprimanded. He nodded. "But Master Hiito is right; you have evaded me. Did you even know you did so?"

I swallowed and straightened. *Boden and the hooded stranger. They'd taken me, but Adnan rescued me.* We had suspected they'd been working for the king.

"When I ask you a question, you must answer." Cruelon examined his fingernails, but the veiled threat was unmistakable.

"I suspected," I managed. My ribcage flared a little at the memory of Boden slicing his knife through my skin. I rubbed my hands down my skirt to dry the perspiration. *Those wounds healed.*

"Interesting." Cruelon laid his hand in his lap. "Benkei and—"

My lips parted, but I withheld from gasping. *Benkei. Adnan. What?* Thoughts slid through my mind too fast to hold on to. *But it wasn't him. The man in the hooded cloak from that kidnapping wasn't Adnan—just ... looked like him.*

"*Boden*," the king finished, drawing my attention back to him. His eyes bored into me, and I knew he'd seen my reaction. "That little capture and escape was less than desirable. But my men don't believe you escaped on your own, so who helped you?"

Adnan saved me.

"Juliet Barrows," Cruelon uttered, accentuating each word. "A bit of advice: when I ask you a question, not only should you respond immediately, but you should also tell the truth. I don't tolerate lies." His voice filled the room, harsh and imposing.

"My apologies ..." I hesitated.

"My lord, will do," Hiito hissed from where he stood.

"My apologies, my lord," I said, taking a step away from the wall and inclining my head. "A friend rescued me."

"Hmm. Some friend. He may have rescued you, but did he know who he was taking you from? Did he know who he was defying?"

I opened my mouth.

"It doesn't matter," the king continued. "You have been very difficult to find. It makes me wonder what you have been up to since the day you escaped from my men. Where have you been hiding?"

The creak of the door opening saved me from having to come up with a plausible answer. Cruelon watched as a servant entered with his head low, the tray in his hands shaking from his nerves. He left it on another low table and bowed his way out of the room.

"Sit. Eat," Cruelon ordered, gesturing.

Sitting down on the back of my heels, I stared down at the table. Succulent vegetables in sauce, meat shining with glaze, and rice with steam curling up assailed my senses. My stomach growled.

"It's not poisoned." Cruelon laughed. "Go ahead, eat."

Silence fell as I began to eat. The food was good, but Master Hiito and Cruelon watched my every move. My skin prickled. It didn't take long before the food began to taste like ash. I drank some water, enjoying a little relief as it flowed down my tight throat.

"Come here." Cruelon's eyes gleamed. He waited until I approached. "I want you to swear your fealty to me, Juliet Barrows, also known as the Otherworlder."

I nodded.

"Do you know what that means?"

I glanced from Hiito back to Cruelon. "You want my loyalty?"

"Yes, but more than that, I want you to join my court. Be a lady of the court."

Triumph filled my heart. *This is what we want. This is what I need.* I could feel the elements of Tristan's plan falling into place. *I was captured, I haven't been killed, and now I'm being placed in the exact position we want.*

But I can't seem too eager. I cleared my throat and bowed. "My lord, forgive me if I seem a little reluctant. What does it mean to be a lady of the court? What happens if I don't swear fealty?"

Cruelon lips thinned as he grinned. "It is the highest honor a woman in this land can hold. You will follow where I go, and you will have fine things to wear, good food to eat. You will want for nothing." His posture stiffened. "As for what happens if you don't swear fealty, it might be better if I show you."

Goosebumps spread over my skin as he rose.

"Come."

Master Hiito ushered me before him as we followed Cruelon out of the room. A pair of the king's private guard fell in behind us as Cruelon led the way. From the room, we walked through a large corridor that branched off, down a flight of stairs, through a series of small rooms, and down another flight of stairs before arriving at a door flanked by yet another two black-clad men. They stood aside to let us pass.

A dank and musty scent assailed my nostrils as we wound our way down a passageway. It sloped deeper underground, following a strange, snaking path. The air grew colder, and water dripped from the ceiling, running in thin rivulets down the walls onto the uneven floor. It created puddles, and where the water ran, the stone was slimy. The footing was precarious. The torches in brackets lining the wall every few yards hindered as much as they helped. Flickering light created dancing shadows, reflecting off the slick, wet surface of the floor.

"You've fallen into an abyss!" Hiito huffed, glancing at me. "And there's no going back now." He held up his robes, his small calfskin-clad feet struggling to keep up with us. His breathing filled the wet air. "Almost there." Hitto chuckled, wheezing. "Aw, never mind, here we are." He turned on his heels to follow Cruelon through an open doorway, flanked by a set of guards, into a long corridor spaced in even intervals with heavy, barred doors.

Are there people hidden behind those doors? My palms were slick with sweat, and my breathing grew ragged. *Will I join them?* I shivered.

Cruelon stopped before a door located halfway down the long corridor. Water dripped next to him, but he ignored it and waved a hand. One of the guards came and slid the bolt across with a grating rasp. The sound echoed up and down the passageway, rebounding off stone and unhindered by the damp wood. A screech sounded as the guard pulled the heavy door open. Goosebumps raced up and down my skin.

The cell was a patch of black untouched by the light from the torches, an abyss, as Hitto had said. My eyes strained as I peered into the shadows. A torch blazed into the space as a guard brought one near, driving away the murky darkness to reveal a thin, shivering form.

The figure—a woman—raised her head, her greasy hair falling back to reveal a face starved with hunger. She stared at me, at us, without a word. Her eyes were void of feeling, as though her soul had left the body behind.

"See?" Cruelon whispered near my ear.

I jumped.

"She used to be one of the ladies of my court." His voice slid over me like silk. His breath was warm against my neck as he leaned close.

"What did she do?" I whispered back, unable to speak any louder, unable to tear my gaze away from the petite woman cowering on the floor.

"She failed. She defied me, defied my wishes. I gave her a second chance, but she ignored it."

I had to strain to hear him.

"A third time, Juliet Barrows. A third chance, and that, too, she didn't take. Now she must bear the punishment. She swore fealty to me and then broke that oath."

A guard slid around us to enter the chamber. He grabbed a handful of the woman's hair and hauled her to her knees. His hand slid down, and a sharp rasp preceded his curved sword sliding out of its sheath.

My breath caught in my throat, and my heart pounded. The air grew stifling. I took a step back.

Cruelon's hand found my lower back, and he stopped me. "No, Juliet Barrows. Watch."

The woman stared at Cruelon, wavering as she struggled to remain upright. "You won't get away with this," she uttered in a hoarse voice.

With a fluid motion, the guard beheaded her.

I gasped, closing my eyes tight, but it was too late. I had seen the sword slide through her neck. I had seen the blood spray the walls and the dank hay lying on the floor.

"This is what happens when someone defies me." Cruelon pointed into the cell, but I refused to look again. "Do you swear fealty to me?"

"I do," I whispered, fear clutching me within her tight grasp.

"Very well." Cruelon's teeth flashed in a smile. "Welcome to my domain, *Lady* Juliet."

He turned to lead the way back up into his mountain fortress, leaving but the echo of his words ringing in my mind. A tear slid down my cheeks. My whole body trembled. I was one of his court now. *Lady Juliet.* A fine line existed between life and death. And now, more than ever before, I felt as though I toed that line.

CHAPTER EIGHT

The same guard who had beheaded the prisoner nudged me forward. Cruelon and Master Hiito had left. It was almost a relief that I struggled to breathe. I worried maybe I could smell the blood in the air if I could. My feet began walking forward, following the other guard as we headed back up the sloping passageway. The silence was a welcome relief—Cruelon and Hiito were gone. Yet it felt oppressive all the same, because I was alone with my thoughts and alone with the images I struggled to thrust out.

I had a vague recollection of corridors, rooms, and stairs before ending up in a narrow, wood-framed doorway. One of the guards slid the door open, and we passed through. Sunlight streamed through the large window. It was a simple but comfortable space. I took in the plush mattress on the floor, the thick cushions about a low table, and the wardrobe that stood against one wall.

The door slid closed behind me. I turned. The guards had left. I let out a sigh, expelling the pent-up breath I'd been holding. Taking off my boots, I stretched my feet and stepped up on my toes. My feet ached. I stepped toward the bed, exhaustion filling my limbs. What now?

A slight knock sounded, and I turned my head. The swish of skirts and lightness of foot alerted me before I saw them. Two women gazed at me.

The elder held up a hand as she stepped forward. "Shh, we won't harm you." Small lines creased her face, but they weren't from laughing or even from old age. Sadness and pain filled the brown of her eyes.

"Who are you?" I asked.

The elder woman slid the door closed with a soft click. "Come." She beckoned before leading the girl to a door I hadn't noticed before. They slid it back and went through.

After a moment's hesitation, I followed. Inside the small annex, a deep tub waited, filled with steaming water. I watched, listless, as they approached me. The moment they began to remove my clothes, I held up a hand. "I can do it myself."

The girl stared.

"It is part of our job," the elder explained, an unspoken plea in her tired eyes. She pushed her graying braid back over her shoulder so that it hung down her back. "Please let us do this."

I nodded.

Done, I lowered myself into the hot water and watched as the girl took my clothes out of the room, holding them as though they'd give her some disease. The water encased me within its warm hold, and I leaned my head back against the sharp metal rim. Lashes fluttered against my cheeks as my eyes drifted closed. The heat seeped through my tired, aching body.

A finger grazed my skin, and I came out of a daze. I looked down and saw the wound Boden had bestowed there, red and angry.

"How did this happen?" she whispered under her breath.

I shook my head, unable to find the words or the strength to speak.

"It will scar," she murmured, straightening as the other girl entered the room. Not another word was spoken as the two of them scrubbed my skin with rough towels until it was raw and cleaned my hair and scalp, lathering and rinsing repeatedly. The sweet but pungent smell of lavender filled the air, driving away the cold numbness of my body. I groaned as what had started as a dull aching grew. It was everywhere. My limbs hurt deep inside, incapacitating and constant. That darn horse. Four days of riding after weeks of not having ridden was taking its toll.

The rest happened in a blur. My body was rubbed dry until it glistened bright red. The girls massaged me with a sweet, floral-scented lotion until my skin glowed, and then I was dressed in a floor-length robe, tied under my bust with a long sash. At last, I was helped into bed: a wonderful, plush mat, softer than anything I'd slept on in weeks. I sank into the cushions and the pillows set behind my head, exhaustion commandeering my body until there was no resistance whatsoever.

Saya's vision must be coming true. She'd seen me in fine dresses. It was one thing for Cruelon to tell me I was joining the court, another to experience it. I couldn't help but feel pampered and removed from what had happened in the dungeon just a short time before. *But what will the cost be?* I closed my eyes. Death faced me no matter my choice. I heard the wind rattle against the fortress walls. *Winter is coming.* Sleep began to steal over me, but I jerked as I felt movement beneath my legs.

"We still have work to do," the older woman ordered, leaning over me. "We must wax your legs and pluck your eyebrows."

"What?" I raised my head.

"We may have to do her upper lip too," the younger piped up. "But there isn't much there, perhaps a bit at the corners."

"We should begin. Just try to relax, my lady."

"No. Wait."

"Try to rest," the older woman hushed. She gave a small shake of her head. "There is no use protesting."

Tired as I was, I couldn't sleep. The long strips of wax pulled on my skin until the hair was ripped away and my skin reddened, irritated. The pain kept sleep at bay.

A hand rested on my arm, jostling me to full wakefulness.

"We're done," the older woman said. "Drink this."

I stared into the cup she handed me.

"It's just tea with a little honey," she encouraged with a faint smile. "It will help."

Help what? I touched the rim of the cup to my lips and drank. It was warm and sweet and soothed my throat. I didn't realize how irritated it was from the tension I had faced. I gave her the cup and sank down into the pillows.

"Now sleep. We will leave now."

Too weary to respond, I watched from under half-closed lids as they bowed and left the room. I was alone. The memories of the past days eased away as sleep stole over me.

A heavy fuzziness filled my mind as I woke up. I blinked several times, struggling to leave the heavy sleep behind. Shifting, I took in the dull gray light filtering in through the large window in the wall.

"Aw. You are awake."

I struggled to sit up, pulling the blankets with me to ward against the chilly air.

Master Hiito stared at me from the foot of the bed where he sat. "The king will see you now. You really did wake up with perfect timing, as I was about to wake you myself." His eyes roamed me, lingering on my face. "I suppose I'll leave you to make yourself more presentable." He pointed at the wardrobe. "I will send in your maids." With a swish of his robes, he was gone.

I stood, wobbling, my legs struggling to find balance as sleep still held me within her sway. With each stumbling step, my body began to feel alive again. I opened the wardrobe door. A dozen or so dresses stared back at me, hanging on stiff wooden rods. I brushed my hands over their silkiness and turned as I heard a door open.

The two women from the day before stood in the opening. A fleeting smile crossed the younger's face as she bowed. Her ebony hair stayed in place, tied in a tight knot at the back of her neck. The elder regarded me without a flicker of emotion. Together, they strode forward.

The elder examined the clothes with a practiced air. "This one will do," she began, choosing a dress. "It is modest, but will still show her off. It presents a bearing of humbleness and quiet strength, which is what she'll need today. It will please him."

My lips parted to speak. "Who?" I asked, but I already knew the answer. *Cruelon.* My legs trembled as the day before came rushing back in full force. I swore fealty. The woman in the dungeon. I licked my lips. She was dead now. *Will that be me at some point?* I swallowed down the lump that had formed in my throat.

Neither servant answered me. In a flash, they undressed me and slipped a garment over my head. Hands tugged at my waist, drawing the material in. They drew me forward to a tall mirror.

I gasped, almost unable to recognize myself.

"You've changed," the older woman whispered.

My face was pale. *I look like I belong here.* The dress hugged my figure as though made for me, and the vibrant green accentuated the blue in my eyes. A hiss escaped my lips as something was pulled tight around my torso. "What is this?" Air left my body with each tug.

"It is customary."

They finished lacing up what seemed like a fancy green corset, accentuating my already trim waist. My eyes sought that of the older woman.

The younger motioned to a stool. "Please sit." She didn't waste a minute in taking my hair in her small hands.

The elder knelt in front of me and opened a small box. "Close your eyes," she instructed.

I waited, feeling every movement of my hair being pulled, the prick of pins in my scalp, and the touch of the woman's hands on my face as she applied powders and tinctures.

"You may stand and look in the mirror now," a stern voice said. "We are done."

I walked to the mirror and froze, staring at my reflection. "This isn't me."

"Yes, it is!" the young girl replied, bouncing just beside me.

Where did I come from? Makeup accentuated my blue eyes, and my eyebrows had been darkened several shades as though to illuminate my tanned skin. My hair had been swept into an ornate bun, with a few loose tendrils hanging around my ears. A thick, loose curl hung over my shoulder. My jaw tightened. *And the dress.* The skirt was narrow, reaching down to the floor, opening out mid-calf to fall in soft folds. I fingered the fabric, the shade of palest green—sage—a color of late spring. I raised a hand to the corset and pulled the material up a little.

"What are you doing?" the older woman bit out.

"It's a bit indecent."

"No," the younger answered. "You are hardly showing. This is modest compared to the other women in the court."

I looked back at myself, askance, and pulled it up just a tad more. Ignoring their frowns, I squared my shoulders.

"You'll do," came the harsher voice of the older woman. "You had better."

I tilted my head to stare at her. *What did she mean?* I watched as she bustled over to the side, putting away the box and the hairpins in a small chest.

"Aw, I see you are done now. Good."

I jumped as Hiito's voice boomed through the room.

"Come, come." He beckoned me forward. "I don't know what the king has in store for you, not that you need to know anyway." He led the way out of the room, waiting for the two guards outside to fall in behind us.

I winced. "Where are we going?"

"To see the king, of course," Hiito responded as he waddled down the corridor. The guards fell in behind me, not so close as to be touching, but close enough that I felt their breath on the back of my neck and could smell their musky body odor. Hiito looked at me before hurrying his step. "Almost there, almost there! Guards, keep her hustling!"

The guards didn't do anything. It wasn't I who was keeping us from walking faster. No matter how fast Hiito pumped his legs, his short legs struggled to stay ahead of our longer ones. After walking down the length of the corridor, we entered a narrow hallway that stretched on, wooden doors marking at regular intervals. I wondered where they led. We ascended a flight of stairs at the end of the hall. I gaped as they opened up to a wide landing, at the end of which lay a set of tall, imposing double doors.

Hiito stopped in front of them and waved a hand. "Here we are!"

I stared up at them, feeling the silent men close behind me. I'd not seen this area of the castle before. *What's behind there?* Air hissed through my clenched teeth, and I ran my hands down the front of my gown. The guards, dressed in tight-fitting black, flung the doors open.

Sunlight streamed through the doorway from a window behind me, throwing a wide ray of light upon the floor. My shoulders tensed as I took in the many guards lining the walls, all dressed in black. They were men short of stature, but each one rippled with muscles under the tight material. Emotionless, swords hanging at their sides, they didn't have to look at me. I knew they were aware of me and every movement in the room without betraying a single eye twitch. There were so many king's guards. Adnan had told me of these men. Cunning, ruthless men not to be crossed. *Men as dangerous as their king.*

I took a deep breath and strode forward. Behind the men stood people dressed in finery—Cruelon's courtiers. They peered over the shoulders of the guards, their gazes curious. The thin slippers I wore made little noise on the stone floor. Head tall, I walked between the immense stone pillars lining the room. Every sound, every sight felt magnified, as though a spyglass had lowered before my eyes. At the far end, the king sat on a large, black throne.

So this was the throne room. With every footstep, my posture fought to slump, to recede into itself. *No. Stay strong.*

His fingers drummed on the side of his chair, but he leaned forward, his dark eyes watching me. He made a lean and imposing figure. As though in slow motion, I watched his tongue flick out to wet his lips.

A snake.

A trickle of sweat ran down my back. I struggled to keep my body from trembling.

Master Hiito passed me and halted just short of the throne. He bounced on the balls of his feet, his eyes darting between the king and me. When I didn't move, Hitto glared and gestured for me to follow. Each step felt like an eternity as I approached the end of the room. It wasn't until I stopped before him that I was plunged back into reality, suddenly aware of all who watched. Hiito motioned down and, with a shallow breath, I stooped into a low bow.

"Lower," hissed Hiito from where he bowed to the ground. When he rose, he repeated, "Lower."

And lower I went, until I felt it was a yoga pose I performed and not a bow. The tight dress pulled back down over my chest, and seeing the view I was giving the king, I grimaced and rose without waiting for a command. Master Hitto licked his lips, still staring, but Cruelon cleared his throat, capturing my gaze with his own as a tantalizing smile wreathed his mouth.

He will not break me. A bead of sweat formed on my brow, and I took a deep breath to steady my nerves. *But he cannot know that, not yet. To him, I must be broken; I must be pliable.*

An oppressive silence filled the room. Hiito's twitching worsened as he shifted his weight from side to side.

"She is even more exotic than I realized," Cruelon said. "What a prize you have brought me, Hiito."

"Yes, my lord," Hiito replied, his lips almost splitting in delight. "Quite beautiful."

"Juliet," Cruelon began, each word striking the air like thunder, the aftermath of lightning. "How do you come before me?"

I tilted my head. *What does he want?* My mind raced. "With loyalty, my lord."

Cruelon's eyes narrowed. "And what do you pledge?"

"My fealty, my lord."

He leaned forward. "Who do you serve?"

"You, my lord." The words stuck in my throat. I felt as though Cruelon would see every lie shining in my eyes. My heart raced. *Calm down, calm down. Don't let him see!* Breathing in deep, I shoved everything down so deep I wondered if they'd ever resurface—the fear, the pain, but above all, the uncertainty. I had to have confidence. Without it, I would lose before I'd even begun. *This was the moment I hadn't foreseen. He wants a show. He wants his men and court to see me swear to him too.*

"And who is the rightful king of this land?"

"You, my lord." I kept my eyes averted, hands by my sides. Good. The shaking had stopped. I threw the key to the box deep within myself, far away where I could not find it, could not open it, could not let my fears consume me.

"And what do you promise to do with your life?"

I did not hesitate. "I promise to serve you."

To pretend to serve him even as I sought a way to kill him. *Even if it kills me.* My chin raised as I looked up into Cruelon's pale face, his dark brows drawn together with concentration. *I'm not broken.*

"Rise." The command reverberated through the room, sending echoes through the wooden beam supporting the ceiling. Triumph blazed in his black eyes. He lowered his voice so that only Hiito and I could hear. "You will be a loyal servant and subject to me. Cross me one time, and you will not live another day. Please me, and you will receive more than you could ever desire. But do not give me a reason to doubt your pledge of loyalty." Each word cut like a knife. His eyes glinted, and his lips compressed. "You will soon realize what honor I have given you, what privilege you now have as a lady of my court." He smiled. "You are beautiful." His eyes trailed over me as I fought to keep my face impassive, my eyes straightforward, uncaring, unfeeling. "Master Hiito," he continued, raising his voice so everyone could hear. "Tomorrow I shall hold a party. It will be her introduction to the court." He laughed like a schoolboy in a candy shop. Whispers sounded throughout the room as the courtiers reacted to Cruelon's announcement.

I glanced at them over my shoulder. What would Cruelon have me do? I wasn't so ignorant as to believe that the room, dresses, and parties would make up my life from now on. He had plans for me. I just didn't know what they were. How long until he somehow found out what I meant to Tristan? How would I be used then?

Cruelon gestured. "Hiito, take care of the details for tomorrow's celebrations. Guards, please escort Lady Barrows back to her chambers."

A hand took hold of my arm.

"No, no," Cruelon admonished. "None of that. She is a lady and will be treated accordingly."

"My king," the guard murmured, letting go.

Another two guards took up the flank as we walked, their leather uniforms making no noise as they slid into positions around me, their boots soft on the floor, their footfalls controlled and even.

One of the guards peeled off without a word when we reached the hall outside the throne room. I watched him go, his form vanishing around the corner, as quick and silent as a wraith.

"He'll make sure food is brought to your chambers, my lady."

"My name is Juliet," I said before I could bite the words back.

It was as though he hadn't heard me. There were few we passed on the way back to my rooms, each and every one a servant, their eyes on the floor and their shoulders hunched. Their fear misted through the air, stifling hope and driving away any comfort I sought to find. All that was left in its wake was an inescapable nightmare.

Let the game begin. I gritted my teeth. *Watch yourself, Juliet.*

Chapter Nine

Footsteps echoed. They were my own, but they were also in front of me. I couldn't catch up. They were always too far away, just behind the next shadowed door, in the next hazy room, or around the next bend in the corridor. My feet flew over the ground as I ran, but still I could never see who the steps belonged to. Something else drove me as well. The need to run grew. I was running from something.

Sweat coated my body, and my hair clung to my neck in limp strands. The farther I ran, the more my drive grew. Thump. Thump. Thump. My heart raced in my chest. The feeling that something was at my heels grew, but whenever I looked over my shoulder, there was nothing but emptiness.

A door clicked shut, the small sound reverberating through the hallways. The edges blurred, sharpened, and blurred again. Shadows grew darker and I stopped, listening.

The footsteps grew louder—

I blinked. Gone were the hallways and corridors. The stone ceiling above my head gleamed gray in the early morning light. *A dream.* I blinked again and rolled onto my side.

"Oh, you're awake." The girl from yesterday walked up to the bed and smiled down at me—her footsteps ...

I sat up. "How long have you been here?"

"Not long, perhaps ten, fifteen minutes at the most. Did I wake you? We were trying to be quiet."

It was just a dream. Hers were the footsteps I heard.

I shook my head.

"Did you sleep well?"

My shoulders rose in a shrug. The nightmare continued to dance on the edge of my thoughts.

"Emi," a sharp voice spoke. "We must busy ourselves. We have much to do."

I pushed the blankets off and stood up from the mat. "So you're Emi," I echoed, cementing the name in my mind. I watched as the older woman strode to the wardrobe, her gray hair appearing darker in the dim light of early morning. "What is your name?"

"I'm Kin."

My jaw dropped and I reeled back. *Kin.* My lips parted and closed again. *She's the spy.* My heart flew within my chest, and I fought to keep my excitement from spilling out. I contemplated the two. *Does the girl know? How am I supposed to talk with Kin if Emi is around?* I stared, wondering what Kin thought of. I didn't have any information to give Tristan yet, other than the fact that I was now part of the king's court.

"The ball," Emi said, bouncing on her feet.

I regarded her. Emi's figure had yet to bear the brunt of what the elder servants here did. She was not bowed down by the weight of serving the king. "What ball?" I asked.

"In your honor," Emi explained, a hint of excitement pulsing with each word. "And to introduce you to the court."

A knock sounded on the thin door. Emi went to the door and came back bearing a tray.

"Why don't you sit down?" she suggested with a small smile. "I ordered a light repast, as your stomach will still need time to adjust. Perhaps you should try drinking some tea first."

While Emi poured me a cup, I watched Kin disappear back into the bathroom. I took the mug from Emi, wrapping my fingers around the cozy warmth. I tried not to look down at the food, but I didn't need to. My stomach growled at the knowledge of it even existing in the same room as me.

I didn't realize I'd been reaching my hand toward a thin piece of meat until Emi laid a hand on the top of my own. "Wait until you've drunk some of your tea, my lady. Let your stomach wake up a little."

I hesitated, but I could see the consternation and nervousness shining in the depths of her young eyes.

She took a step back and clasped her hands together in front of her. "But if you don't want to, that's fine, my lady. Whatever you would like."

"No," I agreed, taking the cup. "I'll drink the tea first."

Emi relaxed and smiled.

"Emi," a sharp voice said from the bathroom. "There is work to be done."

Emi smiled again at me and bowed. She disappeared through the doorway.

I sipped at the cooled tea, the nutty flavor of toasted rice filling my mouth. Its tantalizing smell and taste reminded me of the inn and the times I'd drunk tea in Tristan's mountain fortress. My mouth salivated at the comforting taste. I wrapped my hands around the small cup, reveling in its warmth.

Tristan is gone. Saya is gone. I sighed and took another sip. *And Adnan ... who knows where he is or what he does now. Is he here?* My hands trembled. Would I see him? Did I want to see him? I grimaced as I took too big of a gulp and felt the hot tea rush down my throat. *What do I fear more, that he is here working for the king or that he isn't here and that I won't see him?*

I set the tea down and picked up a small piece of dried meat. Chewing slowly, I watched as Emi and Kin reentered the room.

"The bath is drawn, my lady," Kin said. "When you are done, we'll begin the preparations."

⁙⁙⁙

The water was hot, and I enjoyed being washed, scrubbed, and massaged with lotions until the sweet scents of jasmine filled the air. Eyes closed, I let them decorate my face with makeup and do my hair.

"All right, stand up." Kin bustled about me, her concentration fully on what she was doing.

I followed her orders, listening to the creaking of the bamboo mat as it bore my weight and feeling the same creaking echo in my bones. I knew I couldn't say anything, not with Emi around, but I longed to talk with Kin, to have some sort of assurance from her. She had to be the Kin Tristan spoke of. I lifted my arms, letting them take my robe and slide a gown over my head. It was soft, shimmery, and slid over my skin as smooth as water.

"Keep your eyes closed," Emi whispered, "and lower your arms."

I lowered them as though they were wings, my body pulled as they tugged on the corset-like portion over the gown.

A gentle hand patted down my skirt. "You can open them now."

My lips parted as I took in my appearance in the reflection before me. The corset's shade mirrored that of the dress—a deep, dazzling blue, almost black, which drew out the tinges of green in my blue eyes and highlighted the blonde of my hair. The morning light reflected off the silvery hem of the dress and sleeves. Smoothing the narrow, swishing skirt with my palms, I fingered the broad blue sash, gathering the material high on my waist, just under my bosom. It all but covered the corset underneath, and the ends of the sash fell in graceful folds.

"Almost done," Kin said as she rubbed a gel onto my bare forearms, chest, and neck.

I peered closer. "Why am I glowing?"

"It is a secret concoction, my lady." She attached small silver earrings to my lobes and straightened the dainty black ribbon woven through my hair. "You'll do. Now go, the guards are waiting." Her voice brooked no argument, not that I would have argued. I took a deep breath and squared my shoulders. Taking one last glance in the mirror, I turned to the door.

One of the men outside raised a brow as his eyes scanned me from head to toe. The other nudged him with a quick shake of the head. They fell in behind me, giving me directions with lowered voices as we went, as though to give the illusion that they were my bodyguards rather than my captors. And we weren't alone; the castle teemed with activity. Music drifted through the stone corridors with an eerie echo. The faint beat of treading feet filled the air, accenting the voices of those in servitude and the guests, which droned in the background. I paused at the familiar tall double doors, listening to the sounds drifting through from the other side, louder now. Torches in metal brackets blazed on either side of the entryway.

With a deep breath, I squared my shoulders and kept my gaze forward as the doors to the throne room swung open. I took one step through and into the blazing brilliance before me. Everything glittered in the glow of dozens—no, *hundreds*—of candles and lanterns. An enormous chandelier filled with scores of cream candles hung above the gathered assembly, throwing a radiance down upon the bright shades of pinks, blues, oranges, reds, and greens glaring at me from every direction. The colorful materials adorned both men and women, and jewels flashed and winked from their vantage points on fingers, necks, ears, hair, and even clothing.

The faces of the crowd before me were blurred, but I could hear the laughter, chatter, and whispers as the sounds swelled and ebbed throughout the large ballroom.

Another step forward. And another. My light slippers made no noise, my own movements drowned out by the noise surrounding me. A feeling of being alone stole over me. I glanced over my shoulder. The guards remained rooted behind me, next to the doors, but their eyes tracked my progress like a hunter stalking his prey. The room grew silent as more and more became aware of my presence. The silence spread like a wildfire, and the crowd fell back before me, clearing a straight but narrow path through their midst to where Cruelon waited at the end of the room. My breathing came quick and shallow, but I managed to keep my head high and my shoulders back, heavy as if burdened with an invisible weight. Outside, I resonated strength—I hoped—and inside, jelly.

Cruelon strolled toward me, his deep golden robes swishing in soft folds around his long legs. But this was no fairytale prince striding toward me. I froze, unable to look away from the sneer that curved his lips. His umber eyes glittered as he neared, meeting me in the middle of the room. He held out a hand, and I took it. My heart pounded. His skin was icy to the touch, but his grasp was firm and demanding. He twirled me around in a slow circle around him. It was so silent. I could hear the rustle of my own dress as I glided across the floor.

I'm a parrot, a monkey on display, and he, my master. I licked my lips. *Stay strong. Remember your role.*

Cruelon brought me close to his side. "What is it, my dear?" His breath blew against my ear. "Fire burns in your eyes, the flames so bright I cannot tell if it is the reflection of the candles or passion deep within you. I broke you to my will, Juliet—"

I shivered. My name felt like a caress on his lips. I forced a slight smile to my face as I glanced at the watching crowd.

"But," the king continued, his voice soft, "I have not killed your passion. No, do not deny it—your passion is what fuels you; the fire inside is what I find ...

irresistible." He looked over the crowd and called out, "Lords and ladies of the Court, I present Lady Juliet Barrows, the Otherworlder."

The whispers began slowly but grew until they filled every corner of the room. Cruelon smiled, his teeth flashing.

A woman stepped forward and bowed low. "My lord, the *Otherworlder*?"

The man beside her placed his hand over her forearm, drawing her back into the crowd. Within moments, they disappeared, lost in the sea of faces.

"Must I repeat myself?" Cruelon sneered.

"How do you know?" a masculine voice called out, hidden in the mass. Cruelon's lower lip twitched as his jaw clenched. But he did not answer the question.

The hair on my arms stood straight up when Cruelon whispered in my ear, his hand brushing against my shoulder. "Well, Juliet, a small question before we continue: Where is the portal?"

"Portal?" I asked, feigning surprise as a clammy feeling stole over me.

"Don't make me ask again, Juliet." His thumb moved in small circles on the top of my hand.

Why does he want to know? Bile rose in my throat, and I swallowed against the nausea roiling in my stomach. His touch, his breath against my face, hot and stuffy, the heat from all the bodies filling the hall, pressing in close as they whispered with staring eyes and sardonic, uncaring faces ...

I averted my eyes as Cruelon pulled me closer. "There is no portal, my lord."

He shot me an amused glance. "We both know that's not true."

Out of the corner of my eye, I saw two guards forcing the woman who had questioned him out of the room. The knot in my stomach grew. *No wonder the man with her had pulled her back. Too late though.* I swallowed. Would she end up like the woman in the dungeon?

"It disappeared. I couldn't return home," I whispered, surprised at how easily the lie came. "It's gone."

Cruelon's fingers gripped my arm, and I winced.

"We shall continue this stimulating conversation later," he growled. He released me and beckoned someone forward.

My jaw dropped. *No.* I stared, unable to move or speak. *It's not possible.*

Before me she stood, straight as a statue, her petite height somehow imposing. Bold shades of gold and scarlet adorned her, and unlike every other woman here, her hair hung free, the natural tones I remember so well glinting in the candlelight. Her almond eyes stared into mine.

The woman who had found me and led me to Umi no Machi. How? My lips parted, but then I remembered where I was. I couldn't speak freely, not here.

The king took her hand, drawing her closer. "Natsumi, may I present Juliet Barrows, the Otherworlder."

From a distance, his words filtered through to my frozen mind and body. I blinked, glancing at him for a moment before returning to Natsumi. The voices around me faded away until it was just her and I.

Natsumi turned her dark eyes away from mine and smiled at the king. "I congratulate you, my lord. The prize of your dreams! Now you may rest easy."

Did she remember me? The lost girl in the woods? The girl who thought herself in a dream?

That girl was no more, but neither was Natsumi. I took a step back, bringing Cruelon's attention to me. Natsumi inclined her head to me, and one by one, the rest of the crowd followed suit. Time slowed as I clenched the fabric of my dress and surveyed the sea of bowed figures. Beyond them the guards, all dressed in black, stood straight and tall, ever watchful, ever still and silent. They contemplated me, a silent recognition, but of what?

Time sped up and everyone straightened, their eyes burning into my own, threatening to unlock my secrets and bare my soul for the world to see and judge.

Natsumi faded into the crowd without a word, not sparing me another glance. *Why is she here?* I wanted to follow her, to speak with her. There had been no recognition of me on her face. Cruelon watched her go until she faded away into the bright ocean of colors. The soft music that had begun moments before tinkled through the air, wavering on the breeze blowing through the narrow windows high up on the walls, building up and falling back, playing with the emotions without thought or reason.

Cruelon turned to me. "Come."

The hours slipped by in a dreamy reality, filled with a whirlwind of introductions: important personages such as the royal advisors, a grim and serious-faced group who left me unsettled, and after them another person of prestige and another. Men, women, smiles, glares—some overly bright, others serious—all left me with a confusing myriad of questions.

I didn't know my lines in the play unfolding about me. Their faces and names blurred into one another, melding together until I couldn't distinguish one from the other. I suspected the drink I'd been given had something to do with it; my brain became fuzzy, my eyes straying, hard to focus on any one person or object. The heat of the crowd stifled me, pressing in until a breath of fresh air or a cool breeze on my skin was but a distant memory.

I drank more.

Cruelon left me, and the hours passed by in a dazzling blur. I wandered the room in a haphazard manner, speaking to no one, finding nowhere to sit, no way to escape the new prison in which I found myself, nothing to jolt me back to wakefulness from the nightmare holding me within its clutches.

"You met Natsumi," a bitter voice spoke, the tone sharp and piercing.

I flinched, turning around to face another beautiful woman.

Her face hardened. "You're quite pretty yourself. No wonder he wants to keep you."

"Excuse me?" I asked, noticing some in the crowd who watched us as though waiting for something to unfold.

She laughed and raised her glass to her lips.

I took a step closer. "Who are you?"

"I am Lady Amarante. Ironic, is it not?" She laughed again, her voice catching.

Another actress. Another who hides behind a shield. I blinked and stared at her. "Is it?"

"I suppose you do not know—how could you? You are rather new to this country." She reached out and touched my hair with a long finger, lowering it to follow the contour of my cheek. "You stand out amongst us all, Juliet Barrows," she whispered, her eyes crinkling at the corners as her eyebrows drew together.

Longing filled her, but also ... I frowned. *Is that jealousy?* I stepped back, out of her reach. "Who are you?"

She looked over my shoulder, and I followed her line of sight. When I turned back, she had gone, disappearing as fast as she had appeared.

I squinted, feeling waves of dizziness wash over me as I took in the luxury in the light from the multitude of courtiers. I caught a glimpse of the king, his golden robes and small jewels sewed into the hems and folds catching every ray, a glittering ensemble.

He turned and strode toward me. I leaned against the wall where I stood, exhaustion filling my limbs. My head spun. He stopped in front of me and bent over my hand, kissing my skin with wet lips.

"Come." He tucked my hand under his arm and led the way through the now-quiet crowd until we reached the hallway. There he released me to my guards without a word or even a look.

How did I do? I wondered as I made my way through the corridors and down the flight of stairs back to my room. *Natsumi is here, of all places.* Dozens of faces and names flitted in and out of my thoughts. Out of everyone, I had all but forgotten her. Natsumi. Her voice that day, questioning my appearance coinciding with that of the northern slavers, had been one voice amongst the many, and then she had faded out of sight and out of mind. *Does she remember me?* I remembered her. The smell of cinnamon and freshly baked bread, the dazzling brown of her almond eyes, and the ageless beauty she carried. *She is here.*

Chapter Ten

I drew my knees up under my chin. The coverlet covering my legs was thick and soft. "Who is Amarante?"

Emi stiffened and glanced at Kin, who regarded me with pursed lips. An eerie silence fell. *What does she want to say but can't?* There was something in the way Kin's gaze flickered toward Emi. I knew she fought an inward battle.

Kin's mouth opened, closed, and opened again. "It is best you learn not to ask questions here, my lady."

I gave a soft smile, but I knew it didn't reach my eyes. "I won't tell if you won't."

Emi cleared her throat. "Kin, if—"

"Emi," Kin barked, and Emi fell silent, toeing the floor as she stared down at her feet. "My lady," Kin began, "you don't realize how dangerous questions are here."

"Who is she?" I pressed, stretching my legs out in front of me. "She was there last night, and I need to know. Please, it should be a harmless enough question." I kept my voice low, unsure of how much the guards stationed outside my door could hear.

Kin continued to watch me, but Emi shifted, glancing back and forth between us.

Kin sighed with resignation. "Lady Amarante is head of the king's harem; his favorite, and most revered and respected of all the women."

I gaped. "His *harem*?"

"Yes." Kin didn't bat an eye as she walked over to the closet. "He has quite an extensive one. Some of the most beautiful girls in the kingdom have the honor of being part of it. You saw many of them last night at the ball."

My mind whirled. *What am I here for? Not ...* I struggled to take control of my wayward thoughts. "So she's not his queen?"

"No, much as she would like to be. No, there is no queen, not yet."

Natsumi and the king. Amarante. A harem. The pieces began falling into place. "Natsumi, she might become queen."

"No more questions," Kin responded in as gentle a voice as I had yet heard. "A hint to the wise: listen, but do not speak, and do not—whatever you do—ask questions. Ask the wrong person, and it can be detrimental. No one in their right mind would want to face the consequences."

"Does she refuse?" I asked, leaning forward. "The king wants her, doesn't he?"

Kin pulled Emi after her. "Be careful, Otherworlder. More goes on than you know." She opened the door but hesitated on the threshold. "Stay strong, my lady," she whispered.

Before I could ask her what she meant, she left, the door sliding closed behind her. I leaned back against the pillow and regarded the ceiling.

"Stay strong," I repeated. "Do I have any strength left?" I waited, listening, but there was no answer in the quiet stillness. I was alone. My eyes closed. Exhaustion filled my mind and my limbs. It had only been two days, and yet my hope dwindled. I lived on edge, unable to relax. My sleep was not restful, and I felt like an automaton, going through the motions. Pretty dresses, makeup, and parties were all that seemed to make my life here. I struggled to stay above the surface, learning the ways of the courtiers, learning what Cruelon wanted of me.

I rolled over. The mirror next to the cabinet stared back at me. Kin's firm fingers always smeared makeup under my eyes, covering the dark circles, hiding me behind a mask. She and Emi went through the motions as well, performing their parts with perfection. There was so much I wanted to say to them, but I didn't. The words never came to my lips.

I blinked and shifted back to look at the ceiling.

The love Kin had for Emi was motherly, yet I didn't think Emi quite realized that. Kin tried so hard to curb her, put her in her place to keep her safe. It was in the small gestures, the warnings she gave Emi, and the way she softened when she looked at her.

As the hours passed, I slept fitfully, never quite asleep and never quite awake. The room grew colder with the fall night air as it blew in through the open window. Once the first gray streaks of light heralded dawn, I stood and walked to the window. I couldn't see the lake from my vantage point, but I could see the plains, and beyond them, the forest. In the distance, the sounds of swords clinking, one upon the other, could be heard. I often heard them. The men practicing. The sharp clanking, sword upon sword, sword upon shield—then the louder clang as shield clanged on shield. Grunts intermixed with groans. Sometimes, I heard a voice calling commands. Even in just two days, I recognized that voice whenever I heard it. It bespoke youth, strength, command ... one who knew what he was doing. Another taisa? The same one who had commanded the patrol which had captured me? Sometimes I heard him call out commands in a different language, but it was unrecognizable, too far away to distinguish the words.

For some reason, his voice reminded me of Adnan. But I bit my lip and turned away from the window. Adnan wasn't here. Tristan wasn't here. Saya wasn't here. I straightened my shoulders and buried the despair deep down as I steeled myself for another day.

⚜ ⚜

No one came for me. Kin and Emi dressed me, brought me food, and then left before reappearing with more food a few hours later. But they did not speak a word to me, and I soon gave up trying.

Is it a relief? Cruelon was busy with his own affairs. He was not concerned with me. *Yet how can I help the rebellion if I'm stuck inside a room all day, every day?* I sighed and paced the room, my feet treading its familiar bamboo flooring. Would indents from my footsteps begin to appear?

Then another day passed, much the same as the day before. But now I'd begun to recognize my guards through the open doorway whenever Kin and Emi appeared and disappeared.

Six.

Two taking a shift at a time, rotating through three total shifts for the day, then three at night. Once I opened the door, tried striking up a conversation—without success. They stared back at me blankly, puppets pulled on strings.

I felt myself pulled downward, the listlessness spreading over me, chasing away the emotions I didn't want to feel. My mind grew blank as I spent hours staring out at the gray sky, or the wall, or the ceiling as I lay on the mat. The one thing that kept me awake was the fear of sleep. It hovered there, never going away no matter how much I wanted the numbing sensation to drive that away as well. Nightmares plagued my sleep, the times I'd wake up sticky, covered in sweat from whatever dreams had held me within their grip. I never remembered my dreams except for one—one flash more clear and vivid than I could've thought possible. Every morning I chased it away as though if I didn't, that memory would kill me, or the fear of it would.

It was me.

I lay there, blood pouring out of wounds that covered my body, pale, gone from this world. It tormented me. I worried what the castle was doing to me, what I was doing to myself. What did the dream mean? I knew Drielle had seen a world without Cruelon in it, and I reminded myself of it, yet I couldn't shake the fear that I wouldn't live to see it.

And so it continued until dawn on the third morning. The skies were dull and lifeless, and a chill wind swept through the window, leaving goosebumps over my skin in its wake. I wondered at the plains and breathed in. I gazed past the brown plains to the forest beyond. The trees stood tall and proud, blending in with one another in a sea of green. Eyes closed, I took one last deep breath of the air tinged with the faint smell of smoke. Baying broke the quiet silence. *Dogs.* I leaned out of the window, trying to see where the sound was coming from, but my view was limited. It sounded like many of them, hungry, and almost angry. *They want their freedom too.* I closed the window and turned. *It's time. It's been long enough.*

Without waiting for Kin and Emi, I dressed myself and strode to the door. My feet needed to wander, to take me away from the dreams and from the memory of them. Three days had been long enough.

The guards stared at me and I at them. But this time, instead of closing the door and turning away, I stepped through. They didn't move an inch. Keeping my eyes on them and the swords hanging from their waists, I took a small step. They didn't move.

Another.

They still didn't move.

I turned my head and, two steps later, heard the light sound of leather moving against itself following me. *I don't have to remain in my room.* With the realization, a smile curved my lips. A chilly breeze whistled down the passageway from the windows, and I wrapped my arms around myself for warmth. Winter was coming faster than I'd expected. The mountains were peaked with white blankets, and I'd heard Kin telling Emi how quickly winter approached in this part of the country. The rain last night had drummed against the walls and roof, soothing my soul with its presence. *When will it snow here?* I wandered down an unfamiliar passageway and paused in front of a narrow and darkened corridor.

"You cannot go that way."

I jumped at the guard's harsh command and glanced over my shoulder at the man who had spoken.

"My lady," he said, inclining his head as he gestured for me to exit the passagewayI hovered upon entering.

I peered down it. "What's down there?"

"Why, Miss Barrows."

I started, and the guards stiffened, their eyes peering over my shoulder. *That voice.* Inhaling, I turned, taking in Amarante's slender figure.

Amarante smiled and gestured to the woman beside her, her white teeth flashing. "I had almost forgotten you were here. This is Lady Suki."

"Lady Suki," I repeated, inclining my head.

"Lady Juliet." She nodded, her dark brown eyes wide and clear.

Lady Juliet. The title sounded strange to my ears.

"Welcome," she continued, her voice meek compared to Amarante's confidence. "Perhaps you should join us sometime—"

"Oh, a fabulous idea," Amarante interrupted, examining a glittering ring upon her pinkie. "Why did I not think of it? You are welcome to join us. You are part of the court, at least for now, so you should join in on the court activities."

Suki folded her hands together in front of her. I couldn't tell if she even noticed the censuring glance Amarante had shot her.

"I would love to join you," I said, clasping my hands in front of me to show my feigned excitement.

"I'll send for you sometime." Amarante waved a hand, making as though to leave.

"I hear you are a wonderful hostess."

Amarante faced me, one curved brow lifted as she regarded me. A faint tinge of pink flushed her cheeks. "I am. Would you like to join us tomorrow?"

I bowed. "I would, thank you."

Amarante smoothed down her deep red skirt and tugged a little on the corset, bringing attention to her ample bosom.

I frowned.

Anger flashed across her face. "Come, Suki. *Miss* Barrows, until tomorrow." Her lips thinned. She squared her petite shoulders and whirled around, the folds of her dress swishing.

A far cry from the servants around here.

Amarante and Suki walked with heads held high, backs straight, while those in servitude kept their heads lowered, their gazes to the floor. The alarm in their eyes, their posture, and their shuffling feet radiated outward in waves until I felt their fear.

The guards followed close behind me. I halted as a young girl wearing an apron passed me. *She can't be more than ten or eleven.* Even Emi wasn't that young.

She kept her head down and hurried along, like all the others. I continued, watching the servants while also trying to make sense of the winding maze of the keep. Whenever I found a stairwell, I went down, looking for the bottom floor. I never tried any of the closed doors. The need to map my way through the main corridors and hallways of the keep was more important.

Sometimes whispers followed us from the mouths of the servants who would pass, but only from those who held their heads higher. There seemed to be a hierarchy, even amongst the servants. The few who didn't walk with bowed heads were also dressed in finer clothes.

Stepping through a square archway framed by gleaming polished wood, I stopped short. Before me stood the main doors, closed, barring me from the outside world. Locked from the inside, they were meant to keep people out.

Not for me. In my case, they keep me in. I twisted a few strands of hair around my fingers. *Dare I?* I felt the two men standing behind me, waiting. What would happen if I tried to leave the fortress? How far was I allowed to wander?

Freedom.

It swirled around me. I closed my eyes. *One day I'll feel the sun again.* Inhaling, I imagined breathing in fresh air before I sighed and turned away. I could almost feel the wind in my hair and remember the warmth of safety. My gaze drifted about the main entryway. Polished wood gleamed beneath my feet, and paintings hung from the walls, the colors vivid as the brushstrokes depicted the artists' imagination. Bright blue waves tipped with white foam, lined trees full of pink and red cherry blossoms, birds with long, slender necks, and other creatures. My lips parted as I slowly walked about the room, studying the paintings.

"Hello, Otherworlder."

I stiffened. The voice broke into my thoughts. *I know that voice.* I turned around. My mind raced to remember.

"Or should I say, Lady Juliet Barrows?" A shallow smile curved the man's lips, and his voice was smooth and low. "You are quite fetching when you are all cleaned up." He smiled, but it never reached his eyes. He studied me as he approached on quiet, cat-like feet. A curved sword hung from his hip, and his black clothes encased his body like a glove. *Another of the king's private guard.*

But who is he? A shiver ran over my skin. *There is something familiar ... I know that voice.* I stood my ground. "I don't believe we've met."

He smiled and stopped, his body mere inches away. "Have we not?" He waited, as though looking for me to move away.

What do I do? My hand twitched. I felt like it was some sort of test. *Just wait.* My breath caught as he peered at me.

"Perhaps it is best that you return to your room. There are dangers even here that you do not know of."

"Like what?" I challenged. *Who is he?* His face was unfamiliar, but still ... there was something about him.

"Do not try me," he replied, his voice hard as he raised it.

The man from the courtyard. He was the one who I had heard calling commands the past three days as the wind carried his voice up to my window. I cleared my throat. "You know who I am, but who are you?"

His lips tilted upward in an amused smile. "I am the Taisho of the Black Guard."

"What does that mean?"

He blinked. "The commander, if you will." He stepped back and gave a swooping half bow. "At your service, my lady. Earlier, you sighed, why?"

I gaped at him. *The front doors. How long has he been watching me?* My eyebrows drew together as I thought.

The man nodded to my two guards, who stepped back a few yards, giving us some space. I returned my attention to the slim man in front of me. His face was emotionless, showing nothing of what he thought.

I made to move past him into the passageway beyond, but his tall frame stepped in front of me, blocking my path.

"Not so fast, my lady Juliet."

My hands trembled. "I recognize your voice."

Shock radiated across his face, but he pulled his mask back in an instant. "From where?"

"The courtyard. I've heard you the past few days."

The man's shoulders relaxed a little. "Ah, yes. My men and I often spend time training throughout the day—those who aren't on rotation, that is." He inclined his head. "Let me begin again. I am Taisho Kohei Hirose, my lady. I command the Black Guard, of whom I think you are aware."

I snorted before I could take it back. "I have. They are the ones who guard me, after all."

He regarded me for several slow seconds. "How do you like it here?"

I blinked. *How does he expect me to answer that?*

"No, perhaps you shouldn't answer that question." He laid a hand on the hilt of his sword as he leaned against the wall. "For then I would be wondering if you were indeed answering honestly or not."

"Were you there, the night at the ball?"

He glanced about the room before lowering his voice. "No, I wasn't there. But I heard you were the king's personal guest, the belle of the ball. Quite the honor."

I crossed my arms.

"Aw, you think not?" He laughed. "Believe me, you caused quite the sensation. The men all talk of you, and the women are jealous of you. It was quite the shock to the court." Hirose smiled, his white teeth gleaming.

Be careful. His smile was charming, andI fought against wanting to be at ease.

"So," he began, "you have figured out you may leave your room. Have you tested anything else?"

"I can't seem to leave my guards behind."

"Yes, well—" Hirose glanced at the black-clad men. "They are here to keep an eye on you and to keep you from escaping. Don't try, because it won't happen." He took a step closer. "I'd be careful," he whispered.

My jaw locked. *Is that a warning or a threat?*

"I have a matter to attend to." Taisho Kohei Hirose bowed. "My men will make sure you get back to your room safely." Without a backward glance, he strode toward the doors as the men on either side opened them to let him pass. Bright sunshine poured through the gap from the now-cloudless sky.

I found myself leaning forward, straining to get more of a glimpse. But the doors slammed shut, and the walls of my captivity amassed around me. I was cut off. *What does Tristan want me to do? What can I do?* A sigh escaped my lips, and I turned, determined to keep exploring. Hirose filled my mind as I slipped out of the room, aware of my ever-present guards behind me. There still seemed something familiar about him, and it went beyond recognizing his voice calling out commands.

It doesn't matter, I told myself. *The Uprising matters, not him.* Casting him from my mind, I focused on exploring and memorizing the layout of the fortress.

Chapter Eleven

A small fire blazed, driving away the morning chill. I stood still as Emi and Kin dressed me in a soft, clinging gown of blue so pale, it was almost white. Closing my eyes wearily, I felt them sweep my hair up and secure it with pins. *Almost time.* Amarante's summons had come an hour earlier. She'd kept her word.

Kin backed away. "All right, my lady, you are ready."

I sighed and walked to the door. "Please lead me to Lady Amarante," I said to the guards outside. One took the lead while the other fell in behind me. I glanced through the open door—Kin stood with her back to me, her deft hands straightening the sheets on the mattress, but Emi remained still and silent, her small, pale form watching me go.

I took one step and then another. Each one carried me farther away from the safety of my room and the quiet company of my maids. I didn't recognize the way. The unfamiliar passageway stretched out before me, narrow but gray and bleak like all the rest. A chilly breeze swept down the corridor, and I shivered, slowing as the guard stopped and motioned to an open archway. The archway led to a wide terrace.

No wonder it was so cold on the way here.

The faint smell of smoke wafted through the air from the braziers, which burned bright with glowing coals and small flames. Their warmth permeated the air, fighting against the crisp winter wind. I shivered beneath the thin sleeves of my tunic, sucking in a breath.

Amarante approached me, wrapped in a thick fur. "It isn't even the dead of winter yet, Miss Barrows. Shall you survive, I wonder?" Over her shoulder, a dozen or so women sat in small groups around the braziers, their gowns a bright array of color against the dull, gray backdrop. She gestured, a bored note underlining her words. "You already know some here, but I shall introduce you to the rest."

"These are the ladies of the court?"

"Only some." Amarante laughed. "These are the ones I deign to invite."

"I'm surprised I'm included."

She smiled. "Yes." One eyebrow rose as she examined me.

A cold breeze swept through. I shivered. "Why?"

"Why not?" She laughed again. "Come, let me introduce you."

It was a blur of faces, names, titles, and forced replies to commonplace phrases. Amarante had been right. I did recognize a few: Suki was there, Amarante's companion of the day before, and Kaida as well, an older matron with harsh features whom I had met the night of the ball. Seeing her had sent a ripple of fear down my spine then, and it did again now. Her cold, dull brown eyes, narrow face, and pale features cast an unearthly aura of doom into the surrounding vicinity. Relief washed over me when I found myself seated between Amarante and Miya, a young woman with a quiet voice.

I stared down into the cup of tea I had been handed, watching as the steam rose in tantalizing swirls of mist. The porcelain warmed my stiff fingers, and I let out a little sigh of pleasure. *Rice.* The smell wafted through the air. Tilting my head down, I brought the cup to my lips and took a sip. The liquid scalded my tongue, and I winced before taking another, more careful sip. The hot tea warmed my insides, and I felt my shoulders relax a little. The young woman next to me kept her head down, staring straight into the cup she cradled on her lap between her small hands.

"Lady Miya," I whispered to her, making sure no one around us was paying attention.

She jumped, the tea running along the rim, threatening to spill out of her cup and onto her lap before settling. We both glanced at Amarante, but her attention was on another.

"Who are you, here at the court, I mean?" I asked, taking another sip.

Her watchful eyes darted around the terrace before returning to my own, then back to her cup. "I am of the king's harem," she murmured, neither blushing nor looking away. "I am new here, so I have yet to become acquainted with the court's ladies."

My mouth opened and closed. "I have to admit ..." I took a deep breath. *What are you going to say? What do you say to someone like her?* I squared my shoulders. "We don't have harems back where I live."

"It is an honor," Miya hissed. "An honor to be chosen by the king. It is my privilege." She receded into herself, her face blank and pale, her eyes so downcast they looked closed.

I shifted on the backs of my heels and adjusted my skirt to rid it of the wrinkles that had formed. "Did you get a choice?"

Miya's face paled until she looked like a porcelain mannikin. "An honor," she repeated.

"Do all of you believe it to be such?" I glanced at Amarante, the queen of the party. She chatted, smiled, and laughed, maintaining the brightness of the small gathering. The other ladies showed her a marked difference, a certain respect and reserve they did not show to one another.

"I will not answer that," Miya replied, returning my attention to her. "It is not something you should ask."

"I'm sorry." I looked down. My tea no longer steamed. The air had cooled it already. "I'm just curious," I added, trying a different tactic. "How long have you been here?"

A pang of longing filled her voice. "Long enough."

"And have you—" I hesitated. "Have you *seen* the king?"

Miya stared at me, her eyes meeting my own for the first time since our conversation had begun. She looked like a fine china doll, so delicate she could break with the slightest push.

"I'm sorry," I said again. "I shouldn't have asked that."

"I have." Her face paled.

Does she regret her answer? I glanced at the gray sky threatening to send either rain or snow down upon us. The chatter of the other ladies filled the sharp air. I stared at the nearest group, three ladies who giggled and examined one another's rings and hair pieces.

"And you are right," Miya muttered. "You should not have asked. We are not just ornaments, you know. We are here for a purpose."

Ornaments. Are they more than that? I twirled my cup in my fingers as I figured out what to ask next. "Do you have children?"

She shook her head. "No."

"And the others?"

Amarante's laugh rose in the air, and Miya seemed to shrink back into herself again. I finished my tea, watching the ladies flock around Amarante, as though trying to win her favor.

"We stick together," Miya said, breaking me away from my thoughts.

"What?" I blurted.

Miya shot me a glare. She waited a moment before answering. "All of us. Those in his harem. We must. If we do not, who will?"

"Are you happy?"

Miya's shoulders tensed. "You should be careful," she whispered.

"Of what?"

She shook her head. "Of whom."

"All right, *whom*, then?"

The laughter and chatter surrounding us faded into the background. Miya stared into my eyes, her own wide. She pursed her lips.

"Miya," I pressed.

"Everyone," she whispered, starting as Amarante's voice called from across the terrace.

"Miss Barrows, come here. I want you to tell us about your home. We are curious." She tucked a loose tendril of hair behind one ear.

My heart began to race as I rose to join her. I glanced over my shoulder at Miya, who remained seated, her eyes trained on her cup of tea. *A mouse hiding from a cat.*

"Tell us of your homeland," Amarante commanded, beckoning. "There is much I would like to know." Her eyes glittered as they swept over my figure.

I approached, ignoring her gesture for me to hurry. Kneeling on a cushion, I felt the cold from the stone floor seep up through it. I shivered. My lips parted to speak, but Amarante's smile grew as she stood, her attention on something behind me. I looked over my shoulder to see Hirose approaching us.

Amarante waved a hand. "Taisho Hirose, a pleasure."

"Lady Amarante, likewise. Ladies." He bowed, his lips quirking into a small smile as his eyes caught mine. "Lady Juliet."

Amarante's smile froze as she strode past me to stand next to Hirose.

"Taisho," I greeted, nodding. "A pleasure seeing you again so soon." The words came so easily to me. *Did I mean them?* I fingered my skirt. *Maybe a little.*

"What brings you here?" Amarante asked the taisho.

Hirose didn't turn away from me. "I am here to bring Lady Juliet to the king."

I stiffened. Smothered gasps rent the air from a couple of the women.

Amarante flinched but otherwise showed no sign of her displeasure. "He asks for her?"

Hirose inclined his head.

Amarante pressed her body closer to his. "Might we interest you in some light repast first?"

"No, my lady. I must return immediately. Lady Juliet?" He held out a hand to me and, after a brief hesitation, I took it and let him help me up. As I turned away, I caught a pitying glance from Miya. Goosebumps spread over my flesh, and not from the cold.

Hirose transferred my hand to his arm and escorted me off the terrace, signaling the guards to fall back from us, just out of earshot. "Why do you tremble?"

"I do not."

"It is quite the honor," he continued, ignoring me as he led the way down the corridor to the left. "Receiving an invitation from Lady Amarante, and to one of her select tea parties no less. Rather curious ... you have to wonder why she issued the invitation."

"I doubt it's because she likes me," I mumbled as we turned into another hallway that branched off.

"Not many win her favor," Hirose said, scanning me from head to toe. "Then again, she has been known to keep her enemies even closer than her friends." He pressed my arm a little, stopping me in front of a large, imposing door.

I know that door. It was the same one that led to the room where I had first met Cruelon.

Hirose dropped my arm and turned to face me. "Be careful with her, Lady Juliet. She is not one to play with."

That doesn't surprise me. I shrugged and glanced at the door behind him. "What does the king want with me?"

Hirose shrugged his narrow shoulders and crossed his arms. "I don't know."

"Don't know, or you refuse to give me an answer?" I kept my tone respectful, even though deep down, I wanted to demand the answers I knew he could give me if he chose to. *One does not become the taisho of the king's private guard without knowing secrets ... And knowing how to keep them.*

"I truly do not know. Let me give you a warning, Lady Juliet."

I waited. *There are a lot of those going around.*

"Use wisdom in your words and actions, no matter whether you think you are alone or not."

Miya flashed through my mind. But not just her: Kin and Emi too.

Hirose tapped a finger against his temple. "Even the walls have ears."

Eyes forward, I focused on breathing, on not letting the doubts arrest the focus I'd commanded of my mind and body.

"Do not test the king. Do whatever he commands. I mean it, Lady Juliet."

"I will." My breathing quickened.

"Whatever he commands, do," he repeated firmly.

"Why are you helping me?"

"I give you words of caution." He knocked once and the doors swung open. He took my arm again and led me through the anteroom and into a familiar, small study. The black chair sat between the two windows, same as before. But this time, Cruelon sat before the low table near the wall. He looked up from his desk and the papers lying scattered over the surface. Hirose lifted my hand from his arm, squeezed it with a slight pressure, and left, the door clicking shut behind him.

I'm alone with the king. I was alone, the perfect opportunity. *This is what Tristan wants.* But I had no weapon.

"Do you like it here, Juliet?" Cruelon's suave voice filled the room, breaking my train of thought. The hem of his robes brushed against the floor. "It was not a rhetorical question, Lady Juliet." The chair creaked as he sat down.

"Pardon me, my lord. It is a complicated question."

A laugh rang through the window. "Yes, I suppose it is, is it not? Come, sit down." Cruelon gestured toward a cushion at his right, and I took a hesitant step forward, then another, until I could sit in the chair. His rancid breath blew over me, the potent and sharp smell of garlic saturating the air. "What do you think of these, Lady Juliet?"

"My lord?" I asked, looking down at the papers covering the desk. It was hard to read them when they were upside down, and my nerves made it hard to focus.

"You come from a different world, yes?"

What does he want to know? I nodded once.

"Look at these papers," Cruelon ordered. "Tell me what you think. Go on. Take your time."

I slid forward in my seat, my palms sweaty, and lifted the first paper. I scanned it. Numbers, full of numbers. The longer I studied it, the more I saw. Troop numbers, guard numbers, population concentrations, amongst others. Another sheet held information about rations, farms, trading ... the papers were endless. As I waded through it all, understanding little, one caught my eye. I slid it out from where it had lain hidden beneath another paper.

Strategies.

Formations, movements, plans, ideas—it was the top page of a small stack, and the rest held much of the same information. Then I saw it: the old rebel base. The one we had had to leave. I scanned the paper. It was a rough blueprint of the underground cave system. *How did he get this?*

"That worked out worse than we had hoped," Cruelon said, watching over my shoulder.

I stiffened, keeping my eyes on the paper.

"We captured some, but they were hardly the numbers we expected." His voice lowered as he leaned closer. "Our intel was not as good as we thought. We had not expected other ways in and out of the tunnels, but I suppose we should have. Who picks a base with only one entrance and exit? And the rebels have proven themselves far from ignorant. They are more resilient than I could have imagined. Have you had any dealings with them?"

"The rebels?" I echoed, forcing myself to keep breathing.

"Yes, you've heard of the Uprising, I assume?" As Cruelon spoke, he made his way around the table.

I picked up another paper to avoid looking at him. It contained an even more detailed map of the base. "I have, my lord." I noticed the route we'd taken to escape wasn't marked. *How did he get this? It's not even complete.* As I went to set them down, I noticed the name printed in small letters on the inside corner where my thumb had rested. *Lanevrog.* What does it mean?

"It would be a pity," Cruelon said with a sigh. "I had hoped you might be of some use to me. Why keep you around otherwise? If you haven't already noticed, Lady Juliet, those who prove themselves useful, entertaining, a possible enemy, or likable enough are allowed to be part of my court. You have not shown yourself to be useful yet, you are too quiet and serious to be entertaining, a possible enemy, I somehow doubt, and—well, yes, I concede I am coming to like you. You are quite pretty and have a beautiful smile. But you have not entertained me." The last sentence was said in a silky, childish sort of voice. It sent shivers through my body.

I looked up from the map I'd been studying and pushed away the thought of who had drawn it, of where it had come from—

"So you see, Lady Juliet, I have to want or need the people who are around me. Otherwise they mean nothing. Do you mean nothing?"

My mind raced. *Then why make me part of the court at all?* The manipulation Cruelon portrayed seeped through the still air of the room. I wished for one of the windows to be open, to feel a fresh breeze on my skin.

"No, my lord."

"Good!" Cruelon nodded, a small smile appearing briefly. "Tell me, what sort of use could you be to me? Have you had encounters with the rebels? Or perhaps stayed with them for a time?"

My chest constricted. I stared at the desk, unseeing. There was a spy. There had to be. *How else could he have received these plans?* I glanced down again at the papers as my mind flashed through the variables of what I should say and what would be the consequences. The air felt stagnant yet full of electricity, as though waiting for the very moment I misstepped to zap me into oblivion. *What if he does know I was with the Uprising? With Tristan?* Sweat beaded on my skin. *I have to seem like my loyalty is with him, not with the rebels.* I set the papers down and licked my lips. *This could give me more opportunities to speak with him ... to get close to him.* I cleared my throat. "I have had an encounter with them."

The king smiled. "There now, that was not so bad."

He did know already. Relief filled me and I felt myself relax. I had made the right decision.

Cruelon swept around the table. "Why did you lie to me, Juliet?" He grasped my chin, forcing me to look at him. A full whiff of his breath entered my nostrils. His fingers tightened. "Why?" he snarled.

"I did not think, my lord. I thought if I told you the truth, you would kill me. Please." In the space of seconds, I'd chosen to become a pitiful, woe-begotten girl, a girl who had panicked and now begged forgiveness, someone helpless, without strength, without fire. "I'm sorry, please forgive me." Fear held me within its fiery grip. *I must convince him.* My legs grew damp from perspiration.

"You are forgiven," he murmured, his face mere inches from mine. "But if you dare to cross me again, there will be consequences. I will not sully your pretty ears. Know that you will not like your fate. It will be nothing like the glamorous lifestyle I have granted you now. But show loyalty to me, honor me, live your life for me, and you will have nothing to fear. Your existence will be one of peace and happiness. Believe me, Lady Juliet, you would do best to obey me, for your sake as well as mine." He released my chin and waved a hand. "What have your dealings with them been?"

What does he know? What has the traitor told him? I cleared my throat. "I was held against my will."

Cruelon's eyes glittered, and his shoulders rose as he leaned closer. "Why?"

"I saw something I wasn't supposed to, and they said they couldn't let me leave."

"What did you see?" Cruelon pressed, tension radiating from him.

My breath caught. "I came across that." I pointed to the underground cave system on the blueprint. "But they captured me before I could get away."

Cruelon drew back and stroked his chin. "You found their hideaway," he mused, tilting his head to regard me. "An impressive feat."

"I wasn't looking for it. I was traveling, trying to find a way back to my home." I let a tremor enter my voice. "I had just escaped when your men found me."

"Aww," Cruelon purred. "You exchanged one sort of prison for another." He slapped a hand down on the table. "Now go. I have work to be done. Tonight, you shall join me for dinner."

I had the vague sense of my lips moving, but I heard nothing. In a daze I rose to my feet, my heart pounding. I turned and walked away, leaving behind the blueprints with Lanevrog written in a small corner and all the other papers that could be of vital importance.

"Wait, one more thing—"

I stopped at the sound of Cruelon's voice.

"I have a spy in Tristan's camp, someone close enough to him when seen in comparison to the information he sends. His name is Lanevrog. A curious name," he mused, staring down at the table. He stirred. "Do you know who he is?"

There was no need to feign ignorance. I shook my head. "I don't know anyone by that name."

Cruelon sighed and went to his chair. "No matter. He, Lady Juliet, has chosen to give his life for king and country, and continues to do so through the dangers that beset him. But you, what will you do?" Cruelon waved another hand, dismissing me as he sat and gazed at the wall, lost in thought.

As I left the study, I knew I had to see those papers again. There had to be something there that would give an explanation or let me know something, anything, about the traitor within Tristan's uprising.

Outside the room, a guard waited, ready to escort me back to my room. When he opened his mouth and spoke, I hardly heard him. The game had changed. I now had information. A name.

Lanevrog. It seemed familiar somehow.

Chapter Twelve

The door rattled before slamming against the wall. My heart raced as Kin and Emi rushed into my bedroom.

"What's going on?" I asked, turning away from the window. Tension filled the air along with the rustling of skirts as Kin hurried to the wardrobe, Emi to the bathroom. "Did something happen?"

Kin spoke, her voice curt. "No time to explain. Come, my lady, we must hurry."

"What is it?"

"My lady, there is no time. Please." She beckoned, her face paler than usual.

I took a step forward.

"You've been summoned to dinner," Kin explained, pulling on my arm to position me where she wanted.

I raised an eyebrow. "Yes, I know."

Kin blinked. "You do?" She turned to the wardrobe and fingered through the many dresses that hung there.

"Yes, this morning the king told me I would be joining him."

Kin glanced at me, her mouth agape, before pulling herself together. "Do you know why?" she muttered under her breath.

I glanced over my shoulder, but Emi hadn't come out of the bathroom yet. "No," I whispered. "Kin, I—"

"Not now." Kin frowned and grabbed a dress. "Emi, hurry it up, girl!"

A light clatter had me glancing over my shoulder. Emi reached down to pick up the fallen item, her arms full of brushes and combs.

"Do you know if it's dinner with just the king?"

"No, no," Kin muttered as she concentrated on her handiwork. "Close your eyes, my lady."

My breathing lightened. *Not just with the king.* I remained quiet as their gentle hands touched my face, applying lotion and makeup.

"No. The king allows a select few to grace his table each night for the evening meal, but to invite you—" Kin hesitated. "You had best be careful, my lady."

Something had her rattled.

"What do you mean?"

"There will be others there tonight," she continued. "Some you will know and others you won't. Don't speak unless you must, keep your eyes downcast, do nothing, *nothing*, to draw attention to yourself. And do not forget the dictates of polite society you have learned while you have been here. This is a test, Lady Juliet, a test you cannot fail."

I opened my mouth to speak, but she continued, "There, you're done. Now go."

In a blur, I was pushed toward the door and out into the hallway. The guards must have already known about the summons, as they herded me along without a word. It was an unfamiliar route. I couldn't keep the turns straight as we headed deeper into the heart of the keep, along narrow passageways lit by single torches, before we entered into a room with one other set of doors.

My breathing came light and fast by the time we stopped in front of the sliding door. I glanced at my guards, unable to hear even a whisper of breath from them, their chests barely heaving after the long walk we'd taken to get here.

I wrung my hands in front of me, my fingers grasping the fabric of my skirt. *Do I go in?* Clothing rustled at my side as my guards moved off down the hallway, slinking along as they melded into the black shadows and disappeared. *I'm alone.* Something dropped far off in the castle, a dull thump that resounded down the stone passageways and corridors, sending chills over my body as I glanced from side to side. Another thud echoed from somewhere deep within the keep, and I took a step forward and away from the eerie echoes. In unison, the doors opened as though someone knew I stood there, waiting to be admitted.

I have no choice, I reminded myself. Sound filtered through as though I were underwater. Light spilled out from the room beyond, lighting the path before me like a royal carpet. I stepped through and halted.

The doors closed behind me.

The room was so silent I could have heard a pin drop. It was an uncomfortable quiet, one that felt like it had to be filled with something to break the awkwardness. This group of people were not at ease with one another. I stayed quiet, feeling the hidden undertone of danger.

My arms fell to my sides, and I focused on unclenching my fingers one by one.

The rectangular table glistened in the soft candlelight. There was one seat left. The rest were taken by the king, Amarante, Natsumi, Taisho Hirose, Miya, Suki, along with five others I didn't recognize. *Twelve, including me.* I took a deep breath and strode forward. *Six women and six men.* My dress swished against my slippers. There wasn't a sound. The air felt charged with static electricity. I blinked. *No, there is no static.* The buzzing in my ears increased.

Hirose rose and bowed, followed by the other men. Only one man did not rise. Cruelon gazed at me from under thick lashes, his umber eyes appearing darker in the dim lighting. His tongue flicked out over his lips.

Run.

Every part of me wanted to run away from them all, run back to my room, back to the semblance of safety I had there.

But I bowed in return.

Hirose strode forward, his footsteps smooth and catlike. His dark hair shone in the gleaming torchlight. He gave me his arm and escorted me the rest of the way to the table, to a seat left of the king. Natsumi watched me with emotionless eyes from across the table, where she sat at the king's right hand. I sat down, making a play of adjusting myself on my cushion as I quickly scanned the rest at the table. Amarante met my gaze, her own icy and cold. She looked away dismissively.

Cruelon waved a hand, and the chatter began. The buzz in my ears faded, only to be replaced with the low murmurs of conversation surrounding me like a soft pillow. I picked up my glass and took a sip. Rice wine. Nutty and reminiscent of toasted rice. I sipped again and peered around the room. It was empty save for the table. Voices carried. It would be hard to have a private conversation in here. *That's probably the point.* I set down my glass. Soon the clatter of glasses, the clink of chopsticks against plates, and the occasional burp from the men commenced.

I picked at my food, eating little but listening. Natsumi and Amarante did an admirable job as conversationalists, neither ever seeming to speak directly to one another, yet keeping the table entertained.

"Are you enjoying the food, Lady Juliet?"

I jumped as Cruelon's voice slithered into my thoughts. *The food?* I hadn't even noticed the taste. I looked down at my bowl of rice and the tantalizing dishes in front of me. "Yes, my lord." I took a sip of my wine, its heady fruitiness rinsing away the sawdust in my mouth, soothing my parched throat, and clearing my voice. "It's delicious," I murmured, taking another sip to forestall any further comments on my part.

"Of course it is. I have the finest chefs in the land."

I looked up as I registered the slurred note in his voice. A gleam shone in his eyes, along with the ruddiness to his cheeks and a general slouch to his normal rigid posture. He laughed at everything the two women said, more often laughing at them than with them, I noticed.

How pathetic. I watched the three of them, wondering if the two women realized they were often the butt of the jokes. *How could Natsumi not realize?* But I knew there was more to her than meets the eye. *Will I ever understand her?* I studied her. She spoke and laughed with a reserved air. Sighing, I took a bite of seared beef and chewed. I knew there was no hope of speaking to her privately tonight.

Amarante laughed. Her amusement appeared genuine. She was filled with longing. It shone in her flirtatious nature, in her desire to be noticed, and in how she dressed. She wanted Cruelon for her own.

"You are more dangerous than you appear, my lady," Hirose whispered into my ear, his breath a warm cloud on my neck.

"Taisho?" I kept my eyes straight ahead, wondering how much he had drunk.

"You seem to be an innocent, gentle sort of woman who keeps to herself, but you are proving to the Ladies Amarante and Natsumi that they have something to be worried about."

My gaze shot toward Cruelon, but he was too busy listening to Amarante to notice our hushed conversation. "But they don't. I haven't done anything," I breathed, my eyes seeking Hirose's.

"Not openly, not yet. But it is obvious there is more to you than they realized. The king placed you in Amarante's seat." He leaned closer, his lips brushing against my ear. "She has been cast down a notch, but it shouldn't come as a complete surprise, even to her. I told you she does not issue invitations to her parties from the goodness of her heart. You are competition, Lady Juliet. Even your invitation to tonight's dinner tells everyone here something, and soon everyone in the entire castle will know. You'd best remember my words of caution, my lady. You are playing a dangerous game, a very dangerous game."

I drew my hands into my lap. "But I don't want this," I whispered.

"I know, but do they know that?" He sat back and took a deep drink of his wine.

Natsumi inspected me for a millisecond so brief that the chattering king did not notice.

I stiffened, aware again of the muted conversations surrounding me. *Had she heard anything?*

"See?" Hirose murmured; his words were so low I had to strain myself to catch them. "You are always watched, Juliet—watched more often than you realize and by more eyes than you realize. Do you know what game you're playing?"

You've already asked me that, I wanted to say. I bit my lip. An icy shiver ran up my spine, and I took the glass of wine in my hand, wrapping my fingers around it and bringing it to my lips, too late realizing how my hands shook.

Hirose watched me. "If not, then you'd best figure it out." He shifted away from me, turning to the woman who sat on the other side of him. But Amarante stared at me, her brows drawn together, and her full, red lips curved playfully as she cocked her head to the side and raised her glass to me.

I raised my own in a salute, watching as she winked. *What did she hear?* I knew Hirose had spoken loud enough at the end for anyone to hear. *No one will know what he meant by telling me to figure it out.* My thoughts started feeling a little sluggish. I took my chopsticks in hand but had a harder time using them to pick up a piece of pickled cucumber.

A boisterous laugh broke from the king, shattering the moment that existed between us for those few brief moments. It rang through the room, echoing off the dark wood panels set into the white-washed walls.

Why am I here? I touched the rim of the glass to my lips but hesitated. *Why does it seem fuller than I remember?* My eyes widened. How often had it been refilled? How much had I drunk? I set the wine down and reached for the water instead. *How much do they see?* Relaxation filled my limbs, fighting against the tension radiating from my position at this table. *It's only temporary.* I pushed the glass of wine away from me. It only provided a temporary illusion, a façade.

"What?" Cruelon's questioned with a slur. "Do you not like my wine?"

I frowned in concentration as I replied, "It's delicious, my lord, as is everything else."

"Then why push your glass away?"

The table went silent.

I ignored the ten faces watching. "It is so good I'm afraid I have done it enough justice." My breathing sounded loud in my own ears.

Cruelon's laugh rolled out, high and reedy. A long tendril of dark hair hung near his ear where it had fallen out of his bun. "Fair, fair."

How similar and yet how different he looks compared to Tristan. Yet the speech is the same ...

A servant stepped forward.

"It is time," Cruelon said, nodding to him.

"Time?" I repeated under my breath, not intending for anyone to hear.

"Dinner is over," Hirose answered as chatter resumed about us. He rose and helped me to my feet. "Never more than two hours, never less. The king likes to be punctual," he added in a low voice.

I let him lead me out behind the others. One by one, those who had gathered peeled off as they headed toward their rooms for the evening. Hirose moved aside to catch a man I didn't know and, after a moment, Miya stepped up next to me.

"Some of the ladies and I are going for a ride in the morning," she said, her voice barely above a whisper. "I wanted to see if you would come."

I blinked and leaned closer. "Outside?"

Miya blinked. "Yes."

"I'll go," I blurted out. "But is it allowed?"

Miya glanced around. "There should be no harm in asking, especially if you say it is at the invitation of Lady Amarante."

"Is it?"

"No, but who will know?" Miya's eyes twinkled, transforming her face into one even more beautiful. I could see how she had become a favorite of the king's, but then felt a pang of guilt and horror at the thought.

"How will I get there?" I breathed, watching as the group dwindled down to Hirose and an unknown man, Natsumi, Amarante, and Cruelon.

"I'll send word to Kin and Emi to ready you, and to the guards that Amarante has issued orders for you to join her on her morning ride." Miya's pale face reddened a little. "It would do her good to be taken down a little."

I raised an eyebrow at her deviousness. "Is this for me, then, or more for her?"

"Can't it be both?"

My lips parted. *There's more to this than I thought.*

Miya straightened and shifted on her feet. "I should go. Until tomorrow, Lady—"

"Call me Juliet, please."

Miya acknowledged, "Juliet, then."

I didn't watch her leave. A roar of laughter from the king turned my attention to him. He turned from Natsumi, who he had escorted out, and slid Amarante's arm into his own. "Come, m'dear," he said, his words like the hiss of a dangerous snake, a viper soft-spoken but on the threshold of a bite.

I approached Natsumi. She stood alone, staring after the king as he and Amaranate moved down the hallway. The familiar scents of warm bread and cinnamon washed over me. Hirose was deep in conversation, not paying attention to us. *Take your chance,* I told myself as I stopped.

I glanced aside at her. "Natsumi."

Her brown eyes flicked over me.

I opened my mouth. "You—"

"Beware the pretender, Lady Juliet."

Her words blew over me with a clap of thunder. *Those words.* I had heard them before. It seemed like so long ago when she had spoken those words to me. *Beware the pretender.*

The hairs on the back of my neck rose. I glanced over my shoulder to see Hirose approaching. I realized then that the low hum of his voice had quieted. There was no sign of the other man he'd been speaking to.

When I looked back, Natsumi was already down the hall, walking with slow, sure strides.

"An interesting woman." Hirose's shoulder brushed my own. "She's quite fascinating," he noted. "Full of mystery. It's no wonder the king keeps her around and caters to her every whim, even when she refused to become queen or join his harem."

"Refused to become queen?" I echoed, my mind racing. Her warning. *Am I the pretender?* Was it meant to warn me that she knows, or did Hirose overhear? Who were the words for?

"Yes. Why? You seem surprised." He nodded in encouragement.

I struggled to make sense of the conversation through the muddled effects of the wine. *Her warning. Queen.* I couldn't remember why it seemed important, just that it did. "Did I?" I asked. "I just hadn't heard."

Hirose eyed me but didn't question. "For now, Natsumi's position is a good one. But things can change quickly here, as I think you are aware."

I opened my mouth to respond, but exhaustion pulled at me and I couldn't remember what I was going to say. Everything felt sluggish, as though I struggled to make my way through thick water.

Hirose waved the man he'd been speaking to forward. "My taisa will escort you to your room, where your guards await. He is my second-in-command."

The taisa, a small man with hardened features, offered me his arm.

I took it, not trusting myself to make my way back without support, not through the slight fuzziness in my head and the oddly clear clarity in which I saw everything. *Not that I have the choice anyway.*

"Goodnight, Lady Juliet," Hirose said. "Until we meet again."

His words followed the taisa and me as we made our way out of the room and into a darkened corridor. *Beware the pretender.* Natsumi's words, Natsumi's voice. I swallowed and slumped a little as I walked. *She must mean me.*

Chapter Thirteen

K in and Emi showed up the next morning with a beautiful scarlet riding habit. I tried convincing them to let me keep my hair down, as I knew it would come loose while riding anyway, but they refused. In the end, we compromised by doing a half updo.

Emi took the now-empty pitcher in which she had brought hot water. "I will go fetch your breakfast now, my lady."

Kin nodded, her hands falling from where she had put the last touches to my hair. The door closed behind Emi. We were alone now. Not a sound penetrated the imposing stillness.

I broke the silence. "Kin—"

"We don't have long," Kin interrupted. "Do you have anything for me to pass on?"

I was right. Relief washed over me. I grinned. "Yes, I do."

"What is it, then?" Kin tapped a slippered foot on the floor. "I will send it as soon as I am able, hopefully by tomorrow."

I stared at her, at a loss for words. My excitement dwindled.

"Lady Juliet," she said in a softer voice, stepping forward. Her shoulders lost some of their tension. "We don't have long. What news do you have for Lord Tristan?"

I shook myself. "There is a spy."

Kin's hands clenched into fists.

"His name is Lanevrog. At least, that's what was on the papers I saw in Cruelon's office."

"Do you have the papers?"

I blinked and shifted on my feet. "No."

"Very well," Kin muttered, glancing toward the still-closed door. "Do you have proof of this?"

"No ..." I knew the way to Cruelon's office. I knew where they were kept. But I was never unsupervised. I bit my lip as I thought. "But I think I can get proof as long as I can get away from my guards."

"Good. If you can, get the papers you speak of. It will also give you a chance to see what else may be of use. Is there anything more?" She stiffened as soft sounds filtered through the door from outside.

"Cruelon wants me to join his harem," I whispered, the words plunging out of my mouth like a waterfall. "I'm stalling, though."

Emi entered the room and Kin strode away from me without a backward glance. "Here you go, my lady," she said, setting the tray down. "You don't have much time to eat."

I hurried over and wolfed down the eggs, rice, and pickled vegetables. Kin and Emi busied themselves about the room while I ate. I took a drink of tea, grabbed my cloak, and left the room.

Miya stood outside, waiting near the guards. I raised my eyebrows and drew close to her as we walked down the corridor.

"I'm assuming you have a plan?" I whispered, hoping the guards behind us weren't close enough to hear.

"Yes." Her lips quirked into a small smile. "The king has a rigorous routine. By now, he should be returning from his walk, where we will happen to meet him. Here he comes."

A pang of apprehension settled over me, but there was no time to back out or question her.

He caught sight of us. "Lady Juliet, Lady Miya, a pleasant surprise this morning. Juliet, the habit becomes you. You will wear red more often. It lights you up like a fire. Where are you ladies off to?"

I licked my lips, unused to the bright gaiety with which he spoke. "My lord, Lady Amarante has invited me to join her and some of the ladies for a ride." How easy the lie came to my lips. "I would like permission to accompany her."

"In such a dress as that, I would find it hard-pressed to deny you. You may go." He waved a hand in the air. "You are free to come and go as you please." But

I could see the unspoken limitations in the depths of his eyes. "I will accompany you."

I started, as did Miya. This was not what either of us had expected.

"I will join you shortly. Please tell Amarante." He turned aside to the guards while we continued.

"He's coming?" I whispered to Miya once we were out of earshot. "That wasn't part of the plan."

"Hush, not here. It is not wise to voice such thoughts out loud."

"The guards fell behind," I reminded her. "They can't hear me."

Miya glanced over her shoulders, her tension fading as she relaxed. "I hate him," she exclaimed softly. The intensity in her voice was overwhelming. "I cannot stand being around him. Sometimes, I hope he will forget about me, what with all the other women he must choose from."

"Why did you become his mistress?" I asked.

She chuckled, but it was dry. "I didn't have much of a choice in the matter. It is an honor to be chosen by the king. It brings honor to my family, as well as wealth and rank. They never see me. It makes it all easier. And there are the other women. I am not alone in this."

"Do the others feel the way you do?"

"No, not all." She shrugged. "Some do, others do not. And still others hide all personal feelings when it comes to who we are."

I was at a loss for words. *What do I say to her?* What words of comfort could I offer when I could not even begin to understand that kind of lifestyle?

The rustle of the guards' clothing as they approached forestalled any more conversation between us. Miya stared straight ahead, her expression peaceful, her face giving no hint of what she'd said to me.

It's as if it never happened.

I felt the guards fall in right behind us. Miya's hand trembled the slightest bit, almost imperceptible to the eye. I brushed my shoulder against hers. Her jaw locked. The booted footfalls of the men behind us reminded us that we were never alone. *Hirose was right. There are always ears listening.*

Ahead, the two men flanking the doors opened them. The wood creaked, and as they did, natural light fell across us. My breath caught in my throat as we stepped through. In the courtyard beyond, horses nickered and stamped, restless with energy. Amarante stood near them, her blue dress a stark contrast to the brown of the horses and the dullness of the courtyard. I lifted my gaze to the sky: gray skies, gray clouds.

"Miss Barrows," Amarante spoke, her voice icy. "What are *you* doing here?"

"The king says to tell you he will be along shortly," Miya said before I could respond.

Amarante's face brightened like a ray of sunshine. "Well, this is a welcome turn of events I hadn't seen." She turned away, calling as she went, "Please have the king's mount saddled! And a few extras, as well. He will probably bring some escorts." She did not give me another glance.

I was forgotten. *For now.*

The stable hands hurried to do her bidding. I gazed around the courtyard, reveling in the fresh air and enjoying the dulled brightness of the overcast morning. Beyond the men tacking horses, cherry blossom trees stood, stretching to the corner of the main keep, their branches bare.

Conversation became muted, and I turned to see Cruelon approaching. He wasn't alone. Hirose and a few of the black guard accompanied him.

Taking the reins of a horse, Hirose approached me. "My lady," he greeted. "Your mount."

I placed a foot in the stirrup. Swinging my legs over, I watched as he joined me on a dappled mare. I cleared my throat. "Does the king not want you to ride beside him?"

"He has his company."

I looked to where Amarante sat upon her mare, chattering to the king, her voice too low to hear.

Braying cut through the air. I stiffened, listening to the frenzied barking as it grew closer.

"Ah, the king's hounds," Hirose said by way of explanation.

"I've heard them before." I shivered as goosebumps ran over my skin. The dogs appeared in the doorway of one of the smaller buildings, ushered through by their keeper, a burly man whose long, dark hair was tied back.

"Come, my precious hounds!" the king cried. He laughed as the dogs' excitement grew.

"Does he take them out often?" I asked, trying to calm my mount.

Hirose was spared answering as Cruelon took off, the others close behind. My horse needed no encouragement. He sprang after the rest, his strides short and quick. I struggled to maintain my seat. Breathing in, I managed to rein in my horse to a more manageable pace. Hirose followed close beside me as we exited the fortress.

I surveyed the plains we rode through. The fortress lay there the whole time. No matter which way I looked, it always seemed to be there, if not in sight, then in my mind. I took a deep breath. *At least I get a taste of fresh air.* The cloak I wore rippled across my shoulders as a breeze picked up.

"You are quiet," Hirose called, speaking over the hounds' barking as they fanned out around us.

My fingers whitened as I tightened my hold on the reins.

"No matter. Enjoy the breath of fresh air."

While you can. The words hung in the air, unsaid. I peered across the never-ending brown plains. In the distance, a forest stretched, short to my eye, but I knew if I could just ride closer, the trees would loom tall before me. Behind the fortress, mountains loomed, their peaks white with snow. Grand and imposing, they hemmed in the valley as a natural barrier. I turned to look west, across the lake with its quiet waters. *What is Tristan doing now?* I followed the rest of the group as they headed back to the castle. *Can Saya see me now?*

⁕ ⁕

Emi waited in my room when I returned from the ride. She motioned me forward to stand in front of a mirror.

I glanced toward the door to the bathroom. "Where is Kin?"

Emi scanned the closed door where the guards waited outside. "She is unwell, my lady."

I grabbed her arm. "Is everything all right?"

Emi pulled away and hung my riding habit. "Yes, my lady."

"Is she sick?"

Emi brought me a simple tunic and pants from the wardrobe. Without another word, she helped me dress and bowed.

I held out a hand. "Emi, wait."

"No, please, my lady." Emi ran out of the room, her young face pale.

Frowning, I walked over to the window and leaned my forearms on the sill. I could see the same tree line off in the distance—a sea of blurry green, still and unmoving. The wild grass and weeds growing between here and there blew in the breeze.

I sighed and propped my head on my arms, looking up to see the still, heavy grayness of the sky. There hadn't been any rain all day. The last few days always looked like rain, but it never fell. Instead, an overpowering dreariness lay over everything and left me with an ache for sunshine. Even rain would be better than nothing. I stared at the sky, hoping something would happen.

Am I the only one who wishes for rain? I wanted it to drum against the ground, to relieve the oppressive silence I found myself in the midst of, but my wishes were never answered. At the least, it would provide some sort of sound other than the guards' chatter and laughter in the courtyards below.

I was left alone the rest of the morning. At some point midday, a servant appeared with lunch and disappeared without a word. Expecting a couple of hours before Kin and Emi would arrive to dress me for dinner, I rolled up the sleeves of my tunic to practice some of the self-defense tactics I'd been taught before leaving the safety of the mountain. I trained in silence, trying to make as little noise as possible so that no one would know what I was doing.

Tired, I flopped onto the bed.

The door opened and Kin appeared.

"Kin," I exclaimed, sitting up.

"You've been summoned, my lady." Kin closed the door and walked across the room.

Summoned. I stood up, tension rippling through my limbs. *Where's Emi?* "Kin, where were you this morning? And where is Emi now?"

Kin opened the wardrobe. "I was unwell, my lady."

"And now you're better?"

"Able to serve you, my lady." She fingered through the wardrobe.

She's stalling. "Is Emi all right?"

Kin took out a dress and motioned me toward her.

"Kin?" I raised my arms and donned the dress, holding my breath as Kin laced up the tight, corset-like material.

"I sent word to the Uprising," Kin said as she began brushing my hair. When I felt her fingers go still, I twisted my neck to look up at her. Her eyes were wide, her mouth open, but no sound came out.

"Kin?" I whispered.

"I ..." she began, her voice weak.

"Go on," I encouraged.

Her lips pursed, and her fingers busied themselves in my hair again. I felt my hair lift off the back of my neck as she pulled it up into a bun and secured it.

I took a deep breath. "Kin, is there something else going on?"

Kin looked like a cornered animal—unsure of whom to trust, unsure of whether someone was a predator about to rip her to shreds or a friend in disguise of one.

I extended a hand. "Kin, you can trust me. We're in this together."

"The king questioned me," she murmured.

"What?" I blurted out, rising.

"Hush," Kin reprimanded, her hands pushing on my shoulders.

I sat back down. "About what?"

Kin slid pins with dark blue jewels in the shape of flowers into my hair. "About you. There, you're ready. I had nothing to tell him."

"And Emi?" I asked, fingering the tendril of hair that curled down my shoulder.

"I believe she is also being questioned. She's been missing for a few hours."

I stood and reached out. "Oh Kin, I—"

A fist pounded on the door. I jumped, my hands trembling.

"Don't trust anyone else. Be careful, Otherworlder."

The knock came again.

Kin crossed the room, her usual, unreadable demeanor back.

A guard outside said, "Is she ready?"

Kin stepped aside. "She is."

I passed her, but her gaze remained glued to the floor. *Am I ready? Another night, another dinner.* Would Cruelon demand an answer? I felt my silent guards fall in behind me.

I stood in front of the double doors, knowing Cruelon and the others sat inside. The single window in the room let in a dim stream of light as the sun set. I was a little early. The guards left as they always did. I was alone. I bit my lip. *I'm not being guarded.* My mind raced. *The papers—now's my chance.* My heartbeat quickened, beating in my chest like a set of drums. Turning, I lifted my skirt and ran out of the room. Down the corridor, into another room, and then into the dark, narrow hallway that branched off. Soon I stood before the king's study. I hadn't seen a soul. Cold air filled the fortress, sending everyone to the areas warmed by fires. Reaching out a hand, I touched the door and slid it open. *Why isn't the room guarded?* I stepped inside, sliding the door closed behind me. Striding over to the low table, I saw the papers had gone. My heart fell. I spun on my heel.

There. A chest sat against the wall, low and deep.

It wouldn't open. I knew time was ticking by. I swallowed and took a deep breath. The air felt stifling. Leaning down, I took one of the long pins out of my hair. While a jeweled flower decorated one end, the other was sharp and pointy. Taking another pin, I inserted both ends into the lock. In my world, I used to unlock doors with bobby pins. *It can't be too different.* I bit my lip as I felt resistance. A sharp click rang through the air.

My hands trembled as I pulled open the lid. Inside were stacks of papers, ink, and quills. I rifled through, my fingers shaking from the pressure. *Lanevrog.* The name stared up at me as I looked down at the blueprints of the underground caves. Slipping the paper out, I rolled it up and stuck it down my bodice.

A high-pitched voice spoke outside. "Why isn't there a guard here?"

Shoving the papers back into the chest, I closed the lid and scrambled to find a hiding spot. Lying on the floor behind the low table, my cheek pressed against the cold wood, I listened as the door opened with a dull rasp.

Mincing footsteps pranced into the room. "Hello?"

I held my breath. *Master Hiito.* I hadn't seen him since I'd arrived.

"Hello?" he called again.

I peered around the corner of the table. Hiito clasped his pudgy hands before him as he finished surveying the seemingly empty room. He turned on his heel and left, the door sliding shut behind him. Letting out the breath I'd been holding, I slipped to the door and glanced into the anteroom. It was empty. The flame from the torch flickered as I ran past it, my tight skirt preventing me from taking long strides. I could feel the roughness from the paper on my skin. Within minutes, I stood in front of the closed doors to the dining room. Fighting to even my breathing, I slid my fingers through my hair, trying to push the hairs that had come loose back into the high bun. I reached for the door, but it jerked open before my hand made contact. Warm candlelight spilled out of the dining hall. My jaw dropped as I saw Hirose standing before me, his brows furrowed, his eyes almost as black as the clothing he wore.

"Lady Juliet," he greeted, his tone icy.

Did they know? I cast the fear aside as I bowed. "Taisho."

"Come." He stepped aside to let me pass. Cruelon lowered his glass, and those seated at the table went silent. I bowed low before sitting down.

"Why so late?" Cruelon purred, his voice filling the air with a quiet roar.

"My apologies, my lord. I had a"—I hesitated—"a slight wardrobe malfunction."

"I sent Taisho Hirose to go and find you," Cruelon explained, his dark eyes searching my face.

"I am sorry to keep you waiting, my lord. It won't happen again."

"See that it doesn't." Cruelon raised his glass and signaled those present to begin eating.

All too aware of the paper hidden beneath my dress, I raised my glass and took a long drink of the sweet wine. It flowed down my throat, chasing away a little of the tension filling my body. I turned my attention to the pandering undertones of the dinner conversation.

⚶

With weariness filling my limbs and weighing down my shoulders, I entered my living quarters. A small sigh escaped my lips. A figure near the window turned.

I straightened. "Kin—"

Footsteps approached out of the small bathroom.

"Emi," I greeted the young girl with relief. "Are you all right?"

A shadow fell over Emi's countenance. "I was unwell, my lady, but I feel better now."

I thought I saw her cheeks redden, but I couldn't tell with the shadows falling across her face. Kin shot me a warning look as she turned to the wardrobe. My eyes struggled to stay open as she made to help me out of the finery.

"Kin," I muttered, edging away from Emi. "Tonight was very interesting." My eyes narrowed, and I slid a hand down the front of my dress.

Kin's jaw tightened, and a muscle pulsed in her neck. She nodded. "Emi, please bring me a nightshirt." Not another word was spoken as they exchanged my dress for a long, loose shirt. I felt a sense of relief, knowing that the paper was now out of my possession. The heady aroma of jasmine wafted through the air, and Emi backed away from where she had lit some incense. I sank onto the thick mattress and lay back with a sigh. The feathers within provided a plush softness beneath my weary body.

Footsteps approached. I opened my eyes to see Kin looking down at me, Emi close behind.

"I will take care of this," Kin said, her face betraying no emotion. "Good night, my lady." Kin's lips curved up in the barest hint of a smile. She and Emi bowed.

"Good night," I whispered to their backs. They took the lit candle with them, leaving the room plunged into darkness. I pulled the blankets up to my chin and burrowed beneath them. The night air was growing colder with each day that passed. The empty fireplace was just that. Empty. No fire warmed its hearth. As I drifted off, I wondered how long it would take before Tristan heard of the traitor, before he received the proof. Was Lanevrog even real? Or was it something made up? My thoughts slowed even as sleep stole over me.

Chapter Fourteen

The next two days passed in a flurry, much like the coming winter. I had used every moment I could to either train or explore the mountain fortress, committing hallways, corridors, and rooms to memory. In the safety of my quarters, I drew floor plans, slowly putting together a map. It had been easy to obtain paper, a quill, and ink. They now sat on the little writing table I had requested.

Each night I tried to speak with Natsumi, and each night she evaded me beyond a greeting. Cruelon ignored me, leaving me free to watch and listen. Both nights I returned to my room and sank into bed, relieved beyond measure to be away from him and the ever-present thought of assassination.

I stared down at the paper in front of me. The fine black lines showed the first floor of the keep, with the main entrance opening into the anteroom containing the paintings and the various rooms, some filled with weapons, the rest stocked with food and provisions. There were a few rooms I didn't know what they contained, as they were always locked. I laid the map aside and looked over the second. With a sigh, I finished marking the dining hall on the second floor and retraced the route from that to Cruelon's study. The stairwells to the first floor were all marked, but there were fewer from the second floor to the third.

Lunch came and went, and the sun traveled across the sky as the afternoon passed. I barely noticed the heat from the blazing fire as I again stared down at the maps. I tapped the feather against my chin. They were ready. I laid the quill to the side.

A knock rang through the air. I shot to my feet, rushing to the wall where the wood paneling ran up to meet the beam supporting the ceiling. I slid the papers into a thin gap and stepped away, my heart racing, just as the door slid open. Kin and Emi came in, Kin's sharp eyes narrowing as she saw me shift on the balls of my feet.

"Emi, go get the bath ready, please." Kin waited until Emi disappeared to order water to be brought up. "My lady," she whispered. "What is it?"

"I have something for you." I peeked over her shoulder. The door remained open, but Emi was still out of sight. "Here." I slid the papers out and gave them to her.

In one fluid motion, Kin rolled them up and slid them under her tunic.

Light footsteps heralded Emi's return.

"Thank you, Kin," I spoke, loudly enough for Emi to hear. "The fire is perfect. It's been warm enough in here." I hid my wince at how formal I sounded.

Kin bowed and backed away to help Emi. There was nothing for me to do but watch as servants appeared bearing pails of hot water. It took a few rounds before the last of the servants left the room and the door closed, shutting off the draft wafting in from the hallway.

"My lady," Kin began, "your bath is ready." She ushered me into the bathroom, where steam rose in heady curls from the water in the tin tub. An aroma of jasmine pervaded the small space. I slipped out of my clothes into the cold air, clutching my arms around me as I raced on tiptoes to the tub and slid in. The initial burst of fiery hotness on my skin and a deep cold inside my body warred with one another before the heat from the water won over. My eyes closed as I relaxed.

"I'll be right back," Kin said.

As I watched her go, I traced a finger along the rim of the tub. She and Emi spoke in low tones.

Footsteps marked Kin's return to the bathroom. "How was dinner last night?" she asked in a whisper. "You barely spoke a word after you came back."

My mind flashed back to the night before, to the dinner I'd rather forget than remember. It had been identical to the others: the same people, the same delicious food, the same overwhelming amounts of wine and sake consumed around me, the same boisterous laughter and conversation, the same rowdiness, and above all, the same disgust that filled my entire being the longer the night went on. The lecherous ways of the king with the women at the table, or with the wives with the husbands of the advisors, sickened me. A nauseous feeling grew in the pit of my stomach. And always, the fear nagged at me as I wondered what Natsumi would do. *Am I leverage?*

"My lady?" Kin laid a gentle hand on my shoulder.

"It was pretty much the same as it has been, and I'm sure it will be the same tonight. Kin, when—"

Kin hushed me, her fingers held across her lips as Emi's footsteps came closer and she entered the room.

"Is there anything else I can do before I take these downstairs?" Emi asked around the armful of bedding.

"No, thank you, Emi. I'll come down and help with them after I'm done here," Kin responded, a soft look in her eyes.

Emi turned and left. We listened as the door closed behind her in the outer room.

"You love her," I noted, my voice just above a whisper.

Kin didn't say anything, but neither did she move.

"Does she have no one?"

"No one except for me."

"She's lucky," I murmured, "and she knows it."

A harsh laugh broke from Kin's throat. "Really?" Her question grated on the air like chalk on a board, harsh and chilling. "What have I done or said to show her my love? Nothing. She knows me as a stern, overbearing, emotionless woman, Juliet Barrows. You have seen through my façade, but she has not." Kin strode to the door and paused a moment. "I live a lie—a lie I may have to live until I die." She turned to face me. "But that's all right, Juliet. I am working for a cause worth dying for, worth everything I have done and will do. Though Emi may never understand, I do this for her and for others like her."

You and I are more alike than either of us realized. I stared at Kin, taking in the lines about her eyes, the gray streak at her temple, and the heavy cast to her shoulders. *I have been lying every day since I got here, and I am seeking a way to kill the king.* With each day that passed, it was but another chance that I could end up dead or in the dungeon. I tried not to think about it. It was easier to focus on the tasks at hand, and I never forgot that with Cruelon gone, these people could live in safety. No one else like Mari would have to give up their lives.

"Juliet?"

I looked up.

Kin hugged herself. "You were lost in thought."

I shook my head. *Emi.* We'd been talking about Emi. "Why don't you trust her with the truth?" I asked.

The lines in Kin's face deepened. "She is young. I am protecting her. I am surprised you ask. Do you want harm to befall her?"

"No, not at all!" I fought to bury the defensiveness I felt rising. "I was just curious. Kin, believe me when I say I don't want you or Emi to be hurt." My voice cracked from emotion. "I don't want anyone to be responsible for either of your deaths."

Kin smiled wearily. "Oh, Lady Juliet. If something happens to me, or to Emi, it doesn't mean it's your fault. If I am found out, do not take that upon yourself. I am making my own choices. I live my own life." She backed away. "I must go."

I slumped as I watched her leave the room.

Chapter Fifteen

I glanced at Cruelon from under lowered eyelashes, Hirose's voice fading in the background. Cruelon's eyes gleamed as he stared at Natsumi, but I couldn't make out their whispered conversation. With a small smirk, Cruelon set his wine down and rose from the dinner table. Glasses clinked as the rest of us followed suit and struggled to rise quickly. The rustle of clothing and the jostling of cushions sliding on the floor preceded heavy breathing as the men and women struggled to remain standing, inebriated as they were.

More so than my first night. The first night, I hadn't been careful enough, and the wine had been a welcome heady relief. Now, I was much more careful. It was the sixth evening Cruelon had me join him for dinner, and while the same men and women graced the king's table, I wondered, with the number always being six men and six women, whose spot had I taken. Hirose had told me I had taken Amarante's seat, but who had she replaced?

Hirose's shoulder brushed against mine for the briefest of moments as he passed me. Feeling more than just his attention on me, I looked about until I saw Natsumi staring at me, the light from the candelabra reflecting in the dark brown of her eyes. She turned to follow Cruelon, but he turned away from Amarante to face her.

"Natsumi," he murmured, his glass-like voice shattering the quiet. He extended his arm and Natsumi took it, her gaze flickering toward me. My chest tightened. *Beware the pretender.* The words lay between us, unspoken. The king moved away with Natsumi on his arm.

Hirose turned to me and offered his arm. "Courage, Lady Juliet," he whispered as we followed the king and Natsumi out of the room.

I stiffened.

He patted my hand with his free one. "No, no, you're stronger than that. Master your emotions like you want to be able to. Control them so that no one around you knows how you feel. For example …" He leaned closer to me, his head almost brushing my own. "You want something, don't you? I see how you watch Natsumi and Amarante. But if you don't want them to see your desire to be like them, then don't let them feel the stiffness in your posture …" He trailed off as his fingers traced the skin around my wrist. "Or the softness of your skin, or the pulse in your wrist, rapid with anticipation, nerves racing …" He shook himself and raised his gaze back to mine. "Control it until it lies deep within. You need to be better at pretending."

Pretending. Does he know? My lips parted, but Hirose brushed quick fingers across my lips. We stopped. My heart raced. The rest of the courtiers and advisors spilled out behind me, all waiting on the king—all waiting for something.

Cruelon let Natsumi's arm drop. Two slow steps later and he faced us, but he turned toward me. My shoulders rose, and I forced a smile to my face. *You enjoy his conversation,* I told myself. *Act like it.* In one fluid motion, Cruelon slipped my arm under his and dragged me out of the room. I looked back over my shoulder to see Hirose standing there, emotionless.

What is he doing? My eyes darted around, looking for the answer. *Amarante.* The fury reflecting from Amarante's face was terrible. I trembled.

Cruelon slowed after we rounded a corner and pulled me to a stop. A torch was set into a bracket on the wall, providing a dim light. As he breathed out, the sickly sweet smell of wine and spices blew into my face. A draft blew through the narrow space, sending the flame flickering.

I shuddered as his lips brushed against my ears.

"You are so pretty," he slurred. "One of the most beautiful women I have ever seen. Not like Natsumi, mind, but you have an exotic—" He waved his free hand in the air. "Something about you. It's quite … intoxicating."

"My lord …" I said, trying to take another step back, but I felt the wall against my back. My feet froze to the floor, and the cold stone pressed into my skin through my dress. Cruelon's body leaned closer. The air grew stifling and hot.

My dress is too tight. My heart felt as though it would jump out of my chest.

"Isn't Natsumi the exotic one?" The words burst out of me as though a dam had broken.

"What?" Cruelon's features scrunched together in thought.

"I look more like your people. *She* is the one who does not look like those from your homeland."

His face came even closer. "Interesting. And what do you know of our history?"

I remained silent.

"Do you also know that custom dictates I am to marry from my home-land?"

Not Amarante. Nor Natsumi. Why is Natsumi here, then? My lips parted and closed. *But Hirose said Cruelon wanted to make Natsumi his queen.*

Cruelon squeezed my arm, and all the thoughts inside my head disap-peared. "You could become part of my house. It is an honor."

For me or you? But the words would not come out. "Part of your house, my lord?" My voice trembled.

"Every woman would jump at the chance," Cruelon purred.

He's forgotten about Natsumi. She doesn't jump at the chance. I blinked. "Your wife or your concubine?"

Cruelon's smile widened. "Which would you prefer?"

I bit my lip.

He leaned even closer. "You are not from my home country, Juliet Barrows, the *Otherworlder*. You may look like it, but you are not. So, I ask again, will you become part of my household?"

I sniffed. I could smell the sake in his breath. *Your concubine. Can you not even say it?*

"Is there another?" His hand tightened over my arm.

"No!" I exclaimed, but two faces jumped to my mind.

"There is," Cruelon sneered.

I looked him straight in the face. *Steel. I can be steel. Strength, think of strength.* Taking a short breath, I shook my head. "I'm overwhelmed, my lord. Could I have some time to think about this?"

Cruelon's smile widened. "Of course, my dear Juliet." He giggled, but it was more like a deep cackle. "Just don't take too long." His fingers trailed along my arm, the thin fabric the only barrier between his searching hand and my skin.

I closed my eyes, hoping he would see it as my being overwhelmed rather than disgusted. Every nerve hung on the edge as though on fire, sending a warning to every part of my body to be ready—though for what, I couldn't guess.

Something pinged far down the corridor, echoing down the narrow corridor. I stiffened the slightest bit, a new wave of tense emotion running over me. I looked back at Cruelon, startled to see his face with its sharp angles so close to mine. I jerked my head back, wincing as a sharp pain spread like wildfire across the base of my skull.

He changed in an instant—his figure rigid, fingers gripping like iron, digging into my skin. He loomed over me, all symptoms of his drunken stupor gone, as though it had all been a farce.

"I could make you." He gripped my chin in his other hand, forcing me flat against the wall. "I am the king. I could make you do anything."

I waited, my heart rising and falling as I tried to regulate my breathing. One thought stayed clear in my mind: *I can't lose it; I have to stay in control, stay focused.*

His eyes stared into mine, dark and furious. We stood there for what seemed like an age, long enough that my arms went numb.

"My lord."

I could have cried. Hirose stood a few feet away, but I didn't dare turn my head all the way.

"What is it, Taisho?" Cruelon snapped, releasing me.

"It can wait, my lord." Hirose bowed and shuffled backward.

"No," Cruelon snapped. "Why did you interrupt me?"

Hirose straightened, not once looking at me. "A messenger has arrived. It is urgent."

"And it can't wait until morning?"

I flinched as Cruelon bit each word out.

Hirose bowed again, his eyes flitting over me. "You did ask that I alert you when he arrived."

Was that compassion? I stared, my back pressed against the wall, but he didn't look at me again.

"Very well." Cruelon sighed. Striding past Hirose, he disappeared around the corner. I slumped against the wall and closed my eyes. I couldn't look at Hirose, couldn't stand to see what might be in his eyes. For then I might lose what little control I had left. But when I opened them, he'd gone. In his place waited the taisa, ready to escort me back to my bedroom. *Why did Hirose interrupt?* I couldn't shake the suspicion that it hadn't just been because of a message.

I led the way as the taisa followed, my mind busy as I mulled over the events from the evening. A shadow of Cruelon's fingers still traced my skin, and the memory of his hot, inebriated breath lingered.

Chapter Sixteen

Master Hiito pranced into my bedroom, his bulk quivering as he bubbled over with excitement. "Aw, Lady Juliet Barrows, the Otherworlder!" He clapped his pudgy hands together. "Come, come."

What is he doing here? I stepped away from the window.

Hiito glared at me. "Lady Juliet, when I said come, I meant come." He tapped his foot. The fire crackled as though warning me.

I glanced at it but walked forward as ordered. "May I know why I am being summoned?"

Hiito giggled. "Yes, but not now. Come."

I went to grab my cloak, but Hiito waved a hand.

"You won't need that, Lady Barrows."

The glee filling his step and voice raised goose bumps across my skin. *What's going on?* Even the guards' familiar presence felt somehow more intimidating. I peeked over my shoulder. They were closer than normal. *What is this?* My mind raced. Kin and Emi had both appeared for breakfast. They had seemed fine. Kin would've told me if something had happened.

I didn't notice where we were headed until I saw the door up ahead, flanked by two men. I stopped in my tracks. One of the guards prodded me forward.

"Keep walking, Lady Juliet!" Hiito ordered. "We must not keep him waiting!"

"Who?" My heart pounded.

"King Cruelon," Master Hiito answered, pointing to where the king stepped out from an open doorway. He waited, his black robes hanging about him as he watched me approach.

"Lady Juliet Barrows." Cruelon smiled. "You haven't answered my question. It has been long enough, I think, for you to have made your decision."

His question. The harem. I felt more than saw the guards waiting behind me, Hiito grinning, his morbid curiosity palpable, and Cruelon, a snake ready to strike. *It was just last night…* I took a deep breath, every nerve taut with tension. *Stall.* I took a deep breath and bowed low. "My lord, I accept your offer to join, but—"

"But?" Cruelon echoed. Tension rippled through the air like a wave.

"Amongst my people, it is customary to have a period of celebration." My mind raced. "Would you honor my people's tradition?"

Cruelon considered me.

The room felt deathly silent. My lungs burned from holding my breath. I forced myself to remain still.

Hiito leaned forward, a look of cruel glee gleaming on his face. I didn't dare look over my shoulder at Hirose and the guards.

Cruelon shifted on his feet, breaking the heavy stillness. He laughed, an unearthly sound as though it was rarely done. "How long does this celebration take?"

The number popped into my head. "Five weeks," I breathed.

"And what is done within those five weeks?"

Think. "There is preparation of the body," I began, my voice growing stronger as the idea cemented. "And then a time of eating little, filled with meditation to prepare the mind. After that, there is time spent with friends—women—to honor the time of being single and time past. Lastly, there is a period of feasting to celebrate the coming union. I know it is a lot to ask, my lord."

Cruelon held up a hand. "Five weeks is not long. I can wait. I will grant you this time to honor the tradition of your people."

Elation almost sent me dancing in relief, but I held back and instead bowed low. "Thank you, my lord."

"Now," Cruelon began, "I have something to show you." He gestured for me to follow as he turned and went through the guarded doorway.

A lump grew in my throat. I knew that doorway. I'd been here once before, when Cruelon had me watch a woman in the dungeon die.

"Move!" Hiito exclaimed with a little jump.

With each step I took, my footsteps grew stronger. There was only one way forward. I passed between the black-clad men, listening to the soft footsteps of my guards following. Cruelon's black robes swished across the floor. A dank and musty scent assailed my nostrils as we wound our way down the passageway. It sloped deeper underground, following a strange, snaking path. The air grew colder, and water dripped from the ceiling, running in thin rivulets down the walls onto the uneven floor. It created puddles, and where the water ran, the stone was slimy. The footing was precarious. The torches in brackets lining the wall every few yards hindered as much as they helped. Flickering light created dancing shadows, sometimes reflecting off the slick, wet surface of the floor and other times creating illusions.

We reached the long corridor interspersed with barred doors. Cruelon halted in front of the nearest one. The rasp of a bolt sliding back echoed up and down the passageway. A screech sounded as a guard pulled the heavy door open. Goosebumps raced up and down my skin. The cell was dark. A patch of black, untouched by the light from the torches.

"You lied."

My mouth felt dry. *The maps. He found out.* I glanced over my shoulder to see the guards looming close behind. *No escape.* I looked at Cruelon.

"We have an understanding, Juliet Barrows. In five weeks, you will become part of my harem. But you still lied, and that cannot go unpunished." Cruelon clasped his hands before him and nodded to the empty cell behind me. "You will experience a taste of being in my dungeons. No food, no water. Tomorrow, you will be released and may begin your preparations."

"My lord," I pleaded, bowing. "I don't understand—"

"*You* don't understand?" Cruelon challenged, a gleam entering his blue eyes. He came toward me, his robes giving the impression he glided across the floor. "Three nights ago, you were late to dinner. Because of a wardrobe malfunction, yes?"

I licked my lips. "Yes, my lord."

"And yet," he paused, circling me, "you didn't require the help of your maids?"

Kin. Emi. They'd been questioned, but that was before I stole the maps. *But Kin never said—* I shook my head. The musty air felt thick and stifling. "I—"

"No." Cruelon tapped my lips with a slender finger. "No more lies. Tomorrow, I shall ask you again." His head jerked and he turned away.

The guard shoved my back, and I gasped as I stumbled into the small room. My foot caught on something and I lost my balance, falling to the ground. The floor welcomed me with a cold, wet hardness, the dampness from the stones seeping into my clothing as I struggled back to my feet.

Master Hiito smiled and waggled a couple fingers at me as the door closed with a loud, clanking thud. The scratchy pitch returned as I listened to the bolt sliding home. Plops of water dripped from the cracks in the ceiling, and the murky darkness billowed in around me. Shivering, I leaned down and felt around the floor. Something soft but bristly poked the tips of my fingers. *Hay.* It was also damp and smelled musty. My nose crinkled. *It's moldy.* I sighed and moved toward the farthest corner of the cell from the door. Dropping down, I wrapped my arms around my legs, trying to retain what body heat I could.

I closed my eyes against the cloying air and focused on breathing in and out. *Don't let the darkness overcome you.* My heartbeat calmed. *It's one day.* "You can make it one day," I whispered, closing my eyes against the consuming darkness.

My stomach rumbled.

"No food," I whispered. *Don't think about it.* I hummed to myself, trying to distract my mind from all the unknowns. There were so many. And I had one day and one night to figure out what I would tell Cruelon tomorrow. *Why didn't Kin warn me?*

⚜ ⚜

Sleep eventually claimed me. When I awoke, there was no way to tell what time it was. Though the temperature hadn't grown colder, my body struggled more and more to stay warm. The chilliness pervading the dungeon crept through every crack and through every piece of stone which touched me. My thoughts were scattered, full of half-thoughts drifting in and out of a semi-conscious state.

I reclined against the wall, my head nestled in my arms, shivering until my limbs shook with the force of trying to keep warm. What I wouldn't give for a thick, heavy feather quilt weighing me down under its bulk ... or a blazing fire, almost stifling in its intensity as its glow captivated the eye. *Just a few more hours.* I had my answer for Cruelon. He must know the truth, but not all of it. Partial truths were more believable than lies.

The rasp of the bolt sliding back brought me to my feet. The door slammed open and I blinked, struggling to see the silhouette outlined by torchlight.

"Come!"

I took a step forward, groaning as an iron hand grasped my forearm and pulled me into the passageway.

"Move!" The guard pushed me in front of him.

I licked my lips and drew as much moisture from the walls of my mouth before I spoke, my voice raspy. "Where are you taking me?" My lips ached from the lack of water.

"Just do as you're told."

The guard walked me up and down the corridor, forcing me forward each time I began to lag. Soon the shivering stopped. Circulation had returned now that blood pumped through my veins. When we exited the corridor leading down to the dungeon, I felt tears of relief sting my eyes.

The path we took was a familiar one. Whenever we passed a window, I could hear the wind howling outside. *A storm.*

We halted in front of the dining hall. The doors opened as I entered to see Cruelon sitting at the table. The smell hit me. I found myself pulled forward as aromas filled my nostrils. *Food.* My eyes widened and my mouth watered. The vast repast arranged on the table before me was so close and yet just out of reach. Steam rose from several dishes. *Oh my...* The thought went unfinished as I took in the large head of an octopus staring back at me, the tentacles artfully arranged to curl around other dishes on the table.

"Magnificent, is it not?" Cruelon twiddled a glass in his fingers, his lanky form relaxed in a chair. His eyes narrowed and he laughed. He took a drink, my eyes following his every movement. "Sit."

I sat on my usual cushion, at Cruelon's right.

"No, no, not yet," the king spoke, as if to a small child. "Do you know how long a person can survive without food?"

My glands began salivating as my eyes shifted from him to the feast before me: rice, meat, and vegetables swimming in succulent sauces, the spices prevalent in the air. I shook my head, a slow, painful movement.

"Or water?"

When I didn't answer, he sighed. "Well, I do, Miss Barrows. I know how long before a person is sure to break, how long before they die of starvation, how long they can go without water. It does not matter who the person is, or what they can take. They all break, eventually. I even know the difference between a child and an adult. So, Miss Barrows," he continued, laying the tips of his fingers against my cheek. "Do you wish to test for yourself how long that is? How long it takes for *you* to break?" He brought his face ever closer to mine. "I know you have not broken yet," he whispered. "I can see the fire in your eyes. Oh? You think I cannot? Would you die before you admitted it?" He straightened and leaned back in his chair. "You were without food and water for twenty-four hours. Do you want it to be for longer?"

Anger filled me. My hands trembled, but I shook my head.

"Now, Juliet Barrows, why did you lie to me the other night? What were you doing?"

My throat ached from thirst and the tension. "I wanted to explore without my guards. So when they left me at the door, I took my chance."

"And?" Cruelon asked, tapping a finger on the table.

"I wanted a way out," I admitted, casting my gaze to my lap. "I wanted to be free again." *That is true. But not yet.* I wouldn't be free until Cruelon's life on this earth ended.

"Oh, yes. Miss Barrows." Cruelon smiled, his white teeth flashing. "Doesn't the truth help? I knew there was something the matter. Your maids both swore there was no wardrobe malfunction that they knew of."

"I'm sorry, my lord," I whispered, putting as much repentance into my voice as I could muster.

Cruelon laughed. "Your time in the dungeon was but a taste, Lady Juliet. Do not cross me."

That night, it was as if the previous day hadn't happened. Kin and Emi readied me for dinner. There were no questions of where I had been, what had happened, nor was there a chance to speak with Kin alone. The same went for the dinner itself. In five weeks, I was to become part of the harem, yet no one seemed to know.

Day two, Kin and Emi knew. They'd been sworn to silence, but so began the preparation of the body. Baths, oils with essence, hair removal, and grooming filled the days, along with a new wardrobe. Fittings under Kin's watchful eye, rides and walks to promote exercise, and a tighter guard through it all.

As the dinners continued, so did the eating, the drinking, and the merrymaking—the same two hours night after night. The men and women there grew more comfortable with my presence. They didn't accept me, but they tolerated me, and that meant I could listen.

A week into the preparations, I gazed out of the closed window, watching as the first snow fell. Soft flakes, large and gentle, fell through the air.

"Emi." Kin's sharp voice broke into my reverie. "Come here, I have an errand for you. Now," she snapped.

I watched as Emi walked out of the room, her movements slow and sullen. Turning back to the window, I stared at the dreary sky beyond. It had become easier to be more relaxed. Cruelon had hardly spoken more than a few words to me, but even then, I always carried an unsettled feeling around him. His eyes and ears seemed to catch everything, and sometimes it felt like he could see right through me. It was more than a feeling; I feared it.

"Juliet."

My head jerked.

Kin approached me and looked out the window. I followed her and stared out to the plains and the forest beyond as a soft blanket of white began to cover them. Somewhere out there, Tristan and Saya waited.

"I received word," Kin muttered. "Good work on the traitor."

"That's it?" I breathed, raising my eyebrows.

"Yes," Kin whispered back.

"Did you tell them I have five weeks before I am to become part of the king's harem?"

Kin nodded.

"And Lord Tristan didn't say anything about that?"

Kin shook her head. "Perhaps he hasn't received that news yet."

"Four weeks isn't long," I said.

Kin didn't have to say a word. I knew she agreed. I knew what we were both thinking. We stood in silence, watching the snow fall. Ever since I had questioned Kin about why she didn't warn me, we had come to a better understanding. Emi. It all revolved around Emi. Kin knew Emi would deny a wardrobe malfunction. She knew the king only asked because I must have used that as an excuse to get the proof of the traitor, yet she couldn't back me up. I still wondered why she didn't warn me. *Because when it comes to Emi, the Uprising becomes second place. I become second place. Maybe I should share more with her, help her to understand why it's better I be prepared.*

I glanced at Kin. "The king knows I was with the rebels," I told her.

"What?" Kin hissed. "How does he know that?"

"He guessed part of it, and I decided it might be to my advantage to tell him some half-truths. I had to give him something, Kin. He needs to think I'm loyal to him; whether by choice or by force, it doesn't matter. He has to *believe* it."

"So he knows why you are here."

"I don't think so, though we still don't know what all the traitor has said." *Cruelon can't know how important I am to Tristan.* My breathing quickened, and I whirled to look ather. "Which means the traitor cannot be close to Tristan. Only a select few knew of our plans or why I'm here. For all they know, I was captured against my will. Why would I have left Tristan? Why would I have left our courtship if I welcomed it?" I grinned. "The courtship serves as proof, Kin! If the king knows of it ..."

"He must know," Kin agreed, "which worries me."

"But it can't be someone close to Tristan," I pressed. *It can't be Adnan.* I shook my head. *There's no reason to think it was him.*

"It could." Kin's words felt like a pail of cold water in my face.

I forced the tremor from my voice. "What do you mean?"

Kin shrugged. "It's possible Cruelon isn't telling you all he knows, or that the traitor is keeping some information to himself. We don't know all Cruelon knows or does not know, or whether the traitor is choosing to share everything.

There are three games being played out here, and Cruelon may not be as open with you as you think he is."

I crossed my arms and shivered. "What three games?"

Kin smoothed down her simple green dress. Her brow furrowed as she thought. "It's possible that whoever the traitor is is playing both sides, and so will not share all with Cruelon. Another possibility is that Cruelon is playing you, and so while he does know more, is not sharing it with you to see how you react and what you do with the knowledge. Third, Cruelon isn't playing you and is actually telling you the truth."

Using my fingertips, I rubbed slow circles on my temples. I shivered again. It was cold, the coldest morning yet. With every day that passed, I could feel winter pushing fall out of her spot, replacing her coolness with his frosty blanket.

"Tell Tristan to be careful," I whispered, watching my breath blow in cool clouds in front of my face. "He doesn't know who he can trust. The king has something underfoot, but I don't know what."

A light knock interrupted me and I jumped, my heart pounding. I turned to face Kin.

"Anything else?" she asked.

"No, nothing."

Knuckles rapped on wood again.

Kin nodded and began walking toward the door, her footsteps slow and sure.

"No, wait!" I held up a hand as though I could grab her. "Ask him if there is news of the Unknown. He'll know what I mean. Oh, and is there any chance I could have a fire?" I turned back toward the window, unable to hear whatever message had been passed to Kin.

Kin winced and bowed. "I'm sorry, yes. I'll send someone to light one for you."

Light footsteps approached from behind. I closed my eyes, feeling the cool draft from the open doorway.

"Here," Kin whispered. "Take this tonight."

"What?"

"A sleeping draught," she replied.

I looked down to see a small vial resting in the palm of Kin's hand. "Is this because it's become harder to hide my exhaustion behind makeup?"

I knew the makeup didn't cover how sleepless my nights had been. Even Hirose had made a comment to me at dinner the night before. Kin frowned, and the smile disappeared from my face.

"What?" I pressed. "What was said to you?"

She shook her head. "Just take the herbs tonight. Get some sleep. Now I must go. The household is tiptoeing right now because the king has been expecting a messenger today and he hasn't arrived yet." She turned and left the room.

I fingered the small vial. A messenger was expected. Exhaustion pulled at me, beckoning with a longing touch. I never left my room after returning. It would be suspicious. I sighed in relief and examined the clear glass with the amber liquid inside. I was willing to try anything to rid myself of the nightmares that plagued my sleep. My hands trembled, and I lifted the container to my nose and sniffed. A herbal, savory aroma, with just a hint of sweet spice, entered my nostrils. *Cinnamon, like Natsumi.* I tipped my head back and drank.

Through the window came the barking of dogs. *The king's dogs. His blood-hounds.* I sat on the edge of the bed. Hirose had told me about them. They were the most prized in the land. "Give them someone's scent and they will track to kingdom come or farther." Hirose's words had sent chills down my spine then, and the memory of them did now, as did the frenzied barking coming through the window.

I lay down and stared up at the ceiling. *Sleep will come.* Just a few more hours.

⚜

I stirred and stretched. It was early, but I had slept. The herbs Kin had given me had helped. I sat up and rested my chin on drawn-up knees as a soft knock preceded Emi entering the room. "Where's Kin?"

Emi shook her head. "I don't know. No one has seen her."

I straightened. "No one?"

Emi shook her head. "I was told she is unwell, but I—I don't know, my lady."

Worry wormed its feral way into my mind. I'd heard rustling the night before, footsteps in the hallway, but this morning everything felt hushed, as though someone had thrown a blanket over the castle. *Maybe it's just the herbs and the deep sleep that had accompanied them.*

"You are to join the king and Lady Amarante for a ride," Emi said, breaking into my thoughts. "The king asked for you personally."

"He did?" I echoed, a sense of foreboding worming its way into my mind.

Emi nodded.

The thread of worry turned into a web. I felt like a zombie without any sense of self-direction as Emi dressed me and I was escorted through the keep. When the large doors opened and bright sunlight streamed down on me, everything seemed otherworldly. It was too beautiful a day. I hesitated, shivering in the cold, my breath misting in front of me. If it had been dreary, wet, and gray, it would've fit the dark mood and made me feel better, but instead it clashed. I pulled my cloak tighter around me, tense.

The guard shoved me forward toward the horses, through the midst of men-at-arms as they scurried about.

They are more active than usual. And why are there more of them? I took in every detail, every movement, filing away the information for later. *The messenger.* I had to find out what had happened.

I schooled my features. I stopped beside Taisho Hirose, who stepped forward to help me mount. I took a breath as I settled myself in the saddle and then wished I hadn't. As the weather had grown colder, the rains had begun, driving away the remaining brown from the summer sun and bringing in the cool, lush greens, but it hadn't taken away the odor of stale sweat and dung.

The saddle creaked as I adjusted myself. Feeling eyes on me, I looked up to see the king tapping his finger on his thigh. Seeing me watching, he beckoned as he urged his horse forward. After a brief hesitation, I followed. I could hear Amarante's snort as she was brushed from first into second place. I straightened my shoulders, not daring to look her in the eyes as I passed her to join Cruelon at his side.

Baying sounded through the air as Cruelon's hunting dogs joined us. I twisted in the saddle to see the hounds tearing after us. A gust of wind blew through the air. I shivered and wrapped my long cloak closer around me.

As we neared the main gate, the harsh chink of chains grated on my ears as the thick metal portcullis was raised. Behind us, the horses' hooves beat a gentle rhythm on the ground, a soft cadence complimenting the fading noises of the busy courtyard behind us. A slight boom drowned out the horses as the gate dropped. The hounds baying grew more frenzied, as though they'd caught scent of something. I looked over my shoulder just in time to see Miya gasp, her face white and her eyes wide in horror. She clapped a hand to her mouth. My horse neighed as I pulled him to a halt and followed her gaze.

I stared for several moments, seeing without seeing. A long wooden pole stuck in the ground, standing straight and tall, and at the top sat Kin's head, high above us. My hands began to tremble. Kin's long black hair blew in the slight breeze and blood still dripped from the severed arteries, trickling down the wood and onto the ground. Her face was frozen and pale, her lips parted as though she wanted to say something, even in death.

My throat constricted, and the murmurs died away. Even those on horseback seemed to disappear until it was just me, the king, and Kin. I gripped the reins, my knuckles white against the leather I held. Tears stung my eyes, threatening with every breath to fall. My chest heaved, my lungs burned, and a piercing pain formed in my temples.

I knew Cruelon's eyes burned into me. My throat ached as it continued to tighten, stretching the muscles in my neck taut. *Don't let him see.* I couldn't, for by doing so I felt I would betray Kin and give Cruelon the satisfaction.

Just yesterday she'd been alive and well. If she'd had an inkling of what the morning would bring—would she have told me what she knew? Would she offer to send my message? Did she even send it? My jaw began to ache.

"Consequences come to those who defy me," Cruelon said, speaking loud enough for everyone to hear. "She proved herself disloyal to her king. An example had to be made. Everyone has to abide by the choices they make, Lady Juliet. It is the way of the world."

I couldn't open my mouth. If I did, I would be dead before the day was out. I blinked back the tears, determined not to let him see them fall. A wave of revulsion swept over me, and bile rose in my throat. I tore my eyes away from Kin and looked at the reins clasped in my whitened fingers. My horse skittered, pawing the ground, and I struggled to bring him under control.

"Is your horse nervous, Lady Juliet?" Cruelon asked in a mild tone.

"No, he's fine," I murmured without looking at him. The horse tried to dance to the side, frisking his head from side to side as he did so, his tail whipping back and forth and stinging my legs.

"Someone is, then," he observed.

I looked up, frozen. Of course. The horse sensed my emotions. Breathing in and out, I began clearing my mind, relaxing my legs, and loosening my grip on the reins. The horse began to quiet, jumpy still, but no longer about to bolt off with me on him.

"Interesting," Cruelon uttered, leaning over his horse, who was as still as a statue.

I hated him—with every ounce of my being—as I'd never hated a person as I did now. Hate may not have even been a strong enough word. I turned away. If I didn't, I knew he'd see the fire within.

I could kill him. I can kill him. Rage filled me, giving fuel to the fire. *Isn't this what Tristan wants anyway? What does it matter who does the deed as long as he dies?* I took a deep breath. Kin—Mari—they had sacrificed everything. *It's my turn now.*

"Keep it up there for another week," Cruelon called over his shoulder to Hirose. "As a reminder to all."

As a reminder to me.

I didn't look at Kin again. She had branded herself into my mind, a burning image behind my eyes. Cruelon knew something; I had been naïve to think he didn't. I thought I was fooling him, but I was the fool.

❧ ❦

The door to my room closed behind me, and I saw Emi approach with a smile on her face. My heart clenched tight within my chest. *She doesn't know.* "Emi," I began, fighting to keep my voice from breaking. "Emi, Kin is dead."

She froze, her face paling. "*What?*"

"She's dead." I couldn't hide the tremor in my words. "The king had her killed."

A sob broke the silence. Emi's small body sank to the floor. She looked even younger then, a defenseless little form curled so tight she barred herself from the world.

I sank down beside her and she jumped, trying to hide her tears. Gathering her into my arms, I murmured, "Emi, I'm so sorry."

She buried her face in my shoulder, her cries so quiet they were almost unnoticeable, but she still shook.

Words came to my mind, but none of them felt right. *What can I tell her?* Kin was dead because of me. I knew it. The king knew it. But Emi didn't know.

"Why?" Emi gasped, throwing all of her hurt and confusion into that single word.

The ache in my chest grew. What could I tell her? That I was the reason? That Kin was dead because the king wanted to warn me? A tear slid down my cheek. *Please, let me never have to tell her the truth.*

Without warning, Emi sat up and dried her tear-streaked face on her sleeve. "My apologies, my lady. I'll help you out of your riding habit." She stood, focused on the wall over my head.

She's so young. She's just a girl. I shook my head. "Nevermind that now, Emi. I will do it myself. Just—"

"No, I will help." She stuck her lip out, clenching her fists at her side.

"Emi, please be careful," I whispered. "Don't give them any reason to think you're anything but my maid."

Emi looked at me then, a childlike pleading in her posture. "Is that why Kin is dead? Did you have something to do with it?"

My lips parted, but no words came out. *Is it my fault?* Yesterday I had given Kin another message. *Was she caught?* Emi faded as I grew lost in thought. *But the king expected a messenger.* My foot tapped a quick rhythm on the floor. Was there a connection? *How?*

"You don't need to answer." Emi's words were sharp daggers.

I started and focused on her.

"Come, my lady. I'll have your lunch brought to you soon after."

What if it is my fault? But how can I explain? I stood, letting her change my gown into a simpler one. *There is nothing to say.*

Not another tear fell from Emi's eyes.

Chapter Seventeen

Miya's shoulders rose as she tensed. "You've been quiet," she murmured under her breath. When I said nothing, she laid her hand over mine and gave it a brief squeeze.

"Have I?" The words sounded as though they'd come from someone else.

Miya inclined her head before surveying the rest of the ladies sitting around at the afternoon tea party Amarante hosted. "Ever since your maid Kin died," she responded.

"You mean, ever since she was murdered."

"Shh," Miya hissed. "Don't say that here."

My heartbeat quickened. I blinked, my hands trembling with pent-up anger. *Control.* Closing my eyes, I fought a losing battle. *The breathing technique.* I folded my clenched hands in my lap. *In for seven, hold for four, out for eight.* Soon the shaking stopped and I was able to breathe easier. It had been too long since I'd used that breathing technique. But since Kin's death the day before, I had felt on the brink of breaking. If my strength and concentration wavered for even a second, I thought I would explode. It was now only three weeks until I would become part of the king's harem. Soon, the time of meditation would begin. The trembling worsened. Time was flying by. I took a deep breath. *In for seven, hold for four, out for eight.*

"How is your maid?" Miya whispered, gazing at me over the rim of her cup. Her full lips were a striking pink against her ivory skin.

"Emi? Emi is ..." I trailed off as I watched Amarante laugh and eat some sort of fruit from a small plate.

Miya shifted and her lips curved in a soft smile, but it was full of sadness. "My maid told me she is young. That she and Kin were close."

My jaw clenched. Emi hadn't said a word since it happened. "She is heart-broken." My thoughts wandered. *She's my mannikin who does my bidding, but nothing else.* "How would you take it if your mother was killed?"

Miya stiffened. "Her *mother*?"

"In all but name." I leaned forward, keeping my voice lowered. "If she was ripped away from you without warning, without reason, without anything you could do to stop it, how would you feel if it was your master who was responsible? Who didn't even do it to get back at you but at someone else?" I bit my lip, pausing. "And you had to serve the one responsible. Yet you could never say anything, and neither could she. You don't even know she's responsible. Perhaps you suspect something. But you still have to go on day after day, and not just you, but her—she also had to go on day after day without being able to speak to anyone, without asking forgiveness—without asking forgiveness from herself, knowing she can't give it." I fingered the tendril of blonde hair that had slipped over my shoulder.

Miya's face paled.

"And everyone around both of them goes on as if nothing had happened." I swept a hand around the room. "Luncheons, dinners, morning rides, as though life had not thrown any obstacle in their path." I paused and looked away, listening to the tittering laughs from the other women.

It grew hard to breathe. The air felt stifling and cold. I stood up and Miya jumped, but she made no move to stop me. No one did. I left without a backward glance. The guards fell in behind me, with the familiar musky scent of leather following. They followed everywhere.

"My lady," a voice rang out from behind us. "The king requests your presence."

I blinked. *Those words.* I had dreaded hearing those words. Bracing myself, I turned to see another one of the king's personal guards standing there.

I waved a hand. "Lead the way, then." I had wondered if Cruelon would send for me. It was clear the day Kin died that it was a warning to me. *Don't be rooted in fear,* I reminded myself. *Why was it a warning?* I focused on watching the guard leading us, his short strides quick but sure. His worn leather uniform made little sound, like a snake among his brood—serpents slithering about, silent and deadly.

We walked down a familiar path, one which led to Cruelon's small study, where I had taken the maps. I almost stopped short as it struck me. *Has he realized they're missing?* A lump formed in my throat.

The guard looked over his shoulder at me as we approached a dark wood door. I entered the small room. Gray light streamed into the room from a narrow window, casting its dreary light onto a table where Cruelon studied some papers. He straightened, and I bowed.

"My lord." I squared my shoulders, my back ramrod straight as I waited.

"Lady Juliet, welcome. Would you like a cup of tea?" Cruelon slid his sleeves up his arms and gestured to the table.

I struggled not to show the sudden stiffness in my body at the sound of his flippant voice, not to show the anger threatening to curve my hands into fists—I couldn't show any of it to him, the one person who wanted that from me. He had won a battle, but if I let go of myself, he would begin winning the war.

"Yes, thank you." I curled my toes in my shoes, fighting the urge to run away.

Cruelon grinned and poured me a cup, steam curling up from the hot liquid. He slid it across the table, its smooth porcelain gliding along the polished wood. I took the small cup and wrapped one hand around it, letting the soothing warmth seep into my skin. I glanced at the pages strewn across the wooden surface. More maps, more strategies, more papers covered with a messy scrawl I assumed to be Cruelon's.

"How long were you with the rebels, Lady Juliet?" Cruelon asked as he handed me the tea. "I believe you mentioned they took you against your will and kept you in captivity?"

I looked up, my hesitation so brief I hoped he hadn't noticed. "Yes. It was for a couple of weeks." *A couple of weeks. What a lie.* It had been far longer, but I didn't want him to know that. The longer I was there, the more he'd assume I'd know about them and their movements. I glanced down at the hot liquid. "I was kept in solitary confinement most of the time but had meals often with the rest."

Cruelon tapped his fingers on the table in soft staccato. "What are you doing here?"

I watched the rhythm of his fingers, then glanced at the paper underneath them—*Lanevrog. That name again.* The name that had been on the map to the first base Cruelon had overrun. *Now here it is again.*

"I hope I do not need to repeat the question, Lady Juliet."

I jerked, the tea almost sloshing out. "Question?"

"*What* are you doing here?" For the first time, a hint of impatience entered Cruelon's voice.

"I wanted sanctuary." I averted my gaze. "It was awful there. I escaped, and one of your patrols found me."

"But *why*, Juliet? Why come here? Why not go back home?"

"I couldn't." I shook my head and felt a pin loosen. "Tristan took me before I could go, and I have no idea how to get back to the portal."

Cruelon steepled his fingers. "So there is a portal?"

My heart hammered, and I winced. The pin loosened a bit more. "Maybe, I don't know. There was one when I came, but I don't know if it disappears after someone comes through or not. I have no idea where it is." *But Natsumi does.*

"There will be plenty of time yet," Cruelon mused.

I flinched as Cruelon's voice grew icier. *Time for speaking to Natsumi? No.*

"No matter. I have much to do here before I could concentrate my efforts in another world. Do you need another maid?"

"What?" As I jerked, my hair loosened from its bun a little. The loose pin threatened to let hair cascade down. *Another world? Much to do?* Cruelon's words echoed in my head. *I need to tell Tristan—Kin's gone.* The realization I had no way to communicate with Tristan hit me for the first time. I fought to keep my emotions under control. *What is Cruelon planning?* The room felt hot.

"It is a simple question." Cruelon examined his fingernails. "Do you need another maid? I hear that the girl, Emi, has been doing all the work. Is she competent enough, or should I assign someone else to you as well? Now that Kin is gone."

"Emi is fine," I bit out. *I have to do this on my own. I have to kill him.* There were only three weeks left before I would join his harem. Three weeks to figure out how to get close enough.

"Good, good." Cruelon stood up and strode toward me. "Very well, Juliet Barrows. You may keep Emi." He sneered as he gazed down at me.

The pin. The thought flitted through my mind. *The pin.* My eyes widened and I slipped a hand up as though I was fixing my hair. The pin was long. It was made of metal.

"Very well." Cruelon reached out and slid a finger down my cheek. "We are done today. You may go."

My fingers froze. The pin was there, cold and slick. I stared at Cruelon, who had already returned his attention to the table before him. The pin moved an inch as I began to slide it out of my hair. A fly buzzed somewhere close by.

"My lord."

The voice sounded like a thunderclap in the rectangular room. I stopped and lowered my hand as I turned on my heel.

Hirose rose from a bow, his eyes glittering as they swept over me before fixating on the king.

Had he seen? My hair threatened to fall down around my shoulders.

"Lady Juliet, why are you still here?" Cruelon asked as he sat down.

Not this time. A sense of relief and also irritation battled within me. I bowed and shuffled backward, feeling his eyes bore into my back with every step.

"Oh, Lady Juliet, one more thing," Cruelon began, his tone mild.

I froze, my hand raised to open the door. The room suddenly felt hot, unbearably stuffy.

"Unless you end up needing a new maid entirely, you had best be careful." The words hung in the air.

I waited, my hand clenching around the piece of worn wood. *Why hadn't I been faster?*

"That is all," he dismissed. "You are free to go."

I could have sworn I heard him chuckling under his breath as the door closed behind me. If Hirose hadn't interrupted, the king could have been dead. My skin felt hot and feverish. I stood there for several moments, welcoming the cold breeze in the passageway.

⁓⟫⟫⟩ ⟨⟨⟨⟨⁓

Ever since Kin was murdered, the smallest sounds startled me and I always felt on edge. Cruelon hadn't spoken to me at dinner after I was called into his study, he didn't show up for the morning ride the next morning, and there was no word for me the following night.

Two days. Two days since I had spoken with Cruelon. Two nights filled with tossing and turning. Worry affected my every waking thought and the dreams that plagued me when I slept. There were no more sleeping draughts.

Kin had to have been sending the messages somehow. *Another servant?* I knew it wasn't Emi. And I hadn't come to know any of the other servants. They kept their distance from me. *Who can I trust?*

I pushed Miya away. She gave up trying to speak to me at Amarante's tea parties, and Natsumi ... Natsumi was never there. Emi also kept to herself. Now there was no one to break through the walls I'd erected around myself.

The fifth day dawned.

I stared into the mirror as Emi decorated my face with makeup and did my hair up into an elaborate bun. In the hour or so spent readying me for dinner, she hadn't spoken one word. My lips parted as I stared at my reflection.

"You are beautiful," Emi whispered from behind me. "You look more regal than the rest of them." She had managed to hide the circles under my eyes as skillfully as Kin ever had.

I raised an eyebrow as I looked at her through the mirror.

Emi tucked one hair into place and stepped back. "I am sorry for how I have been treating you." She averted her gaze and wrung her small hands. "I think I blamed you when I shouldn't have. You didn't—" She sighed and shifted on her feet, her narrow shoulders drooping. "You didn't kill her," she whispered.

I sighed. "There isn't anything to forgive, Emi." I stared at my reflection as Emi moved to stand next to me. Gold combs with emeralds sparkled in my hair, bringing out the gray in my eyes more than the blue. I rose. Smoothing down the dress, I admired the deep green, so dark it was almost black. *Tristan's favorite color on me. If only he could see me now.* "It's not me."

"What do you mean?" Emi moved so we stood side by side in front of the mirror.

"It's not me," I whispered. Before it was Tristan and Kono. Now it was Cruelon and Emi. A new ruler, a new maid. *But the same color.* My shoulders rose and fell. "Look at me, Emi. I look like some dark queen out of a movie, as though my very touch could destroy a life. When did I grow so cold? Life has sucked the warmth out of me, Emi. The wind has chilled me inside as well as out, and the walls have enclosed around me, growing ever tighter with each day." My vision wavered, blurring a little as I took in the room I stood in. "What am I doing here?" I murmured into the mirror, but if it hadn't been for watching my own lips form the words, I wouldn't have realized I'd spoken them out loud. Cruelon had asked me the same question. Did I know how to answer it anymore?

A warm hand wrapped around my own and gripped it. Emi walked in front of the mirror, tearing my eyes away and down toward her small face.

"Juliet." Her voice was plaintive, hesitant even. "You have strength and warmth within you that you aren't aware you have, but you will—in time. The only walls that enclose you are the ones you construct. They are your greatest fear. Defeat them, and you will find that no walls can truly contain your spirit. Even when everything looks bleak and all is black, there is a light at the end of the tunnel, a light that will grow brighter if you let it." Emi took my other hand, clasping both of them in hers. "Stay strong, be true, cast away your doubts, and live in hope—without hope, there is nothing. Don't let them defeat you."

Everything around me faded away until only her words were left. "Emi," I began, "how—"

"I remembered it all." Tears welled up in Emi's eyes. "I didn't forget a single word. She had me memorize it, over and over until I could say it in my sleep." She blinked, letting one single tear escape down her left cheek.

"*Kin,*" I realized.

Emi reached to wipe her wet cheeks. "She told me something might happen and if so, I was to pass on her message."

"She knew? She knew, and she didn't tell me?"

Emi shook her head, her loose dark hair flying about her face. "No, I don't think she knew, not for sure anyway. But I think she was afraid what path you might go down if something did happen to her. It's easy to be suffocated here, especially when you don't have support and friendship. You wouldn't be the only one to give in, and you wouldn't be the last."

"Why do I feel like you just matured more in the last week than I have in years?" I sniffed, feeling an urge to smile and cry at the same time. "You are too young to be speaking like this."

"Those weren't my words, my lady. I'm just a messenger."

"Did Kin—"

"I should go." Emi pulled away, but I tightened my grip on her arm. "You'll be late if you don't leave now. I hope Kin's message helps."

"It did," I replied, walking to the fire and staring into its bright orange flames. "It does. More than you could possibly know."

Emi gave a soft, sad smile and dipped her head in a brief nod. "I'm glad. I should've told you earlier, but I hadn't wanted to say it before tonight. I don't know what you both meant to one another, but I know Kin liked you; she liked you a lot, and—" Emi took a deep breath. "And I hope she didn't die for nothing. Whatever you're doing, don't give up. If she didn't want you to, then I don't want you to either."

I knelt on the small cushion next to my mattress. "Emi," I whispered, aware of the guards on the other side of the door. "Kin loved you. Don't you forget that. You helped me, Emi, you and Kin both." I smiled at her, and as it grew wider, I realized I meant it. It was a genuine smile because, for the first time, I felt a lightening of my load.

Emi bowed and turned away without another word. Her bustling faded to the background as I stared at a piece of white paper lying on the small bedside table. A messenger had come the night before Kin died. *She'd sent word about Lanevrog. Had Tristan caught him?* Taking up a quill, I dipped it and wrote, *Lanevrog.* I sat back and studied it. The name wouldn't leave my mind. There was something about it, and it had to do with the spy. The word had eaten away at me, but it still didn't make sense. I tapped the quill against the paper, splattering ink across the page. It looked like a signature on the blueprints. Cruelon called the spy Lanevrog. I knew no one by that name in the Uprising. *Or could it be a word to mean something else?*

A small gasp escaped me.

"My lady?" Emi asked, poking her head around the corner from the bathroom.

I waved a hand. "Nothing."

She nodded and disappeared again.

Lanevrog. I wrote it again, as though signing my own name. Hovering over the paper, I watched as the quill dripped ink. Lanevrog was different. It stuck out because the phonetic system was different. Adnan, Tristan, neither of them had a name like those born of this country ...

I frowned.

A knock sounded on the door. I rose and stuffed the paper into the small fireplace. Watching it burn, I ignored the mutter of voices at the door. Soft footsteps approached.

"My lady," Emi spoke from behind me. "You've been summoned." She bowed her head.

I turned. "I know I'm summoned to dinner."

Emi shifted her weight. "No, by Lady *Natsumi*."

My shoulders stiffened. "What?"

"She has requested your presence, immediately."

"But it's almost—"

"I know, so you should go now." Emi strode to the wardrobe and removed a light cloak. "Here, just in case. It's cold out there. Winter is upon us, my lady."

⚘ ⚘

I wrapped the cloak tight around me as I hurried down the corridor after the servant, my two guards close behind. A chill breeze swept through the corridors, and the wind whistled outside the fortress.

What does she want? Why now?

A door was flung open, and I hurried through onto a wide, open-air veranda. The air was biting with a cold fury, more so with the harsh wind that now flew against us with a passion.

"Well, well, here she is, gracing us with her presence." Amarante's silky voice shook a little as she inclined her head to me. Her soft, full lips tilted up in a cold smile.

Amarante. I blinked.

"Lady Juliet," another voice spoke. "Thank you for joining us." Natsumi stood in her familiar attire of deep scarlet, a thick coil of hair falling over her shoulder. She clapped once. "Bring Lady Juliet some tea."

"Why is she here?" Amarante asked, not caring if I heard or not.

Natsumi regarded her with a quiet, regal sort of air. "Because," she began, a small smile playing about her lips. "In two weeks, Juliet is to become closer to you than she already is."

Amarante stilled, her cup halfway to her mouth. "What do you mean?"

"She is to join the king's harem."

Audible gasps rang out across the veranda. Everyone had frozen in place, watching Natsumi, watching Amarante, and now, me.

Amarante's lips moved, but no words came. Drawing herself to her full height, she sent a mocking smile toward me before saying, "Why two weeks?"

"It is to honor the traditions of Lady Juliet's people," Natsumi replied without hesitation. "Today begins week four, a week of meditation." She glanced at the maid, who still stood unmoving as she listened. "Did I not instruct you to bring Lady Juliet some tea?"

Out of the corner of my eye, I saw a maid scurry to do her bidding. Natsumi's dark gaze met my own light one. She inclined her head before turning away and continuing a low conversation with one of the other women. The others watched, shock showing in their widened eyes and mouths agape.

A light hand touched my arm. "Lady Juliet, will you join me over there?"

"Miya," I said with a little relief, having to speak louder over the wind. "How are you?" I followed her over to a more secluded corner, the farthest away from the burning braziers.

She checked to make sure no one was within hearing before speaking. "You are to join the king's harem," she noted, ignoring my question.

When I didn't answer, her face paled. "Is it true?" she asked, her hand trembling.

"Yes."

"In two weeks?"

"Yes." I forced the word out behind the lump in my throat. Gazing about the veranda with its worn wood flooring and weathered beams, I closed my eyes, enjoying the brisk, cold air. I took a deep breath through my nose, smelling the damp mountain air. The sky above billowed with dark gray clouds. I wondered if it would snow.

Crossing my ankles, I looked at Miya, taking in her hair in its intricate bun and her eyes framed with black lashes. "This is the first time Lady Natsumi has invited me."

"This is the first time for all of us, I think," Miya replied, her voice low. "I've not known her to give a tea party before. She sometimes goes to the ones Amarante hosts, but never is the hostess herself."

I shivered and wrapped my arms around myself. "And Amarante?"

Miya frowned and took a sip of tea. "I don't know what you mean."

"I think you do," I said in a hushed tone. "I've never seen them both together, not like this. Have you?"

A maid approached and neither of us said a word as she handed me a small mug of tea and disappeared back into the crowd of ladies.

"No, I haven't." Miya looked into my eyes. "Juliet—"

It was the first time she'd ever used my given name.

"What's happened?" she asked. "Something's changed."

"What do you mean?" I focused on the tea I held.

"You've changed. I don't know exactly how, but it almost reminds me of the glimpses I thought I saw when I first met you weeks ago ... but different somehow. I can't put my finger on it." Miya leaned forward as she spoke, as though she didn't even realize what she had done. "You're not a shell anymore."

"I'm still me."

Miya shook her head and tilted it to the side as she regarded me. "No, you're more than that. At least, you're more than the person you've become while you've been here."

I smiled, feeling a little more relaxed as I smelled the warm, toasty aroma rising from the tea. "Are you saying you didn't know the true me?"

"Maybe you should tell me."

I took a deep breath, feeling the air bite into my lungs, and raised the mug to my lips with shaking hands. The liquid scalded my mouth and throat.

"I don't blame you," Miya added, smoothing down her fine blue skirt. "You don't trust me, and I'm not sure I trust you, but I want to."

I gazed down at the deep green of my dress. *Tristan's favorite color.* I looked up. "This conversation doesn't make much sense, Miya." But that was the thing—it all made perfect sense in a weird sort of way. I needed someone to trust.

Miya was careful, but she was also unhappy. *And I'm desperate. I only have two more weeks.*

"I think you know it does as well as I do. I like the change, Juliet. You have a fire burning beneath your skin that I'd not noticed before."

Fire ... Cruelon.

I shook my head.

"Am I wrong?" Miya inquired, watching me.

"No, it's not you." I took another sip of tea, my grip steadier now.

"You're not the only one who's changed. All of this—" Miya swept a hand across the veranda. "Something's in the air, affecting everyone here, especially Natsumi and Amarante. They're different, you're different, and even this tea is abnormal. I feel as though it's been building up and now everything is reaching a climax."

I looked around, the noises fading into the background until they sounded like a dull buzzing, too inconsequential to take much notice of. The vibrant colors of the gowns and cloaks disappeared into a blur of indistinguishable shades. Natsumi stood at one end, resplendent in her scarlet gown bright as blood, whilst Amarante lurked at the other end, almost as beautiful in glittering gold, edged in black.

Miya was right, I realized. It all felt different, weird, off-setting ...

I blinked and turned to face Miya. "Why are you telling me all of this?"

"Because I can't go through it alone, not now. There was one person here I felt I could trust, who I loved, and she is gone."

A spark ignited inside me, and as realization dawned, my heart beat faster. *Kin. How?*

Miya looked down with a sad smile, her eyelashes heavy against her cheeks as she closed her eyes. "Stay strong, Miya," she whispered.

Kin had spoken like that to me. The same words. "Kin," I exclaimed. I leaned forward and lowered my voice. "How?"

"She was my maid when I first arrived, and though it didn't last long, I loved her. And I think there was something between you and her as well, maybe not as strong as my bond with her, but I know you felt something when she died."

My tea lay forgotten in my lap, growing colder with every second. "She—did she tell—"

"I hadn't seen her much the last few months."

Miya's words made my jaw clamp tight, disappointment gnawing away at me as the hope that Miya might be part of the Uprising died. *Dash it, Juliet.* I'd almost given myself away because of another woman opening herself up to me and making both of us vulnerable. *But why didn't she tell me this before instead of fishing for news about my maids?*

My heart tightened in my chest. I took a mouthful of the warm tea and forced it down. I stood up, mumbling something about a headache or needing to have enough time to get ready for dinner—I knew it wouldn't satisfy Miya.

"Juliet." Miya rose and laid her hand on mine before I could move away. "What happened?"

"Nothing," I murmured, extricating my hand out of her grip. "Nothing at all."

And everything.

Chapter Eighteen

"There," Emi murmured as she set the last comb in my hair. "And another new gown." She motioned for me to stand.

I looked in the mirror. *Another beautiful gown. Another palette of make-up masking my weariness and stress.* I reached up and touched my hair. "Flowers?" The small jewels looked almost like real flowers, except for the way they flashed in the light.

"Yes. Delicate, but somehow they make you look stronger." Emi looked up at me and smiled. "I thought they would go with your dress. You don't look dark, you know."

I laughed and stepped away from the mirror. "What do you mean?"

Emi cocked her head to the side as she examined me. "You should laugh more often. You look prettier when you do, and your eyes light up like I've never seen them before."

"I don't have much to laugh about these days, Emi. But I don't think I've ever looked better. You've done an amazing job."

Emi beamed, the first smile I'd seen on her in days. She hung the dress I had been wearing and closed the wardrobe doors.

"Kin would be proud." I knew the light would leave her eyes, as well as the smile, but I had to say it. Inside, my heart clenched as I saw the lines reappear on her face.

A fist hammered on the door from outside.

"It's time." I drew my shoulders back and cast one last glance in the mirror before walking to the door.

Emi's voice trembled. "Be careful."

"It's just one more dinner. I'll see you in a couple of hours." I tried to sound lighthearted, but I still couldn't shake the feeling that something was wrong. It had been eating away at me ever since the tea party that afternoon.

"You've been quieter," she whispered, following me with quick steps. "Something is wrong, isn't it?"

I shook my head and forced my lips to curve upward. "No, nothing is wrong. I'll see you tonight."

"Are you sure you don't need to talk?"

My step hesitated, but I made it to the door. I glanced over my shoulder. "No, thank you, Emi." *She's too young.* I repeated in my mind. *She's just a girl.* Her full cheeks with their soft curves framed her small face. I smiled at her. "I'll see you later tonight."

In the hall, I waited for the guards to fall in behind me before I strode toward the dining hall. The path had become as familiar to me as the mountain. Entering the anteroom, I strode across to the set of double doors and didn't hesitate before opening them. Energy raced through me as adrenaline kicked in. Still, the feeling persisted that something was going to happen, something unexpected.

I strode into the room, my eyes jumping to the three empty chairs. *Wait.* My step slowed. Amarante sat at the king's left again. Beside her were three empty seats. My heart rate sped up. Licking my lips, I walked forward.

Cruelon lifted his glass to me, a lopsided smile on his face. "Lady Juliet, you look radiant tonight. Please sit there." He gestured to the middle of the empty seats.

Why? I inclined my head and sat down. Smoothing my skirt down, I peered around the table. Cruelon's eyes trained on the wall beyond us all, twirling a glass of sake in his hand. The clear liquid sloshed against the smooth sides. Natsumi and Amarante were quieter than normal. Everyone was quieter than normal. With a silence like death hanging over the table, I could have heard a pin drop. I had to keep reminding myself to breathe, though the room was not stifling.

A fly buzzed close to my ear, and I flinched.

Amarante cleared her throat, and we all watched as Cruelon stopped twirling his glass. His eyes shot daggers at her. She looked away, her shoulders tense. I rolled my shoulders back. Red moved. I looked across the table to see Natsumi staring at me. Her scarlet gown hugged her in all the right places, and a necklace of gold filigree hung around her slender neck. She twirled her glass between her fingertips. I licked my lips, feeling thirsty as I watched. She traced a slender finger along her cheek, from her eye down to her full, rosy lips. *She's trying to tell me something. But what?* I squinted as I focused. *Eyes, mouth ...* She slid her finger across her lips with a quick movement. *Lips, close lips?* My brows furrowed.

Footsteps approached from the door. Cruelon set his glass down. I shifted in my seat, feeling the hairs on the back of my neck tingle, and took a sip of wine to settle my nerves. A knowing, appreciative smile crossed Amarante's face, and she fluttered her lashes. The king took Natsumi's hand and stroked her upturned palm. A shiver traveled up the length of my spine.

Clothing rustled as two forms sat to either side of me.

"Lady Juliet," Hirose whispered as he settled himself on my right—between Amarante and I. He winked, but there seemed to be lines there that I didn't remember.

"Finally," Cruelon exclaimed with a sigh. "Taisho."

I looked up from my lap then.

No. Shock rippled through my entire being. *How?* My body froze, and everyone and everything faded from around me. *It's not possible. How can this be?* The question pounded inside my head. It took all my strength to remain silent, to turn away and place my trembling hands in my lap where no one could see them.

"Benkei, I am glad you are here." The king steepled his fingers as he leaned forward. His eyes traveled over me.

Benkei. The word bit into me. I stared at my glass of wine but didn't dare pick it up for fear everyone would see my shaking hands. *Why is he here?* I took in a deep breath. *In for seven, hold for four, out for eight.* The shaking began to subside and breathing came easier. I didn't dare look at Hirose. He noticed everything, and I couldn't have him suspect anything or ask me any questions.

I glanced once at Adnan, but it was as if I wasn't there as his gaze traveled over me and down the table. Tristan couldn't have been right ... but why was he here? Fear clutched my soul in its iron grasp. I gripped my thighs, needing something to hold onto, but froze as I saw Adnan so close to me, mere inches away. My head throbbed and pressure built behind my eyes. Voices were dull and distant.

It was as if someone had dunked me underwater and even now held me just beneath the surface, a surface so close and yet so far. Blurry faces drifted in and out of view, my sight impaired through a foggy lens.

There was only one voice that I didn't hear. One voice I knew I could distinguish from all the others. I ached to hear it, yet feared it all at once. My heart constricted, and my throat grew raw against the onslaught of emotions.

"Lady Juliet." Hirose's voice broke through like a tidal wave. "Are you not hungry?"

I looked at him then, his dark eyes searching my own. *Don't give him the answers he seeks.* Forcing a smile on my face, I murmured, "I am tired, is all." Taking my glass, I raised it to my lips and sputtered as I realized the servants had poured me sake instead of wine. *They know I don't like sake.* I raised my eyes to see Cruelon raising his own glass in a slight toast to me. *It was him.*

Amarante frowned at me before turning her attention back to the conversation at hand. Chopsticks chinked against china plates as Adnan reached forward for some meat. He was so close I could almost feel him. The barriers I'd built around me began to crumble.

It's too soon. I set the sake back on the table and took up the chopsticks. *He shouldn't be here.* I fought for air in the small but warm room. *Why is he here?*

The next two hours disappeared in a quick blur. I hadn't realized what time it was until the servants came forward to clear away my empty bowl, and then my wine glass. I didn't remember eating and drinking. Not a word was exchanged between Adnan and I, yet I could not get him out of my head, nor could I look at him. His muted voice in conversation was unignorable.

The king stood, giving us the signal for the rest of us to follow. Hirose took my arm as usual, escorting me into the antechamber outside. I could feel Adnan at my heel, could almost hear his footsteps through those of the others, feel his breath on the back of my neck ...

I stopped when Hirose did, waiting for Cruelon to finish up his current conversation and choose whom he would escort to his chambers for the night. Natsumi waited as well, not speaking or staring at me, her graceful form still and silent. She regarded Adnan before returning to me. *What does she think of? What does she know?* I wondered how she did it, how she managed to keep the king wrapped around her thumb and still live, still have his favor. The thoughts distracted me. *She must remember Adnan from Umi no Machi.*

"Lady Juliet," Cruelon greeted, tapping me on the shoulder. I jumped, my breath catching. Flashes of the last night he'd done this flew through my mind. I still had two weeks left. Panic bloomed up in place of the numbness I'd felt leaving the dining room. *Keep calm, keep calm—* I felt far from it. Everything around me spiraled downward so fast it felt like I'd plunged into a dark abyss.

I stared into Natsumi's emotionless face as I took Cruelon's arm. *I am but a puppet.* Tension raised the hairs on my arms and stiffened my limbs, but I'd been trained well. I moved through the motions without a single hesitation, without a sign of the war just under the surface.

I thought I saw Natsumi nod her head to me as we began to depart, but when I turned and blinked, she'd recoiled back into her stony beauty. Amarante shifted next to Natsumi, her eyes shooting burning daggers my way. There was no one to stop Cruelon. *Why tonight?*

Adnan remained behind me, his presence the biggest distraction of all. I couldn't look at him, not when I might see what lay in his expression and dissolve what little strength I had left, what little strength was currently keeping me from seeing his familiar face, his eyes that would twinkle or the soft, rare smile that would light his face up.

But what if Tristan was right?

I stared at the floor as the king turned to say something to one of his advisors, catching sight of Adnan's familiar, worn leather boots. I knew they were his. I'd seen them so many times before. Closing my eyes, I squared my shoulders. *Don't look up.*

The king began walking, leading me along until I was sure I could open my eyes again. Master Hiito trailed along behind us, his high and reedy voice breaking the silence. I tried to listen to what they spoke of, but I couldn't. It required too much focus. I never thought I'd be so glad for Hiito's presence—for anyone's presence. *But why is he here? Where are we going?*

As we left the others behind, I could hear the soft footfalls on stone fade into silence but for our own. As I heard Adnan's distant voice behind us, every nerve in my body tensed as I tried to resist the urge to cry out to him. I knew what I wanted to say—the words came so quick, so easy—but I wouldn't voice them out loud. I couldn't. My dress rustled with every step, mingling with the sounds of Hiito's heavy breathing and the swish of Cruelon's robes.

I recognized the corridor. It was the same one I'd traversed a couple of times during my imprisonment in the dungeon when I'd first arrived. Did Tristan know about my impending marriage of sorts? What had Kin reported to him? *Had she even had time?* And Saya, did she know?

The farther we went, the more flashes of dark memories shot through my mind—hunger, thirst, cold, dripping water—it all surrounded me in a building cacophony until I wondered if Cruelon could see and hear them. I glanced up at him, but if he knew I watched, he gave no sign.

We walked into the dungeon, down several flights of stairs, past the dozens of cell doors, and into the farthest room, but it was no cell. Candles blazed with light, showcasing books, scrolls, and maps littering the large table at the center of the room. Smaller tables also overflowed. It was a haphazard mess. Mildew permeated the air, making the dank room seem even worse. The room wasn't guarded, but then again, it was well hidden. It looked like just one more cell.

Cruelon released my arm, and I stood still as he turned to face me.

"Don't worry, Lady Juliet. This isn't your cell."

"My lord?" I inquired with dry lips.

"You have done so well the past few weeks. I am so proud of who you have become, who you are becoming still. I knew when you first arrived it would not be easy to break you, but you have learned to master your emotions beautifully. It is alluring, the way you clutched my arm as we walked down here. I could almost see your thoughts playing out in your eyes, the widening of them when we entered here, the stiffness of your body walking next to mine, and the feverish heat beginning to rise under your skin."

I stiffened and forced myself to seem more compliant and welcoming of his affections.

"You play a dangerous game, Lady Juliet." He laughed. "You act so innocent I have doubted myself more than once. But I finally have proof, Juliet. I commend you for it. I have not met a woman with more bravery—or we could even call it foolishness—than you."

"My lord, I am not sure what you—"

"Do not play games with me," he snapped. "No more. You thought you could hide the truth, but you forget who I am, Lady Juliet. I am the king of this country. I have more power than any other man here." His voice echoed off the four stone walls. "And you, fiancée of the Uprising's leader, have been found out. Oh, I suspected you were up to something, believe me. How could you have evaded capture all this time, only to end up here out of the blue? But I will admit, you are good. I began disbelieving myself in the last few days. You play your part well." Cruelon glanced back at Hiito, who remained in the doorway. "Even Master Hiito began to have doubts about you, until our spy confirmed my suspicions— the rumors circulating the rebel encampments—an assignation between the rebel and the Otherworlder. Unless there are two Otherworlders that have come, then you, Juliet, are engaged to the one man who challenges my rule." Cruelon's robes rustled as he paced the cell. "You have yet to shrink away from speaking your mind, Juliet, so why now? That is one thing I like about you. You have guts, but what to do with you? I now have you and the rebels in the palm of my hand. If he truly cares for you, then I can now make him do whatever I would like, but if he does not, then that puts a damper on things."

I took a deep breath. "I'm not his fiancée." It didn't sound convincing enough.

"No? And why should I believe you?" Cruelon leaned closer, his face so close I could smell the alcohol on his breath, feel the heat blowing against my face.

"I'm not," I pleaded, stepping closer. "I swear. I don't know who gave you that information—"

"A trusted confidant of their leader, a man who works for me."

My breath caught. *The Unknown, Adnan. It can't be true.*

"Master Hiito wishes to make an example of you," Cruelon continued as though Hiito wasn't within earshot. "But I feel like that would make you into a martyr. The Otherworlder, killed by the king's hand, for the crime of having become engaged to his enemy. A romantic story. The people would soak it up. Rather than scaring them all into hiding, it would fuel the resistance. Many would flock to their banner."

Master Hiito shuffled his feet behind me, but I stayed stock-still, frozen in place.

Cruelon smiled, but it never reached his eyes. "See, you have a rare strength about you. A resilience I wish more of my own men would have." He tapped his finger on my cheek. "On the other hand, we could use you against the rebels. They all look up to you. You have grown in stature, commonly known as the Otherworlder. If you were seen in public, as one of my court, someone who admires and respects me, it could weaken them—crush the resistance. A supporter of your king and country."

"I already am one of your court," I agreed, "so that plan could work. They haven't even made a rescue attempt," I spat, throwing all my present despair and fear into my voice. "I'll do whatever it is you want. They've abandoned me here."

Cruelon threw his head back and laughed. "The fire!" He slid a hand into my hair. "You are beautiful, Juliet Barrows." His voice chilled. "And a fool."

"My lord?" I whispered, rolling on the balls of my feet.

Cruelon slid the pins out of my updo. My hair fell and cascaded down around my shoulders.

He examined the pins in his slender hands, turning them over so that the jewels glittered as they caught the light from the candles. "Did you think I don't know what you tried to do? Hirose saw you. He saw your fingers clasped around one much like these. Were you going to kill me, Juliet?" My name felt like a caress of his tongue.

I shivered.

"Do you know why I've let you continue wearing these? Because you haven't had a single chance to use them since that night. I have not given you a chance." Cruelon twirled a lock of my hair. "It's a pity. I actually thought you might be telling the truth."

I opened my mouth.

"No." Cruelon tapped a finger over my lips. "No arguing. You're not going to change my mind. You will do as I say, otherwise I will have you killed, and I don't think you want to die."

Hiito cleared his throat in the background, and I heard rustling as he shifted on his feet.

"Why do you think I could stop the resistance?" I whispered. "If I had meant so much, wouldn't their leader have tried to get me back by now?"

"Words, words," Cruelon interrupted, fluttering his hand in the air. "Enough. You will do exactly as I say when the time comes, whatever it is."

"I won't do it," I breathed.

"Easy for you to say now," Cruelon replied.

"You'd have to kill me. I won't betray them. You hold nothing over me besides my life. And I value my own life less than those of my friends. Is that a hard concept for you to understand, Cruelon?" I laughed. "You, who hold yourself most dear and who don't care for the lives of your people. Everything you do is for yourself, so how can you understand? You would trade anyone's life for your own. But I am not you. I care for others more than myself. I would never betray a friend to save my life."

Cruelon chuckled, low and deep. "Spoken well." He clapped his hands together. "Bravo, Lady Juliet."

Fury rose in me. I bit my lip to keep it down, so hard I bled.

Cruelon stepped forward and brushed a rough thumb against my lip, then looked down at the blood on his finger. "Juliet, see how easily you bleed? I will make you bleed. Those few days in the dungeon—those were nothing compared to what I can do. Do you really want to put yourself through that?"

I gritted my teeth. *No!* Every fiber of me wanted to yell the word out. But I thrust those thoughts down, deep down, and concentrated on the throbbing of my lip. I didn't need to say anything. Cruelon could see it in my eyes.

He rubbed his thumb again, wiping the blood off on my skin. "Very well. You have made your decision. I will break you, then build you up into who I want you to be. The last time was just a taste of what is to come. You have no idea what is ahead of you."

I forced a smile to my face. "All words, Your Majesty?"

Cruelon growled. "Master Hiito, take her away."

Hiito snapped his fingers. I hadn't realized we weren't alone. Footsteps sounded behind me.

"I hope you sleep well, *Lady* Juliet," Cruelon purred. "And Juliet, you will still have the pleasure of joining my harem."

I glared at him as a hand gripped my arm, dragging me backward. *Hirose.* The man who now held me in his grip pulled me by force down the corridor. He didn't look at me once.

"Hirose—"

"Quiet," he snapped, clamping down on my arm.

I winced and stumbled, my feet trailing along the dirty floor before I could get them under me again. With every door we passed, I expected to be thrown into a cell, but door after door receded behind us, and soon, we entered the long corridor sloping up into the rest of the keep.

Where is Adnan? I couldn't help but look for him as we went, but there was no sign of him. What did I expect? Turmoil wrapped me within a thick blanket, making my thoughts race and sending confusion flooding over me.

Four guards joined us at the entrance as though they'd been waiting, falling in around us into a tight formation.

"Why the show of force?" I asked, throwing as much condescension into my voice as I could manage. "Where are you taking me?"

They didn't answer but rather picked up their pace. We turned down a familiar hallway.

"Why are we here?" I asked. "What are you doing?"

Hirose shoved me forward hard enough to cause me to stumble. "No questions, king's orders."

I slammed against the side of the wall as we rounded another corner and heard a distinct rip from a seam in my gown.

A guard in front of us strode forward. A door slammed open, the door to my room. Hirose and I entered, and I realized something was different. But what? *There.* Next to my mattress—except there was no mattress, not anymore. Now two iron rings were mounted into the wall a few inches above the floor, another two set in the boards a few feet away.

Metal clinked behind me. Before my scattered thoughts could come together, I was thrown to the ground. A yelp escaped my lips as my hip thrust into the wood and pain flared up my back.

I struggled as the four guards attached the cold manacles to my wrists and ankle, the heaviness of the iron driving my limbs to the ground. "Hirose," I panted. "Please, don't do this." A ripping sound tore through the air. I glanced down to see my gown come away at the shoulder seam.

Hirose folded his arms and looked away. "Let's go," he ordered when the men had finished.

"Hirose!" I yelled, straining against the cold metal. "Hirose! Who told the king about me? The traitor? Or was it Benkei?"

Hirose froze, his silhouette black against the light pouring in from the corridor outside. He continued without another word.

The door slammed shut behind him, leaving me alone and in darkness. My heart pounded. It had all happened so fast. One moment I was at dinner, just another night in the castle, and the next Adnan was there. *Adnan—where is he? Does he know? Does he care?*

It didn't matter now. I'd lost my chance. I should've tried to say something at dinner. Tears pricked at my eyes, and I let my head fall back between my arms. The iron hurt; it bit into my skin, and it was cold. The fire was out, the shutters wide open, letting all the cold night air flow into the room. Within ten minutes I was shivering, the thin material of my dress inadequate for a chilly winter evening.

Chapter Nineteen

Within a few hours, I stopped feeling any pain or even the cold seeping into the room. The ashes in the fireplace lay limp and dull in the hearth. The room was dark. No moonlight shone through the window, which was but a dim shape on the wall near the dark, vague shadow of the wardrobe. The wind whistled outside.

The door opened, and I lifted my head from where it had lolled against my raised arm. I blinked at the familiar small figure. "Emi?" I asked, my voice croaking.

A small flicker appeared as Emi lit a candle. "Come, my lady. It is time to ready you for the day." The flame spluttered and grew brighter. It was Emi. She looked so real. She walked over and held out a hand to undo the bun falling into my face. Her skin brushed my own—so soft, so warm.

She's real.

"Emi?" I repeated, but she didn't answer. Two guards entered the room, assuming places on either side of the door.

Emi waved a hand at them. "Please, at least turn your backs."

They glanced at one another but did so.

"We don't have long, my lady," Emi whispered. "I'm just going to wash your face and hands and smooth your hair a little."

"Hurry up," a guard ordered.

Emi rushed to the bathroom and came back with a damp cloth. I winced as the cold material touched my face. She lowered the cloth to my hands. "I'm sorry. There is no time to heat water."

"S'all right," I said, slurring my words through the towel. My chapped lips threatened to break open and start bleeding, so I didn't try to speak again.

Emi leaned back. "She's ready."

The guards moved forward, and the manacles shifted as the key twisted in the locks before dropping with heavy thuds. I fell back against the ground as my arms were freed. The guards placed their hands under my shoulders and heaved me to my feet. My legs trembled, unable to bear my weight after having been in the cramped position for so long. I stumbled along behind Emi, propped between the two men.

"Did you hear?" one whispered to me, his face otherwise expressionless. "Benkei has asked for you."

His words ran through my mind in slow waves as I struggled to comprehend. *Benkei—the Unknown ... Adnan!*

"He wants *you*, Otherworlder." A gleam entered his eyes. "Doesn't take much to wonder why. I wish I could have been gifted you instead."

He wants me.

The other guard snorted.

Wants me in that way. Goosebumps ran over my skin. *Was I just a toy? A plaything to him?* Cruelon said someone trusted in Tristan's eyes had told him about me, and Adnan showed up the same day. *Did I mean nothing to Adnan?* I didn't speak but stared straight ahead.

"From what I hear, he has to have you." The guard chuckled, his shoulder almost brushing against the wooden walls as he strode beside me. "He begged the king for you to be his gift. He said he would break you for him as he uses you." The guard paused and placed his hand on my jaw, forcing me to look at him. "I can't say I blame him." His eyes raked over me from head to toe. "Even through the dirt and crumpled clothing, you're an attractive slip of a thing."

My jaw clenched. Disgust filled me, and a pit grew in my stomach. I swallowed down the nausea.

"You think I—*we*"—he chuckled and gestured to the other guard—"haven't noticed? If King Cruelon notices you, how could we not? Especially when we've guarded you day and night."

Ahead, Emi's shoulders tensed.

Why does she have to hear this? I licked my dry lips. "What did Cruelon say?"

"He laughed. Thought it was the funniest thing he'd heard in a while. Probably struck a chord within himself. Everyone knows he wants you too. Suppose you'll just have to wait and see who gets you first. Who do you want warming your bed?"

I glanced downward, unable to fight the bile rising in my throat.

Silence fell as we approached a busier part of the keep. It seemed like ages had passed since the night before, when I'd seen Adnan and then been thrown in the dungeons, but it had been mere hours. I rubbed my wrists and pulled my sleeves down as far as I could to hide the angry red marks. They flared as though I'd been burned. Chilly air blew against the open skin on my shoulder where the sleeve had torn away from the bodice. I shivered as I was reminded of how cold I was. The night had been bitter, and my body struggled to remember what it felt like to be warm.

The guard ahead opened one of the doors leading out of the keep, and we stepped through. The sun glared down on me, too bright and strong. It had been far longer than I had thought. I had spent the whole night in those manacles. I lifted a hand and shielded my eyes. Amarante, Natsumi, and several other court ladies stood waiting by their mounts. Silence fell as they watched me approach.

My first impulse was to look away, pretend nothing was wrong, that my appearance was perfect, but I reined in my resolve and looked them straight in their faces, watching some school their features to perfection, whilst others, including Miya, did not. I had no idea what they knew or didn't know, but I guessed what they assumed. How could they not, when I'd left on the arm of the king and even now approached in the same dress, torn along one shoulder seam, hair in disarray, and with a drawn and tired look on my face? I could imagine how I looked to them. I could see their conclusion in their eyes and downturned expressions, in the anger flaring on Amarante's flushed face. *They think I was with the king.*

I jumped as a voice hissed in my ear, startling me.

"You are not to say a word about what transpired last night to anyone. If you do, the king will kill those you care for one by one. Think of Emi." With that parting warning, the guard nudged me forward to my horse.

The women began chatting again, but none addressed me. *That's fine,* I thought as I stroked the nose of my horse. Leaning against him, I felt sleep drifting over me. I was too tired to talk anyway. *Just a few seconds of sleep.* It could have only been moments later that I felt myself stumble and fall sideways. I caught myself against the horse's shoulder and grabbed a fistful of its mane.

"Juliet?" Miya's soft voice broke through the bubble I'd wrapped myself in.

I looked at her. "I'm fine," I muttered. *Don't talk to her. Don't put her in danger.* My shoulders jerked as the horse shifted on its feet. Grabbing the saddle for balance, I felt my legs wobble. A lean, cloaked figure appeared in the corner of my eye. *Adnan.* I swung my head, searching, but he wasn't there. *Am I seeing things?* I could've sworn he had been standing there. Swallowing past the lump in my throat, I focused on remaining on my feet.

"Let us go," Amarante announced in a lofty tone, not bothering to hide her glee at my present state.

A rustle of skirts alerted me to Miya striding off to mount her own horse. I'd forgotten she'd been standing there.

⌇⌇⌇⌇⌇ ⌇⌇⌇⌇⌇

A daze had fallen over me. It wasn't just the ride. My steps were slow as I meandered back to my room. After the ride around the castle, I'd attended a tea party where I wasn't allowed food or water, just tea, and then another walk. It felt purposeful on their part. No rest.

My door loomed in front of me, no longer a comforting sight. Weariness pulled at my limbs, and adrenaline buzzed at the edges of my mind and body. I made to step in front of the mirror, but Emi caught my arm.

"Don't." Though petite, she pulled with a greater strength than I knew she possessed.

I stopped and a dry chuckle escaped my lips. "Do I look that bad?"

"Of course not," she said, but still draped a blanket over the mirror. She quickly dressed me in a gown and combed my hair before slipping it up into a simple bun. "There." She secured a small, ornate comb and stepped back. "Now go, before you're late."

As I walked to the dining hall, all I could think about was food and sleep, or maybe sleep and then food. *Do I care which comes first?* My stomach growled as tantalizing smells wafted down the corridor. I licked my lips and entered the room.

Everyone was there.

Hirose nodded to me as I took my seat. I couldn't look at Adnan. But I could feel him, just there beside me. I stared down at the glass of sake in front of me and the small bowl of rice with the wooden chopsticks beside it. My stomach growled as the savory aromas assailed my nostrils.

Something brushed against my left leg. I glanced down. Adnan was so close. My breath caught. *Was it by accident? Is he trying to tell me something?* I bit my lip, feeling a recent scab crack under the pressure. Fresh blood trickled into my mouth.

"Biting yourself again, my dear?" Cruelon smiled around a mouthful of food. "We can't have that. Be more careful."

I gritted my teeth. "Yes, my lord."

"Hirose, pass her that napkin, if you please."

I took the napkin with shaking fingers and dabbed at my lip. Cruelon clasped his hands together, spoke thanks to the gods for the food—not a customary thing for him to do—and began to eat.

What was he about? I blinked. It didn't matter, not now. Right now, I needed to regain some strength. I cast the question from my mind and shoveled food into my mouth, closing my eyes as the juices from the tender meat worked their way down my throat. The steamy crispness of the vegetables with the spices and sweetness coated my taste buds. Desire broke over me a hundredfold. Food had never tasted so good.

When I opened my eyes, I saw Miya staring at me, her mouth hanging wide open. I tried to slow down my eating, but it was too late. Pain shot across my stomach as it cramped. I struggled to keep it in check, to wait it out. It had only been twenty-four hours since my last meal. *Is it poisoned?*

Before I could stop myself, I stood up, struggling to keep my balance as my legs tangled themselves in the gown. "I have to go," I burst out, clasping one hand to my mouth and the other to my stomach.

Hirose reached out, but I ignored him and ran out of the room. Acid burned my throat and esophagus. Even through my haziness, I realized when I was back in my room. I stumbled toward the wall as the guards shoved me from behind. Without grace, they flung me onto the floor so that I hit it in a heap, my arms and legs flailing.

Salty tears rolled down my cheeks. "Have I been poisoned?" I licked my lips and closed my eyes.

"Put this on her," a voice growled. "The king doesn't want any more of her dresses ruined."

"Please!" I pleaded, curling as another cramp wrecked my stomach.

"You're not. Be quiet," the guard snapped.

Through half-closed eyes, I watched Emi approach and felt her movements as my body was divested of my clothes and I lay there, shivering on the bare floor, before being redressed.

Afterward, the guards strode forward and each grabbed a hand, shackling my wrists to the iron rings mounted in the wall. They were rough as they did the same with my legs. The manacles weighed down my ankles, and the heavy chains bit into my skin. Cold to the touch, they weighed me down as they seeped what little strength I had left out of me.

They all left. Even Emi. I stared up at the ceiling, dark above me. The breeze blowing through the open window grew colder as time passed. Before long, my eyes began to drift shut. I sighed as my head dropped forward.

A faint hammering filtered through my sluggish thoughts.

It grew louder. *Bang, bang, bang.* Two pans collided with one another repeatedly. The sound pierced my ears and echoed about in my head. Waves of shooting pain almost blinded me as I stared up at the guard in front of me.

"No sleeping. King's orders."

I bit back a groan and ignored him, closing my eyes once again.

"Not on my watch," the guard growled. "The king would have my head." He slapped me. My head flew to the side from the force of the blow.

Again and again, all night long. I would fall asleep for but a few minutes before the barrage of noise. As the hours passed, the guards had to become more creative with their methods. My cheeks swelled from the slaps, and my body ached from where they would press their fingers into my nerves until I cried out for them to stop. When they'd leave, tears would sting my eyes before sliding down familiar paths along my cheeks. The room that had become my sanctuary over the past few weeks had now become my prison.

I felt nothing when Emi came in the morning. She brought strong black tea, steeped until it had become bitter. I gulped it down anyway, feeling the heat flaring inside my belly and spreading out like a web.

"Come on, my lady," Emi said when I finished. "You can eat this on the way."

She held out a small roll with a thin slice of cheese and ham. I ate it so fast I couldn't taste it. I looked at the crumbs on my lap. *I have no memory of the taste. Or even of having chewed it.* Saliva pooled in my mouth and I longed for more, just one more bite. My stomach growled, hungry, awake, reminding me of its emptiness. My senses sharpened a little, and that was what I needed.

"Come, my lady," Emi whispered again. "It's time."

⁙⁘⸙ ⸙⁘⁙

Another ride, another morning where the women dared not speak to me. What they knew, I had no idea, but they feared something. Maybe they had been told not to converse with me. Miya did try once, but the guard's warning flashed through my mind. *Could they be killed just for speaking to me?*

No, I couldn't talk to her. She was the closest thing to a friend I had left other than Emi, and I didn't want either of them to end up like Kin. The hours passed, slipping by, one by one. I wasn't allowed to sleep. I wasn't allowed to eat. Before I left for dinner, I was given another small cup of strong black tea. It helped a little. One of my guards helped me to the dining hall, as I was unable to walk on my own. My legs were too unsteady.

Adnan wasn't there.

His cushion was empty. I managed a few mouthfuls of food, but not much. My eyes drooped and my jaw ached. I waited, watching, but he never showed. His seat remained cold.

Then another night. It came and went, filled with banging, with lack of sleep, and with the guards keeping me company. I loathed my room now. The bare walls mocked me, the wardrobe filled with beautiful dresses laughed at me, and the window reminded me of the freedom I had lost. Freedom the birds outside my window had but I did not. They could fly where they wished; I couldn't even walk across my room.

The nightmares came day and night, any time my mind floundered, any time my eyes closed for just long enough to doze. But it wasn't just in my sleep. My nightmares had become real. They filled every living moment of each day, even more horrific because they weren't just dreams. No more tears came. I had no energy to think, let alone move. I sucked in air. Breathing was hard enough.

The third day dawned, and I was escorted down to the courtyard, unable to move my legs on my own. I stumbled, moving like a child learning to walk. The guard helped me onto the horse, and I slumped over the mare's head. Through bleary eyes, I saw Miya watching, her face pale.

When the women spurred their horses forward, I gave a half-hearted attempt but lost my grip on the reins. The ground rushed toward me, and I felt weightless as I watched. My body hit the dirt, and I gasped as the air was knocked out of me.

Just let me die. I stared up at the overcast sky and closed my eyes as I heard footsteps approach. Strong arms picked me up like a sack of potatoes, and the familiar scent of rain filled my nostrils.

Adnan.

I stiffened as I looked up at him. *I'm dreaming.*

"Shh," he whispered.

It's not a dream. I wanted to say something, but I couldn't. The words wouldn't come.

"This way, Benkei," a guard spoke from somewhere behind me.

I heard Master Hiito's voice talking, but I couldn't make out what he said. *Master Hiito ...* The thoughts filtered through my mind, slow as molasses. *Where has Adnan been?* Exhaustion crowded my thoughts, slowing them down until I couldn't figure out how much I even cared. I felt torn. *He is a traitor. Lies, lies, lies ... that is all he has ever given me. Lies and secrets.*

Adnan didn't look down at me until we were well inside the castle walls.

"Juliet, what are they doing to you?" he hissed, lowering his head.

"You—" I tried. "They—"

"What is she saying?" the guard asked from up ahead.

"Nothing," Adnan responded, gripping me a little tighter. "Just mumbling."

The guard grunted.

"They're waiting for me to break," I murmured as I fought hard to keep my eyes open. "I'm so tired," I whispered. "Adnan, I'm so tired. I can't do this …"

His grip tightened as my head lolled against him. This was different. I could feel it coming.

"I'm going to black out," I managed, unable to fight against the darkness creeping in around my vision.

"Hold on, Juliet. You have to stay strong—" His words faded, but I saw his lips moving. I couldn't hear anything as a soothing blackness overtook me.

Chapter Twenty

A familiar face loomed over me, the light casting flickering shadows over his skin. The guard waved a hand over my eyes and I shifted, hearing the clanking of the chains as they moved. "Good, you're awake." He leaned back, still crouched low. "Master Hiito was afraid you'd died on him. Come on." He hoisted me to my feet.

Shackles. I'm not shackled. The realization was like a slight jolt of electricity. I looked down to see them lying on the floor, coiled in a heap as though in waiting for my wrists and ankles. *I must've jostled them when I moved,* I realized. The guard pulled me away, and another joined us in the corridor. Between the two of them, they half-carried, half-dragged me down the hall. Flickers of ornate wall tapestries, glimpses of servants, and closed doorways passed us by as I flitted in and out of consciousness.

My eyes opened, closed, and opened again. Vague shapes moved, the motion of being carried, a door, a room—then someone shook me before thrusting me into a chair. I blinked several times, peering through blurred vision at the king.

He looked up from his papers and his eyes narrowed. "Leave us."

I heard footsteps and a door close. *We're alone.* I blinked. *Where are we?* The familiar two windows flanked Cruelon as he stood between them, one hand on the rim of the black chair. His study.

"Well, amazing what a few days of less-than-ideal treatment can do to a person."

My tongue flicked out over my dry and cracked lips. "You're despicable."

He smiled, and his bun bobbed as he nodded. "Perhaps I am. Is it working?"

I shook my head.

Cruelon leaned over the table. "I will ask you this once only. Choose your answer wisely."

A period of silence stretched out. Every nerve in my body felt taut.

"Will you work with me to bring down the Uprising? Do you swear allegiance to me?"

Blasted man. I chuckled, and my body shook from the force of it. *Why am I laughing?*

Cruelon's lips thinned. "Your answer?"

"No. And I never will."

"So you would rather kill yourself?"

"No, but I know you'll do it."

He steepled his fingers together. "Interesting."

I watched him even as he watched me. It took all my energy to keep upright. *Death may just be a welcome gift.* It would be better than wasting away, watching as those around me suffered and not knowing what happened outside the walls of this fortress. Nothing broke the silence. Cruelon's chest rose and fell as he breathed. He wasn't dead ... but then again, neither was I—not yet.

"What am I to do with you, Juliet?" Cruelon's voice dropped into a soothing purr. "I offer you everything. You turn me down. I threaten your life, and you still are willing to sacrifice it for your friends. What if I offered to let you return safely to your own world? All you have to do is tell me everything you know."

"No."

Cruelon clasped his hands behind his back. "Have you ever wondered how I knew about you?"

I blinked, confused at the sudden change in tactic.

"My seer saw you arrive in this world."

His seer. My lips parted.

"I immediately sent men out to find you," Cruelon continued in a mild tone. "Benkei and Boden came close—the closest—until you turned yourself in to the patrol."

"It's not possible," I whispered, shaking my head, my hair lashing the air like a whip. My shadow flickered with the movement.

Cruelon cocked his head. "Why not?"

"Because …" I choked the words down. What was I going to say? That Adnan and I had been together before and after that? *Give him up.* The thought poked at me, urging me to tell Cruelon, to give up on my hopes. *No.* I pursed my lips.

"There is much you do not know, Juliet Barrows." Cruelon paced the room. "And Benkei is an enigma for you, isn't he?" He threw his head back and laughed.

I shuddered. *Benkei … Where is Adnan?* He was here, and after our little exchange, I remained more confused than ever as to his loyalties. I cleared my throat. "I thought you hated seers."

"Oh, I do." Cruelon waved a hand in the air. "But would I really be stupid enough not to keep one close to me? She has been quite helpful in many ways. She saw you being helpful." He snorted. "More than that, she saw you helping me take down the Uprising and securing my throne."

I shook my head. *No.*

Cruelon's face reddened and grew livid, almost matching the red of his robes. "I will give you everything you desire. *Everything.* Tell me who the leader of the Uprising is. Tell me where he is."

"Why hasn't your traitor told you?" I tensed as Cruelon stepped toward me.

He stopped and forced a smile to his face. "He plays the game."

My heart felt like it stopped beating. *No.* Tristan's suspicions came flooding into my mind. *What if Adnan is playing both sides?*

"Tell me who he is," Cruelon pressed as he advanced another two paces.

I backed up a little. "No," I whispered.

Before I could do more than blink, he stood in front of me, his hands around my throat. I gasped as he hoisted me out of the chair and brought my face close to his.

"I offered you everything! You worthless girl," he yelled, spittle flying from his lips.

Spots danced before my eyes, and my vision blackened at the edges. I was but a rag doll in the hands of a giant bent on destroying it. His grip was of iron, and my defense was weak. I raised my hands and raked them down Cruelon's face. Red streaks flared across his skin, and he howled—deep and loud—like that of a wounded animal. He hurled me to the side, and I hit the floor. My head slammed against the wall. I drew in deep breaths, trying to move, but my limbs wouldn't respond. Sounds filtered in as though I had fallen under gallons of encroaching water. My breaths were loud and rasping. Still, I couldn't move.

Cruelon doubled over, clutching his face in his hands. "Guards!" he howled.

Something crashed outside; the sound was dull but reverberated through the closed door.

"Guards!" he yelled again, letting go of his face and glaring at me through red-rimmed eyes. "I will kill you myself!" he exclaimed, a knife appearing in his hand from somewhere in the folds of his robes.

Fear lanced through me. I sent every command to my body that I could think of, shaking as I tried to tell my limbs to move, but they had frozen as though held immobile by an invisible force.

Cruelon strode toward me, light from the candelabra glinting off the sleek, silver blade.

I opened my mouth and screamed. The sound was bloodcurdling as all my pent-up shock, hurt, confusion, and anger filled the room. All my emotions unleashed at last.

Cruelon hesitated before continuing, his eyes alight with a sort of maniacal brightness. A tiny drop of blood rolled down his cheek from where I'd gouged him with my fingernails.

The door crashed open, banging against the wall with a loud thud.

"Cruelon."

I know that voice. It was the calm against the chaos. I couldn't see the speaker around Cruelon's robes.

"Your time has come."

It's, it's… I struggled to see around Cruelon.

Cruelon shifted, his gaze locked on someone over his shoulder. His fingers whitened as they gripped the blade's handle. He whirled and released the knife. It flew, and there was a thunk as it struck wood.

"Any last words?" the voice asked, filling the room with a deep-throated power.

Who is that? The voice was familiar.

Cruelon snarled, and another knife appeared in his hand. His robes swished as he ran forward. In the open doorway stood a hooded figure, a sword in hand, bright with red blood.

The painful throbbing in my head continued. I struggled into an upright position, watching as Cruelon stopped, frozen. The hooded man lowered his sword and Cruelon's body crumpled, falling against the floor with a thud. A look of surprise lay frozen on his upturned face, and a dark stain appeared on his chest.

The figure drew back his hood.

"Tristan?" My heart thudded in my chest. *I knew that voice. He's here.*

"Juliet." Tristan rushed forward and kneeled beside me. "Come on, we have to get you out of here."

"Wait, how—what—" I spluttered, my body trembling.

"Can you walk?"

I shook my head. "No."

"Benkei," Tristan barked. "Get in here now."

Adnan. My eyes widened. Adnan backed into the room, peering at us over his shoulder.

"Help me with her," Tristan ordered, putting an arm around me.

I started, "But—"

"Shh, not now," Tristan replied. "Let us get you out of here."

Between the two of them, they supported me whilst sporting swords in their free hands.

Tristan hefted his sword. "Let us go."

"But—"

"Hush," Adnan whispered, his voice so familiar, so normal. I closed my eyes. The sound of his voice calmed me like nothing I could've imagined.

They're together. Adnan is here. I fell silent. It was all too much. Everything was happening too fast. We moved out of the study. Distant shouts echoed down the hallways, and booted footsteps grew closer.

"There." Tristan pointed. "Give the signal."

Adnan dropped his arm from around me and strode to a brazier next to an open window. Drawing an arrow, he set fire to the tip and drew the string, his cloak falling back as he freed his arms. I couldn't see his face under the shadowed cowl. I tried to take a step forward when I felt Tristan shift beside me, but my legs collapsed.

Tristan grunted as I fell against him. The arrow loosened, Adnan strode back and slung my right arm over his shoulders. I gasped for air.

"This isn't working. Carry her," Adnan said, releasing me. Before I could protest, Tristan swung me over his shoulder like a sack of potatoes. The wood floor moved down below, and I listened to the quick footsteps of Adnan and Tristan as they moved forward.

I smelled the smoke before I saw it. The main gates were ablaze; the courtyard seethed with roiling men—clashes of sword against sword, clanging of weapons against shield or armor—the screams of the dying, the screams of the triumphant, and the screams of those without hope. Commands were called from both sides, each vying to be louder over the mesh of entangling bodies.

Moonlight shed its cold, pale gleam over the courtyard, and the smell of blood permeated the air. It rolled in waves toward us, carried on the night breeze. It was the smell of death.

Tears coursed down my cheeks; even so, I felt empty. I saw everything upside down, as if gravity had shifted, yet everyone but me remained glued to the ground.

He stood amidst the many. Shifting in and out of view. Even upside down, I recognized his lean, cat-like figure.

Hirose.

Always moving, hacking, whirling, fighting for his life as well as those of his men. For one moment, our eyes met across the expanse of bodies, and it was as though time stilled.

What does he think of right now?

He turned back to the battle at hand, and everything slammed back into reality. Tension radiated from Tristan's shoulders. The constant barrage of noises battered my senses, leaving me more drained than from a whole day in the dungeon.

Tristan moved forward and my head slapped against his back. The ground blurred, and the night grew blacker. Everything around me faded away as I lost myself to oblivion.

I blinked, my vision sharpening as the face above me came into focus. "Adnan."

He leaned forward. "How do you feel?"

I swallowed and raised my head. With a grunt, I dropped it back on the pillow. "Awful."

"You look it."

"Where am I?" I looked around the unfamiliar space. It was small. Other than my mattress and a couple of cushions, there was nothing. A crackle alerted me to the small fire in a brazier.

"A room here in the fortress," Adnan replied, crossing his arms. "We thought it best you didn't wake up in your old room."

I swallowed.

A creak drew my gaze to the doorway. *Saya.* My jaw dropped.

Saya strode in with a sad smile.

"Saya," I murmured, clutching the sheets.

She knelt down next to my mattress. "I wanted to be here when you woke, but it's for your own protection."

I raised an eyebrow.

"To keep Shizukana in line," she explained with a hint of humor. "He's not happy with you."

Adnan stared at me, his arms crossed over his chest, his face deadpan.

"I did tell him to save it for when you have more strength," Saya continued. "But I'm not sure he has ever listened to me."

What? Confusion fueled the ache in my temples. *Why does this all feel as though nothing happened?* I pressed my fingers to the sides of my head, rubbing the area just behind and above my ears.

Tristan appeared in the doorway. "Benkei, Saya, may I have a few moments alone with Juliet?" He stepped aside, waiting for them to file out of the room.

I struggled to sit up. "Adnan—"

Tristan moved forward. "Shh, it is all right. You are going to be fine."

"But what—how—" I watched as Tristan and Saya left.

Tristan sighed and crouched next to my mat. "I was wrong. I am so sorry, Juliet. I was wrong about him."

"What do you mean?" I whispered.

Tristan shrugged his broad shoulders. "He is not a traitor. He worked his way into Cruelon's circle to help our cause, but he did not tell me, and that is where it all went sideways."

"So ..." I left the thought unfinished. *There is someone else. Adnan isn't the traitor.* My eyes swept the room. *The traitor is still out there.*

"Yes, you can trust him."

Had I ever really stopped?

"Now, I have to go. There is so much to do, but I will visit you later." He took my hand and pressed a gentle kiss to my skin before standing. "Do not mention it to him, Juliet. I did not tell him I told you. Best leave it in the past."

"I—"

"It would hurt him, I think." Tristan leaned over and brushed a finger down my cheek. "I am sorry, love, but I do have to go." He was gone before a single word could come to my lips.

Saya and Adnan came back in.

Everything was happening so fast. My temples throbbed. I waited until they sat down. "What happened? I don't remember anything after we arrived in the courtyard."

"You passed out moments after we left the keep," Adnan began, his voice so deep and familiar. "We took the castle."

I shifted under the blankets. "That's it?" My body ached.

"You wanted to talk to her, Shizukana. Here's your chance." Saya grinned.

I stared at her. I'd seen the changes happening before I left, but now she seemed a new person, joking, laughing. What had happened in the weeks I'd been gone? *Does she know what happened to me during those four and a half weeks?*

Adnan's eyes crinkled with mirth as he glanced at her. "When we left the keep, we walked right into the midst of the fighting. We didn't plan very well, putting you in danger like that. But the entire evening didn't quite go according to plan." He shifted to stretch his long legs out in front of him. "We were supposed to get you out of there, then give the signal for attack. But things went wrong when the king requested your presence. I'd already snuck Tristan into the keep, so getting to you was the easy part." He ran a hand through his hair. "The fighting was fierce and ended quickly. We found a spot in the stables to wait it out. Within the hour, the castle was ours."

"And Cruelon?"

"Dead."

I felt my body relax. *He's dead.* "What about Hirose, Miya, Emi, and the others?"

Adnan's brows furrowed. "I don't know. Tristan is out there now, dealing with everything. Trying to, at any rate. It's all chaos. He was crowned king yesterday morning."

King? My breathing quickened. "How long have I been here?"

Adnan and Saya exchanged glances. Feeling a sense of alarm, I sat up and my head spun.

Adnan's arm shot out to support me, and he lowered me back onto the pillows. "Careful." He cleared his throat. "You've been out for three days."

My head throbbed. "Three days?"

"In and out of consciousness. But I'm not surprised you don't remember those moments. Even then, you were barely awake."

"He's been here all that time," Saya put in, casting me a knowing glance.

A feeling of warmth spread over my body, and I could feel myself softening. It all just felt too weird, as though none of this was real. And Adnan ... I didn't know how to act around him anymore, or what to say. I still didn't understand. He'd gone from being a traitor to not ... He was gone when I left, but then appeared at the castle ... I shook my head. It was too much. I closed my eyes against the pounding.

Adnan's voice was quiet. "Enough. Saya, why don't you fetch some food? I'll stay here."

I heard the door open and close. Everything ran through my mind like water over ice. Memories flooded my thoughts. As they faded away, one question remained. "Adnan—"

Adnan's warm but rough hand smoothed my hair away from my face. "We need to talk. Not now. But soon."

"No, I have to ask this," I protested. "It can't wait."

Adnan's jaw locked, but he nodded and laid his hands back in his lap. His shaggy brown hair fell into his face, longer even than when I'd last seen him.

"Did you tell Cruelon about me?"

Adnan's face darkened and his green eyes appeared like emeralds. "No."

I swallowed and clutched the blanket closer about me.

"Juliet, I never would've done something to intentionally put you in more danger." Adnan laid a hand on my lower thigh. "I didn't tell him about you and Tristan. He found out through someone else." He paused. "Not me."

I breathed through my parted lips, bobbing my head slowly. *It wasn't him.* My chin trembled. Deep down, I'd known it wasn't him, but I had to hear it. *The traitor.* It had to have been the traitor.

"I'm sorry I couldn't get you out sooner," he whispered.

I tilted my head to look at him.

He ran his free hand through his hair, his other still resting on my leg.

"I know," I murmured, smiling through tears that threatened to fall. I'd missed him. I'd missed the way he spoke, his presence— "I thought about you." There it was. The words were out, and I couldn't take them back. He didn't know just how I'd thought about him—the confusion, the betrayal, the hopelessness I'd associated with him, especially after I had seen him with Cruelon.

Adnan smiled, but it was sorrowful. "Close your eyes and get some rest. Saya will be back soon, and I'm sure Tristan won't be long behind her."

Was that a bitter note? I examined his face, but he stared down at his hands. *Why did so much have to change?* There was so much I wanted to ask him, but what to say, what to ask ...? Sleep drove my thoughts from my mind.

⁂

A soft kiss on my brow woke me.

Tristan leaned back, his blond hair impeccable and his clothes without a wrinkle. "Hello, beautiful."

I glanced past him to see Adnan still sitting by my bed.

Tristan helped me into a sitting position. "Here is some food." He placed the plate on my lap. "We have a lot of catching up to do, and I want to know everything that happened to you here."

Everything? I stared down at the food without touching it. *What had been the point? I had suffered. I had felt pain. But in the end, I hadn't done what I was sent to do.*

"Juliet?"

"I failed."

Tristan took my hand and entwined his fingers in mine. I tried to pull away, but he tightened his grip.

"Tristan—"

"No. I will not have that. You did help." He didn't let go of my hand. A wave of exhaustion fell over me, and I looked over his shoulder at Adnan. He gazed back at me, but with his old mask on, showing nothing of what lay beneath.

"You were the instrument to Cruelon's downfall," Tristan continued, his thumb drawing slow circles on my skin. "It was because of you we were able to take the castle that night. Your maps were instrumental. You are a brave one."

A brave one? I didn't feel brave. To avoid answering, I took a bite of meat, but it was tasteless. *The traitor—Lanevrog.* After chewing and swallowing, I asked, "What about the traitor? The one who sent Cruelon his information?"

Tristan frowned. "What traitor?"

I pushed my food aside. "I had Kin send word about him. Cruelon had papers in his office with a name on them, Lanevrog."

Tristan cast a wary look at Adnan. "Juliet, I did not receive word about that."

I shook my head. "I know she sent it." My hand shook.

"Lanevrog?" Tristan echoed. "I do not know anyone by that name, if it *is* a name."

"But—"

"Shh," Tristan soothed, sliding my food tray back onto my lap. "I will look into it. We will search Cruelon's study."

I nodded and took another bite of food. "Adnan, why did you come? What happened after Kin died?"

Strange looks were cast between the two men, and Tristan's brows drew together as he returned his attention to me.

"I came as soon as I knew where you had gone," Adnan murmured.

Tristan's jaw clenched.

I'm missing something. But it was just out of reach.

Adnan cleared his throat. "My mission took me a few weeks. I only returned a little over a week ago and made straight for the king's stronghold. I knew they would take me in without question. They have been wanting me for years, so I could play completely into their hands. It proved to be far easier than I had even imagined. I'd been in the castle for almost two days before I joined you for dinner that first evening you saw me." His eyes clouded, and I found myself leaning forward as he continued. "I heard whispers all the next day of something afoot, but didn't know what it was till I saw you at dinner. And the day after that. Those were some of the hardest days of my life," he added in an undertone.

Tristan squeezed my hand. "One of my contacts sent word to me that same day the tables were turned against you. Using him, I was able to hash out a plan with Benkei. Risky, but it was high time. Now or never to take the castle. And I could not lose you." Tristan brought my hand to his lips. "You are safe now, Juliet. Do you forgive me for the treatment you have suffered under for the past weeks?"

"There is nothing to forgive," I responded mechanically. "None of that was your fault. I chose that path, and I must live with the consequences."

Adnan stood up and strode to the door without a second glance. I lifted a hand and my lips parted.

"Leave him be," Tristan urged. "His nerves have been wrought the past few days. I am not sure what has gotten into the man." Tristan scooted his chair closer to the bed. "Now, if you have the strength, tell me everything that happened."

"Everything?" I echoed, flashes of the past four weeks flying through my mind. There was so much.

"I love you, Juliet Barrows." Tristan's blue eyes sparkled. "I want to share in the good and the bad. I must know what happened."

But the words sounded hollow, feeding the emptiness already inside me. *Perhaps it would help to talk about it.* For the next hour or more, I recounted my tale. But I found myself holding back on the more intimate parts, the ones I couldn't speak of out loud, not now, not to him. I knew my story sounded vague in some places, but I couldn't open myself up completely. *Weeks of remaining silent around Cruelon, and now it continues.* I brushed over the suffering as though it were a distant memory, though it felt the opposite. It was too recent, the memories too raw. Tristan's enraptured listening reminded me all too much of Cruelon's apt attention. My gaze flitted between Tristan and the wooden ceiling. He didn't press me for more details, so it was easy to hide. *Just like it had been with Cruelon.* It was too easy to stay silent, to say what he wanted to hear and nothing more. Give a semblance of truth, but nothing more. *Isn't this how Cruelon made me feel?*

Chapter Twenty-One

S aya strode into my room and pulled the covers back. "Come on. I have fresh clothes for you, and there is a bath waiting for you in the next room."

"Maybe tomorrow."

She shook her head and grabbed my arms. "After your bath, we're going on a walk and then getting some food."

"Saya—"

"Honestly, I'm shocked neither of your suitors are here to get you up and moving."

"Suitors?" I echoed, crossing my legs under me.

Saya's eyebrow rose. "We should talk, but after your bath." Her nose crinkled. "You smell awful."

I followed her out of the room and to the bath.

She sat on a cushion near the tub and looked me up and down. "You're a lot thinner than when you left."

I sighed as I sank down into the hot water.

"I don't think living in our country does your health much good," Saya continued. "I—" She hesitated. "I wish it had been otherwise."

I eyed her. "You don't say."

She grinned, but her smile faded. "Want to talk about it?"

"No."

"It might help." When I didn't answer, she cleared her throat. "I know I haven't been there in the past for you, but I am here now, for what it's worth."

I sighed and sank further into the hot water. "I know."

She raised her eyebrows and grabbed a towel.

The hot water eased away some of the tension and aches. "Maybe another time," I whispered.

"I'll be here when you're ready."

I stared up at the white-washed ceiling. "You were right, you know. Your visions. I did become part of Cruelon's court. I did help bring about his downfall. We now exist in a world without him."

Silence fell.

I looked at Saya.

"It doesn't mean it was an easy road to get there. And it wasn't just my vision." The last words were spoken so quietly I almost missed them.

I cleared my throat. "Are you still working with Drielle?" Cruelon's words slammed into my mind. *His seer.* He had a seer, someone close by. My thoughts whirled with that possibility. Was she here in the castle?

Saya's face fell. "Not anymore." She wrung the towel between her hands.

I crossed my arms over the rim of the tub and rested my chin on them. "What happened?"

"She died."

"*What?*"

"During the battle, a few nights ago." Saya's eyes narrowed. "It was strange, really. She and I had been given orders to stay out of the battle, as Tristan didn't want either of his seers in any danger of being killed, and yet we found her body in the aftermath."

"You saw her?" I stood up and took the towel from Saya.

She shook her head. "No, but I was told someone slit her throat." Her gaze grew distant.

Something wasn't right. It didn't add up. "You weren't with her before she disappeared?"

Saya jerked. "What? No. Well, yes, but I don't quite remember what happened. A lot happened that night."

I finished dressing and Saya stood up. She didn't say a word as she led me out of the room and down the corridors I'd walked through so many times during my weeks here. It was different now. No guards following me, no fear of whom I might meet or who might speak to me. But I trembled when I saw the door to the dungeons. Two men stood there, talking with one another.

Saya stopped and glanced between them and me. "What's wrong?"

"Nothing, just bad memories." My feet carried me forward, farther down the hall. "What did you mean about my suitors?"

"What do you think I meant?"

"That's not an answer."

"Answer me this, then," she demanded. "Can you spend the rest of your life with Tristan?"

I almost stumbled, and my breath caught in my throat. *Could I? He was sweet, kind, yet there was no thrill when I thought of it ...*

"You would become queen," Saya continued. "You'd make a good queen, I think."

I laughed. *Queen?* Queen of a country that wasn't mine. *Is it mine now?* Would I ever return home? Thoughts of home seemed so distant now. It had been so long. So much had happened. *I'm torn between two worlds, between two lives.*

"Shizukana won't wait forever." Saya glanced at me. "I'm serious, Juliet."

I reeled. Hair fell into my face with the movement. "What are you talking about?"

Saya rolled her eyes. "Do you *still* not see it?"

I tucked the hair back behind my ear. "See what?"

She stopped and turned to face me. "You are more than a friend to him. You have to see it. There have been times I thought you felt the same way, but then you fell for Tristan. He could have given up on you since, but he hasn't. You know, the moment he found out you were gone and where Tristan had sent you, he up and left in the middle of the night, *against* Tristan's orders. He went after *you*, Juliet. And if it wasn't for him, you may not be alive now."

"But—I thought Tristan ..." I hesitated, the thoughts swirling around my brain like a tornado. "Tristan knew Adnan was here?"

"Of course he did." Saya eyed me, confusion shining in her eyes. "You thought he didn't? Yes, it was Shizukana who connived the plot, who snuck Tristan and his men in, and it was Shizukana who stayed by your bedside for three days and nights as you drifted in and out of consciousness." Saya threw up her hands. "I'm not saying Tristan wouldn't have, but he had much to do."

"Saya, Tristan said ..." I trailed off. *He said he didn't know Adnan was on our side. Why would he say that if he knew why he was here?* "Saya, did Tristan know Adnan was here before?"

Saya blinked and her slender shoulders rose in a silent question.

"Before I left the mountain, I heard Adnan was here. Did Tristan know *why* he was here?"

"Of course he did. He sent Adnan as a spy, not that the king knew that. We're getting off topic, though. I think it's time you decide between the two of them. Would your heart break if you never saw Tristan again?"

"No," I whispered, and I knew it to be true with my entire being. *How did it come to this?*

Saya strode to a nearby window and peered through it. I followed her and looked down into the courtyard. Men busied themselves, still cleaning up from the battle, bringing bodies out to burn piles out on the plains. Others were readied for burial.

"Where is he?" There wasn't even an echo left when I realized I had spoken out loud.

"Shizukana? He left at dawn this morning."

I jerked. "Why?"

"I don't know," Saya replied. "Tristan knows something about it."

"Another errand?" I asked, unable to keep the bitter note out of my voice.

"Most likely. Tristan has an overabundance of missions for his favorite."

"He really left?"

Saya nodded. "He didn't say goodbye to me either. I heard from a messenger."

He left ... again. Why didn't he say goodbye?

Saya held up a finger. "I want to know one thing. Even if it was Tristan who was solely responsible for your rescue, would you marry him?"

"No." And I meant it. Tristan wasn't the one.

She smiled. "I know. I wanted to make sure you did as well." She crossed her arms and regarded me for a few moments. "The rest can come later."

"Wait, the rest of what?"

Another quick grin. "Shh, you don't want to overexert yourself."

I glared at her. "I thought you were the one who pushed me toward Tristan in the first place."

Saya returned her attention to the landscape out the window. "I did."

I looked out at the trees under the gray skies, trying to ignore the small figures on the plains in between them and the fortress. They were like busy bees, digging graves for those who had died. "I feel torn," I began. "Like a piece of glass that has fallen, and in that single millisecond when the tip has impacted against the floor, and pressure is threatening to shatter the glass again, but yet all is whole, trying to stay strong, knowing in a single moment it will be broken into thousands of tiny pieces ..." I took a deep breath. "I feel like that piece of glass—shattered—even though you can't tell yet. Some turn to dust to be blown away by the wind, and others lay hopeless, beyond all care." With another deep, shuddering breath, I closed my eyes. My hands trembled. *Tristan. The seer. Adnan. Saya. Cruelon.* "Saya, you said the seer's throat was slit?"

Saya crossed her arms. "You want to speak about death after that little speech you just gave?"

"Please, just answer the question."

She sighed and turned away from the window. "Yes, it was."

"During the battle over the keep?"

"Yes ..." Her eyebrows rose and she placed her hands on her hips.

"Where were you?"

"Not with the seer. Juliet, is this some sort of interrogation?"

"No, I'm sorry." I chewed on my lip. "I'm just trying to understand. Why would the seer come to the battle in the first place?"

"I don't know." She shrugged. "Tristan ordered both of us to come, but we didn't talk about it. We didn't really have time to. We were given the orders an hour before we left the mountain. As to where I was, I stayed at the back, where Tristan placed us. We were both to remain behind the lines, where we were safe—or should've been."

"And you haven't seen the body?"

"No," Saya retorted. "Why would I?"

I ignored her question. "Do you know where it is?"

"Most likely with the other bodies awaiting burial."

I glanced out the window again, but I couldn't see the main courtyard from this angle. "Can you show me?"

Saya took a step away from the wall, and I followed her. "I don't understand why you want to see it."

I put a hand on my side, against the stitch I felt growing there as we walked down the stairs into the lower levels. "You don't think this is all a little strange? She was Tristan's most prized possession, so how was she allowed to die? And why no word?"

Saya paused a moment in thought at the front doors to the keep. "He is dealing with a lot right now, Juliet. It is not so strange, especially with our customs, to have a more quiet, reserved honoring of the fallen. No sign of outward emotion does not mean there isn't any. Besides, just because she died doesn't mean she was *allowed* to die."

I murmured thanks to the guards as we passed through the door. They were so different. No black leather, less disciplined, their features unschooled as they chatted and laughed. A light drizzle of rain fell, and the ground had begun to dampen. My feet sank into the earth a little.

Saya pointed. "There they are."

My throat constricted. There were more bodies than I'd expected. Each one was laid out, so still under the falling rain. A man watched us approach. I gasped as the smell hit me. Covering the bottom half of my face with my sleeve, I gagged against the strong smell of rotten meat and the putrid smell of old blood. The smell of death and decay that no one would want to breathe in or have to describe.

Saya called out to the man watching us. "Where is the seer?"

He gestured over his shoulder and led us to a covered corpse. "Don't know why you would want to look. Not a pretty sight."

"What happened to her?" I asked the man watching.

"Got her throat slit," he articulated with a grunt.

"Did you see?"

He shook his head and walked away.

Saya stooped and grasped one corner of the cloth. With a quick jerk, she drew it away. I forced myself to stay still though every nerve surged with energy. My brain sent abundant signals for me to run—run away from the smells, run away from the sight of all those bodies—but I stayed.

"Cover her back up, Saya." *It's Drielle. She is truly dead.*

Saya placed her hands on her hips. "You satisfied now?" She walked off, her short legs almost running.

"I wanted to be sure," I called after her as I followed.

She whirled around. "Why? Why do you care so much?"

I shrugged. "Something just doesn't seem right. I don't understand how she got separated and why she was without protection. Slitting her throat—someone would have had to get close enough to her."

"I think it's time for you to go get some rest." Saya's voice was icy. "You need some time away from all this. You're not thinking clearly."

I tossed my long hair over my shoulder. "Maybe so." My steps slowed as we reached the doors to the keep. "Saya—"

"Later, Juliet."

But I couldn't return to my room. I knew I wouldn't be able to sleep. I wandered the castle as I used to. It was so different now. The faces had changed, the guards had changed, and the servants—their faces were brighter and clearer. Frowns had transformed into smiles, glares into polite bows, and timidity into boldness.

I strode down a corridor on the second level and peered out the window as I passed. My attention was arrested when I saw a familiar face in the courtyard below. Turning from the window, I ran toward the stairs that led to the lower levels of the keep. Something inward drove me—an unexplainable urge—one which led me on beyond distraction. I could almost feel the pieces of the puzzle coming together, but something held them apart, something tangible—if I could just place my finger on it.

Where is she? I scanned the courtyard. *There.*

"Emi," I called out.

She stiffened, but continued walking as though she hadn't heard.

"Emi, wait!" I struggled to catch up, my breath coming in heaves as I weaved my way through the crowd of men, muttering apologies as I bumped into one person and then another. I caught Emi's arm at the door leading to the kitchens. A waft of fresh bread sailed through the open doorway.

"My lady." She curtsied.

"Call me Juliet. There's no need for the title, not anymore."

She shifted on her feet.

"Emi, I'm sorry. I'm sorry for the act I put on before. But I had to. And I'm sorry for Kin's death. It's not what I wanted. I know how close you two were." The words tumbled out of my mouth. "I didn't know he would kill her. She was already working for the Uprising. I wish to God she hadn't died."

Emi glanced up at the skies.

"What are you doing now?" I asked.

"Working the same as I was before, my lady. King Tristan kept on most of the servants."

"And the rest? What about the rest of them? And those who survived the fighting? Did Taisho Hirose survive? And what about Miya?"

"He did. They both did." Emi shifted on her feet and lowered her voice. "I don't know if I should say if you do not know."

"What's going on? What do you mean?" I drew her to the side, further away from prying ears.

"They're all in the dungeons, miss." She stared at the ground.

I shivered. "What? Even the servants?"

Emi shrugged and her hands shook. "No, the king kept the servants freed so they could serve. But that's not all." Her eyes shifted back and forth, and her lips thinned.

"Tell me, please," I pressed.

"I don't know how I should. You being the king's fiancée and all." Emi glared at me as though I had betrayed her.

"Emi, ignore that. I am still my own person. I have not changed. Trust me."

She sighed. "Very well. They're not being fed right, miss, and they are slowly freezing to death. Tristan is giving them the same treatment Cruelon gave you. Some of them are not going to last much longer."

My throat tightened. *What is Tristan doing?* My eyes flicked across the courtyard to make sure no one was within earshot. "How long have they been down there?"

"Almost three days. Not long after the battle."

My hands clenched. I knew what that meant ... how it felt. "Why did you say it was like how Cruelon treated me, Emi?"

"Because, miss, that's what Tristan said in his command concerning the prisoners."

I whirled around and made for the keep, taking the shortest route to the dungeons that I knew. *Tristan has always done what he thinks is best. He's a planner.* My breathing quickened, and my hands clenched into fists. *I can't speak to him yet.* My stride quickened as I wove through hallways on the main floor. I had to see for myself.

Two guards flanked the heavy oak door.

"Open it," I commanded, unable to stay still as I rocked back and forth on the balls of my feet.

They hesitated.

"Let me through," I repeated.

The two men exchanged glances, but they opened the door, and I stepped in.

My feet pattered on the hard floor. Small plops from water dripping grew louder as I continued, and the air became danker. I tried not to breathe through my nose as the smell worsened. There was no light here, none except for the torch I carried. My hands trembled. I didn't want to go down there. Not again. Not ever again. It was so silent. I tightened my resolve—I had to. Because of what I'd gone through, because of Cruelon's treatment of me—because I had to confirm with my own eyes what Emi had told me and because of the slivers of suspicion and cut-off threads dangling in my mind. I needed answers.

It was silent. I passed two more guards, but neither made a move to stop me. The smell was fetid. I clasped a hand to my nose as I looked through grating after grating. If anything, it was worse than when I'd been detained down here.

In each cell, men and women were clustered together like sardines in a can. There wasn't much movement from within. A sick feeling grew inside me and nausea filled my stomach. I could feel the urge to vomit growing.

I couldn't stand it any longer. Bracing myself against the wall with one hand, I closed my eyes, swallowing against the bile rising in my throat. I had to get out of here. Guilt tore at me, followed by anger. All of this, in my name. The anger gave me energy, and I looked up, hearing approaching footsteps.

"Fetch food and water for all the prisoners," I ordered as the guard neared.

"But our orders—" the man protested, raising his torch.

"You have new orders now."

"King Tristan—"

"I don't care. You will do as I say. Bring food and water and blankets," I added. My command rang through the dungeon.

"Otherworlder." He bowed and left.

I hoped it was to do my bidding. Leaning against the wall, I waited. As much as I longed to escape the smell, the memories, I knew I couldn't leave. I had to see this through.

⚘ ⚘

When the guard returned, Emi was one of the servants who accompanied him. She flashed a small smile over the pile of blankets in her arms. I followed as they went from cell to cell, handing out food, water, and blankets. Over their shoulders I peered into the small rooms at the prisoners.

I found him in the last cell.

"Hirose," I murmured, my voice soft.

"Why, Lady Juliet, I did not expect to see you here." He grinned, but it didn't reach his eyes.

I leaned down next to him and gave him a mug of water and some bread and cheese. "Here, eat this."

He eyed me, a question evident, but began eating, slow and methodical. "My men?"

"They're being taken care of. I'm sorry." I crouched down. "I didn't know about any of this until this morning."

Hirose laughed. "You're sorry? We treated you the same way."

"So I should turn around and do the same? No. It's wrong, no matter who does it. Perhaps you do deserve to be in prison, but not ill-treated."

"Your king and *fiancé* would disagree."

He does. I pushed Hirose's statement aside. "I'll make sure your people are fed and kept warm. Don't worry on their account."

Hirose regarded me before relaxing back against the wall. "You don't hate me?"

I considered the question. Hirose's gaze didn't leave my own as he waited. "No. No, I don't."

His eyes widened. "Why?"

"How do I not hate you?" I repeated. "I don't know. You betrayed me; you stooped to the lowest level to obey your king. I know you were obeying orders, but I think you knew it was wrong." I stood. "You're a better man than that, Hirose. You could be—if you follow your heart and are man enough to stand up for what you believe." I left the cell, not waiting for a response. He didn't call after me.

"Where's Hiito?" I asked the guard after the cell door clanged shut.

"He was executed yesterday."

"What?" I took a deep breath. "Executed?"

"The king's orders. Hiito and a few others were executed as there seemed to be no doubt of their loyalty to the past king. Those here in the dungeons still await their sentencing. But most likely they will all follow suit." The man smiled and rubbed his hands together. "You're just giving them one last little pleasure before their lives are over. Rather a waste of food and resources, it seems."

I tensed, feeling the anger build up. *Calm down. Not now, not to him.* "Then it is a good thing you're not in charge." I turned and strode back up the corridor. *Have we just exchanged one cruel tyrant for another one similar?* I shook my head. *Don't think that way.* My steps slowed. *Tristan cares. He cares about what people think of him. He cares about loyalty.* Water dripped onto the floor from the ceiling.

Tristan has shown a dark side before. When he'd ranted about how important his cause was, I'd seen the darkness within him. The battle that seemed to be losing then. *Who is our king now?* The thought had taken root, and now those roots spread.

I don't know Tristan as well as I thought.

Chapter Twenty-Two

Saya appeared out of a room farther down the corridor. She frowned as I approached, but I didn't break my stride.

"Did you know?" I said as I passed, but she followed after me.

"What?"

"Did you know what's going on down in the dungeons?" Clouds appeared in the air in front of my face as I spoke. Saya didn't answer. I sped up. *I know exactly where to find him.*

"Juliet, wait."

"No."

The sound of her boots on the floor stopped. I didn't glance back, but her silence felt like a betrayal. Anticipation surged through my body. *There.* I opened the door more forcefully than I had intended, and it slammed against the wall. The drapes over the window rustled, disturbed.

Tristan and his advisors looked up. I recognized Kuro and Shoto, but there were two other men there as well. *Where is Haniel?* He was missing. Tristan's eyes lit up, and he smiled. It fed the bomb inside of me waiting to explode, drowning everyone and everything about me in flames.

"Gentlemen," Tristan spoke, waving a hand. "Please excuse us for a few minutes." He laid a paper he'd been examining down on the table and approached. "You look a lot better."

I took a deep breath. "Why are the prisoners being given no food nor warm clothing?"

A strange look crossed Tristan's face. "Because I ordered it."

My booted foot tapped the floor. "Why?"

"Until they are tried and either released or executed, they will be given the same treatment you were. A crime for a crime."

My hands shook. "I don't think that is the right saying. It was Cruelon's orders, not the people down there." I pointed below my feet. "And he's dead now."

"So he is," Tristan replied, "but they are his people."

I stepped forward. "Do you think you are better than they are?"

"Yes. I have many faults, I admit that, but how they treated you cannot go unpunished." He placed a hand over his heart. "I am avenging you."

"No, you are not. And I don't want to be avenged. I don't want my treatment thrust upon those people down there! Cruelon gave the orders—"

"But they carried them out," Tristan parried, his voice steely.

"Tristan, please." I laid a hand on his muscled forearm. "Stop this. Do it for me."

"I am doing this for you."

I groaned and stepped back.

"Fine." Tristan took my hands in his. "I will stop, if that is what you *truly* want."

I nodded.

Tristan tightened his clasp. "I will give the order for them to be fed until they are tried, but that is all I will do."

"It wasn't right to starve them," I whispered, waves of exhaustion rolling over me.

Tristan let go of my hands. "They killed my family, Juliet!" His face reddened as he backed away. "What would you have me do, give them tea and pastries and apologize for capturing them? No, I will *not* let them get away with this." His fists shook at his sides.

"Tristan," I pleaded, trying to reason with him. "They didn't kill your family. Cruelon did. And he's dead—you killed him. Don't take out your anger against those under him."

"Juliet, you are naïve, and that is not a bad thing, but in this case, you need to listen to me."

I snorted. "*Listen* to you? I am listening, Tristan."

"Juliet—"

"No, not right now. I'm done talking." I turned and walked to the door. He didn't try to stop me, and I was glad. I shook as I slammed the door behind me, wanting to take out my frustration and anger on something, anything, but no relief came.

"Argh!" I yelled, closing my eyes against the onslaught of stinging tears. Something creaked. A servant stood in front of me, mouth open wide. She started and disappeared around the corner.

My feet ate up the floor as I hurried toward my room. Inside, I stopped, staring. The walls stood bare and looming, threatening to either crush me by falling over or close in about me until I would be smashed between them. Cold air rushed in through the open window, blowing about me, invisible and icy. The metal chains and hooks had been removed, but they couldn't hide the evidence, the jagged, circular holes in the ground and on the walls, or the sifting of sawdust as it swirled across the floor.

I lay down on the mat but couldn't sleep. Hours slipped by as I regarded the ceiling I had come to know so well over the past weeks, a ceiling full of discoloration and cracks that I had memorized from living under it. I drew the blankets up around me, curling into a ball as I rolled onto my side and stared at the closed door. No longer was this my prison. *Then why does it feel like it?*

A footstep passed my room, but whoever it was moved on. I watched as the shadows grew longer and listened as the wind picked up. It smelled like a storm was brewing. With a sigh, I pushed the blankets back. A glint of white caught my eye. A piece of paper lay on the ground. *It must have fallen from the blanket.* I stooped down and picked it up. Taking it over to the single candle which burned on the bedside table, I sat. My hands shook as I saw the signature. *Adnan.* I forced myself to slow down and read from the beginning.

Juliet,

This must serve as my goodbye. I didn't have time to find you. I had to leave, but I will return as soon as I can. There is something I must look into. Someone. Do you remember your nani? I need to make sure she is well.

Be careful.

Adnan

I read it again. *Nani.* My nani? I chewed on my lower lip. *Nah-ni.* My eyes widened. Tristan's nani. She was his caregiver—had been—before she died. This note was a warning. *Why look into her?* I refolded the paper and tapped my chin with it. The unknown traitor, and now this. I stood up and grabbed a cloak. I couldn't stay here anymore. Sleep wouldn't come.

I left and walked down the darkened halls of the fortress. Memories of the last few weeks swirled about my mind, intermixed with those from today. *So much has happened.*

"My lady?"

The voice penetrated my innermost thoughts like an arrow piercing flesh. I took a step back, raising a hand ...

"My lady? Are you all right?"

I peered at the speaker as I spiraled back down into harsh reality. *That door. The dungeons.*

"My lady?" the man asked again.

"I'm fine. Please open the door."

"I'm sorry, but the dungeons are off-limits right now. Lord Tristan's orders. There are some unruly prisoners down there from the battle."

I squared my shoulders and put on a pleasant demeanor. "I want in. You can bring it up with Tristan if you'd like, but I think you should let me through now."

The guards exchanged glances and stood aside. I brushed past them and hurried through the door, already able to feel and smell the dank corridor leading down to even worse cells. In my rush, I'd brought no candle. I pressed on into the close, murky blackness, my hands stretched out as my fingers trailed against the sides of the passageway. Three times before I had been down here. But going down of my own accord didn't seem to help. I breathed in, remembering the fear with which I had gone down, the relief each time I had left. The dripping of water onto rock threatened to send the memories flooding back. The woman who had died in her cell, my imprisonment without food, water, or light—a warning, a punishment. *Flowers.* I focused on a sea of flowers under the bright sun, listening to imaginary birdsong and seeing an imaginary breeze blow, sending a vibrant wave across the warm field. *Keep the walls up.*

Soon I saw the first of the torches burning in the wall bracket. My field of flowers disappeared. Another set of guards stood next to the final door leading down to the dungeons.

"A lantern, please," I requested. Taking it, I brushed past the two men. The floor sloped downward, and the air grew musty. I passed the first cell door, and then another. Four more were left in my wake before I paused in front of one, like all the rest, yet different to me. Different because it had been the one I'd inhabited for a night. I trailed my fingers along the rotten wood.

"Is there anyone in here?" I asked, shifting the lantern to my left hand.

The guard shrugged.

A grunt escaped my lips as I shoved the rusted bar back, the metal grating through the narrow corridor as it slid back. The light flickered, sending the shadows dancing on the walls and floors. I looked back the way I'd come, but all I could see was my own silhouette, elongated and deformed, stretching out over the floor behind me.

The door creaked open, and I shivered—*dim, cold, lonely; noise, never-ending noise.* I blinked away the memory and took a step forward into the cell.

"What are you doing here?" a voice croaked, almost animalistic.

I raised the lantern and peered at the heap lying in the far corner. "Amarante?"

The figure laughed, but it was more like a cough. She sat up and leaned against the wall. "Have you come to gloat?" Her matted hair fell back, revealing dark, luminous eyes on a mud-streaked face.

"No, I—I didn't even know you were down here."

Amarante laughed again. "Of course you didn't. Because what, you would have stopped it if you had? Just as I tried to influence Cruelon to have mercy on you? Laughable. I knew where you were, what you went through, and I didn't lift a finger to help you, so why would you help me?" She took in a deep, wheezing breath. "I'm dying, Juliet. I'm dying, and don't pretend you care. You came down here to see me one last time, if not to say something, to show me you—alive and healthy—have won." She shot forward, leaning over to peer up at me, and I jumped, almost dropping the lantern. "Just remember that it doesn't always last, no matter how much you may wish. People change, times change, powers change, tides turn, often faster than we can comprehend. Be careful, Otherworlder."

"Amarante, I—"

She waved a hand through the air and leaned back with a sigh. "Beware who you choose, Juliet Barrows. Benkei or Lord Tristan. Two men with much to lose or gain, both with an immense amount of power within their grasp."

"How do you know Benkei?" I licked my dry lips, that name foreign on my tongue.

"How do *I* know him?" Amarante turned toward me. "His coming to rescue you was not his first visit here, and maybe it won't be his last. I heard he left—gone at dawn—a common occurrence with him, I think."

How does she know he's gone? I crouched in front of her. "Amarante, how many times has he been here?"

Amarante leaned against the wall and began drifting off to sleep.

"Amarante!"

She started. "He's rather handsome, isn't he? Are you torn between him and Tristan? He won't have me, you know. Believe me, I tried." She spat out each word, her voice bitter. "He only had eyes for you, Juliet. You never saw, I don't think, but I did."

Adnan. She was watching Adnan.

"He was clever," she went on. "You captivated him. He always ignored us ladies, no matter how hard we tried. But I can see you didn't even notice; you couldn't see how he looked at you."

My mind reeled. "How often has he been here?"

"Two times," she admitted, tucking her black hair behind her ear. "Beware, Juliet Barrows. There is much you do not know, and even more that you do not understand."

I backed away toward the door.

"Wait—" She flung out a hand. "Did you know Adnan had been here before?"

"Not for sure."

"You didn't." Her eyes flashed triumphantly. "That means he's keeping secrets from you. Secrets, secrets, secrets. Otherworlder, they are your whole life, aren't they? What other secrets does Tristan keep from you? What secrets does *Benkei* keep from you?"

I turned and fled, away from her bright eyes, her cackle, her words—words of a viper—words, words, words. I fumbled with the lantern as I closed the door and ran back up the passageway, almost throwing the lantern into the guard's hands as I made my way past them and up into the keep.

Liar, liar, liar. The words sang inside my head until they filled every crevice. *He lied to me. Tristan lied. Why?* I didn't even feel like crying. There were no tears stinging my eyes, no lump forming in my throat. *Lost.* I was lost. The corridors were empty, as though all within were wary of me. *Why so many questions without answers?* The past, the present, the future, the unknown—so much was unknown.

I opened my door and almost stepped on a tray that had been set inside my room. Bending down, I picked up the folded note.

Juliet,

I came to bring you some dinner, but you were not here. No one has seen you in hours, and when you did not show up for dinner, I heard you were not feeling well this afternoon. Please know that if there is something going on, you can talk to me. Eat and get some rest. If you are feeling well enough, please join me for breakfast in the morning.

Respectfully,

Tristan

The note fell from my hand, floating down until it came to rest on the floor. I picked up the plate of food and sat on the mat. Each bite was methodical, and I hardly tasted the meat, vegetables, and rice. As my stomach filled, I glanced down at the note again. *Tristan.* I frowned and picked it up. There was something familiar about the signature. I stared at it, but the memory danced at the edge of my fingertips. With a sigh, I lay down and pulled the covers up. A heavy drowsiness stole over me as I stared up at the ceiling. With each passing second, the thoughts flaring inside my mind slowed and stopped. My eyelids fluttered as the war within me raged. *No time to sleep.*

Yet sleep won.

⚓

Dim light filtered in through the window. I blinked away the last vestiges of sleep. Something white shifted on the floor. *The note.* I sat up and everything rushed back in—*Tristan, Amarante, Adnan, the prisoners, the executions*—but another note caught my eye. A new one lay near the other, having been slid under the door.

I slipped out of bed and hurried over. Leaning down, I picked up the small, white piece of paper and unfolded it. *Saya.* She wanted to speak to me later that morning. Judging by the dreary morning light, it was still very early. I ran my fingers through my hair and looked down at the gown I wore. Wrinkles covered the material. Biting my lip, I strode to the wardrobe and opened the doors. Inside hung an array of gorgeous gowns in a rainbow of colors. From the bottom shelf I grabbed a pair of tight, black pants and a deep burgundy tunic. I belted the tunic. Grabbing the thin, flat shoes from beside the mat, I slid them on and left. Footsteps receded somewhere to the right, but I ignored them and went left. Rounding a corner, I saw Saya's figure up ahead.

"Saya!" I called out.

She stopped and swung around. "I thought you'd be asleep."

"I saw your note. What did you want to talk about?"

"I'll tell you later."

I stopped in front of her. "Why not now?"

Saya crossed her arms. "Very well, but not here." She beckoned for me to follow as she moved off. "I think even the walls have ears."

I froze mid-step. *Who said that to me before?*

"Coming?" she called.

"I just—someone said something similar to me once." *Was it Kin? She'd warned me that Cruelon had ears everywhere—but if not him now, then who? Tristan?*

"Here." Saya held open the door to a small closet.

I quirked an eyebrow. "A broom closet?"

Saya shrugged and closed the door behind us. The dim lighting from the wall sconces in the corridor was cut off, and we were thrown into darkness. "I've been asking around. No one saw Drielle die. Her guards had had orders to bring her to the battle after the rest of us had already left. Apparently, she wasn't even going to be there in the first place."

"What do you mean?"

"It means there shouldn't have been a reason for her to die. She must have been targeted. There's no other explanation. Tristan called for her to come, switching the original plans, but I don't know why."

My vision sharpened as my eyes grew accustomed to the blackness of the closet. "Saya, wait, why now? You didn't want to think anything was wrong yesterday, so why now?"

Saya's silhouette slumped. "I'm sorry. I thought your time here had changed you, and it has, but I assumed that was why you were so determined for there to be a reason for Drielle's death other than wrong time, wrong place."

"Have I changed that much?" I whispered.

Saya shook her head. "Never mind that now—I have something else to tell you. Her detail of guards was ordered last minute to leave her and guard the entrance to the keep from any possible rear attack."

"Who gave the orders?"

"Tristan."

My heart sank and I leaned against the wall for support. *Why?* Tristan would've wanted to keep her guards around her, not send them away.

Saya stepped forward. "Maybe he didn't do the deed himself, but he took away her protection."

"Saya, wait, you know her, you trained with her—was she incapable of protecting herself? She should have had some defense skills, or Tristan wouldn't order her guards away so recklessly after insisting she be there. Why didn't she stay with the guards?"

"She wasn't completely defenseless," Saya retorted. "She kept a dagger on her person at all times, two actually. One in her boot and one strapped to her arm under the sleeve of her robe." Saya waved through the air. "And she's fast—I couldn't tell you how many times I saw her catch something in midair that fell."

I stared at the floor of the broom closet. "So she knew her attacker, then."

"No, she couldn't have."

"She could," I pressed. "I don't know how, but she must have. It's the only explanation. Knowing the predicament, she stood in without her guards, she must have been on the lookout. Her senses must have been heightened. She couldn't have let someone approach close enough to slit her throat without trying to defend herself, and if she had, how did they get such a clean kill?" I took a short breath before continuing, my mind racing as the thoughts connected like hundreds of thin, interconnecting webs. "She has no other wounds, none that would warrant her having been in a fight. She knew her attacker," I repeated. "She didn't expect to die. It's the only explanation."

Saya slapped the palm of her hand against the wall. "But it doesn't make sense. Who would want to kill her?"

"I don't know, but more importantly, who had reason to kill her? Who would gain from her being gone? And how did they know Tristan would call his men away? They wouldn't—" I hesitated as the realization took hold. "Unless they knew of his orders. Unless they gave them."

"Haniel?" Saya asked, knowing as well as I did he was the one person Tristan put absolute trust in. "He wouldn't—what would *he* have to gain?"

"There must have been something the seer knew, and Haniel was afraid she would tell Tristan. A vision, maybe?"

"It's possible," Saya admitted. "But it still doesn't make sense."

"It doesn't have to make perfect sense, not yet anyway." I paced the small room as I thought. "We don't have all the facts. Haniel was absent when Adnan and Tristan rescued me—he was the one who gave the orders to the guards, wasn't he?"

"He was," Saya affirmed. "That much, I was able to find out." A shaft of light shone into the closet as she opened the door and stepped out. "I'm going to find out."

"Wait, Saya!" I called, walking after her. The hallway was empty but for us. "What are you going to do?"

"Talk to Haniel," Saya growled, swinging away from me.

"Wait, please."

Saya turned back to me, her cheeks red with anger.

"Please don't do anything, not yet. Let me think about all of this."

"Don't?" she repeated, her voice taking on a deadly edge. "You're not in charge, Juliet."

I hesitated. *She's right.* "Just don't do anything, not yet," I pleaded. "Let me think, but don't rush into things, not without talking to me first."

"Who put you in charge?" she sneered.

I reached toward her. *Why should I be in charge?*

Saya spun around.

"Just wait, please," I called after her. "I don't think we should alert Haniel of our suspicions until we know more." I winced as she charged down the hallway, her footsteps receding faster than a bird flying with the wind.

Chapter Twenty-Three

I watched the servant leave the kitchen, holding a note from me canceling breakfast with Tristan on the excuse of a headache. *It's not an entire lie. Just a partial one.* Taking a wafer off a tray, I munched on it as I left the kitchens. This early, there was almost no one about.

I brushed the crumbs off my hands and rounded the corner into a passageway. Tristan waited near my door; his arms were crossed as he stared at the wall opposite. I hesitated. He hadn't seen me yet.

"You're not in bed with a headache," he stated without facing me.

I let out the breath I had been holding and approached. "No."

"So why did you cancel on me? No, do not answer that. I do not want to know."

I shifted on my feet, clenching and unclenching my fingers as I tapped a nervous rhythm on my thigh.

He turned and looked at me. "It was important, you know. I had something I wanted to ask you."

"Oh?" I stilled. *The traitor.* "There's actually something I want to ask you too."

Tristan let his arms fall by his sides. "Go ahead."

"Did you find anything about the traitor?"

A muscle pulsed in Tristan's neck. His jaw clenched. "The traitor?" he echoed. "No. We searched Cruelon's study, but there was nothing there."

I frowned. *Why is it gone?* I fingered the hem of my tunic. *Did he find something?*

Tristan's eyes shifted to the side and back again.

Is he keeping something from me? I shifted on the balls of my feet and glanced at the door to my bedroom.

"We will keep looking, Juliet." Tristan stepped closer. "I believe you, but we do not have much to go on right now."

Then the traitor is still out there. My body tensed. We were no closer than when we started.

"Now, Juliet." Tristan took my hand. "I did not even want to wait this long since rescuing you ... I thought it best, but I cannot wait—*it* cannot wait."

A sudden wish that someone would come upon us, that there would be some interruption, swept across me.

Tristan leaned closer. "Will you marry me?"

I could feel my face paling as the blood rushed from it. *Marry?* My mouth opened and closed.

"Tomorrow?" he continued. "At dawn, we could marry, and you would be crowned queen right after. In a few weeks, after everything is sorted, we can have a more formal crowning in front of the nation." He leaned closer, his head tilted down. "Become my queen, Juliet."

I turned away before his lips could touch mine.

A frown marred his features before being replaced with a teasing smile. "I needed to ask you. It couldn't wait any longer. But *I* can be patient. If you prefer to wait to kiss until we marry, I will respect your wishes."

My head spun and I took a step back. "Tristan, I never—"

"Juliet." Tristan's voice whipped through the air, and I jumped. "If your hesitancy is because of the prisoners, I promise I will stop. I only did to them what they were doing to you. An eye for an eye, a tooth for a tooth, is not that a saying? But if you would rather I do nothing, then nothing is what I will do. I have work to do, so I will not see you until the morning."

"Tristan!" I protested. "I'm not—"

His blue eyes twinkled. "I will arrange everything. Do not worry about a thing." He opened my door. "I will give orders for a gown to be prepared for you. You have made me the happiest man in the kingdom. I love you, Juliet."

Everything was happening too fast. *Wait.* My hands clenched and I stiffened. "But I—"

He pressed a firm kiss on my brow and disappeared down the hallway. I continued to stand there, frozen. The wind whistled through the window in my bedroom and blew around me as I stood in the open doorway. My own thoughts echoed the low-toned moaning. *Marriage? Why hadn't I been able to say anything?* It was as though my brain had stopped working, my limbs frozen. I stamped a foot and let out a grunt of frustration. Had he not realized I wanted to speak? I had been at a loss for words or action. It wasn't all my fault. Tristan hadn't given me room to speak. I groaned and rubbed slow circles over my temples.

"Juliet?"

The question startled me. I felt like I'd been drowning, but that voice drew me back to the surface, out of the depths of shock and oblivion, up into a dreary day where everything was real. Pain and heartache met me.

"I saw Tristan pass by." She halted in front of me. "Juliet, what's happened? Are you all right?"

"Saya."

Her hand clasped my arm, a pinpoint of comfort and an anchor to the present. She drew me into the room and closed the door. "Tell me what happened."

"I need to go for a ride—clear my head. I have to get outside."

"I'll go with you." I knew she'd spoken, but the words floated through as though on a thin cord, weaving in one ear and out the other ear.

A servant passed us, and in a vague blurriness, I heard Saya give the girl curt orders. When we reached the stables, the girl thrust a heavy black cloak into my hands.

"Put that on," Saya ordered. "Otherwise, you'll catch your death out there."

I took it with numb fingers and slipped it on, pulling the hood over my head.

The horses stamped and neighed in the stables, the musty smell familiar. A stable hand rushed forward, his young face flushed from the cold.

"Saddle two horses, please," I requested.

"Yes, my lady." The lad jumped to obey, a delighted look on his face.

Saya scrutinized me with open curiosity as we waited, but I didn't say a word.

"Pardon me," a guard interrupted my thoughts.

I turned to face him. "Yes?"

The stable hand brought the horses forward, their hooves sending up little puffs of dust. I waved a hand in front of my face to clear the air. But the guard rocked on the balls of his feet. "No one is allowed to go out of the castle grounds, my lady."

I licked my lips. "No one, or just me?"

The guard's eyes shifted to the stable hand and back.

It's me.

"Upon whose orders?" The question left my lips, but I knew the answer.

The guard took a small step back. "King Tristan's, my lady."

A sharp breeze cut through the air. I clutched my cloak closer around me. "And will you stop me if I go?"

The man drew himself up. "If I have to, my lady."

"Juliet, let's just go back to your room," Saya pressed.

So close. With one running leap, I could make it onto that horse and ride as far as he would last. I'd never have to look back. *How far could I make it?* But knowing Tristan, not far enough. Besides, I wasn't alone. Saya was here. And Adnan was ... somewhere, looking for Nani. Yet another mystery.

I stalked back across the courtyard and into the fortress, Saya's soft footsteps following behind me all the way. I hardly noticed her presence.

Back in my room, I closed the door behind us and leaned against it.

Saya planted herself on the mat. "Tell me what happened."

I strode to the window. "Tristan was waiting for me outside my room. He proposed."

"*What?*"

"Well, he didn't *actually* propose. It was more like he told me that the marriage is set for dawn and didn't give me a chance to reply." My heart raced in my chest as I paced. "He's even having a gown made up, and I don't know what to do." I sank down onto the mattress.

Saya's face was a blank mask, but her eyes darkened. "I don't understand."

I let out an exasperated sigh. "You and me both. I feel like a prisoner, not a fiancée." I raked my hands through my long hair.

"Juliet ..."

"No, you know I'm right. There is something more going on here." I tapped my knee as I spoke. "There are too many pieces at play."

Saya curled her legs beneath her. "What pieces?"

I raised an eyebrow.

"Yes, I know about Haniel—and Drielle—and now your engagement. A very short engagement," she added under her breath. "But is there something else you're not telling me?"

"It's mostly just a feeling, I guess," I confessed, drawing up my knees. My foot tapped impatiently.

"Go on," she prodded.

Thoughts buzzed as they flew around in my head. "The Unknown isn't here because Tristan sent him somewhere."

Saya blinked, her long lashes brushing her cheeks. "What?"

"He left me this." I reached under the mattress and handed her Adnan's note.

Saya scanned it once, twice. She looked up. "I don't understand, who is Nani?"

"Do you remember what Tristan told us the first time he met us? About his nurse, Nani?"

"Yes ..." Saya said with some hesitation. Her eyes widened. "Oh."

"Not my nani. Tristan's," I confirmed, resting my chin on my knees.

"But why?"

I shrugged. "I don't know. But it's not just that. It's also the fact that the traitor is still out there"—I waved a hand—"somewhere, and Tristan has no clue who it is."

"Traitor?" Saya asked. "What traitor?"

I had evidence. I stole it. I pushed the thoughts away. "Cruelon told me of a traitor named Lanevrog, someone close to Tristan. At first I thought it was the Unknown, but that's not the case. I gave Kin blueprints of the cave system with Lanevrog written on them, but Tristan said he never received anything." I chewed on my lower lip and lifted both hands in the air. "I have no idea what happened. Kin said she sent them."

Saya's face darkened as she thought. "So now it's Drielle's death, Adnan's secret mission, a traitor, and a quick engagement."

I grimaced.

"There's more?" Saya asked with a pensive tilt of her head.

"There is one other thing I should tell you. It doesn't really have to do with anything, but it's still a mystery." I crossed my legs. "There is a seer that worked for Cruelon."

Saya gasped. "What?" Her face paled.

"He said that's how he knew of me in the first place. It's why he sent Boden and someone he called Benkei. He'd been searching for me from the time I got here, Saya."

Saya rocked back on her heels. "But he hated the seers. He killed them, and those he didn't were driven out."

"He must have seen the importance of keeping one close to him."

"Who is it?"

I shook my head. "I have a guess, but I'm not sure."

"We need to find him—or her."

I nodded and stood up. "I could question Hirose. If anyone knows, maybe he will."

"Who?" Saya asked, standing as well.

"Hirose, the taisho of the King's Black Guard. He's down in the dungeon." I strode to the window and gazed out at the gray day. Small snowflakes drifted down, sticking to the ground far below.

"Juliet," Saya whispered, joining me at the window. "About Tristan ..."

I tensed and gripped the windowsill. My breath blew against the glass, fogging it.

"You don't love him."

My hands whitened. "You know I don't. I don't think I ever did. I liked him, but I never loved him. And now, I don't know that I can ever like him as more than a friend."

"Why didn't you tell him?"

"He didn't give me the chance." I stared at the far-off trees.

"What does that mean?"

"I don't know him. Do you realize that everything somehow revolves around him?" At Saya's questioning look, I explained. "The traitor close to him, his order to call away Drielle's guards, his nurse, and now the engagement, not to mention the prisoners down there." I pointed at the floor beneath our feet.

A soft knock filtered through the thick wood paneling on the door.

"Come in," I called.

Emi entered, freezing when she saw Saya. "I can come back later."

"What is it?"

Emi took a step forward. "Are you leaving?"

I reeled. "Why do you ask that?"

"Answer me this: Do you know what the king plans at dawn tomorrow?"

"Yes," I replied, not hiding the bitterness I felt. "My wedding."

Emi's eyes widened in surprise, but she shook her head. "Nothing else?"

I glanced at Saya. "No."

Emi hesitated, her gaze sweeping over Saya, who stood next to me.

"Go on, Emi. Anything you say to me, she can hear."

"There is a rumor going around that he plans to execute the rest of the prisoners the moment you and he are joined together in matrimony."

I opened my mouth, but no words came out. If I had ever felt the least bit out of control of a situation, this surpassed them all. I closed my eyes, willing everything to disappear. But when I looked, Emi and Saya still stood there, and I was as visible as they were.

Emi reached out. "My lady? Are you all right? Should I call someone?"

"No!" I barked.

Emi jumped, and even Saya shifted on her feet.

I rubbed my face. "I'm sorry." I drew myself up, ideas bouncing around my head until they threatened to burst. I had seen everything this far, and I had to finish. I had to see it to the end. *Whatever that might be.* "How can anyone be so perfect?"

"What?" Saya started. "What do you mean?"

"Everything! His manner, his bearing, his looks, and a king to boot? A prince out of a fairytale. And that he would choose me, a woman from a different world, a woman whom he just met, to be his queen." My lips curved sardonically. "How could I have been so deceived?"

"You?" Saya shook her head. "Juliet, slow down. We were all deceived, and we still don't even know quite what we were deceived of, other than he doesn't keep his word."

Adnan is gone. Anger filled me. Anger that he'd left again, that he wasn't around for this, anger toward him because he had dropped me like a sack of potatoes—*no, that's not fair. He's not here, and that's that.* "What time is it?"

"Almost time for the midday meal," Emi replied, confusion ringing in her voice.

"Emi, go about your work as though nothing has happened. But listen, and anything you hear that you think I should know, find me. Saya, you should go about whatever you normally do as well. We can't let Tristan suspect anything. I don't think anyone will find it amiss if I keep to my room this afternoon."

Saya shrugged. "What are you thinking?"

"Well, I'm not going to sit around and do nothing."

She gave a grim, thin-lipped smile. "It would be easiest for you to escape and leave this all behind."

No. I'm not running. I took a deep breath. "I can't. And I don't think you would either."

Saya nodded, her bun bouncing with the movement. "Not that we *ever* take the easy route."

I picked up my cloak from where I had discarded it earlier. "This definitely won't be easy. I have an idea, but I need to think more. Emi, please send up some tea."

"Yes, my lady." She turned and left the room.

"She's young," Saya observed, crossing her arms. She tilted her head to the side and looked at me. "Very young."

"I know."

Saya let her arms fall by her sides. "Just remember that."

"I do!" I protested, following her to the low table near the mattress. A stick cracked in the fireplace. *I do.* I bit my lip and sat down.

Saya nodded and adjusted herself on the cushion. "Are you still going to speak to Hirose about the seer?"

I stared at her. Cruelon's seer. *There isn't time.* The minutes ticked by, bringing me closer to dawn.

Hope shone in Saya's gaze.

"I should, yes," I said, unable to say otherwise. My head began to throb. "Saya, I don't have much time," I whispered, shaking my head. *One day.* I gritted my teeth. *Less than a day.*

Saya let out the breath she'd been holding. She threw her shoulders back and grunted. "What is the first step, then?"

"The first step?" I drummed my fingers on my thigh. I stared at the floor. Saya faded away, as did the soft crackling of the fire in its hearth. Even the wind outside had stilled. "I think we need to find out more about Cruelon's seer and what happened to Drielle." I looked at Saya and shrugged. "I can't marry Tristan."

Saya snorted and tucked a loose tendril of hair behind her ear. "What do you want me to do?"

"I want you to go down to the dungeons. See what you can find out from Hirose about the unknown seer."

Saya stood but hesitated. "And you?"

"I'm going to talk to Haniel."

"May the gods be with you." Saya's voice had a sardonic lilt to it.

I raised an eyebrow.

"I haven't seen him since we stormed the castle," she explained. "He might not even be here."

I haven't seen him either. I waved a hand. "I'll find him. Meet back here when you're done?"

Saya took a deep breath and nodded.

Leaving my cloak on the mattress, I glanced about the room before leaving. I closed the door and turned.

"My lady?" Emi asked, confusion ringing through the air. "I brought the tea."

The tea. Emi's small, heart-shaped face was pale with worry, and exhaustion showed in the lines about her eyes. "Emi," I began, placing my hand on her forearm. "I'm sorry. I have to go do something. Could you—"

Emi's shoulders slumped a little. "What are you going to do?"

"Try to save lives."

"The gods be with you," she muttered, turning.

"Wait, Emi!" I stepped closer. "Have you seen Tristan's right-hand man, Haniel?"

The confused look shadowing Emi's face lifted. "Yes. He has been overseeing the placement of the men. You may be able to find him in the smaller building nearby."

I frowned. "What is in there?"

"Food, storage, rooms for the Black Guard ..."

"Thanks, Emi." I watched as she took the tray back down the hallway. Now alone, I strode to the nearest set of stairs. Taking a turn at the bottom, I made my way to the main doors of the keep. This time I barely noticed the paintings that hung on the walls as I stopped. The guards on either side watched me with curiosity.

Now to see if Tristan even lets me outside. I squared my shoulders. As I neared, one of the two guards opened a door. I walked through without a word. Cold air bit into my skin and I gasped, wrapping my arms around me for a little warmth. Quickening my pace, I hurried to the small building that flanked the wide courtyard.

I stepped through the open doorway and hesitated, blinking as I let my eyes adjust to the dim interior. A musty scent of mildew and unpleasant body odor washed over me.

"What are you doing here?" Haniel stood to my right. He waved a hand at the man he'd been speaking to, who bowed to me and left.

I swallowed my dread. "I want to talk to you."

Haniel raised an eyebrow and clasped his hands behind his back. "Come in, then."

I followed him into a small room. Torches hung in their brackets on the walls, and Haniel's blue robes were a stark contrast to the plain wood floors and walls.

He sat down and regarded me. "Well, Otherworlder?"

I sat down, my back to the door. My lips parted. *Ask him about Drielle.* I cleared my throat. *How do I ask without alerting him?* I tugged on my tunic. "Have you found the traitor yet?" *That wasn't what I was going to ask.*

Haniel didn't blink. "No."

I froze. *He knows about the traitor.* The thought flew around inside my head. *He knows. Tristan knows.* "But—" I paused, my mind racing. The room felt stifling.

"We are still looking," Haniel said. "You seem surprised."

"I thought the information I had sent was mislaid," I admitted before biting my tongue. "I must have been mistaken."

"Is there anything else?" Haniel asked, glancing at the doorway behind me.

"Yes." I looked over my shoulder to make sure we were alone. "Why did you order Drielle's guards to leave?"

Haniel started. "What?"

"You heard me. Why?"

Haniel sat back on his heels. "Why do you want to know?"

"Because I'm trying to get closure for a friend, for Saya. I think you know what that feels like," I added. Despite our differences, the three of us had gone through that day at the village together. I waited, breathless, keeping my gaze locked with his.

Haniel's eyes grew distant for a moment before clearing. He gave a slow nod. "Tristan said they were needed elsewhere."

"Why?"

"He didn't say." He leaned forward. "Juliet, I am sorry that Drielle died. I hope Saya knows that. I didn't know that was going to happen." Haniel's face paled as he spoke, as though he realized the suspicions I had not voiced. "I did not want her dead."

Truth rang in his voice.

He didn't kill her.

"Juliet?" Haniel asked, his voice ragged.

I laid my palms on my knees as I leaned forward. "I believe you. Who did, then?"

He blinked. "I don't know."

Chapter Twenty-Four

Saya waited in my room. She looked up from where she sipped tea as I entered. "Here." She motioned to the table. "Emi brought some repast a little while ago. It's still hot."

I sat down and stared at the cup she handed me.

Saya eyed me. "Drink. I'll go first. You look like you could use some food too." She gave me some rice and meat. "Hirose claims no knowledge of the seer." She took another sip and raised her narrow shoulders. "I think he's telling the truth. I told him why I was asking, and his bearing changed when I mentioned your name."

"Does he suspect anyone?" I took another drink of the rice tea.

"He thinks if it's anyone, it would be one of the women from the harem."

My eyes widened. *Of course.* I set the cup down on the table with a dull thud. "Why hadn't I thought of them?" *Amarante?* My eyes widened. *Natsumi.* Both were close to Cruelon. *But Natsumi—*

"What did you find out?" Saya asked.

I shook my head, clearing my thoughts away. "It wasn't Haniel."

"How do you know?" Saya set down her own tea.

"I said he didn't want her dead, and I believe him."

"And Tristan?"

I frowned. "Haniel doesn't know why Tristan gave the orders." As I picked up the rice bowl, I saw a bit of white on the floor. Reaching over, I pulled out the two notes I'd hidden under my mattress, one from Adnan and one from Tristan. I tucked them into my pants.

Saya raised an eyebrow.

"I'm not sure I should leave the Unknown's note lying around," I explained. "Something isn't right—it hasn't been right. I think I need to search Cruelon's study."

Saya held up her hands. "Juliet, I thought Tristan already had it searched? To find out about the traitor?"

I shook my head. "Not that study. Cruelon has another one. And Haniel admitted knowing about the traitor. Tristan was lying." As soon as the words were out, I felt like a little bit of the world had been lifted off my shoulders. *Tristan is lying.*

"Wait, Juliet. You can't say that."

I pushed my anger down. "Why not?"

"Because Haniel could have found out after you asked Tristan."

"No. Haniel didn't contradict me when I mentioned the information being mislaid. He already knew. Which means Tristan already knew."

Saya gazed down at the table. "I don't drink, but I think I could use something a little stronger." She shot me a wry smile and stood up. "I'll be back."

"What are you going to do?"

"I need to take a walk." She leaned over and squeezed my shoulder. "I won't be long."

As the door closed behind her, leaving me alone, I stared at the untouched food lying on the table. There were still so many pieces to the puzzle, and none of them quite fit. I took out paper, an inkwell, and a quill. *Whatever happens will be done by tomorrow.* I took a deep breath and wet the tip of the feather in the ink.

⁓⁓⁓

I laid the quill down and stretched my fingers and wrists as I stared down at the table. My writing stared back at me, roughly drawn diagrams of what I knew, connecting to other pieces, trying to fit together in a haphazard way. *The traitor—Tristan knew after all, Adnan leaving to look into Nani, Tristan calling Drielle's guards away, which led to her death, my impending wedding, the executions to take place at dawn ... I* rubbed at my tired eyes. *Tristan is at the heart of all of it.* I knew he had to have a plan. He *always* had a plan. *But why all this?* I leaned my elbows on the table and rested my chin on my hands.

A knock startled me. I jerked and my elbow slipped off the table. The door opened, revealing Saya and Emi. I sighed in relief.

Emi set down the tray she'd brought as Saya approached and stood next to the table.

"What's this?" she asked, gesturing to the papers littering the table and floor.

Emi handed me a cup of tea and some bread. I shoved a bite of the roll into my mouth and took a small sip of the hot tea.

"Burn them," I said around the mouthful of food.

She raised an eyebrow but did so. We all watched as the papers caught fire, blackened, and shriveled.

I took a deep breath. *This isn't just my life on the line.*

"I'm all in, Juliet, for better or worse," Saya murmured as if she had read my thoughts.

"As am I," Emi spoke up in her soft voice. "I trust you."

Trust. I hope I don't let them down. Taking a deep breath, I took a moment to gather my thoughts. "I'm not going to marry Tristan at dawn, nor are the men and women in the dungeons going to die."

Saya and Emi stared at me, their tea and food forgotten as they strained to hear my low voice.

"So we have to not only free them, but we have to do it by dawn. And I need to leave with them." I shrugged. "I have a plan." *Or at least part of one.* I inhaled and took another sip of tea. "But it's pretty simple."

Saya snorted. "Simple? Even the very idea doesn't sound simple."

"Shh," Emi hushed, staring at me.

I couldn't help the small grin that crossed my face.

Saya rolled her eyes but gestured for me to continue.

"Emi, do you know how Kin created the sleeping draught she gave me?"

Emi's eyes brightened and then glistened with pent-up sadness all in the same breath. She nodded, unable to speak.

"I want you to make it for me."

"For you?" she whispered, her voice breaking. "For you?" she repeated, stronger this time.

"Not for me to take, but I am going to need it."

Emi's small head tilted up. "I'll do it. How long before you need it?"

"As soon as you can. Also, meet me at the entrance to the dungeons and bring a loaded tray for the prisoners."

Emi stood up.

"I also need you to have the servants prepare a bath for me. Have it ready when you return from the dungeon."

"What?" Saya asked, staring at me. "Juliet, this isn't the time."

I looked at Emi, who waited, shifting her weight from foot to foot. "Emi, have them prepare it. As soon as you return, I want you to remain in my chambers so that if Tristan comes by, you can tell him I'm bathing and am being fitted for a new gown for the wedding, so I cannot be disturbed."

"Yes, my lady," Emi murmured. She muttered my instructions under her breath. "Anything else?"

"No, I'll give Saya her instructions soon ..." I hesitated. "If ..."

Saya's eyebrows rose over her wide eyes, an unspoken question hovering in the air.

"Are you both all right with following me in this?"

"Yes!" Emi exclaimed, clasping her hands together.

Recognition shown in Saya's gaze. I knew she remembered our earlier conversation where she'd asked who made me the leader.

"Yes," Saya replied. "I'll follow your lead."

I blew out the breath I'd been holding. "Good. One more thing before you go, Emi. Are you both sure you want to take the risks? If this goes wrong, Tristan could imprison us." *Or worse.*

Their silence was answer enough.

Saya regarded me and shrugged her petite shoulders. "You are not of this country, Juliet, nor even this world, and yet you are risking your life yet again for it."

"You're wrong," I whispered. Saya quirked her eyebrow. "Perhaps I am fighting for this country, but not for it in and of itself. I am fighting for my friends, and for the injustices being done."

"I still think that qualifies as this country," Saya put in.

I waved a dismissive hand. "All right, Emi, you may go. You know what to do." I smiled, but my heart wasn't in it. I couldn't bear to look Emi in her eyes as she left the room.

"What do you want me to do?"

"I need you to help Emi create the sleeping draft, or at least another one. You know herbs, and you've done this before."

A light shone in Saya's eyes.

I licked my lips. *The slave traders.* It had worked then. "A draft large enough to knock out anyone who eats and drinks tonight. But I also need you to keep an eye out for who comes and goes during dinner, and I need you to be the one who drugs the food and drink, or however you want to go about it. Emi needs to be covering my absence here."

"Ah." Saya drank the rest of her tea in a gulp and set the cup down. "And then?"

"And then I want you to come back here and fetch her. You both need to be ready to leave with Hirose and the others. You can't stay here after this."

Saya threw her head back and sighed. "How has it come to this? Have you considered talking to Tristan?"

"Of course I have!" I slapped my leg. "But I don't think he'll listen. I can see now the ways in which he has manipulated every situation to how he wants it, how he has manipulated *me*. I can't do anything that will make him suspicious. He has to think I'm all in, or at least willing." My breathing slowed as I forced myself to calm down. "He wants power, Saya. I think I was always just too blind to see it." I didn't realize how much time had passed until I went to take a drink of my cup of tea and realized it was stone cold and still full.

The silence stretched on for a couple of minutes. I took a piece of fruit but didn't eat it, my appetite gone. There was so much with my plan that could go wrong. *And my part might be the hardest.* I hadn't told Emi or Saya what I was going to do. Part of me felt like if I voiced it out loud, I would give in to the fear and dread building in the pit of my stomach.

"It's not a perfect plan," Saya admitted, rocking back on her heels. "But we don't have time to work out all the kinks. I'll go get started. We don't have long before dinner will be served." She stood up and I followed.

"Try your best." I gave her a quick hug, her soft brown hair brushing against my cheek as I pulled away.

Why does this feel like a goodbye? I moved back over to the fire, hoping to hide from Saya the pensive sadness I felt. Stirring the charred pieces of paper with a poker, I watched as they crinkled up, turning to ash. I stared down at them. I could become them if I didn't do this. I had already begun fading like the writing on the papers had faded to nothing, burned up by one more powerful than me, destroyed before anything could be done. But I could do something. The puzzle pieces had fallen into place, and if I was right, if my plan worked, then we could come out of this on the right end.

"Juliet?" Saya asked in a plaintive tone. "What are you going to do?"

My throat constricted. *Break into Tristan's study ... Search Cruelon's secret study.* I set the poker to the side. "It would take too long to explain," I managed. "Go on, Saya. Please, just do as I asked. Be safe."

I listened to her footsteps as she crossed the room.

Saya bowed. "May the gods be with you."

I waved a hand in farewell as she left. *It's time.* I drew my hair back and secured it with some pins before leaving the room. In the hallway outside, I ran my damp hands down my thin, tight pants, straightened the tunic, and took a deep breath.

No one stopped me as I slipped through the corridors and down the stairs to the second floor.

The castle was in an uproar. Servants busied themselves, readying for the morning. Tristan's private guard patrolled, ensuring the safety of the king and soon-to-be queen.

A buzzing in my temples grew as I neared Cruelon's study, now Tristan's. The door loomed before me, imposing, and was made even more so by the guard flanking it.

He cleared his throat. "Excuse me, my lady, but you cannot go in there."

"Is Tristan in there?"

"No, he is not."

"I must see him, though. Please, it's important." It wasn't hard to let tears well up in my eyes and slide down my cheeks. My emotions were already in turmoil. "Do you know where he is?"

The man grunted and moistened his lips with his tongue. "No."

I flung my arms into the air. "I have walked all over this castle, and still I can't find him. Would you go and enquire as to his whereabouts so that I do not wander around the passageways until dawn? I don't think your king would be very happy to have an exhausted bride."

His cheeks reddened. "I—I'm not supposed to leave my post, my lady."

"Oh, please." I batted my eyelashes. "I will stay here and make sure no one enters. You have my word. I can't walk another step." I sighed and swayed.

His arms shot out as though to help and then returned to his side, albeit with a little reluctance. "Very well, my lady. I will return as soon as I find out."

I beamed. "Thank you." I watched as he disappeared around the bend. As soon as he was gone, I let myself into the chamber. It looked much like it had while Cruelon had held office. Papers, pens, and ink littered the surfaces.

I ran to the table and rifled through the papers, flinging one aside, then another. My hands trembled, my breath short. Time was running out. Who knew how long the guard would be. *He must not find me still here when he returns.* I found nothing. Cruelon's papers had gone, or at least the ones with the traitor's name written upon them. And I found nothing else that stood out.

I sighed and walked to the door. Part of me wondered why I didn't just escape, why I needed physical evidence, but the other part knew there had to be something I was missing, something that existed beyond the tips of my fingers.

But there was one more step in the plan. *The next step.* I left the study. The door clicked shut behind me right when the guard appeared around the bend.

"Oh, there you are!" I feigned, trying to control my breathing as I focused on trying to look as though I had been waiting the entire time.

"My lady." The guard bowed. "I found out that he has just returned from looking over the troops. He is now getting ready for dinner in his chamber."

"Oh, perhaps I should go there."

The guard reeled, a tinge entering his cheeks. "He—the king has requested a bath, my lady. I am sorry, but he has asked for no one to disturb him."

Perfect.

"I understand. Thank you so much." I turned and left him behind, my feet finding the familiar path to the opposite side of the fortress, to the door leading down into the dungeons.

There also, two guards stood.

At the end of the hallway, Emi approached with a loaded tray. Her shoulders were bowed under the weight.

I strode up to join her and sashayed my hips as I made my voice rise an octave. "We are feeding the prisoners. Please lend us a torch for while we are down there."

One man made to do as I asked, but the other hesitated. "We've had no word of this from the king."

"I am soon to be queen," I stated, "and I did not wish to bother the king. This will be their last meal. Wouldn't you prefer to have one last meal if it were you down there?"

The men shifted on their feet and stood aside.

"Thank you."

I beckoned to Emi, who followed as I made my way down the passageway. I took a torch from the wall, listening to our boots echo on the stone floor. The drip of water splashed against stone, slipping through small crevices in the ceiling. The walls were damp from the winter rains, and it grew colder the farther down we went.

When we reached the bottom, I whispered, "Emi, did you bring what I asked?"

She nodded and set down her tray.

"Good, save it with something here for the guards upstairs." I gestured to the food.

"Understood, my lady."

While Emi gave some of the prisoners food, I headed for one cell in particular. I slid the bar across and opened the door. A sharp creak rang through the air.

Hirose looked up and uttered a hoarse laugh. "You deceived me. I did not think it possible, but you got the best of me. You should be proud. It's rare someone can surprise me."

I knelt next to him. "You know, then?"

"Yes, I rather think I do. We all do. The king came down to gloat not an hour or so ago."

I breathed a sigh in relief. *That was close.*

"I was not surprised," Hirose continued. "Expected it of him. But you, I really thought you might have been speaking the truth."

"I'm going to get you out of here," I whispered, ignoring him.

Hirose's chin rose. "I'm not leaving my men."

"I'm getting them all out."

"All of them?"

"Yes, I hope. Now will you listen?"

Hirose crossed his arms. "Fine."

"Good." I settled my weight on the backs of my heels and began. "We're drugging the guards. I'll send someone for you when it's time."

"And then?" Hirose asked with a note of interest.

"That part of the plan is still a work in progress," I admitted. "But it's the only option you have," I added as I saw Hirose hesitate.

"Very well. But I might be able to help you with that portion. I do know the castle fairly well."

I bit my lip and sat back on my haunches. *He's right.* "All right. We all have to get out of the castle. The main keep is the only way, and I'm not sure how we're going to get past the guards on duty, especially without weapons." Now that I said it out loud, I realized how many pieces were missing.

Hirose swung his head to toss the hair out of his face. "Well, we could raid one of the armories. There is one on the main level of the keep."

I perked up.

"And there is another gate, a smaller one, near the stables."

I bobbed my head as I thought. "All right. I'll get it taken care of. I have to go." I rose and stretched my legs.

Hirose regarded me. "It's risky, but it just might work. Very well."

It was as though a dam had broken inside of me. Relief washed over me in waves. He was in. I stepped out of the cell and saw it clear of anyone except Emi, who was holding an almost empty tray in her hands.

"I'll be right back," I said to her. "Wait for me."

She nodded, moving away from the water dripping along the wall.

Spinning on the balls of my feet, I ran farther down, into the deepest part of the dungeon. Moss grew on the stones, and I prayed I would not slip. *There.* The door stood waiting, unimposing and unlocked. I entered the paper-strewn room. It looked the same as when I had been here with Cruelon. Tristan hadn't found it. I took a deep breath and scanned over every piece I could grab hold of. Report after report after report.

Frustrated, I noticed a small chest lying on the floor. Locked. Biting my lip, I slid a pin out of my hair and slid it into the small iron lock. I twisted and turned, sweat beading on my forehead as I struggled to unlock it. With a small click, I threw back the lid. My eyes widened as they fell on familiar maps, reports, and strategic formations.

The papers I'd seen when Cruelon brought me into his study. I flung them on the floor and groaned. I'd already seen them. They wouldn't help. But I froze as a name caught my eye. *Lanevrog. The traitor.* I lifted the paper and examined it. There was something familiar about it. It was the writing. I tilted my head and gasped.

Jumping up, my arm hit the table and an ink bottle crashed to the floor, its black liquid spraying out across the shards of broken glass lying scattered across the floor. I took the notes from where I had tucked them into my pants. Spreading them out, I stared at the signatures. My hands trembled. The writing. They were the same.

My heart drummed within my chest. *Tristan. Lanevrog.* They were written by the same person. *Lanevrog.* I started. Taking a quill, I wetted the tip in the spilled ink and pulled the paper toward me. Under Lanevrog, I wrote with a trembling hand, G-O-R-V-E-N-A-L. *Gorvenal.*

Tristan Gorvenal.

I leaned back, the air stifling and hard to breathe. *It's him. He's the spy.* He was the one who had fed Cruelon information. My heart raced, threatening to break out of my chest. *He is responsible for all of this.* Rolling up the map, I stuck it in the waistband under my tunic and burst out of the study. Flecks of water splashed up with every step.

Emi stood outside Hirose's cell, her foot tapping. "Are you ready, my lady?" she asked.

"Come on, then. We have a lot to do." I quickened my step, Emi close behind as we made our way back up into the fortress.

The guards stared at us as we passed.

"Thank you," I murmured to them. "We are done. Oh, and we left some spiced wine and cakes for you both if you are hungry."

The men licked their lips and glanced about.

"Thank you, my lady," one said with a grin.

"We shouldn't—" the other began, but stopped as he saw Emi offer a bottle of wine and two cakes.

"I give you my permission. Drink to my health, and to the king's." Spinning on my heel, I left, loose tendrils of my hair that had fallen brushing against my neck.

"They'll be out within half an hour," Emi whispered once we'd left the guards behind.

"Good. Emi, good luck."

She bowed and turned away. "I'll see you later."

I bobbed my head. *Yes, you will. Be safe.* With each step, I felt strength flooding into me. They all depended on me. And I knew what they didn't ... the next part of the plan wasn't even a plan. The next step, I had to wing it.

Is there anyone watching over us? I looked up at the stone ceiling, knowing night had fallen outside and the bitter, cold winds of winter blew. *If they are, are they listening? Tristan is the traitor.* I ran up the closest stairwell, taking them two at a time. *He told Cruelon about me. It was him.* A bitter taste filled my mouth. *And now he wants to marry me.*

He had played me all along.

Chapter Twenty-Five

Scarlet streaked the sky, battling against the enclosing blackness of night. Fog had begun to descend, casting a haziness over the shadowy courtyard below. Torches blazed on the battlements, and throughout the grounds, large braziers had been lit, providing a little warmth for those who must stay outside. Even now, the vague forms of men huddled around them, their cloaks pulled close around their bodies.

I filled my lungs with crisp air. *It's almost time.* I took in one more breath, pushing back the ache in my temples. The evening was calm, but an eerie sort of calm, as though waiting for the coming storm. *There's no going back.*

The fortress was so empty. Everyone who did not have duties to attend to was in the dining hall for dinner. Tristan would also be there. So far, he had not come looking for me. I had checked in with Emi after leaving the dungeon. I hoped he had bought my excuse of a bath and gown fitting. I clutched my cloak a little tighter, trapping the heat under the material. Continuing, I watched as my shadow flickered in and out with the torches burning in their brackets on the walls.

Footsteps approached. I looked up. A man with shifty eyes, dressed in simple clothing, halted in front of me.

"My lady," he whispered. "It's time."

The next step in the plan. A sigh of relief escaped me. The servant raised an eyebrow but said nothing as he led me down the corridor. He could not know how little of a plan I had for this part. Even Saya and Emi did not know. I had given them few details, hoping they would not realize the large pieces that were missing. *Or perhaps they did notice, but they trust me.* My teeth clenched. *So much rides on me. So much rides on this night.*

The man looked over his shoulder, some yards in front of me. I hadn't realized I had slowed down. I sped up, trying to walk as softly as possible. Who knew what ears could be listening.

We halted in front of a double door flanked by two windows. I glanced through. The sun had almost set; the scarlet rays were no more, and there was but the faintest hint of a dull light in the far west.

Where is he? I looked up and down the corridor. "You may go," I told the servant. "Tell Emi the next step is complete."

"Very well." He left.

I stood with my back flat against the wall. The castle was quiet, and there were few about. Now that dinner had begun, I knew Saya should be on her way to fetch Emi. They had one more thing to do for me. A contingency in case things went wrong. *Please let this all work out.*

I bit my lip in frustration. A hand clamped over my mouth, and I jerked as a body pressed closed behind my own.

"Shh," a voice hissed. The hand released me and I turned, trying to calm my racing heart.

I shifted on the balls of my feet. "Any trouble?"

"None whatsoever, my lady." Hirose bowed. Exhaustion darkened his face, and a weariness lent itself to his posture, but a light still shone strong in his eyes. He was not ready to give up—not yet—and neither was I. "The others will be ready. Shall we?"

I gestured to the doors. "Where are the guards?"

"I took care of them. Don't worry, they're not dead."

I opened one of the two doors, which swung back on well-oiled hinges. We stepped inside, and I gasped. I spun as I surveyed the oval room.

"Impressive, isn't it?" Hirose asked with a smirk. "You can close your mouth now, my lady."

I glared at him and turned my attention back to the objects within the room. Weapons of all kinds hung upon the walls. Katanas, swords, maces, axes, daggers, bows, crossbows, and more. A long trestle table held supplies to make arrows, and sealed casks stood against one wall.

"Tar," muttered Hirose, following my gaze. "Arm yourself. Then we'll gather weapons for the others."

I walked over to one of the walls. *What to choose?* I picked up a beautiful sword, but my arm dropped under the weight of it. Wincing as the point almost jabbed a notch in the floor, I strained to lift it back up onto the hook.

Hirose stepped up beside me. "Here, let me help." He selected two daggers, one slimmer and longer than the other. He handed the longer out of the two to me. "For your boot."

I slid it into my right boot and held my hand out for the second. The steel was cold to the touch. "And this one?"

"Hmm. Here, put it under the sleeve of your left arm. It's flowy enough that it would be easy to get to." Hirose handed me a thin leather harness. "Now, I assume you have little experience with weapons?"

"Not much."

"So a bow would be out of the question, most swords would be too heavy, a crossbow is slow and bothersome ... perhaps one of the lighter katanas?" He ran his slender hands over the hilts until he selected one with a thin, curving blade. "Here, try this."

I hefted the blade and was surprised at its lightness and balance. The silver weapon flew through the air as I waved it experimentally. "Feels good."

"Here's a sheath." He held out a matching leather piece.

I buckled the katana to my side.

"The gods know whether you will have to use it or not, but I hope we can avoid that." Hirose dragged two bags into the middle of the room. "Help me load these up with as many swords and daggers as you can."

The items clinked as we set them in the bags. Metal clanged against metal, and the sheathed sword I wore dragged across the ground every time I crouched down. It didn't take long to fill the bags.

Hirose stood. "Now for the bows." He slung a few quivers onto my back. "We have a couple of good archers amongst my men, so they may come in handy. Is the weight too much?"

My shoulders trembled under the weight, but I shook my head. Grabbing a few bows with my free hands, I waited for Hirose to pick up the two bags.

He grunted. "Don't worry. We don't have far. Let's go."

"We've been too long as it is," I muttered, hoping Saya's drug was working.

Hirose took the lead. "In the end, it only matters that we've tried. Keep your hope alive and your courage strong."

Hope and courage. I pulled the door shut behind us. *That's all we have right now.* I sent up a silent prayer that no one would come across us. We weren't as silent as I wished. The heavy loads of weapons clanked as we went.

"Right through here," Hirose whispered. He knocked twice, then four times in rapid succession. Something heavy slid back, and the door creaked open a slit. "Let us in," Hirose ordered. "Quickly, man."

I was pulled into the room after him, and the metal bar slid into place behind us.

There weren't more than two dozen haggard men in the room. None were taller than me. I winced at the smell emanating from them. "So few." The words slipped out before I could stop them.

Hirose gestured to his men to take the bags and the bows. "They'll be enough." He raised his voice. "They're some of the best and will fight to the death."

"Why will they do this?" I whispered my question to Hirose, hoping no one else would hear.

"My lady?"

I leaned closer, aware of how small the room was. "I know it's not because of any loyalty to me, and any loyalties you and your men had were taken with Cruelon to his grave. I just want to know why."

Hirose's brows drew together. "What would you expect? We are to be executed at dawn, so we fight for our freedom, all of us. And my men's loyalties lie with me."

Out of the corner of my eye, I saw some of the men nearest to us nod at his words. I sighed. "All right."

Hirose bowed and turned to his men, barking out orders. His voice faded to the background as I gripped the katana's hilt and stared at the bare wall.

I can do this. We can do this.

"We're ready." Hirose's announcement broke into my reverie. I looked over the men. Two dozen, all half-starved, but their eyes glittering bright and their grips strong.

Desperation can give strength to the weakest of men.

My hand had just settled on the iron barring the door when a gentle knock came through. We all froze as one. Again, it sounded.

"My lady," a hoarse voice whispered.

I slipped the bar from the door, too late to heed Hirose's whispered warning. But I'd recognized that voice. I pulled Emi into the room. "What's wrong? Where's Saya?"

"She's waiting for me, don't worry. But my lady, there are a few here who want to go as well."

My eyebrows rose. I ignored the snort from Hirose. "Who?"

"Some of the servants."

I chewed on my lower lip.

"My lady," Hirose began with a note of disbelief.

I held up a hand. "Emi, are they ready?'

"Yes. They'll travel light."

"They'll just slow us down. We have to go now," Hirose spat.

"Emi, we'll see you and whoever else by the small gate in the east wall. If not, then Godspeed."

Hirose cursed under his breath. The men shifted, looking back and forth between him and me as I thought.

Not all of us will make it this night. Fear pooled in the pit of my stomach.

Emi bowed low. "My lady." She turned to leave.

"Oh, Emi," I hissed. "The horses?"

Emi looked over her shoulder. "They'll be saddled and waiting for us. The stable master isn't loyal to Tristan. He will leave with the rest of us."

"All right. Remember, even if you don't see us, leave. Mount two to a horse if needed. Scatter. Don't give them only one trail to follow."

Emi beamed.

I keep forgetting how young she is.

"My lady?" She took my hands in hers. "Where will *you* go?"

Hirose muttered something under his breath and turned to his men.

I shrugged and gripped Emi's hands. "Maybe east." It was a mechanical reply. My dread had grown. I had an awful feeling I wouldn't be getting away. Something would happen. I was not one fated to leave at dawn.

"Then I will go east too." Emi's soft voice was of steel. "What are you going to do?"

What would I do? The question hung in the air. Tristan was the puppet master, the one who had been pulling the strings all along. He had acted so perfectly and yet deceived all who knew him. *Could I leave him alive?*

"He'll hunt us until his last breath, or until ours," I murmured.

"So you'll kill him?"

A shiver ran over my skin. "I don't know."

Emi dropped my hands. "Remember Kin." Her small face was pale in the glow of torchlight. "Kill him."

"Can I?" Something stabbed through my heart and tightened within my chest, and panic shifted through my body. My hands trembled. *What if killing him sends me down a path I can never return from?* "If I kill him, who will rise in his place? Another man, the same, or even worse? He isn't the only one, Emi. There are far more like him in this world, in mine—more than we could ever know."

She stepped back. "So you'll do nothing, then?"

I didn't answer her. And when she left, it was as if a small piece of me broke off and left with her. She had proven a true friend in all of this. We had bonded in the past few weeks, and even if I never saw her again, she would always be a part of me. *Her life is also in my hands.*

I followed Hirose out into the hallway. Distant noises echoed through the castle, and I could almost hear Tristan screaming my name, yet I knew I heard it only in the deepest recesses of my mind, the scariest place of all.

This was the last piece of my hasty plan. Even now, I warred with myself over it.

"The gods are watching over us tonight," Hirose whispered as we veered into the final corridor leading to the door nearest the wicker gate in the courtyard.

"Or maybe fate," I replied.

Hirose's stride broke for a moment. "Aren't fate and the gods intertwined? You can't have one without the other."

I shrugged. "You think there is someone watching over us, guiding us, an invisible presence in the darkness?" But even as I spoke, I knew my own doubts. *Could there be someone listening? Someone watching?*

"You don't?"

"I don't know. Maybe. But I can't imagine there being more than one."

"The more, the better, Juliet. Why pray to one when you can pray to all?"

I don't have an answer. I glanced up as though I'd be able to see someone watching, but there was no one. My lips parted, but no words came out. *What can I say?* A breeze wafted down the corridor, bringing with it the smell of sweat, grime, and the foul odor of unbathed men.

"Wait, what are you all—" a husky voice began from up ahead.

The words froze me in my tracks. But not all of us. Hirose and one other, the two closest to the guard who now stood in front of us, lunged forward. One their swords sprang from their scabbards, cutting the man down where he stood.

My limbs were unable to cooperate, my brain at odds with even gathering enough strength to do or say anything. Within mere moments, the man who had stood full of life lay on the ground, his blood seeping out of him. *Had I met him before? Was he in the mountain when I was there?*

Hirose helped drag the man to the side. "Let's go. More will come."

I couldn't take my eyes off the dead man's eyes. They stared into my own, unseeing. "Hirose—"

"Juliet. Now." Hirose's voice snapped out the words.

Almost without thinking, my legs moved to obey his command. There was no way to skirt around the body, so I stepped over it, the blood already trailing in rivulets down the rough stone.

I heard the echo of boots on stone as the rest of the men followed suit. Hirose held his sword in his hand while grabbing my forearm with his free hand to keep me moving. Blood, bright red in the glowing light from the torch Hirose carried, dripped off the tip of his sword.

"Keep it tight," Hirose muttered to those behind. The order echoed until it reached the last of our small group. Up ahead I could see the door.

That was the moment the screams began. Shouts and hoarse cries beat against the door separating us from the shrill voices. We paused for a brief second, yet it seemed a lifetime. Hirose raised his sword above his head, and we surged forward.

We were through.

The courtyard blazed with light from the fires in the braziers. Men streamed out of the gatehouses to the right, buckling on sword belts and milling into one another in the confusion. Even from this distance, I could see the befuddled looks on their shadowed faces. The stables lay to the left, with the small gate beyond. A group clustered there, fighting against some of Tristan's men.

"Hirose!" I yelled, pointing.

Hirose's lips thinned. "We have to give them time." He turned to face us, ordering half his men to engage the men attacking Emi and the others trying to escape. The other half ran with him and me toward those streaming from the gatehouse.

"Their force is smaller than it should be. Looks like your plan is working," Hirose panted, sword in hand.

My plan. The drugs Emi had slipped into whatever food and drink she could. I drew my sword, listening to the harsh cries sounding from the lips of those facing us. They ran forward, swords raised high above their heads, mouths open in whatever chant came to mind. Sounds dulled as though a breeze had carried them away, leaving but a whisper behind. I barely registered the clink of weaponry, the thuds of footfalls upon the packed earth, the pants, the murmurs of hurried prayers, and the shouts.

But the whites of the eyes of those in the courtyard, the sweat beading on their skin, all lay in sharp focus. My mind screamed at me to retaliate. A man—no, more of a boy—raised his sword and swung it down with a harsh cry toward me.

Instinct took over and my sword came up to meet it, the blades crashing hard upon one another. The young man's gaze met mine, and he faltered. Hirose shouted something, but I didn't understand. My opponent's eyes hardened as he drew his sword back and swung it toward me yet again.

I sidestepped, allowing his sword to glance off mine and using the momentum to propel my blade toward his thigh. It bit deep. The blade sunk into flesh, giving a squelch as tissue and tendons gave way, and then a sharp ping as bone impeded the blade's progress.

He doubled over, but not a sound issued from his lips. I wrenched the sword out of his leg, and he fell sideways, rolling onto his back, dark red blood soaking the ground. He stared upward as he breathed in ragged gasps. A single tear coursed down his cheek.

I would never forget the look upon his face. I may not have killed him, but I'd destroyed the life he could have had. I panted and stumbled backward. He was the first to fall victim to my sword.

But another came without respite.

Adrenaline took complete control, along with a deep sense of self-preservation. The boy was the first, but he wouldn't be the last.

Fierce as we fought, we were pushed back, but it worked in our favor. Foot by foot, we gave way, toward the very gate we wanted to make our escape through. Inexperienced as I was, I stood my ground, though not without wounds. Stings like paper cuts were the sole signs I had that any blade touched my skin. I didn't know how much of the blood that soaked my clothing belonged to me.

Through a brief lull in the fighting, I knew I lived because of Hirose and his right-hand man. They protected me from the brunt of the fighting, never straying too far from my person in an intricate dance. Those I faced were but the few who got through. Without my two guards, I would have fallen long before.

Hirose came up beside me. "This is your chance," he yelled over the skirmishes. "Take a horse and go." He gestured to the gate. "My men hold a few there."

I glanced over my shoulder. "What about you?"

"Don't worry about me. Just go." He pushed me forward.

"Not without you," I protested, resisting.

"Don't argue with me," Hirose snapped. "You know there wasn't a chance we'd all get out of here alive."

I opened my mouth and saw Tristan. Everything seemed to freeze, as though in waiting for something to happen. A path had cleared through the fighting, leaving a clear line of sight. He stood there amongst the smoke but a few dozen feet away, his booted feet almost planted in the embers from an upturned brazier. As bright as the embers flared, Tristan's appearance burned brighter, with a fury beyond anything imaginable.

Our eyes locked.

For the second time, the noises of the surrounding battle faded away. But this time I was aware of myself, him, and those around us. Each sense heightened—my fingers tightened around the hilt of my sword. Fear cut into me, vying for control over my mind and limbs. Standing there, staring at him, a brutal battle raged within me. *Run. Don't run. Stay. Don't stay.*

Tristan drew a long, curved katana from his scabbard. "Juliet!" he bellowed.

"Go!" Hirose yelled, spittle flying from his lips.

"No." As much as I wanted to, I knew I couldn't. *Not now.*

Hirose grabbed me by the shoulders. "Juliet, leave. He doesn't want us. He wants you. Draw him away."

Tristan grinned and strode forward, his teeth glistening in the firelight.

Hirose spun me to one side and pushed me forward. "Run, Juliet! Take a horse and run!" His voice, driven by desperation, spurred me onward.

My breath came in short gasps. I sprinted.

A small group of Tristan's guards appeared in front of me and attacked those holding the horses. *No!* I veered to the left toward the keep without thinking. Behind me I heard Hirose's distant shouts, his last orders for his men to flee, to escape while they still could. I couldn't keep myself from feeling a sense of betrayal, my hopes dashed knowing they were leaving me behind. I doubted Hirose had seen me change direction. And even if he had, what could he do? He'd done more than enough. He'd kept me alive. He'd allowed a chance for those in the dungeons and others to escape.

I risked a glance over my shoulder. The footsteps echoed behind me. So close, the echo seemed to be on my heels. I was unable to escape, and my pursuer was relentless.

Tristan was gaining ground.

My dream. A snatch of memory drifted through my mind. I peeked over my shoulder before turning the corner in the corridor. Tristan's perfect face twisted into a sneer, his blond hair dark with the night. From a distance, I could have sworn I heard my name again, but I couldn't stop. Blood pumped through my veins, and my head pounded. Pressure built in my ears and temple as I made it to the door to the keep. I let it swing closed behind me as I took the stairs to the right.

I'd reached the first landing when I heard the echo of the door slamming shut a second time. My breathing quickened. The sounds of battle faded the farther I climbed, but the heavy stomp of footfalls on the stone stairs below continued. I gasped, trying to draw as much air into my lungs as possible, fear driving me forward. The echoes of Tristan's pursuit reverberated through the circular stairwell.

A gasp escaped my lips as I collided with a serving woman. She pressed herself against the wall, terror filling her face.

My eyes followed hers to my sword. "Get out of here," I yelled, waving. I left her as I bounded up the stairs two at a time. My legs trembled, protesting with every step, yet I climbed higher still.

Here was the level I sought. *Please.* This was the contingency plan. *Did Saya and Emi follow through?* I gasped for air. Distant sounds reached me as I ran past the narrow slits in the walls. I was far above the ground now and could see flashes of the empty battlements. There were only two ways out of the fortress, the main gate and the small wicker gate, but neither was an option right now.

There. I hadn't known this moment would come, but I'd wondered. My last command to Emi, and she'd followed it without question. A rope hung on a peg next to the door. I grabbed it and plunged through the open doorway. Here I halted, turning to face the long corridor I'd run down. Tristan came to a stop at the other end. A single torch burned between us, but the light did not reach him.

"Juliet." His voice was hushed, like a caress. "Juliet," he repeated, even softer. His shoulders relaxed, and he held out his hand to me. "There is yet time. Come to me."

I squared my shoulders.

"Juliet."

Now it was a warning. He had seen the stiffening of my body, knew which way my thoughts ran.

"You do not understand—"

"Yes, I do. I understand perfectly, Tristan." Each word was a hammer blow. "You were behind everything. This was all a game to you. You moved your pawns about with ease, bringing everything together for your benefit." I ran my hands over the rough rope. "Cruelon was working for you all along, wasn't he? He just didn't know it. You love playing the game, Tristan. *King* Tristan." I mocked him with the words, adding a slight bow with my arms flung out. "But you couldn't stop with just being king. I realize it now." My voice lowered as my mind became lost in memory. "You've always cared so much about what everyone around you thinks of you, what they see in you. You've used others to get you to where you are now." I gripped the rope tighter and backed up a step. "No, you had to show everyone the conquering hero who saved all, a fantastical ploy where the evil king, the scourge of the land, stole your fiancée and laid waste to your entire family—where you vanquished him, showing your might, courage, and valor." The flame that had filled me with resolve for the Uprising rose again within me, but this time it was anger fueled by betrayal. "I don't even know what to believe anymore. When did you tell me the truth? Or was it all lies?" My voice cracked.

"Juliet." Tristan smiled and lowered his sword hand so that the tip touched the floor. "Why do you think I told you lies? I may not have told you the truth, but—"

I held up a hand. "No, Tristan. You've lied. You lied about the traitor. You did receive the word I sent. So if you would lie about something like that, what else? Are you even Tristan Gorvenal, heir to the throne? Did your whole family really die?" My hands shook from the adrenaline coursing through my body.

"I am truly Tristan Gorvenal. The throne is mine, Juliet." Tristan sighed and raked a hand through his hair. "And I am now the sole heir. There is no one left to take it from me."

His words rang through the air.

There is no one left.

My jaw dropped.

Tristan took a step forward.

"No!" I yelled, mirroring him as I moved back. "Did *you* have something to do with their deaths?" I knew the battle raged outside, but right now, it had all faded so that it was just the two of us standing in the hallway. I could feel the door close behind me.

Tristan's broad shoulders tenses and his hand flexed. The sword tip scraped across the wood with a soft hiss.

"You did," I breathed.

"I did not just have *something* to do with it, Juliet. I ordered their deaths. I was the mastermind behind it all. None of them were fit to rule."

"But you were already heir," I whispered, struggling to understand.

"Yes, but I had to make sure none would rise to contest that right."

"They were your family, Tristan." Tears wet my eyes. I blinked.

Tristan opened his mouth, but I held up a hand to silence him.

"Was I just another piece in your game? Another pawn to maneuver to your heart's content?" I took a deep breath, controlling my thoughts. "You sent me here. *You* gave me up. The act of saving me was a farce. You saved me from a situation *you* put me in. You betrayed everyone." Tears slid down my cheeks.

"Juliet, I love you."

I laughed. "No, you do not. This is not love."

"You love me," he commanded, loud and sharp.

"No, I do not, and I realize now I never did."

"Oh, really?" It was Tristan's turn to laugh. "And you know what love is? Tell me, Juliet, what experience do you have? The Unknown, as you call him? Adnan? Is it he who fills your thoughts, who you long for when you are alone? Adnan left you behind. He does not care for you. He did not even care enough to say goodbye. What kind of man does that?"

The words cut into me more than I wanted to admit. "He's a better man than you'll ever be." *He's been there when you haven't.* I gripped the rope and took another step back, into the open doorway. *And he did say goodbye.* Adnan's note was still tucked into the lining of my pants.

Tristan took a step forward, then another. "Juliet, come to me. Let us forget all of this. Be my queen. Stand by my side." He dragged the tip of the sword along the floor as he walked. "I love you deeply, ardently. I want you."

I shook my head. "No, you have an obsession. A sick obsession. Goodbye, Tristan."

He lunged forward as I slammed the door closed, swinging the metal bolt down into place with my free hand. Sheathing the katana, I hoisted the rope over my shoulder and ran down the stairs and into the vestibule. At the end, a narrow wooden beam extended from it to the battlements.

I paused at the edge and peered across into the shadows. Holding my arms out for balance, I placed one foot in front of the other. *Don't look down. Don't look down.* I repeated the phrase over and over as I focused on traversing the wooden slats. The wind whistled past, almost shrieking at this height. Sounds of battle below filtered up through the breeze, distracting, like a fly buzzing in my ear.

My foot contacted the far side of the battlements, and I looked back. Tristan hadn't followed me, but I could hear him pounding on the door and screaming my name. The clink of swords had faded, and so did the voices. I leaned over the parapet, looking down into the courtyard below. It seemed as if the fighting had ceased. A few men sat huddled on the ground—some of Hirose's men. Tristan's guards stood above them, swords still at the ready. Others milled about, turning over the dead, treating the wounded.

A quiet hush had fallen in the aftermath. It had been a short battle, but fierce. I scanned the faces bathed in the firelight, but I couldn't make them out at this distance. *Where is Hirose? Had he made it out?* Now I knew who Tristan was. And I knew the men down there would not live to see dawn.

Turning my back on the scene of carnage below, I unslung the rope and tied it securely around one of the juts of stone, throwing the rest over the side. In the darkness, I couldn't tell if the rope was long enough, but I had no choice but to believe it was.

Something moved in my peripheral.

My head whipped around. My sword released from its scabbard with a hiss. I raised the tip up in time to block a bone-jarring hit. Tristan pressed his body close to mine, swords locked in between us. His breath blew hot against my face. I shoved him, gaining mere inches with the effort, but it was enough. I grabbed the end of the rope with my free hand and twisted it around my wrist. *This is a bad idea.*

Tristan held out a hand. "Juliet, stay, please. I will not harm you. You will be my wife, queen of this country. You may have anything you wish—"

I leapt over the edge, letting it envelop me, feeling the rush of air as I flew toward the ground.

Tristan screamed in rage behind me, but as the wind whipped against my face and hair, his voice faded. I couldn't see the ground. No moon existed tonight.

The rope went taut, jerking my body to a stop. Something snapped in my wrist, and I yelped in pain as the rope bit into it, taking the brunt of my fall. The pain was numbing. I let go and fell until my body hit the hard-packed earth with a thud.

A groan escaped my lips. I rolled onto my side, struggling to get up into a sitting position. One thing dominated my thoughts: *escape.* I had to get out of there before Tristan found me. My breaths came out in gasps as I dragged the sword up out of the grass and sheathed it.

The distant creak of heavy oak doors opening had me on my feet. I searched, squinting in the darkness as I cradled my injured wrist. The pain blurred my thoughts. Setting off toward a thick copse of trees, I stumbled like a blind man as I ran.

Once in the shadows of the tree fringe, I looked back. Torches flared out in a wide array behind me, streaming from the castle. Then the distant baying of dogs reached my ears.

Cruelon's hounds.

Chapter Twenty-Six

The terrors of the night had escaped my dreams. For hours I walked, ran, walked, and then ran again. My feet ached and my legs burned. The braying of the hounds had finally faded into the distance, but that didn't mean I had lost them. Several times I had thought they had gone, but then the howls would begin again, at times so close I feared they were on my heels. When I'd look over my shoulder, they were never there.

Don't stop. Don't stop. Don't stop. The words rang through my mind, each command a bell pealing with sharp, clanging tones. *Tristan may not be far behind.*

The moon cast a glimmer of light over the landscape, slipping through the cracks in the bare foliage of the trees above me, the leaves having since long fallen. The toe of my boot caught something, and I flew forward, crashing down onto my side. I bit the inside of my mouth to keep from shouting. Cradling my wrist, I rocked back and forth as waves of pain lanced through me like lightning bolts. I blinked as I peered through wet eyes at the forest around me. The tall trees seemed to sway over my head with clutching fingers. Taking deep breaths, I rose and waited, bent over, feeling a little relief as the pain receded into a sharp throbbing.

I stumbled onward, wincing with each footstep. The trickling of water came to my ears, and I followed it to the bank of a brook. Hesitating at the edge, I took a deep breath and entered the icy water. Following it upstream, I welcomed the ease of aches in my feet and calves from the cold. I paused long enough to hold my wrist in the stream until that pain, too, faded.

There. A large, thick branch hung over the stream, the end of it trailing in the water. It was a struggle to mount, weighed down as I was with wet boots and an injury, but eventually I straddled the branch. Inching my way up and over, I dropped to the ground several yards from the stream's edge. Something rustled and I froze, my eyes scanning every movement. The branches whispered in the slight wind. My shadow fell across the ground, broken up by the foliage above, blocking the moon's light.

Dawn was approaching and I still hadn't heard any more signs of my pursuers, but I refused to relax. I kept on, my skin prickling with each slight creak and crack of the forest life around me. But no attack ever came. Sometimes I wondered if each wave of apprehension was brought on by my own mind, thoughts conjuring themselves into false reality.

As dawn shed her first light, driving the throes of night away, I saw a hamlet nestled amongst the small grove with smoke curling up from the chimney. It looked so peaceful, and yet not far enough from Tristan. I watched, teeth chattering, as an entire hour went by. The cold breeze cut through my blouse as though it weren't there.

I sighed. I had stopped moving. Forcing myself to keep going, I crept along until the front door of the small cottage loomed in front of me. I listened to shuffling inside. When I knocked, the sounds ceased. A bolt withdrew, and the door opened a crack.

A voice issued from the darkness. "What do you want?"

"To warm myself by your fire, if I may. And some food, if you have some to spare. I've been walking for a long time without food or rest."

"Do you have money?"

I shook my head.

After a moment's hesitation, the door opened. "Very well. Come in."

I wondered at his sudden change of heart, but exhaustion filled my mind and body. I resisted the nagging doubt to keep moving on and entered. In the dingy, dim interior, I couldn't see who I was talking to until I'd entered the cottage. A man stared at me, not much taller than me but quite a bit wider. He gestured toward the fireplace. "Take a seat. I'm making breakfast. You're welcome to a bit of it."

"Thank you." I sat on the edge of the chair by the fire, aware of the filth surrounding me but too exhausted to do anything but sit there. I turned my eyes away, back to the fire. The glow warmed my body, bringing much-needed warmth and comfort.

Breakfast was a silent affair. The man didn't take his eyes off me. I ate, hardly tasting the food that touched my lips.

He gestured toward my hand, which I had laid on the table. "That looks bad."

"It's fine."

"I can take a look at it."

"It's fine," I repeated, a little harsher than I'd intended.

The chair squeaked as he slid it back and stood, his back hunched and his shoulder stooped. "I have chores to do. Feel free to rest here if you like. I won't be in till noon or thereabouts." His eyes slid over my sword, which still hung at my side.

I resisted the urge to drop my hand to its grip.

After he left, I felt I could breathe easier. He was right. Something was wrong with my wrist. It was useless. I couldn't do anything but cradle it against my stomach, and the pain hadn't disappeared. I stretched my legs out in front of the fire and stared into the low, flickering flames. *Just a couple of hours, and then I'll leave.* My eyes closed.

⚬⚬⚬⚬ ⚬⚬⚬⚬

I woke and blinked in the darkness. The fire had all but died out. Standing up, I rubbed my eyes and stumbled to the door. *What time is it? How long had I slept?* I opened the door and stared out at the bright light that streamed into the cottage. Leaning against the rough oak door frame, I let my eyes adjust to the sudden change in light. Clouds covered the sky, but I knew it had to be past noon. Looking out the way I'd come, I stiffened. Figures moved toward the cottage, too far away to distinguish, but I knew who they were. Who they answered to.

Using the cottage as a visible barrier, I ran in the opposite direction of the approaching men. I climbed a way up a hill and found a vantage point in a crop of rocks. Stooping behind them, I watched as the men approached the cottage far below. A burly man led them.

The farmer.

A distant shout sounded. The cottager fell to the ground in front of the group, no doubt begging for his life. Not waiting any longer, I continued climbing the hill. My breathing came in gasps, and my hand hung limp and useless at my side. The path I'd chosen grew steeper, turning into more of a climb than anything else.

The baying grew louder, hammering inside my eardrums. My arms trembled with fatigue as I clung to the rocks. Beads of sweat rolled down my face. I had long since stopped feeling cold. My clothes clung to me, damp with sweat.

The sun had begun its sloping descent when I reached the top. Sparse trees dotted the landscape, providing a welcome shade. Far down below, I saw a thin curl of smoke from the man's cottage, but nothing moved about down there. In the distance, I could see the spires rising from Cruelon's—now Tristan's—castle. Worry created a crease in my brow. I'd hoped I'd come farther than this. *If I hadn't woken when I had ...*

A bark cut through the air, a high, yapping noise. I froze. The hounds again. Shading my eyes, I scanned the area where I thought I'd heard it, but saw nothing. My blood boiled hot in my veins. I wiped my face with my sleeve, the faint sound of Cruelon's bloodhounds riding on the breeze.

Please. Not again. I closed my eyes, agony filling every limb. *Move, Juliet.* Pushing off a rock I'd been leaning against, I ran. The descending sun was at my back, but I began cutting my way north to angle away from the south—away from Tristan. Even with the few hours of sleep I'd had, exhaustion set in tenfold. *How many had escaped? How many had Tristan killed when we'd gone?* I shook my head, gasping for air, my mouth and throat dry from the lack of water. *It doesn't matter. He only wants me.* I couldn't have gone with Emi and the others anyway, so it was good we'd been separated. Tristan would have followed me right to them.

But where was Saya? Where was Emi? Hirose?

My thirst grew, driving back any other thought. I licked my lips, my tongue thick and swollen. I slowed to a walk, gazing at the hills about me. I shivered. A memory flickered through my mind—a landmark on a map in Cruelon's study—a waterfall. It had to be somewhere near me. *But where?*

My feet ate up slow mile after slow mile until the distant trickle of a stream finally came to my ears. My head cocked, I listened. It was hard to see anything through the dim light. I looked about the forest, noticing for the first time that the rockiness had disappeared and the ground felt spongy underfoot. Tall evergreens surrounded me.

I had to adjust my course a few times as the sound of water faded, grew stronger, and faded again. Taking another step forward, I gasped as my foot encountered empty space. I lashed out, my hand encountering an overhanging branch just strong enough to hold me. I pushed on it, hard, and propelled myself back onto solid ground. Sitting down, my breaths coming in gasps, my head pounding, I stared down at the void below me.

A hole? I skirted it with careful steps, following the sound of rushing water as it grew clear and loud. I felt it before I saw it. The ground grew muddy, and my boots grew damp. *There.* I stooped down and dipped my hands into the icy water running by. It was so dark now. Taking a deep draught, I felt my shoulders relax a little as the dizziness receded. I sank to the ground and leaned against a tree, listening to the sounds of the rushing water. Shivering, I wrapped my arms around myself and closed my eyes.

Chapter Twenty-Seven

My nose twitched. The dream holding me within its nightmarish throes began to dissipate. I blinked, but my eyelids were heavy and fell closed again. *The smell* ... A welcome heat warmed my body. I turned my face and my eyes fluttered open.

A cloaked figure crouched in front of me. I stiffened, my hand dropping to the familiar weight of the katana at my side. It was still there.

"Good morning."

The voice was confident, quiet, and sure ...

Adnan. Relief filled my body. I sat up, my cloak falling away from me with the movement. "Adnan. What—how—"

He stood and moved back a little to sit by the fire.

Anger grew inside of me. "Good morning is all you have to say?" I spat, trying to disentangle myself from the cloak which had wrapped around my legs. "Do you know what's been going on?" I turned my head to dash away the tears that had begun to fall. *Why am I so angry?*

"Here."

I looked up to see Adnan holding out some water and food.

"Come eat. You'll feel better for it." Sympathy poured out of his warm green eyes, but his jaw was clenched, and I could see the tension radiating from his raised shoulders.

My knuckles whitened, still gripping the hilt. I tried to banish the tears threatening to fall.

A hand touched my shoulder lightly. "You're angry because I left."

I stared down at the ground. *He's right.* I *was* angry. I was angry he'd left me on my own again. I was angry he hadn't been there when I'd needed him. "I wish you'd been there," I managed to say.

He gripped my chin and drew it up. "I know," he spoke, his words halting and slow. "I regret leaving you, but I felt I had to leave. I can explain."

I raised an eyebrow. *Nani.* "Did you find her?"

Adnan's hand fell away. He crouched down. "I did." He took my hand in his trembling one, unable to keep the passion and frustration from ringing with each word. "Are you ready to hear me out?"

My lips opened and closed. "Of course," I whispered, feeling the anger extinguish. Even as the words left my lips, I knew I wasn't angry. I was hurt, and even that had begun to ebb away. Now that he crouched down in front of me, his green eyes gazing into mine, I felt as though things might be okay. Stubble lined his chin and cheeks, and weariness filled the lines and dark circles beneath his eyes.

I released my grip on the katana's hilt. "I'm glad you're here."

Adnan smiled. "Come eat." He led me over to the fire and sat down close beside me.

Neither of us spoke as he watched me wolf down the food. I sighed after the last bite disappeared.

"Better?" he asked, handing me a bit of cloth to wipe my hands on.

"It was the first thing I've eaten since dawn yesterday," I admitted. "When did you find me?"

"Middle of the night, not too long after you fell asleep, I think. At first, I thought you might be dead. You didn't even stir when I checked your pulse, and there's barely a patch on you without dried blood, but most of your wounds seem superficial." His eyes scanned me from head to toe. "One hell of a fight it must have been."

"How did you find me?"

Adnan sat back and stretched his legs out in front of him. "I think I'd best explain what happened while I was away, first. Otherwise, this won't make much sense."

I scooted backward. Pain lanced through and up through my arm. I groaned and swayed, cradling it to my chest.

"Juliet! What's wrong?"

"It's my wrist," I ground out. "I can explain later."

Adnan knelt next to me and held my wrist with gentle fingers. As he prodded it, I winced, fighting to keep from passing out. "It's broken. I'll need to reset it. Here, bite on this."

I opened my mouth and bit down on the leather.

"On the count of three. One—"

"Are you sure you know what you're doing?" I mumbled, unsure if he could even understand me. My heart raced.

"Three."

With a sharp crack, fresh, furious waves of pain wracked my wrist and arm. Tears stung my eyes and ran down my cheeks. A ripping sound bit through the air as Adnan tore a strip off his cloak.

He took hold of my arm. "Here. We'll need to fashion some sort of splint. Keep your arm as level as possible."

I nodded, watching him through the haze of tears. Adnan fashioned the splint and then secured a sling around my neck and shoulders. The pain had receded some, but it still throbbed as though all hell had broken loose.

With a gentle touch, Adnan reached up and wiped away my tears.

"That hurt like—like—" I spluttered.

He smiled. "You'll feel better for it."

"Perhaps," I replied as a shiver wracked my body. Without a word, Adnan sat next to me against a tree, pulling the cloak over both of us.

I leaned my head against his shoulder as I stared into the fire. "Your story?"

He took a deep breath and cleared his throat. "My suspicions began when we stormed the fortress to rescue you. I couldn't put my finger on what, exactly, but there were certain pieces of information that were missing or didn't make sense." He paused and shifted a little. "When I got back and found out everything that had happened in my absence, I—Tristan wanted to rescue you."

I watched the green branches of the tall evergreens rustle in the breeze. *He's not telling me everything.*

"In private, he was all reserved," Adnan recalled. "But publicly, he acted the torn and ravished man. It stirred his people up. If he had not made a big pretense of holding them back for some hidden reason of his own, they would have all been at Cruelon's castle immediately." Adnan paused and stared into the dying fire. "You really have become a symbol to them all."

I snorted.

Adnan continued, ignoring me. "As it happened, more and more streamed to Tristan's banner. All the while, he received word that yet more would come. He held me at bay, kept me from council meetings, kept me from acting on my suspicions because they were just that—suspicions. When it came time for the attack, it was easy." Adnan looked at me. "Cruelon wasn't expecting it. No one was." He halted, and I shifted my head to glance up at him. He stared straight ahead. "Are you engaged to him?"

"Adnan, it's not that simple."

He stiffened.

"It's an unfair question," I protested with a small shake of my head.

"It just requires a yes or no answer."

"It's not that *simple*," I retorted. "He asked me, and I didn't say no; I also didn't say yes. I didn't know what to do, and part of me was attracted to him. He was charming, handsome—"

Adnan barked out a bitter laugh, startling me.

"But I don't love him, and I never did," I said as I wondered why I felt such a strong urge to reassure him. "I regretted that decision from the beginning. I thought I was doing it for you, for Saya, and for everyone else living under Cruelon's tyranny. Little did I know I played right into his hands." I struggled to sit up so I could face Adnan. "And you, you were so distant. You receded into a shell that I wasn't allowed to enter, even more than normal. It wasn't the first time, but it was the worst time." I let all my frustration with him underline my accusations. *Listen to me,* I thought, hoping he would take my words to heart.

His shoulders folded, and his gaze left me to land on the fire. "I had to leave at first because he held much over the three of us, and I had to follow his orders. This last time, though ..." He hesitated and a muscle pulsed in his neck. "This time, I had to leave because I couldn't stand watching you with him. You were on your way to being engaged, if not married, and I couldn't think with you around. Besides, I had to find Nani. I needed answers."

Hope and confusion warred within me. I waited with my breath held, hoping he would keep opening up, that he wouldn't stop. *Not again.* I ignored the sound of birdcalls heralding the morning.

"It's the last time I'll ever leave," Adnan stated, his voice low.

I tensed, but couldn't bring myself to ask what he meant. A breeze blew through the trees, sending the fire into a dance. I stared into the flames, ignoring the chill that swept over me. "You shouldn't promise that." I felt him take a deep breath and expel it as though gathering himself.

"I won't leave. And this time—" he hesitated. "This time I left a note. I had hoped you would understand the cryptic message."

"I did," I replied. Grimacing, I admitted, "I would've been a lot angrier if you'd left without a word." When he didn't say anything, I glanced up at him. "Did you succeed?"

Adnan blinked and looked at me, a question in his raised brow.

"Did you find her?"

"Yes, but it was too late." Adnan sighed and stirred the fire with a stick before adding a little more wood to it.

"What did you find out?"

His broad shoulders rose in a shrug. "I found her, alive and well." Adnan relaxed a little. "I'd had a suspicion about her for a while now, but hadn't had a chance or a reason to dig deeper. I knew Tristan was sending Haniel somewhere with money at regular intervals, but only had an idea of where, and it wasn't until later that I wondered if she could be the one he was supporting."

I shivered and held my hands out to the small fire.

He paused and tucked his cloak in around me. "She told me she had no idea why Tristan would lie about her being alive, but also that she hadn't seen him in some time, not since the Uprising had really grown in stature and power. And that wasn't all. Tristan lied about how he escaped from his family's massacre—he rescued his nani, not the other way around. He had come to her rooms, gotten her away from the palace, and into the night like he wanted us to believe. But he could only have escaped with her if he'd known the attacks were coming, if he'd had time to plan a getaway and get rid of the entire family, leaving him the sole heir to the throne, without any challengers."

"I know." I picked up the water skin and took a drink. "Tristan admitted to it when I challenged him."

Adnan's jaw dropped.

I could have laughed if not for the gravity of the conversation.

"You already know?" he repeated with his mouth still agape.

"Yes, but what I don't understand is how Cruelon escaped. If Tristan was going to kill his entire family, why leave out Cruelon? And how old was he when he planned this? How could he have had them all killed?"

Adnan sighed, and a small cloud filled the air in front of his mouth. "He was twelve."

So young.

"Why did he leave his nani alive?"

"She truly did—does—love him. That was reason enough for him."

"She helped?"

He shook his head. "No. She knew nothing before that night. But she did become his accomplice after that. Said there's good in his heart. That he had—and *has*—a chance of redemption." A wistfulness seemed to fill his voice as he finished.

I snorted, my body trembling with anger. "If she'd spoken up sooner—"

"No. She wouldn't have if I hadn't spoken to her. He keeps her alive, and she's grateful. She's been twisted by her love for him, and we both know how much of a manipulator he's proven to be."

I ignored the knowing glance Adnan sent my way. My fingers played with the leather of the water skin.

"Tristan is irrational," Adnan snapped. "I think all of this has shown that. A twelve-year-old plotted to have his entire family killed so he could not only be assured of the throne but have no competition or fear of such." Adnan's fingers played with the hilt of his sword. "Cruelon should have died as well, but he was called away without Tristan's knowledge. Cruelon was the one part of the plan that went awry that night. He was not to be found."

I sputtered on the drink of water I had just taken. "You're saying the entire royal family was in the same place, except for Cruelon?"

Adnan crossed his arms behind his head. "Yes. They were at the royal palace. The royal family was not too large, and yes, they liked the comforts of being the royal family and were pretty close-knit, from what I have heard."

"Tristan's obsessive," I murmured. "He's proven that with me. He means to have me." *Like you did, apparently.* The thought leapt into my head. *The guard said Adnan had asked for me, wanted me, and Cruelon had laughed.*

Adnan stiffened, his muscles tensing.

Cruelon practically forced me to join his harem. Tristan tried to force me to marry him. I shook my head and drew my knees up. "No matter what it costs," I continued. "I think he would rather kill me than let me out of his reach." I leaned forward. "I mean it, Adnan. I can see you don't believe me, but it's true. I knew it that night. If he can't have me, he'll kill me."

Adnan didn't answer, but his boot tapped a strange rhythm on the ground.

"How did you find Nani?" I asked, changing the subject.

"I have my ways."

Again with the secrets. I rolled my eyes. "That's no answer."

"It'll have to suffice for now," he replied, looking at me. I glanced back at the trees surrounding us, the light dappling the ground as the rare winter sun shone through the breaks in the clouds. I had to look away. I couldn't see the darkness deep within Adnan's eyes. I'd seen it before, barest glimpses, brief but deep enough to send a thrill of curiosity, fear, and even allure through me.

I clenched my hand under my cloak and shivered. *I want to press him. I want to so much it hurts.* I could admit it to myself, but not out loud. There had been times I'd tried before, and it always ended without answers, without him lowering the shield he kept raised around himself. *Even now, he gazes into the distance, so much hanging over him.*

Adnan leaned forward and added a few dry sticks to the fire. "He won't have you, Juliet."

I jerked a little, startled at the sound of his voice. My stomach roiled as disgust grew from a seed to a pit deep down. "He won't stop."

Kill me. An idea grew from an ember.

"Then you'll leave."

I barely heard Adnan's words. *Paranoid—he's paranoid. He won't stop. It can't be anyone else. He'll want to do it himself. He'll want to give me one last chance.*

Tapping my finger against my leg in tune to the thoughts bouncing around my head, I wondered if it would work. I knew Adnan wouldn't stop until Tristan was off the throne ... or would he? Would he continue fighting? Saya would. *Where is she? And Emi ...*

"What's wrong?" Adnan asked. "You look lost."

The idea burned brighter. "I know what I have to do."

He cocked his head to the side. "Oh?"

I turned from the fire to face him. "I'm the chink in his armor. Think about it."

Adnan held up a hand. "No. You are leaving. I'm escorting you back to the portal you came through. You're done here."

"Adnan—"

Adnan interrupted as though I hadn't spoken. "Whatever you're thinking, Juliet, no. He won't stop. It's time for you to leave. You'll be out of his reach that way."

"But—"

"I won't have you offer yourself up to him."

"I *don't* mean to offer myself up to him," I blurted out, raising my voice. "At least, not like that. I am his weakness, and I think we can use that to our advantage."

Adnan shook his head.

"Adnan, you can't do this. It is my decision to do this if I want to. You can't tell me what to do. You don't have that right." I moved away from him. "We don't know where Saya is, and there are others. Do you want to leave Tristan on the throne?"

He rolled his shoulders back. "No, but it's not our fight."

"Isn't it, though?" I pressed. "Has everything we've done been for nothing, then?"

Adnan's lips thinned as a storm cloud seemed to rest over his facial features.

"I could go home and leave," I agreed, leaning forward. "But I would always wonder, and it would drive me insane! And you—you would move on and leave the people here under a worse ruler than even Cruelon was?"

"Juliet—"

"If we can find Hirose and the others who escaped, they'll help. I know it."

"Hirose?" Adnan blinked. "What does *he* have to do with this?"

I ignored the steely tone of his voice. "I don't know if he's alive or not, but I think he'd help."

Adnan frowned. "Why him?"

"He helped before. We couldn't have done it without him and his men. They protected me."

"Fine." Adnan folded his arms across his chest. "What's your plan?"

"So you'll do it?"

"I didn't say that, but I might as well hear what you're thinking. You'll tell me anyway," he added in an undertone.

"If I were to send word," I began, the idea forming as I spoke, "telling Tristan I would be at some location of our choosing and promising to turn myself in or talk or something of that sort, I think he would come."

Adnan shrugged his narrow shoulders. "Likely."

I shifted into a more comfortable position on the ground. "He knows how much I care for others. I think if I could convince him I'm doing this out of self-sacrifice, wanting his promise that he won't harm anyone, he'll buy it."

Adnan considered my idea. "True, but why should he believe you?"

"Because I've used the same arguments before."

He shook his head. "Sounds like a poor demand to me. He'll see right through it."

"But will he think through it that much if he thinks he'll have me no matter what? So, do we have a plan?"

Adnan sighed. "If you can call it that. Very well. Most of those who left the castle went north. I tracked them a little ways before realizing you headed east and so left their trail behind." He looked down. "Now tell me how you injured your wrist."

A stick cracked. I glanced over my shoulder and watched as it burned. "I leapt over the castle wall."

"What?"

"Yes." I grinned, enjoying his disbelief.

"How? What happened that night?"

I took a deep breath and gave him a quick rundown of the events that led to that night, then how the plan was unfolded. "I didn't *want* to jump off the wall, but in that moment, it was the only choice. I'd waited too long, and I wasn't going to stay there."

Adnan leaned back against the tree again and stretched his long legs out in front of him. Seeing me shiver, he beckoned, and I sat down next to him, my back to the tree.

"That was impressive," he whispered. "Your whole plan, the execution."

A blossom of warmth bloomed within me. "My wedding was to be that morning, you know." The words left my lips before I knew why I said them.

"I know."

I stiffened. "How?"

"I have my sources." He chuckled and beckoned to me.

I scooted over. He drew in the cloak closer around both of us.

"I wish I could take it all back."

He shifted and his arm flexed about my shoulders. "You're not a seer."

"True," I muttered. *A seer.* We still didn't know who Cruelon's seer was. *Would we ever know?* The women were supposed to escape along with Hirose's men, but did they make it out?

Frustration grew inside of me, and my stomach fought against a sudden queasiness. *Do I have a shot at redemption? I've used myself as bait one way or another, become different people, done so much …*

I sniffed. My throat constricted, and I closed my eyes against the agony filling my soul. A pit existed within me. A deep, dark pit. *Who am I? Who have I become?*

Adnan stirred and laid a hand on my leg. I looked up at him. "Juliet, stop."

I blinked. *Stop what?* My hand trembled, and waves of pain throbbed through my wrist and hand.

"No more," Adnan asserted. "Turn your mind away from what I know is tormenting you inside. There is nothing you can change; there is no going back. If you do not move forward, if you do not take the next step, then you are lost. You cannot live regretting your past, not like this. Take these memories, learn from them, use them, and do not repeat your mistakes." He inhaled, and his hand tightened where it rested on my thigh. "By the gods, I wish I could change what happened. I wish I'd been strong enough to send you back, take you myself, before—" A tremor ran through his voice.

"You did try," I whispered.

He didn't break his stare. Anger, frustration, and something I couldn't place radiated out through his green eyes. "I can't change anything either. You have to learn to live with your past, or you don't."

"But—" My voice broke.

"I know you, Juliet. Don't forget that. You are not the only person who makes mistakes. You aren't the only person who has to live with their decisions or things done to them." Adnan sighed before he continued. "I know I bear blame. I know I can't disappear, pretending ignorance or forgetfulness of what we've been through, but you can't either. It would destroy you."

I licked my lips. "It feels like it has only just begun to settle in. As though I stand on the brink of something, and I'm not sure which way I will fall."

"I'm not leaving you, Juliet. I'm here."

I laid my head on the front of his shoulder. The tremble in my hand faded. *He's here. He's always been here in the way that Tristan never was.* I listened to his faint heartbeat. Fear had filled every corner of my body and mind, but now it dissipated, sliver by sliver. Hope blossomed within me, a light that had begun as a flicker but flared into a torch, burning bright.

I know what I have to do. I clenched my jaw. *This isn't over, not yet.*

CHAPTER TWENTY-EIGHT

A rough hand, the movements gentle, brushed against my face before dropping onto my shoulder. "Juliet, it's time."

I tried to open my eyes, but they felt so heavy. I couldn't even shift, my body disobeying the weak commands my brain tried to send. Sleep began enfolding me again—

"Juliet, we have to go." The voice was more insistent this time.

"Yes," I murmured but didn't move.

Adnan pulled me into a sitting position. "Here, drink this."

"I'm awake, I'm awake," I mumbled around a wide yawn. "What is it?"

"It'll help. Just drink."

Too many orders. Tristan liked giving me orders. He *loved* giving me orders. I gritted my teeth and sniffed. My nose wrinkled. "What *is* this?"

"Drink."

I raised an eyebrow at him but sipped at the hot tea, grimacing at the bitter taste coating my mouth. With each drink, energy flowed back into my body in tiny, trickling amounts. Curling my legs underneath me, I shifted my sling so that my arm lay more comfortably.

"It's sunset," I noted, gazing out over the trees.

Adnan glanced up from where he rolled up his pack. "Yes, and we have much ground to cover." He handed me a packet of dried meat. "It's not a lot, but eat up. You'll need your energy."

I took a bite. "I—"

"No," Adnan interrupted with a slight smile. "Rest and eat. I'll make sure no traces of the camp remain."

"How did you know what I was going to say?" I asked around chewing the tough meat.

He turned and slid things into his pack. "Because I know you."

· · ·

Our feet ate up the miles slower than I would've liked. Adnan led the way, and I followed in his shadow. There were things I wanted to ask and say, but what little energy I had was needed for the grueling march. As the landscape passed, so did time. The sun continued its path along the sky, hidden behind gray clouds.

As night drove back the day, we paused on the rise of a hill. Adnan pointed down. "Should be them."

I peered down at a small group of figures at the foot of the hill. A small curl of smoke rose from a fire. "Looks like most of Hirose's men are down there." I breathed a sigh of relief. "They must have made it out."

"What history do you have with him?" Adnan asked, staring at me.

I shifted on my feet and winced as the throbbing grew in my wrist. "What do you mean?"

His lips parted and closed again. "Do you trust him?" he replied.

I considered him, my eyes narrowing as annoyance washed over me. *That's not what he was going to say.* Again, he was keeping something from me. I shrugged. "Not completely, but enough. I think he's honorable. He needs to be given the chance to prove it and given the confidence. It was he who carried out Cruelon's orders," I admitted, remembering the harsh way I'd been treated. "When I was in the dungeon for a day," I explained bitterly.

Adnan's face darkened and fire seemed to blaze within his eyes. "He put you in the dungeon?" His tone was ice cold.

"*Cruelon* did. Hirose was following orders."

"And you trust him?"

I looked back down at the men far below. "No, not completely, but enough to ask for his help."

Adnan took my hand and squeezed it. "What else happened there?"

I shivered. *Do I want to say?* The memories haunted me. How long would they continue to haunt me? "I ..." I began, hesitant. "Cruelon wanted me,

Adnan. Just like Tristan, except, perhaps, not to marry me," I added with a small smile. I peeked at Adnan's hand holding my own. It was rough, calloused, large. "I don't think Hirose is a bad man. I think he truly wished things weren't the way they were, but saw no way to do anything about it until Cruelon was dead."

Adnan studied me. "Every man makes his choices and must live or die by them. Hirose made his with you. But he did save you from Tristan in a way. Did he ever say a word to you of how he may feel?"

My eyebrows rose. "Feel? Feel what?"

Adnan released my hand and brushed his hair back. "A man like him doesn't go to battle for *any* woman."

Again with the secrets! I wanted to yell it out loud. Taking a deep breath, I chose my words with care. "I am really beginning to think you like irritating me by giving me hints of your thoughts and leaving me to figure out the rest of what you don't say." I frowned and picked up a small stick, which I twiddled in my fingers. "Fine, I'll bite. You're saying Hirose has feelings for me, and that's the only reason he did as he did. Either way, he still protected me, to an extent."

"It's no matter," Adnan replied, swiping his hand across the air in a dismissive manner.

"Oh, it's not? Then why did you bring it up?"

A glimmer of laughter entered his eyes. "We probably should head down. At this rate, we won't be there before dusk."

I grunted. "Let's go, then."

Adnan led the way down the slope, his long legs taking slow, measured steps so as not to leave me behind. "Now we'll find out whether it is to be death or life for us."

I rolled my eyes. "Don't be so morbid. Hirose won't kill us."

"We'll see."

⁂

On my knees, I cradled my wrapped arm, Adnan's shoulder brushing my own. "Hirose, listen—"

Hirose shook his head. "I have listened to Benkei. What could *you* possibly have to say that would add to his argument? There is no reason for me or my men to take down the new king. We've lost enough."

"What would you do?" I pressed, grasping at straws. From the moment we had been spotted by his sentries, my hope had been dwindling.

Hirose threw his head back and laughed. "There are many other countries in this world, Juliet Barrows."

"But you owe me a debt. I saved your life."

"And I saved yours," he returned, widening his stance as he stared down at me. "Why not come with us?"

I blinked, my jaw dropping at the suggestion. *Adnan was right.* I ignored the sudden pressure as Adnan's shoulder bumped mine. I knew it wasn't an accident. Ignoring Hirose's question, I almost growled out my next words. "Hirose, this is your country, your people. Haven't you let things go far enough?"

Anger laced his tone. "Excuse me?"

"You are the taisho of the Black Guard. You could do something. You could rally your men, rally those possibly still alive in the castle." My uninjured hand flung through the air as I spoke. "I know you care."

Hirose turned away, his arms folded across his chest.

I sighed, my shoulders slumping. It was no use. *He won't change his mind.* "Hirose."

Adnan's solemn voice broke my reverie. I looked at him, surprised he had spoken. Even Hirose returned to face him, a suspicious gleam in his eyes.

"I know you want to regain the honor you feel you have lost."

Hirose stiffened as Adnan spoke.

My gaze shot back and forth between the two men.

"A debt of honor is everything, is it not?" Adnan kept his voice neutral, but a sort of heaviness seemed to hang in the air. Even Hirose's men had gone deathly quiet.

"Hirose," I interrupted. "You've gone against king and country even before Tristan sat on the throne, haven't you?" I ignored the murmurers coming from the men watching as they heard my words. "You tried to be a shield between me and Cruelon."

Hirose's narrow shoulders tensed. His fingers played with the worn hilt of his sword.

I took a deep breath. "Hirose, remember what I told you. If you had more strength to stand up for your beliefs—"

Hirose's face reddened. "You think I should hang up my sword like some farmer?" Laced with fury, his voice grew in volume. "Turn my back on what I know?"

"You know that's not what I mean." I hesitated, choosing my words with care. "Loyalty is one thing, but to the wrong person, it corrupts you. I think you have more honor than even you care to admit. You care about the men you fight for. You care about the servants. You care for me. You were willing to sacrifice your own life that night so that we all might live."

Adnan stiffened again.

Does he disagree with me?

"Tristan will be a more tyrannical ruler than Cruelon ever was," Adnan interrupted. He stood, and no one made a move to stop him. "He will bring misery and ruin to the Ryujin people. If you abandon this cause, you abandon them. And that is not the way of your people. Your honor means everything. We are giving you a chance to redeem it now."

Sadness filled Hirose's eyes.

"Hirose," Adnan began. "You're a smart man. If we overthrow Tristan, someone will be needed to take his place."

"Adnan!" I exclaimed, stumbling to my feet.

"What say you?" Adnan asked, ignoring me.

"I have made more mistakes than you could ever know," Hirose replied, shaking his head. "You have only known me a few brief weeks, and yet you put me forth as the next king?"

Adnan took a step forward. "I think you could be the man Juliet speaks of. I think even your hesitation now shows it to be true."

Hirose gripped his sword hilt. "What if I don't want to rule?"

"Is there someone else you can think of?" Adnan questioned, glancing about as though someone else who could take the throne was standing there.

"Yes."

The answer surprised me. "Who?" I asked, peering toward Hirose's men who watched us in silence.

"Who else?"

I followed Hirose's line of sight to Adnan, his face registering the same shock as mine.

Why hadn't I thought of that? Why did I not want to think of it?

"No," Adnan said with a frown.

Hirose's jaw tightened. "And why not?"

"I am not the man for the job. I don't want it."

Same answer. Either could take it, yet neither wanted it. I curled my toes within my boots, waiting for one of them to say something.

Hirose smiled with a smug look. He inclined his head in recognition of Adnan. "Even to make sure someone like Cruelon or Tristan wouldn't take it next?"

"Yes, if I had to," Adnan admitted, shooting Hirose a glare. "But that isn't the question here. I know you don't want the throne, same as me. But you know me. You know my history. You should be the next ruler, at least for now. Put the country back on its feet, rule without fear, as it used to be in the days before us."

The two men eyed one another while I looked back and forth between them. The longer it stretched on, the more the air seemed to sparkle with anticipation.

"Answer me this: Why?" Hirose implored.

"I don't want it."

"You don't want the power, prestige, and wealth that come with the throne? To make those under you bow, to be secure in the knowledge of your strength, of the importance of your position?"

Like Tristan. My breathing quickened.

"No."

I couldn't help the sigh of relief that escaped my lips.

Hirose put his hand on his sword hilt and smiled. "All the rumors are false, then."

"Rumors?" I echoed, but neither man even looked at me.

Hirose's smile deepened. "Very well."

"Rumors? What rumors?" I asked again.

Hirose didn't break his gaze on Adnan. "You've told her nothing, then?"

Adnan's jaw tightened, his eyes narrowing before returning to its usual nonchalance so fast I could've been imagining it. But I knew better.

"Adnan?" I reached out to touch his sleeve.

"Hirose," he growled. "I'd advise you to mind your words. You do not know of what you speak."

"Really?" Hirose laughed, but there was no mirth in it. "But I think she does, or at least has an inkling."

I opened my lips, but Adnan laid a gentle finger on them. "Not now." He glanced at Hirose. "Later."

"You promise?" I asked, wary of the secrets he continued to keep. *Tristan knows more, Cruelon knew more, and now even Hirose knows more about him than I do.*

"I give you my word." His head lowered to look down at me.

He means it. I felt the skin of his hand whisper against my own before clasping it—a quick, tight grasp and release. Hirose moved to the side and glanced about as though to make sure none of his men were within hearing distance.

"I have lost the honor required for a position such as this," Hirose stated, hanging his head.

With Adnan close beside me, I followed.

"What do you mean?" I asked, not understanding.

"It would be a lie," Hirose continued, but more to himself than us. "I should have fought to the death; instead, I surrendered to Tristan. Not just my life, but those of my men. I do not even know why they still follow me." He looked up and surveyed the busy soldiers around us.

Adnan stopped close beside him. "They follow you because they are loyal."

"Why?" Hirose's hands clenched, and he took a step closer. "Why!"

"Because you realized their lives were of more value alive than dead. You realized it wasn't a cause worth dying for."

"I had pledged my allegiance—my life—to Cruelon. My job was to die for him. Death before dishonor. I dishonored my position, my men, and myself. Yet I could not do it. I could not take my own life, not while those of my men hung in the balance, but I considered it." A harsh cackle escaped his lips. "I considered it, but I could not do it. What kind of quality is that in a king?"

Silence stretched the air taut.

"I don't understand," I murmured.

Adnan ignored me as he addressed Hirose. "You showed more strength in saving the lives of your men than in sending them all to their deaths, and to saving yours as well."

Hirose's shoulders slumped. "That is not our way."

"I know," Adnan agreed, laying a hand on Hirose's shoulder. "But I think you know what you did was right, though deep down you war with yourself because of what you have grown up with and the things that have been instilled within you."

"It is our culture—our tradition," Hirose spat, but his tone had begun to lose its sting.

"Traditions are not always right. You know this to be true." Adnan pointed at Hirose. "Do you think Cruelon was a just and good king?"

"He was a tyrant."

"And Tristan?"

Hirose gritted his teeth and shrugged. "Cut from the same cloth."

"Hirose, I won't try and change your mind," Adnan said, his voice slow and deep. "This is your battle, but know that because of your decision to defy tradition and risk dishonor for you and your men, you might be the man the people need right now."

Hirose sighed but said nothing.

Adnan clasped him on the forearm. "Now, how many men do you have?"

Hirose cleared his throat. "Just under two dozen. We lost some that night." He glanced at me as he led Adnan over to a tent. The two men's heads were bowed, each vying to talk over the other, already discussing ideas and plans.

Without me. I stared after them, debating whether to follow. Again, I was left out of the planning. This time, it was my idea to begin with. *He hadn't even bothered asking me if I wanted to join.* I stamped my foot in frustration. My wrist bumped against my belly, sending shooting pain up my arm. I bit back a scream of frustration.

A rustle of clothing alerted me to a man striding up to me with some bedding.

"Here." He offered the items. "If you want to rest, lay down close to the fire. When the food is ready, we'll bring some to you."

I glanced one last time at Adnan and Hirose before taking the bedding. The idea of sleep called to me. My stomach growled. *And food.* I took the bedding with my free hand and made my way to the blazing fire.

I'd dozed while waiting for the food and, after eating, dozed again. I wasn't sure how much time had passed before I woke to a slight pressure on my shoulder.

Adnan knelt next to me. "Sleep well?"

"Better than I have in a while," I admitted, adjusting my arm in its sling. "How's it going?"

His eyes hardened. "We're done. It'll happen in two days. Hirose is even now sending one of his men to Tristan."

"Two days," I echoed. *Too short for much planning, too long for anxiety and doubts to fester.*

"I'm going to go get some food." He stood up. "I'll come back in a little while. Try to get some more rest." He strode off without waiting for an answer, but before I could relax again, I heard footsteps approaching and turned to see Hirose.

"Juliet," he greeted, sitting down.

I sat up and then wished I hadn't. It was so cold without the warmth of the blanket. "Hirose, do you know if Saya got out? And Emi?"

"I don't, I'm sorry. I'll send a man out to the east, see if he can catch any word of them. But we've stayed close together, out of Tristan's way, and so we have not even had the whisper of a rumor."

"What's the plan?"

Hirose glanced in the direction Adnan had disappeared. "Benkei didn't explain?"

I shook my head.

"We picked a plateau near the fortress for you to meet Tristan," Hirose explained, searching my eyes with his own as he watched for my reactions. "It's just beyond the edges of a thick forest, where my men can hide. We'll meet at dawn. The rest, you can worry about later."

Or now. I grunted and slid my uninjured arm out of the blanket. "Why can't I know now?"

Hirose blinked. "Because there will be plenty of time later. Right now, it's important you rest."

"Yes," I snapped, my heart beating erratically in my chest. "But if I'm the one at the middle of this plan, I want to know what the plan is."

Hirose held up his hands as though to ward me off. "I'll let Benkei tell you."

I lay back down and stared up at the velvet sky filled with twinkling stars.

"He cares for you, you know." Hirose's words broke into my reverie. "He's a good man."

"I know," I said. Out of the corner of my eye, I saw Hirose glance at me. "Your point?"

"You know what my point is. You're holding back, keeping yourself penned up in a cage of your own making." He paused, and I strained to hear his next words. "Adnan knows your faults, your mistakes, your doubts, and uncertainties, but he also knows your strengths, your sense of humor, your care for others over yourself, your wit, charm, grace, beauty—" His words sounded heavier the more he spoke, and he paused for a moment. "He knows, but he is still by your side. Let him in. Don't push him away."

"I'm not," I began but stopped. It was true. I was letting him in, finding myself drawn to him, wanting to trust him, rely on him, but I had kept a part of myself from him, and he knew it. He wasn't Tristan.

Hirose stood. "I should go. He's coming back."

I glanced over to see Adnan's lean figure approaching. "So?"

Hirose bowed. "We've already talked long enough."

"What is that supposed to mean?"

"Ask him." Hirose smiled and left, his footsteps soft on the cold, damp ground.

"What's with you and Hirose?" I asked Adnan before he'd even had time to sit.

He arched an eyebrow. "Why?"

"Because Hirose just left when he saw you coming and told me he'd talked to me long enough already."

A small smile curved Adnan's lip.

I resisted the urge to flick an annoyed glare at him. "There's something, and I don't understand what it is or why."

"Did you ask him?"

I groaned in frustration. "I did, and he said to ask you."

Adnan shrugged and took a mouthful of food.

I sat up and pulled the blanket close around me. "Is it because you think he cares for me?"

"He's a good man, or will be."

This time I did shoot him a glare. "You didn't answer my question."

Adnan's shoulders rose.

"You're driving me crazy. You won't tell me, will you?"

He shook his head.

"You're really stubborn, and it's annoying." I pointed at him, my movements wild as I unleashed. "Actually, it's more than that. You can't continue keeping everything from me. I've had enough. Hirose said I could ask you, and so I am."

Another shrug, but this time I caught a twinkle in his eyes. He couldn't hide it this time. And then I saw the laughter building up inside him, the relaxed stance, and the playful grin he sent my way.

My insides warmed, and I looked up at the sky, the stars invisible due to the cloud cover. *Was he flirting with me?* I forced a serious look on my face. *He still needs to tell me.*

Adnan regarded me. His green eyes reflected the light from the fire. "Hirose is the other Benkei."

I stared at him, trying to make sense of what he'd said. *The other Benkei ...* I gasped. I could feel my face whitening. The time I'd been kidnapped by the hooded stranger and Boden swept through my mind. The scent of sweat, horse, the drugs—

"Juliet," Adnan murmured, gripping my hand in his.

The voice. I knew Hirose's voice had reminded me of something—of someone—not just from calling commands in the courtyard. *He's the same build.* Who else would Cruelon have trusted to send after me?

"Juliet," Adnan said again, pressing my hand.

I stared at him, unblinking.

"Are you all right?"

"What he did—" I began, unable to shake the fear holding me. Closing my eyes, I tried driving away the memories. They pulled me under, away from the present, leaving me wallowing in pain and hurt.

"Juliet, it is over now." Adnan gripped my hand, his voice a low hum in my ear. "You're safe now. Put them behind you. You're strong. Let it go."

I inhaled and looked at him.

"Hirose was following orders—" He held up a finger as I made to speak. "I'm not excusing what he did. But I think he truly regrets how he treated you."

"So all along, it was him?" I whispered. "He knew who I was when I arrived at Cruelon's court. He had spent a few days dragging me across the country, and I had no idea." My fear began to turn into anger.

"It was him," Adnan affirmed.

"I can't do this." I shook my head. "I can't go with him."

"You're not going with him. You're going with me." Adnan reached forward and brushed my hair out of my face, tucking it behind my ear. "Hirose's heart is changing. He has regrets in his past, same as I do."

I trembled. "I have to think about this."

Adnan scooted next to me and laid an arm around my shoulders. "You need rest. I'll be here. I'm not leaving you."

My gaze found the flames, flickering in the darkness. *Hirose kidnapped me. He made it seem like he was Adnan.*

"Did Hirose tell you anything about the plan?" Adnan asked, tightening his grip to get my attention.

I knew he was trying to distract me. "Not really. And what he did seems really simple."

Adnan gazed into the flames and lowered his voice. "Sometimes, that's the best sort of plan. Are you all right?"

I laughed, a shaky one that shook my core. "No."

"I won't let him harm you, Juliet—I swear."

Tristan. I looked over at Adnan, his shaggy brown hair almost falling to his cheeks, his eyes bright and clear, his stance rigid and controlled as he looked down at me. "I know," I whispered. "But sometimes we can't stop the inevitable."

So many things hung in the air. So many questions, so few answers. Confusion radiated through my entire being, as though so much hung in the balance, things that had attached themselves to me deep inside, a tether so tight it left me a husk around which encircled only questions and doubts.

Adnan had been there. *He'll be here again. It will be all right. Two more days.* I sighed.

Chapter Twenty-Nine

Endless war and bloodshed filled my mind. Panic, fear, tears, and faces—flitters of such—emotions frozen in time and place. Nightmares plagued me. Voices cried out with a hellish reality. Frantic cries from both men and women rent the air. Fear shook my body.

Everything blurred, the dream fading. I rose to the surface, struggling as though in thick, murky water. The sludge fought to pull me down as I strove to escape.

"Wake up!"

The force of the words jarred me. There. A lifeline. I locked onto the voice and opened my eyes. A dark shape loomed over me, and I recoiled. Hands grasped my shoulders.

"Juliet, it's me."

Adnan.

My body trembled. I buried my shaking hands under my cloak and took a deep breath, trying to calm my nerves.

Adnan tightened his grip as he stared down into my face. "Juliet, you're safe."

I couldn't speak. The images were still too real and the voices too loud as they rang in my head. Adnan brushed a hand over my head, his fingers catching in the tangles in my hair.

I took a deep breath. "I'm fine."

"No, you're not." He leaned back on his heels so he could look at me better. "Stop telling me that. More than that, stop telling yourself that. How long have these nightmares been going on for?"

"For a while. Since the village. But they've worsened."

Adnan peered at me and frowned. "There is a look in your face that you didn't use to have. I noticed it before, but I didn't realize it was that bad. What all happened in Cruelon's court?"

I shrugged. "It's been some time since I've had enough sleep. I'm sure that's made it worse."

He grunted. "Stop making excuses."

"I wasn't—"

"Yes, you were," he interrupted, sitting down in front of me. "You don't need to hide from me. Talk to me."

As you talk to me? I wanted to ask him, but the words wouldn't leave my mind and come out into the open. "Some nights are worse than others. It's not always this bad." I looked down at the ground. It felt like my walls were being cracked a little, and I wasn't sure I liked the feeling.

Adnan handed me a water skin. "You can talk to me."

His suggestion battered my senses. Within me, a dam broke forth, and as the words poured out—everything I'd felt, everything I'd experienced—I exposed the innermost parts of my soul to him. It grew easier as I spoke, as though this whole time I'd needed someone to listen, someone who wouldn't ask questions but who would hear every word and who would *understand.*

When I finished, I took a long, deep drink of water. *He hasn't always been there, but he's here now.* He had been there when it really counted, every time. *Unlike Tristan.* I could sense the anger radiating from Adnan in waves. *What is he thinking of?* I had told him all of it, even when Cruelon had spoken to me alone, his questions about my joining his harem, my agreeing, all of it. I continued to wait for him to say something, anything, but he didn't. A storm brewed in his eyes, one that fed the knot of worry plaguing the pit of my stomach.

"There's something else," I whispered, feeling short of breath even though I hadn't moved. "Tristan, he didn't just play me ..." I hesitated. "He played me against you. He tried to convince me you were a double agent or something like that. And I began to believe him. When I saw you that night in Cruelon's court, I believed him. I thought you'd betrayed us—me—and that it was all true." A tremor ran through me, and my voice trembled. "I'm sorry."

Adnan took my hands in his and leaned close. "Don't be sorry. You were manipulated by a master, and I gave you no cause to think otherwise."

The apology rang in his voice. *He pushed me away in the same ways Tristan did, always knowing better, always keeping me at an arm's distance.* "But I doubted you, after everything."

"Yes, but do you trust me now?"

I blinked. "Of course." *But trust is the beginning.* I wanted more of a foundation. *Trust needs to go even deeper.*

Adnan sat back and rolled his shoulders. "Then what's done is done. I shouldn't have left you. There were mistakes on everyone's part." He grimaced, his voice deepening. "No one is perfect, no matter how hard they try. Some are just less perfect than others. And you, Juliet, you are strong, courageous, and wise. You have enough strength to learn from your mistakes and move on, carry them with you, learn from them, and grow."

I lowered my head, and he leaned forward till our foreheads touched.

Adnan's hair fell loose, brushing against my face. He drew back. "Did you ever tell Tristan what you told me?"

"No, I didn't. Well, not what hurt the most."

"Why didn't you tell him?" he asked, his voice gentle.

"Because I didn't feel like I could. I couldn't open myself up to him like that. I knew I liked him a little, but he was a manipulator. I never saw the true him, and I never wanted the engagement. I couldn't say yes when he asked me because I don't love him." Letting go of the blanket I'd been clutching, I found myself leaning closer to Adnan. "Believe me."

A rare smile crossed Adnan's face. "I know I can never—" He growled and ran his hands through his brown hair. "I don't want you to do this. I don't want you anywhere near him."

"Do *you* trust me?" I asked, trying to hide the warm feeling his words had given me.

His lips opened and closed, and he nodded.

"Then will you tell me your past now?"

He chuckled, but it was bitter. "You hadn't forgotten?"

While I hoped it was a rhetorical question, still I pressed him. "Tell me, please. I want to know."

Adnan stiffened, and his jaw clenched. I waited, but he said nothing. Even with the thin moonlight shining from the sky above, I could see the war within him, the fear.

I clasped his arm. "Adnan, I want you to tell me when you're ready. I want to know. Just don't wait too long." I knew the words would sound like a warning, and in part, maybe they were.

"I will tell you. I am going to tell you, but not tonight. It is not a story for the dark of night, nor for when the terrors haunt you." He brushed back some of my hair with a gentle touch and pulled my cloak closer around me. "Tomorrow is going to be a long day. You should get some rest."

I nodded and lay down. I knew he would tell me. He kept his promises.

"I'm afraid to go to sleep." I knew I sounded like a little girl, but after my conversation with him, I felt as though I could say anything. *We've formed a new bond, a stronger bond.*

"I'm here. Go to sleep." Adnan sat next to me, his head tilted up toward the sky, his face cast in shadow.

"Thank you for coming after me, for saving me yet again," I murmured, lying down. "I couldn't do any of it without you."

"Go to sleep, Juliet." Adnan's hand touched my head, and he ran his fingers through my hair and over my scalp. A sort of peace descended over me, my mind free from the terror that had gripped me every time I went to close my eyes. A blanket of safety and security had covered me, and as I dropped off, Adnan's form was the last I saw before falling into a deep, dreamless sleep.

⁂

Dawn heralded us as we readied to leave. Pale beams of golden light rolled over the horizon until they became lost in the clouds overhead.

"Looks like a storm is coming," Adnan said, approaching me from where Hirose and his men loaded up their horses.

I yawned. Exhaustion filled my limbs and weighed down my spirit.

"Can we talk?" he asked, holding out his hand.

I took it and let him lead me out of Hirose's small camp and toward a craggy rock. We sat down on top of it, facing the sunrise. Everything seemed more serene than it had in a long time. The sun's orange and pink rays shot across the morning sky, chasing away the shadows and lingering darkness, and the high-pitched, yet melodic chirping and tweeting of small birds heralded the beginning of a new day. Fog lay low over the valley, misty and curling tendrils as they moved in the wind, and it was quiet, so quiet. For one moment, there was no mention of death or destruction.

My sleeve brushed against Adnan's. He was here. I wanted him here; he was the safety net that enclosed me. He watched the sunrise, his hand running through his hair to push it back out of his face, a motion that had become so familiar to me over time. His hand returned to his knee and stilled, his body motionless except for the rise and fall of his chest as his heart beat a steady rhythm.

"It's not that I don't trust you," Adnan began, hesitantly. "Or perhaps it was at first, but no longer—not in a while. By the time I did begin to trust you, I didn't want to tell you about my past."

I shifted to find a more comfortable position.

Adnan tapped his calf with his finger, inches above the handle of a knife protruding from his boot. "Earth ... where do you live?"

I blinked, surprised at the question. "In the northwest part of a large country. It's a state called Washington." I closed my eyes as memories flooded my mind of home. "Gig Harbor," I continued. "It's a small town lying along the Puget Sound. It's beautiful. There are so many trees and mountains, and everything is green. This—" I gestured with a sweeping hand. "This reminds me of home, but there are fewer evergreen trees here and less water, and it's flatter."

"Gig Harbor." The name rolled off his tongue with a strange intensity.

"Yes."

The birds in the trees chirped louder, their song swelling with the light of day.

Adnan stared off into the distance. "I knew someone else who came from your planet."

My breath caught. "What? How?" The questions tumbled out of my mouth as my foot tapped a rhythm on the rock. "Is that how you suspected? I know you did, back in Umi no Machi. I could tell you knew something about me."

"Yes. I suspected then and knew for sure soon after."

"Who is it?" I asked, watching as Adnan looked at the sunrise.

Adnan sighed. "He was so young when he first came over. Young and naïve, unable to take care of himself or fully understand what had even happened. He never found a way back, even when he tried ... It wasn't long ago that I was an assassin for hire." His shoulders tensed, and his skin paled a shade. "Sometimes, I was an assassin or a spy; other times, I was someone else. I was whomever I was needed to be. Always for war, for bloodshed, for when someone wanted a person dead, or an army thwarted. That's how they all know my name—Hirose, Cruelon, Tristan ... This isn't the only country I've served in some capacity or other. There are many countries, but always two names, Oniwaka and Benkei." Adnan unclenched his fingers and looked down at his hands. "Umi no Machi is where I settled down after a while." His eyes grew stony and expressionless. "I'm good at what I do, at what I've done. Strategist, assassin, tracker, commander, tactics trainer, sword-for-hire—that is the man I became."

I flinched at the pain filling his voice.

"Umi no Machi was a place I could stay between jobs. Nothing has helped banish the memories of what I have done from my mind. But with you ..." He hesitated. "With you, they have grown more distant. There are some happy memories intermixed now."

"Happy?" The question escaped before I could stop it.

"You've made me smile. I haven't done that in a long time."

The pain in those last words cut through me, and I sucked in a breath. "Adnan—"

He continued as though he hadn't heard me. "For years, stubbornness and the will to live has kept me going. My anger at Hirose ..." He shook his head, and his hands clenched. "I'm worse."

He is angry at Hirose. He's angry at what's been done to me. I reached out. "Adnan—"

"Juliet, listen to me. You don't know what I've done, what I've seen. Everything you've experienced is a mere glimpse of the pain and suffering that can happen in this world—in any lifetime."

"I knew you understood," I whispered. "I always knew. I didn't know why, but I knew. Every time I talked to you, every time something happened, you would jump to conclusions—conclusions that could've happened if things had gone a different way." I gripped his forearm. "But Adnan, you're not all you say you are."

His muscles tensed under my touch. He grimaced, and his teeth flashed in the growing light as he opened his lips. "Why do you think everyone has heard of me? Have you noticed how they avoid me? How they skirt around me? They are afraid, Juliet. They are afraid of what I can do, of who I am."

His arm flinched as he tried to move it, but I tightened my grip. "They're afraid of a legend."

He looked at me then.

"Oniwaka. Benkei. Even Saya told me."

Adnan's eyebrow rose. "When?"

"Long ago, back when she first heard Tristan mention those names." I shifted on the hard rock, drawing up my feet to rest on the rock. "But that isn't who you are now."

"Am I not? What have I been doing for Tristan?"

I shook my head. "No. Why else would you have done everything? You helped the townspeople, helped a cause against an abusive king, helped protect me, and even now, you're risking your life to end Tristan's tyranny." My foot slipped and my arms jerked, an involuntary movement. I winced as pain lanced through my injured wrist. "I don't think you are the man you're telling me you are. And I think even then, part of you cared for others more than yourself."

"Juliet—"

"You're not an aimless killer, Adnan!" I burst out.

"I didn't say I am," he said, a small smile lighting his lips. "I appreciate your advocacy for my character, but I'm trying to make you see that I'm not—"

"That you're not an average man," I finished, irritated. "I get it. I won't try to understand it all right now, to demand to know everything—maybe I never will—but I've seen enough of you to know that you are not someone I should stay away from. I know you well enough to know that if you thought you were, you would've left me long ago, knowing it would be better for me to be on my own than to have you near me. But you haven't left." I didn't even stop to take a breath as I continued. "Everyone has darkness within them, some with more, some with less, but I don't believe you to be evil. No one is born evil." I bit my lip and played with the hem of my cloak. "It's what you do with the life given to you that matters."

Adnan recoiled as though I'd slapped him in the face. "'You aren't born evil'?" he echoed. "Juliet, nothing is clear-cut black and white, no world, no creature, no human. Yes, you do have choices, we all do, but those are not always clear-cut either. There is darkness in everyone, *everyone*." Adnan's jaw clenched and his eyes narrowed, but his voice softened as he continued. "I hope you understand that someday."

"I didn't mean ... I think ..." I stopped, unsure of what to say. He was right. I didn't quite understand, and right now, I didn't quite know how to reach him. "People are complicated. This is complicated," I admitted. "But I think, even with the past you have, that your past doesn't define you."

"You're naïve," he said, so bluntly it physically hurt.

The urge to lash back at his hurtful words goaded me. "You think I haven't made mistakes I'm not proud of?" I knew my pain showed. I could feel the tears pricking my eyes as I twisted my hair in my fingers. "I've done things I wish I could take back. I've seen things I wish I hadn't, and those haunt me. Maybe they'll always haunt me, but you taught me to keep going, to learn from my mistakes, to move on, to always go forward without one foot hanging back in the past."

"Everything"—Adnan began, the words coming out strong and deep— "you have seen and done is a mere glimpse of what I've done and what I've seen done. The worst experience you've had pales in comparison to the horrors I've lived through."

In his eyes, I saw the anguish, the lack of fire. A pang radiated from my heart as I realized how far gone he was, how I'd misunderstood completely. My hand twitched, and my lips moved without forming words. Adnan didn't break his stare. Did he know how much I could see, deep inside? As the thought crossed my mind, it was as though a shutter flew closed and his eyes became clear and bright again, hiding his emotions so deep they had all but disappeared, but I saw the muscle in his cheek twitch. Tension radiated from him, washing over me until every nerve jumped with anticipation.

"You cannot understand," Adnan began, much quieter this time. "And I'm glad you cannot. I wouldn't wish it upon anyone, most of all you."

I leaned forward without realizing it as my thoughts turned in a different direction. I hadn't been irritated at him disagreeing; I'd been irritated because he might be right, because he was probably right, and deep down, I knew that possibility more than existed.

"I want to be there for you." I bit my lip, terrified at the words that now hung out in the air. *I have nothing left.*

"This is all a lot," Adnan whispered. "You'll have questions eventually. I'll try to answer them as best as I can. I am trying to make you understand that I'm no knight in shining armor." He flung out his arms.

I scanned him, with his worn leather boots, brown pants, and the travel-stained cloak covering the rest of him. "You could say that again."

Adnan laughed, a deep, throaty chuckle, over almost before it had begun.

"Benkei, Juliet, it's time."

We both turned as one to face Hirose on the ground a little below us.

"Everything is ready."

I took a deep breath. *Now for the next step.* I glanced once more at the beauty of the early morning sky. *Will it ever end?*

Chapter Thirty

The wind whipped my hair around my face, stinging my cheeks, and the long grass wavered, creating a billowing effect around my feet. Branches swayed behind me and leaves rustled. The forest seemed to groan as though waiting for what was to come.

Before me lay the plateau, long, narrow, and bare of anything save the dried weeds and grass, which were dull brown from the sun and the lack of rain. If I breathed through my nose, dust coated my airway, threatening to bring on a sneeze. If I breathed through my mouth, it choked me.

Any time now.

It was mid-morning. Tristan could make his appearance at any minute. *But where?* I shifted on my feet, half from anxiety and half from my limbs stiffening. I felt thirsty, yet I'd drunk not long before. Goosebumps spread over my skin, but I wasn't cold. My hair felt like it stuck straight up on the back of my neck, but it was just a feeling.

I didn't look around as I knew I wouldn't see them. Hirose and Adnan had hidden not long since, melting back into the trees and the scant scrub brush lying here and there. The plan was simple. I was to distract Tristan, keep him talking, until the moment was right for Adnan and Hirose and his men to come out. Another plan where so much could go wrong.

And after last night, even more so. I'd slept until morning, no memories of dreams, no waking up in cold sweats, and no bleary vision, when I awoke to find Adnan still sitting there, watching me. He'd smiled, we'd talked, and then I'd eaten while he gave me last-minute instructions. He'd had dark circles under his eyes, and I realized he'd barely slept.

He'd been watching over me.

A hawk circled high above. *This is it.* The wind shifted, and the faint drum of hooves floated with it. I drew a hand up to my eyes, shading them as I looked to the east, across the plain.

Riders.

With each second, they drew closer, the noise rumbling, the forms growing clearer. Tristan rode in front, the men on either side fanning out as if to form an arrow with him at the head.

An arrow to pierce my heart.

I knew they'd seen me. An eeriness fell over the plateau. The wind picked up until it seemed to whistle across the open plains.

Less than a quarter mile from me, Tristan raised his hand as he reined in his mount. He slid out of his saddle. *He's not coming any closer. He wants me to come to him.* I resisted looking over my shoulder and strode forward. This wasn't part of the plan. But it was only a short way. *Everything will be fine.*

As I neared, I recognized Haniel as one of Tristan's men. He didn't look at me, though I wanted him too. We had shared something deep, back in Haniel's village. We had shared in loss and pain. *He won't face me.*

Tristan's blond hair blew in the wind. The minutes slid by, slow and steady, until I stopped a couple yards in front of him. Goosebumps spread across my skin at the smug grin crossing his face. Why did I feel like I'd just been dealt a bad hand in a poker game? I was now farther from those who sought to protect me.

Tristan's men flanked him. There weren't many. Did he truly think I'd come alone?

I licked my lips, watching as his shirt blew in the wind, rippling across his muscular chest and shoulders. There was no rage in his eyes, nor anger. I stood my ground, willing myself to remain, to not move an inch backward, to not show any of the fear that rocked me to the core, telling me to run, run far away as fast as I could.

He placed his hands on his hips. "Hello, Juliet."

"Tristan," I acknowledged without the customary bow.

"You look lovely, as always." A small smile quirked his lips, and his blue eyes crinkled at the corners. He didn't say anything as his eyes raked over me from the top of my head down to my feet and back up again. I hated it. But that was his intention.

He took a step closer. "So it is true? You will marry me to save your friends?"

"Yes, but I must have your word, in front of witnesses." The words came out in a robotic manner as I followed a script given to me by Adnan.

Tristan grinned and spread his arms out wide. "That is the easy part. Why would I want to harm them? With you by my side and the throne beneath me, I have no qualms about sparing them. It would be an act of mercy on my part, a wedding gift to you." He bowed and swept a hand in a sarcastic salute. "I swear that I will not kill anyone with any ties or association to Juliet after we are married. No one who has her favor will ever be executed." His voice carried the words back to his men. He had brought his witnesses.

Empty words. I knew it; he knew it. An ongoing act, but this time on both of our parts. I wondered how close Adnan and Hirose were. *Can they hear us?* I resisted the urge to flick my eyes to the sides, looking for a single glimpse of Adnan. He was there ... somewhere.

"Why now, Juliet? Why come back? You could have left. You could have disappeared wherever you came from and not given any of us another thought." The words were bitter, but his gaze stayed locked on my own, and he took another step closer. There wasn't much distance between us now. "Does part of you care?" he whispered, his suave voice rolling over the plains, carried by the air. "I know this is hard. I know you are confused. I tricked you, deceived you, but I love you. I promise you that nothing I do will ever harm you. You can be sure of that."

I closed my eyes against the longing deep within the depths of his own, the echoes underlying his voice, earnest and quiet. What kind of fool did he think I was? How many other women had this worked on to gain so much confidence? Had he always been like this?

His family had been murdered, that much I did know. But he'd been a young boy, which is why everyone thought him the victim. Yet he claimed responsibility for the act. Had he always been twisted? Or had there ever been some good in him, even the smallest bit?

"I don't care." That wasn't what Adnan had instructed me to say. He wanted me to play along, but the words slipped out anyway.

"Yes, you do," Tristan said, his voice ringing with confidence. "You care, and that is why you are here. Maybe not for me, but you do care. You care about so many things, Juliet. But I care too. I care about what happens to you and what happens to this kingdom." Tristan paused, considering his words. "What could I do or say that would change your opinion of me? I am not completely lost. You can bring me back to the surface—bring me back from the depths I have fallen."

Beautiful words. Meaningless words.

I had already begun going off-script, so I scrapped the rest of it. "You could let me go back home and never harm Saya or Adnan."

Tristan's face reddened, his eyes seeming to flash fire. "Adnan, or the Unknown as you used to call him, has always held part of your heart, even before I met you. And no matter what I did to rid you of him, he kept coming back, and you continued to care for him. Even when you suspected he had betrayed you and everyone, you still had hope." His fists clenched at his sides. "All those missions meant to make you two distant, to separate you, to loosen the bond, the ties which had formed between you ... all of it was for nothing." Fury filled his words. "But he is gone, Juliet. He left of his own accord, and he never came back. Who knows where he is now? But *I* am here. *I* will take care of you. *I* will make sure he never sees you again." He stepped forward, pleading with me. His broad build moved like a cat, soothing and yet dangerous.

I backed up as his voice became so quiet and calm it was eerie. A stab of uncertainty shot through me. He continued to play a game, and I realized I didn't know what it was. Something was off. I rolled on the balls of my feet.

"Tristan," I began, refusing to glance over my shoulder. *Where is Adnan?* "Think about what you've done, what you are doing. You're doing all of this to yourself. Where has your heart gone? Do you have anything left of your soul, or has it completely sunk in darkness? It's not too late," I continued, shifting on my feet. "You can come back. It'll take time, but we—I—" I recovered, but it was too late. I hoped he hadn't noticed that slip of the tongue. "I can help you. Step down from the throne. Do you remember your mother? You told me a story about her once. You loved her. What would she think?" A trickle of sweat began to slide down my neck.

Pain filled his eyes, though he fought to control it.

I shook my head. "But it hurts, doesn't it? Do you honestly feel, deep down, that your actions are the right ones? That you have a right to control others' lives, decide who lives and who dies—play god?" I felt my hair loosen from the pins as the wind picked up. "That's what you're doing, Tristan. You're playing god, but you're not one. You're a man—a mortal—you can be hurt, you can die, you can disillusion yourself until you believe your own lies. And that's all you've done."

Tristan's fists shook at his sides, but I didn't know if it was from anger or two sides of himself warring with one another. "Beautiful words, Juliet. Any more I should listen to?"

He's not listening. I took a deep breath. "A mere man can't do everything. We're imperfect—full of faults, confidence, self-denial, fear, love, happiness, betrayal, sadness, doubts, and trust. We want to think of ourselves as the center of the universe, but you aren't, Tristan." I stepped forward and pointed at his chest. "You're not, I'm not, none of us are. One of man's greatest weaknesses, I think, is to believe everyone else must revolve around them as the Earth revolves around the sun."

Tristan laughed and crossed his arms. "And you are different, are you? Of course you are, or at least, you think you are, you who care more for those around you than yourself. You could have been long gone, but instead you are standing here in front of me. You could have left the country that night, but instead you gave yourself up to me to free Adnan and Saya." His tunic tightened across his chest as he threw his shoulders back. "You allied yourself with those who imprisoned you. You could have chosen not to go to Cruelon's as my spy, and yet you did. You gave away every chance to return to your world, and they were far more than most are given." Tristan flicked his fingers in the air.

I glanced over his shoulder toward his men but saw no movement.

Tristan approached with a slow tread, and I mirrored the movement, stepping backward, trying to keep a little distance between us. "What do you fear, Juliet? Do you fear anything?"

Another step, and another step back.

My breathing grew rapid. "I—we fear everything and everyone, whether it be a little or a lot. We fear our emotions, our feelings, ourselves—but fear is a fickle thing. Tristan, you can learn to control it; when you begin to see everyone as an enemy, everyone as someone who can betray you, you let fear take root. You let it control you rather than the other way around." The words came to my lips, flowing as a stream over rocks. I paused, wondering how they had come to my mind and out through my mouth. But I realized I spoke from within. I spoke of my own involuntary fears, my own turmoil, and put them in Tristan's perspective.

Tristan chuckled. "And what if I choose fear?"

My voice was so quiet I knew only Tristan could hear my words. "Rule in fear, and your people follow in fear. Rule in love, and your people follow in love, in loyalty." My fingers flitted over the now-familiar leather of my sword hilt. "You're angry, Tristan. Angry and bitter. I don't claim to know all you went through as a child, what led you to this moment right now, but it's not too late to change."

Or is it? I knew that I didn't know if it was too late, if it was ever too late. I hated him, yet pity had begun to take root the longer I stood here. When at first it had been solely manipulation, now truth had ingrained in my words. *Could he change? Was there hope for even him?*

Tristan went rigid, his posture steely, turmoil lighting a fire in his eyes. A bird chirped in the distance, a lonesome sound in the waking hours of morning, gone before it had quite begun. The air felt warm, though I knew it to be cold. I glanced again over Tristan's shoulder to the men beyond. All remained on horseback—I stiffened—all but two. Haniel stood at the forefront, his hand heavy on the shoulder of a slight, hooded figure. He avoided me, instead watching Tristan.

When I returned my attention to Tristan, I was surprised to see a smile flickering about the corners of his lips.

"Juliet, what would you do now if you held the life of a friend in the palm of your hand?"

"What?" I asked, my muscles tensing. My eyes flicked to the small, hooded figure again. A knot grew in the pit of my stomach.

"What will you do?" Tristan raised a hand.

Over his shoulder there was movement. I shifted to the side and watched as Haniel shoved the slight person forward.

Tristan turned and strode back the few yards to join Haniel. Grasping the hooded figure's upper arm, he dragged them toward me. I took a step forward of my own volition.

Where was Adnan? Hirose?

Tristan halted a few feet in front of me. "Well, what would you do if, so clearly, you could feel the responsibility of a life in your hands?"

I couldn't move as I stared, spellbound at the small figure.

"If, with their death," Tristan continued, his voice like steel, "you felt the pain, horror, and terror at what you have done? Would you break? How far would you go?"

A shiver wracked my spine. "Tristan, what—"

"Do you care for her?" he asked as he yanked the hood off.

Dark hair spilled across a face. The figure blinked wide eyes and looked up, the hair cascading back like a wave.

I froze, my teeth clenching. *Emi, Emi, Emi,* I wanted to scream. *How? Why?* It couldn't be possible, yet it was. She stood there, her slight figure bent with the pressure of Tristan's grip, the tight gag in her mouth stifling any sound, and her cheeks drawn and pale. Everyone and everything blurred in that moment.

"This would not be the first time someone has died for you," Tristan said with a sardonic lilt.

In a haze, I swung my head up. "Kin," I murmured. *She hadn't died for me.* Yet I knew she was who he meant.

"Not just her. There are others whose deaths lie at your door. You have not figured it out?" His brows rose and he winked. "Who else, Juliet? Who else?"

The village. My mind raced. *Tristan, the messenger, Mari and her family.* The web grew as my mind connected the dots. "Mari and her family, Haniel's family. You were responsible."

"Responsible? Was I?"

I knew then it was true. Tears misted my eyes. Images flashed, vivid memories flying across my mind like a slideshow on fast-forward.

"I was not responsible, Juliet. You were. Yours may not have been the hand that struck the blow, but it was because of you. Their deaths are on your hands, not mine."

"Why?" I asked, my voice breaking.

Tristan shook his head, his hand laying over his chest. "I did not want to, but it had to be done."

"Why!" I exclaimed, taking another step forward. "They followed you; they loved you."

"You needed something to jolt you into action," Tristan explained with a shrug. He tightened his grip on Emi. "Their deaths were a necessary sacrifice to ready you. It would have taken far too long otherwise."

Tears threatened to spill down my cheeks. "How do you justify that?"

"War calls for sacrifices, for hard decisions. I would not be a good leader if I did not have to make those calls." He sighed and glanced down at Emi, the gag in her mouth keeping her from uttering more than moans. "You are right, Juliet, I am not perfect. But at least I have the strength to do what I think needs to be done, just as I am about to do. I know who I am and what I am. Have you ever killed anyone, Juliet?" His scrutiny pierced me.

"I—" *The battle. The men I killed, some but boys.* I blinked away the red before my eyes.

"How are you so different?" Tristan's tone slithered through my ears like a serpent, forcing me to look at him as though he held some sort of sway over me. A sliver of fear wormed its way through me, cutting through my heart like a knife. We played this game, but there was still something I didn't know, that I didn't understand. It was there, lurking in his look, in the smile curving his lips.

His blue eyes sparkled. "Even now, you need another push, Juliet."

Something glittered in his hand, catching the slightest ray of sun as it broke through the clouds, dazzling my eyes with its light. A knife.

"No!" I screamed, all the pent-up rage, fear, and hopelessness breaking through, giving strength and speed as I leapt forward, even as everything slowed down, time stilling with clarity. I saw the smile formed on Tristan's face, the maniacal gleam of his eyes, the force of his arm as he shoved Emi to her knees, tears streaming down her young face, unwavering even through the glassy stare. My feet weren't fast enough. *I* wasn't fast enough. The knife rose in the air, held within Tristan's grasp, and fell with a quick twist.

Emi's eyes widened as a thin red line formed across her neck. Blood, bright and thick, blossomed as her life drained from her body.

A scream ripped through the air, sending shivers across my aching body, but I didn't know where it came from. I didn't care where it came from. All I could see through the blurry haze in front of me was Tristan, still grinning, and Emi's body slumping as he let go, and she crumpled.

It wasn't until I tried to speak and felt the hoarseness in my throat that I realized the scream had been mine. The long grass tore at my legs, but I reached Tristan and raised my fist before I knew what I was about. He stayed still, barely moving as my fist impacted his chest. His face tilted as he looked at me and grabbed my shoulders like a lion pouncing. Strength rippled through his grip, and I felt fragile and broken already.

No tears fell down my cheeks.

He twisted me around, holding me within an iron grasp as he forced my head toward Emi's body lying in the grass. "You are a weakness, Juliet. You have been and always will be. You were right in what you said, but you were also wrong. It is too late for me. And you," he murmured, his arms tightening until I gasped. "Your choice is no choice at all. You should not have contacted me. You should not have come." His voice grew in intensity until he spoke in a cold fury. "I cannot live knowing you will not have me. I cannot survive with you by my side, weakening me, just as I cannot survive if I let you go. You have become a problem."

Bile rose in my throat as my gut twisted in disgust and fear, but panic also took root, taking charge of my irrational thoughts and turning them into resilience. I tried to wrench myself out of his grasp, but he grabbed my neck with one hand and shoved the back of my legs, forcing me to my knees in front of him. His large hands gripped my throat, squeezing tight as he took my life in his hands.

"I am sorry, Juliet. But this is the best way, for both of us."

I looked up, staring into the familiar blue of his eyes, unable to say anything as I tried to breathe. Spots danced before me, the edges of my vision blackening, the sounds of his breathing fading until I heard nothing, but still I saw the sheen of tears glittering. *Tears.* He was crying.

It had all happened so fast, and he was too strong. My brain grew fuzzy, and my vision was but a dim haze. I stopped struggling, having no more strength to do so; I couldn't breathe as pain lanced across my throat and my head ached with stuffy thickness.

A shout echoed across the open plateau. More than one. Boots rustled through the long grass. Without warning, I was flung to the ground. I lay there, the scratchiness of the grass tickling my face as I gasped, trying to force as much air into my lungs as possible. I drew my hands to my throat, wincing at the raw tenderness there. It hurt to breathe; it hurt not to breathe. Images danced before me, but they were fuzzy. Sound began to return, a slight buzzing in my ears, nothing distinguishable. I didn't move, trying not to succumb to the darkness that opened for me, still threatening to draw me deep into its depths.

So many figures and flashes of light.

The void began to recede as my breathing returned to normal. The buzzing changed as noise filtered in as through a distant tunnel, building into a cacophony of sounds, but one voice stood above all the rest.

Adnan.

I heaved and turned my head slowly, watching him as he ran toward me, but though I knew it was his voice, I couldn't process what he shouted. The seconds ticked by. He was almost to me. Looking up, I saw the sky through slits, the gray clouds enveloping the expanse like a blanket, flitting about and giving the motion of descending.

Someone dropped to their knees, and a hand waved over my eyes before going to smooth my hair away from my face. Each blink lasted a lifetime, but I saw him hovering, a frown marring his features.

"Juliet."

I heard him. The word waded in, misty and far away, but I heard him. I opened my lips. They were gummy and dry.

"Don't speak," Adnan ordered. He lifted me up into his arms, and my head lolled against his shoulder. My lips parted, but when I tried to talk, pain cut across my throat. After several long strides, he laid me down on the ground and crouched next to me.

"I'll be fine," I managed in a croaky whisper. Fire ripped through my throat as I spoke.

"Shh," Adnan hushed, worry etched into his face.

All I wanted to do was erase that concern. "That's how you know," I said, managing a tiny grin even through the pain. "You ... hate it when—I—say that." I had to pause between each word as it left my lips.

Adnan's features softened. "You're right. Maybe I should've left you on the ground back there. Can you sit up?" His hands hadn't left me, dancing over my arms as though if he let go, I would disappear.

I nodded, but as he helped me rise, a wave of dizziness passed over me and I fell back. I shook my head, trying to rid it of the bug that buzzed around my ear before realizing it wasn't a bug. All sounds had faded into the background, and everything was quiet. "I can't hear anything," I panicked.

"It's not you," he muttered. "It's over." He shifted to the side so I could see. Hirose and some of his men rounded up the survivors, whilst others began piling the dead. The dead. Emi's body lay in the grass, so silent and still I knew she was gone. My breath caught in my chest, and a shuddering gasp ripped from me.

"Juliet!" Adnan exclaimed, fear radiating from that single word.

From my name. I didn't look at Adnan. All I could see was Emi's face pale with fear as she looked at me, as Tristan raised the knife and ended her life in front of me, and I could do nothing—she was gone. *Another life gone.* An excruciating pain ricocheted in my neck and spread until it engulfed me. Sobs wracked my body as the tears came. *She can't be dead. She can't, she's not ... it isn't possible.* The words played in my mind, coming from all directions, yet though my brain told me one thing, my eyes and my heart told me another. I didn't even feel Adnan's arms around me, pulling me into his embrace as my body shuddered from the force of grief. My throat felt raw and strained, but it wasn't enough to keep me from crying.

Adnan ran a hand over my hair in gentle motions, and after time passed, I began to grow calmer. Sobs turned into simple tears, which turned into hiccups. He murmured into my ear, but I couldn't hear the words. They were muffled, but his voice was soothing. And the scent. He smelled of fresh rain, earth—the outdoors. I sniffled again. He shifted and I saw a glimpse over his shoulder—Tristan's fair hair standing out amongst the darker heads of his men.

He survived.

I stiffened.

He knelt on the grass, unswerving in his glare.

Adnan let go of me and gripped my face in his hands. "Juliet, don't look at him. Don't think of him. Not right now."

"Adnan, I don't feel anything." I reached out a hand as though to anchor myself to him but began pulling it back before I could.

He grabbed my hand and gripped it. "Juliet, you're in shock. You're not in your right mind. You need rest." His arm came around me.

The world tilted and spun around me, and my vision grew hazy again. "Adnan—"

"Hellfire," he exclaimed. "Don't speak."

I couldn't have spoken if I tried. The blackness pulled me inwards again, and I gave myself to it.

Chapter Thirty-One

My throat was on fire. It ached, filling my mouth with a dry and tight feeling. I blinked, my eyelashes fluttering. It was so quiet. The sky above was blue. Gray clouds drifted across the expanse. It looked like spring. I struggled to disentangle my hand from the blankets.

"Juliet." Adnan leaned over me, his hair tied back at the nape of his neck. "Don't speak. Here, drink this." He helped me sit up and handed me a mug with steam curling up from the surface. "It will help you wake up, and it'll soothe your throat."

I nodded and took a sip of the hot liquid. "Thanks," I croaked.

Adnan leaned back on his heels, his finger tapping his thigh. "What were you thinking?"

I lowered the cup and stared at him. "What do you mean?"

"You didn't follow my orders—" He took a deep breath. "Do you realize he could've killed you? He almost did, and would have if he'd chosen a quicker way, one in which we would not have been able to get there in time. As it was, you were farther away than we'd planned. And even then, you have Haniel to thank. He overheard Tristan admit to orchestrating the death of his family, and he was the one who threw Tristan off you. I didn't think you were alive at first—you were so still—but then I saw you trying to breathe. I thought I wouldn't be able to get to you fast enough."

I swallowed, tensing as I listened to the raw emotion filling Adnan's voice.

"Why did you approach him? You let him control the situation from the beginning."

"I just ..." I sighed. "I knew he wouldn't come. I had to go to him. And then later, I thought maybe I could get him to change his mind."

"You know how dangerous he is."

"Yes, I do. I *do*, Adnan. I know better than most. But I had to try. It wasn't a plan, you know. It just all happened!" I ignored the ache in my throat. "I know Emi's death is on me. I know it's my fault." The words almost choked me. "She was my maid, Adnan. She was my friend, and I failed her. I wanted her to escape, and instead, I orchestrated her death."

"Juliet—"

I fought against the waves of sadness. "She wouldn't have died if it wasn't for me."

"Juliet," Adnan snapped. "That young girl died at Tristan's hand, not yours. There wasn't anything you could do."

"I could've done nothing." But I knew the words were false.

"We all live wondering what we could've done differently. If you take her death on yourself, you'll let her down. You have to live on for her. For all of them."

My chest constricted. "But what if it's too hard?"

"It won't be, not for you." Adnan locked his eyes on me. "You can overcome this, and you'll come out on the other end even stronger for it. Don't forget her, but don't let her death consume you."

I let out a shaky laugh even as I felt a pang of guilt for laughing when I should've been crying. "And the guilt? It hurts so much I don't want to feel anything. It's like there's a void waiting for me, Adnan, away from all the pain and sadness, away from heartache—"

Hands gripped my shoulders and shook me. "Juliet, don't you dare hide away from feeling anything. Emotion is powerful. It is painful, it is beautiful, but don't you dare escape." He paused and continued with a gentler tone. "That is the coward's way out, and you are no coward. You go down that road and Emi's life, Mari's life, will have been for nothing." He loomed in front of me. "Promise me."

"I promise," I whispered. "I'm sorry."

"Stay strong, Juliet." His words echoed inside my mind, going back through memories until I heard Kin saying those very words, until I heard Emi saying them too.

So many. So many voices.

I straightened my shoulders and glanced toward where Tristan and his men sat on the cold ground in a ragged group. "I won't pull myself down. I won't let him win."

Adnan turned to face them as well. "He's already lost. He lost before he'd even met you."

I opened my mouth to speak, but someone interjected.

"Perhaps you two want to carry this conversation on elsewhere?"

Neither of us had heard Hirose approach.

I glared at him, blinking back tears, but Adnan relaxed his posture.

"There's no need," he said, not bothering to hide a hint of irritation.

"Good, because all you're doing is entertaining Tristan and his men. They can see you from where we have them."

Adnan frowned and glanced at me as though taking in the emotion shining upon my face and in my slumped posture.

A drop of rain hit my face, and I looked up at the sky. The clouds that had lain in the sky high above us were darker now.

"Looks like we're in for a shower." Adnan looked at Hirose, who still stood there, watching us. "What is it?"

He beckoned. "Come on, we should talk."

Adnan helped me up. The ground swayed beneath my feet. I wasn't in danger of falling, but Adnan's hand didn't leave my arm as we followed Hirose. His hand was a comforting grasp that anchored me.

"We have to talk about what's next," Hirose spoke, gesturing back toward Tristan and the other men. "What do we do with him? With the throne? What do we tell the Ryujin people?"

"Simple," Adnan interrupted. "Put him on trial in front of the nation's judges and whatever comes. We already know what the verdict will be," he added, his voice lowered.

A shiver ran down my spine. "Death?" I asked in a whisper.

Hirose inclined his head. "I could use your help," he admitted to Adnan. "Both of yours. We should be back at Tristan's stronghold by evening tomorrow." He sighed and squared his shoulders. "There will be much to do."

"No," Adnan interjected. "I'm taking Juliet home."

"What?" Hirose and I said at the same time, though in very different tones.

"I'm taking you back home," Adnan repeated, his voice soft. "It's time."

I ignored Hirose's interest as I stared at Adnan. "No—"

"You've been here long enough. You can't live here forever; you don't even know how long it's been since you left home." His hand dropped from my arm. "I know you miss your family, and the guilt will eat you up inside if you stay. Besides, this isn't your world."

As through a haze, I saw Hirose walk away. I looked up at Adnan, my eyes misting. It was too much. *But why?* Why did I feel as though a hole was opening in my heart? A breaking heart that had just been mending, an emptying soul that had just begun to fill back up. *This is wrong.*

"Juliet," Adnan murmured. "It *is* time."

"What about Saya? I can't leave without saying goodbye." I knew I grasped at straws, but I didn't care.

Adnan's jaw clenched. "I'm sorry, but we have no idea where she is. Hirose told me she made it out, but they parted ways. She accompanied the other women—who knows where. Hirose will give her your goodbyes. I think it's best for you if you leave this world. You've known only heartache here," he ended, shifting on the balls of his feet as though unsure of what to expect from me.

Does he think I'll attack him? I took a deep breath. "But who will I talk to? Adnan, I can't say anything about this to anyone back home. Not to my family, not to my friends. I'll be alone." *Do I not want to go home?* The thought tore through me.

"We're never alone, Juliet." He took my hand and ran his thumb in slow circles over my skin. "Even when we feel ourselves in the darkest place imaginable, we are never alone. Never forget that."

I crossed my arms and watched the sun dip under the distant tree line. Its bright rays shot across the sky, streaking it with magnificent and regal orange shades tinged with pink. The light bloomed amongst the edges of the clouds before being lost in the roiling grayness.

He stood next to me, also watching the sunset. "We'll rest here tonight, but we leave in the morning."

"But what harm would it be to stay a little longer?" I asked, holding my breath as I waited for his answer.

"So that you can see Tristan stand trial? So you can see his execution?" He shook his head. "There's nothing for you here. You need to go home. Watching will not bring you peace." He pulled on my hand, and I let him lead me back to Hirose. We were silent. There were no more words.

What can I say?

Hirose turned his gaze on me, his figure dwarfed by Adnan's. "Will you leave?"

"Yes."

"When?"

"In the morning," Adnan answered. "I'll take her to the portal."

A sad smile crossed Hirose's pale face. "Then tonight we'll eat, and tomorrow we shall say our goodbyes. It will be a sad parting, but one that was inevitable, I suppose." He glanced up at Adnan, and I frowned at the unspoken conversation that passed between them. "Come, sit. I'll have the men bring us some food, and we shall not talk of what has happened here. Tonight will be only getting to know one another as friends so that we may part as such ... at least, that is my hope," he added with a sad smile.

⤜⤛⤛⤛

Darkness surrounded me like an enveloping gray blanket, lightening as the sun began its slow rise over the horizon. A deep breath entered my lungs, bringing in fresh, crisp air and heightening my senses. I stared down at Adnan's figure, bundled in a cloak and stretched out on the ground before my feet. He didn't move a muscle, and neither did I.

The rest of the men also lay strewn about, all tired from talking late into the night. I didn't look, but I could feel the sentry's eyes on me. They'd been on me since I stood up, but he hadn't made a move to stop me.

The rain had stopped for now, but its cold wetness had seeped into each and every one of us. I looked down at the figure before me again, and I reeled back as I saw Tristan blink as he stared up at me.

"Juliet."

I bit back a gasp and clenched my shirt, but my mouth wouldn't move. Tristan maneuvered himself into a sitting position, his cloak falling away to reveal bound hands.

He smiled. "You did not have to come say goodbye."

I forced myself to bend my knees, loosen my stance. "I didn't."

"Then why are you here?" His words fell like a caress on my skin, and I shivered. "You cannot stay away from me, can you?" Even in the darkness, the blue of his irises stared straight into me.

"There was no choice," I spat, my voice shaking. "I didn't have to make a choice. There was only one way for me. How could you think I would ever, ever follow you? You only care about yourself, Tristan." I took a deep breath, my heart hammering within my chest like the rapid beating of drums.

His blue eyes gleamed in the glowing embers from the small fire. "And yet you would align yourself with Hirose?"

My lips parted. I hesitated. *He doesn't know.* I shifted to the right a little, throwing his face into shadow as my body blocked the glow from the embers. *He can't know about Hirose.*

"Do you know all he has done in the name of the king?" he spat, all his calm composure gone.

"And what about you?" I challenged, anger driving away the lingering fear. "How many lives have been lost because of you?"

Tristan grinned. "Is that not similar to the same question I had asked you?" He sighed. "It does not matter."

"That's where you're wrong," I murmured, my voice low.

"You do not know how wrong *you* are. It has all mattered, Juliet." Tristan strained against his bonds as though forgetting they were there. He relaxed. "Every decision I have made has mattered. Kin had to die so that you would be spurred toward what I needed you for. I had to act a traitor so that I could build up the drama before killing Cruelon, thus cementing me as a hero in the eyes of the people." His breathing quickened, his chest rising and falling with each breath. "And Drielle had to die so that she would not give away the final game."

Drielle. Time seemed to freeze. *His orders.*

"Yes, Juliet," Tristan purred. "I killed her."

"Why?" I gasped, my mind racing. "Why kill your own seer?"

"Because she finally figured it out. She put the pieces together because of her visions." Tristan gritted his teeth. "There was no other choice. I wanted her to join me, but she refused. So I called away her guards and slipped back. She did not see that coming. Her visions did not show her death." He laughed, a low chuckle that drifted into the night air.

So many. I closed my eyes, breathing in to calm my racing heart.

"And while we're talking about deaths—"

I started.

"There is another. You now have another death on your conscience, Juliet." Tristan cocked his head to the side. "How does it feel? Did you think of your brother? Do you think of him now?"

I shook my head from side to side, unable to block out his words.

"Two deaths on your conscience," he crooned in a sing-song way.

Stop, stop! I cried inside my mind. I reached up and clutched my head. "You didn't have to kill her," I whispered.

"Oh, but I did." Tristan's teeth flashed as his lips opened. "She was my revenge if you made the wrong decision."

A mocking laugh escaped me. "You were going to kill me no matter what."

Tristan leaned forward, his broad shoulders straining. "You could have had everything; I would have shared everything with you. Is not that what marriage is all about? One flesh, one body, sharing in all of life's ups and downs, through the good, the bad, and the ugly?" He gestured to himself as his eyes traveled up and down me.

I felt sick to my stomach. "No, you're wrong. Marriage should be something good, something purer than anything you could ever imagine, Tristan." My voice grew stronger as I spoke. "You would never understand what marriage is because you have no morals."

Tristan flexed his wrists against the ropes. I jerked back even as my hand reached out in front of me as though to form a barrier.

"Emi died because of you," he snarled. "She died because of your failures, your mistakes, your choices. You have no one to blame but yourself."

I cringed, shrinking in on myself as his words battered me. "She was just a girl—"

"She knew the risks when she became Cruelon's spy, when her actions brought about Kin's death, when her actions caused your imprisonment. And later, when she regretted her choices, she risked all to absolve herself of her past and to atone for her sins. Why else do you think she stayed to help you free the prisoners, to free yourself from me?"

No. It's not true. My breathing quickened. *She was questioned by Cruelon. She wouldn't have done anything to harm Kin.* Trembling, I felt my throat tighten. *She knew I would've lied about the wardrobe malfunction.* I struggled to regain control. *She could have found out Kin was passing messages back and forth.*

"You're lying," I said, but the words sounded weak and trivial.

"No, you know I am telling the truth." He made as though to stand up and grunted in frustration at his bound feet. "Juliet, Emi had been passing information to Cruelon, and thus to me, from the very beginning. Did you ever wonder how Cruelon knew Kin was a traitor? I absolved Emi of her guilt. I took her life, saving her from living a life of self-doubt, uncertainty, and regret. Now she lives on, who knows where, but she no longer has to live with her mistakes. I saved her." A vein pulsed in his neck.

"You're lying," I blurted out.

"No, and you know it. Why do you think she stayed to help you? I think she felt guilt at Kin's death. I do not think she expected it. I think it rocked her to her core. She was just a girl, after all," he added, watching me closely.

My throat ached worse. "You're despicable."

"Am I? She no longer suffers."

Tears spilled from my eyes. "I suppose you say that for everyone you have killed?"

Tristan shrugged, then nodded. "No, not all. Some, yes, but others were necessary pieces to remove."

A harsh cackle escaped my lips, and my next breath bordered on a sob as I said, "You'll answer for your crimes, Tristan. For all of them."

Tristan's hair rustled in the breeze. "Do not be so sure of that. Come here, Juliet."

I shook my head.

"Lean down. I have one last thing to tell you. One last secret."

What secret? My foot tapped on the ground. *What does he have to say?* I bit my lip.

I strode forward and bent down, my left hand touching the ground while my right stayed put in its sling. *What are you doing?* The thought tore through my mind.

Tristan's gleaming smile filled my vision. "You will want to know this," he whispered, drawing me in closer. His breath whispered against my face, but before I could move, his hands shot forward to clasp mine. I bit back a scream as pain wracked my injured wrist, sending shooting waves into my fingers and up my forearm. Dizziness washed over me as my head swam.

"Let her go. Now." Adnan's voice bit through the air like a rumbling thunderclap. Tristan's grip dug in as he pulled me even closer.

"Let me go," I growled.

He pressed harder. The pain worsened and I yelped. He loosened his grip but didn't pull away completely. "Juliet, you loved me. You can love me again."

"No, I never loved you." I shook my head, tilting it back a little as I felt his breath on my face. "I liked you, but it was never more, and now I feel sick at the thought of what I used to feel for you. You sicken me, Tristan. You are twisted. I thought there was hope for you, but if there is, I don't see it. You are so lost I'm not sure you'll ever find your way back, even with help." As I finished speaking, I tried to pull away again, but my wrist screamed in resistance. I swayed as lightheadedness bowled me over.

Adnan's hand came down on Tristan's shoulder and I saw the glint of steel as a knife pressed in close to Tristan's ribs. "Let her go," he said, his tone brooking no argument.

Tristan released me. I wrapped my arms around myself and stumbled back.

"You hate me," Tristan stated with a maniacal smile. "Admit it. Feel the hatred coursing through your veins."

I stiffened as Tristan smiled again but felt a sense of relief as Adnan let Tristan slump back to the ground and walked over to join me.

"Well, *Unknown*," Tristan spat, his eyes glaring daggers. "What are you going to do?"

"Nothing," Adnan answered. "You'll have everything coming that you deserve."

"So you will kill me?" Tristan jeered. "Why not do it now?"

"No, I won't kill you, but I can't say the same for Hirose."

Quiet footsteps crossed the grass as Hirose came up and joined us.

"You'll be judged for your crimes and will receive whatever punishment instituted," Adnan continued, nodding to Hirose. "But it won't be by my hands. This is the last time you'll ever see Juliet—or me—again." Without another word, he tightened his hold around my shoulders and nudged me away.

"You do not know that for sure!" Tristan yelled, almost hysterical.

I stopped, glancing back over my shoulder at him.

"Do not forget what I said, Juliet." Tristan locked his gaze on me. "Do not forget."

Hirose laid a hand on his shoulder, nodding to me to go.

"One last secret," Tristan mouthed.

"Come, Juliet," Adnan urged, putting his arm around my shoulders. "He's not worth it."

He's right. I let him lead me away. *Another secret doesn't matter.* After a few steps, I looked over my shoulder at Tristan. "You were wrong. I don't hate you."

His eyes widened.

"I pity you. Your heart is filled with darkness because you gave up to it. You have no one to blame but yourself, and now you'll answer for it. We all struggle, Tristan, we all make mistakes, but you have gone so far you've buried yourself. Goodbye."

Adnan led the way, his arm still wrapped around me protectively. It must have been some time before Adnan halted. I looked around with some confusion as I realized we'd left the rest of the group far behind and far out of earshot.

Adnan turned to face me and stared at me until I shifted on my feet from the force of his quiet stare. "What were you thinking?"

I opened my lips to speak, but before I could, he took a step forward.

"Juliet, you don't—" A groan escaped his lips, and he ran a hand through his shaggy hair.

A pang filled my heart. His eyes flashed a deeper green, and for a moment, a vulnerable piece of him showed that I saw but rarely. With visible effort, a mask fell over his features, and he returned to his usual self. I sucked in a breath, shocked at the swirling emotions within me.

"Juliet!" Adnan exclaimed, gripping my upper arms.

"I'm fine," I stated, waving a hand. "I was just so mad."

"What?" he queried, his eyebrows raising.

"At Tristan, at everything. I was angry, Adnan," I admitted, staring down at his boots. "I didn't intend to talk to him, and then—how much did you overhear?"

"Enough."

"Did he know you were there?"

Adnan shook his head once. "No. Otherwise, he wouldn't have tried what he did."

My eyes narrowed. "Why did you stay silent?"

He shrugged. "I was curious." He folded his arms and looked across the pasture toward the sun rising in the east. "You're not upset?"

"I am, but I don't hate him, not anymore." I twirled my hair between my fingers. "I woke up, and I just didn't hate him. I don't have enough energy to, or all feeling is drained out of me."

"It didn't, though," Adnan said, stepping closer. "You still feel, Juliet. You told him you pitied him, even after everything he's done."

"Yes, I do pity him; I feel sorry for him, but I'm angrier and more disappointed at myself." I cradled my injured wrist, remembering the conversation, the way it ended ...

"Don't let him get to you," Adnan snapped. Then his eyes widened, and he shook his head. "I'm sorry. Don't let him rule over you even now. You have a good heart and care deeply, and you have to keep living. We all do, no matter what we've done." As he spoke, the air seemed to grow darker and colder somehow.

The sun is rising. Dawn is approaching. I shivered, and Adnan took off his cloak and draped it around my shoulders.

"Come on. Enough for now. You're exhausted. We'll eat and say our final farewells."

"Wait! Do you think Tristan was telling the truth? About Emi?"

"I don't know. It's possible," Adnan admitted. "But we'll never know for sure. Does it really matter?"

I took one last look at the sun rising, throwing pale streaks of orange across the lightening sky. "No, I suppose it doesn't. Not anymore."

Chapter Thirty-Two

Hirose clasped my hand. He let go and fell into a low bow. "It's been an honor, Juliet Barrows. Thank you for everything."

I watched, trembling, as he rose. Heat rose to my cheeks. "I didn't do much."

"You accomplished more than you know. I wish ..." He looked at Adnan. "I wish things could have turned out differently, but I don't expect you to stay." The words were so low I almost didn't catch them, but Adnan stiffened beside me.

Hirose raised my hand to his lips. "Perhaps one day we'll meet again, and I hope in better circumstances."

His words hit me like a thunderbolt. *Why couldn't I come back?*

Adnan shifted beside me and somehow, I knew he guessed what I thought. "You'll do well. Just remember what I told you."

Hirose bowed. "I won't forget. Take care, and thank you."

Adnan brushed against my shoulder. "Let's go."

As I turned, Hirose took a step forward. "Juliet, I'll do everything in my power to find Saya and let her know what happened here. She and any other seers will be left to live in peace and safety."

A slight stinging sensation pricked the back of my eyes. "Don't forget to give her my message."

Hirose held up his clasped hands. "I won't."

Adnan slung a pack over his shoulder. I hesitated, but there was nothing to do but follow. Nothing I could place my finger on. Something felt undone, as though there was still one piece to the puzzle. An invisible piece hanging by a thread right in front of me. I swallowed it down.

"Wait—"

I watched Haniel approach. Somehow he looked far older, as though in one hour years had passed. His hands were bound, and Hirose followed close behind him.

He bowed. "I hope you will forgive me."

I considered his words. Never had we gotten along. He was Tristan's shadow, he had threatened me, and now he was asking for my forgiveness. *Am I angry?* I shook my head. *There isn't anger left in me. Just questions … and sadness.*

"I forgive you, Haniel." I hesitated. *Should I tell him?* My chest rose as I breathed in. "Tristan said he was the one who killed Drielle."

Haniel's expression darkened.

"He had to order the guards away so he wouldn't have any witnesses."

"Why?" he whispered, his posture slumping. Pain filled his face. "So I was the instrument."

"No, Tristan's knife was. You didn't know what you were doing," I added, knowing how it felt to feel responsible for the loss of life. *I still know how it feels.*

"But I didn't question." Haniel gazed at me, a broken man. He inclined his head. "If we don't meet again, Otherworlder, farewell. May you be safe on your journeys."

I took a deep breath. "If you see Saya, let her know the truth. She needs some sort of answer."

"I will." He bowed. "Stay safe."

I watched as he walked back to Hirose. Adnan waited until I rejoined him. After a time, something made me look back. I saw two men watching our retreat—Hirose and Tristan, one standing, the other kneeling, one dark and the other fair. Hirose remained still, but I could almost hear his voice, faint as the breeze carried it our way, but it must have been my imagination. I waved one last farewell.

"Hirose is different and yet the same," I murmured. Adnan kept silent so long I wasn't sure he had heard, but then he spoke.

"He'll be a good king."

My nose wrinkled and I looked up at him. "If you think that, then why don't you like him?"

"It's not that I do or that I don't."

"Then what is it?" I pressed, speeding up to keep up with his long legs.

"He admires you."

I stopped walking and stared. "That's why you don't like him? Because he likes me?" I missed a step and hurried forward to catch up. He grunted, and I couldn't help my lips from splitting into a grin. A sense of relief washed over me as Adnan slowed a bit and I fell into an easy stride.

"It's also how he treated you when he pretended to be me."

I peered into Adnan's face shadowed by his cowl. I hadn't forgotten. Now I knew Adnan hadn't either. I hid a small smile as I looked forward.

"But you're right. I think he will make a good king," Adnan admitted.

I adjusted my arm into a more comfortable position in the swing. This time, watching the ground pass beneath our feet, it was different. This time we weren't running from something or someone. This time there wasn't a rush because our lives were in danger. This time, it was Adnan and me.

I knew we were too far away to make out the camp we'd left behind, but I still couldn't help looking back at the distant ridge. Adnan's boots plunked against the stone plateau. I sighed and turned to follow, but something—a flash of red—caught my eye.

What is that? I shaded my eyes as I peered. A figure in red. *Who ...*

I gasped, and my heart froze within me.

Adnan stopped and strode back to me. "What? What is it?"

My lips opened and closed, and I raised a shaking finger and pointed. Adnan followed my gaze and stiffened.

"What is she doing here?" I gasped out, clutching his sleeve.

Adnan laid his hand over the hilt of his sword. "I don't know," he mused, not taking his eyes off of her.

My feet carried me forward, but Adnan still stood, staring at the distant figure.

"Juliet, wait," he said.

"Adnan, it's Natsumi—"

"Yes, I know. You forget I was there." With a few strides, he caught up to me.

He'd seen her in Cruelon's court, but he didn't know the connection. *He doesn't know.* I kept going.

"Juliet!"

"Adnan," I replied, calling back even as I strode forward. "It's her. She was there when I came through the portal, she was there in Umi no Machi, and then she was in Cruelon's court. She's been there every time." I watched as she walked into the fringe of trees banking the plateau. The trees swallowed her whole. "She's the one none of you recognized, the one you couldn't find."

"That's not possible—"

"It is," I insisted. "I know it's strange. It doesn't make sense. But it's her. I never got a chance to talk to her—we were never alone. Then everything happened, and I forgot. But she's here now. It can't be a coincidence. I have to talk to her. I need answers." The words poured out of me, anxiety filling every nerve. A bird chirped, high overhead, but I filtered it out. Everything around me zoned out and I stopped, turning to face Adnan. "Please."

"Something about this is wrong," he muttered, regarding me with his solemn brown eyes.

I caught a flash of his inner turmoil. He wanted to find out as well, but he didn't want me going with him. And even if he said no, I knew I wouldn't go without him.

He sighed and walked forward. "Fine, yes, let's go."

We broke into a run, Adnan holding my hand, helping to pull me along. My breath came quick and heavy, the blood pounding in my ears. I ignored the dull throbbing in my injured wrist.

We reached the fringe of the woods, the dry sticks crackling beneath our feet, pine needles thrown up with each footstep. Dry leaves crunched underneath us among the sound of the wind dying down. Branches rustled above our heads.

"Why is it so dry here?" I gasped. "It just rained last night."

"We're higher up. Must've not rained up here," Adnan answered, slowing to a walk. He cocked his head as though listening, but I couldn't hear anything. "This way." He didn't wait but headed off deeper into the dense growing trees and the shadowy darkness.

I followed him as closely as I could, stepping where he stepped, concentrating on being as silent as I could. I loosened the folds of my cloak, the coolness sending tingles down my body. *Where is she?* She'd disappeared into the forest like a wraith.

Adnan's movements were stealthy and silent, slow as he listened, his head looking this way and that as he searched for Natsumi.

I reached out and grabbed his shoulder, and he stopped. "There," I whispered. My hair clung to my cheeks, damp with perspiration.

She stood with her back to us, her long scarlet dress hanging about her slim figure, her hair out of its usual bun, rippling in waves down her back.

"Natsumi," Adnan called.

She didn't glance behind but walked on as though she hadn't heard.

"Natsumi, wait!" I yelled, but she disappeared around a tree. Shadows darkened as the forest thickened.

I ran, hearing Adnan's footfalls not far behind me, and burst through the same spot she had been standing, out into a small grove. Shock rippled over me, and I stopped. *The portal.* Adnan careened into me, and I fell forward. His arms caught me around the waist, drawing me back onto my feet.

He grunted. "Sorry. You stopped so suddenly."

"Adnan, it's right here." I gestured, unable to look away. "The tree, it's here. And she went in. She's in there."

"What? I don't understand."

But I remembered. He couldn't see it. The portal, only I had been able to see it ... and now Natsumi. *Who is she? How can she see it?* I took Adnan's hand and pulled him forward. "It's the tree—the portal I came through. Natsumi just climbed up into it. She's up there. It's right here. Give me a leg up." I put my hands on his shoulders, ignoring the suspicion in his eyes, but he did as I asked. As I felt my feet land on the rough bark of the small opening, I glanced back down at Adnan. "I know you can't see me, but trust me."

His eyes searched.

I looked around. Was that a flash of black? A glimpse of scarlet? I didn't wait to see if Adnan joined me. My feet moved almost against my will, carrying me forward into the twisting roots. The scent of dirt encasing them rose into my nostrils.

"Juliet!"

"Come on," I replied, not looking back. "I have to find her." A fly buzzed close to my ear, startling me. I bit back a cry and ignored the falling earth loosened from the roots by my hurried pace. "Natsumi," I called. I listened, but I couldn't hear any footfalls.

"Juliet!"

Adnan sounded distant, and I couldn't see him either. The mass of roots seemed to have gotten bigger, more complex—like a maze. Memories crashed upon me. I opened my lips, but then all thoughts of responding vanished as I stepped into the center. It had grown bigger. Longer, but still narrow. Natsumi stood so close, and yet there, at the end of the small path, her back was to me.

"Natsumi." The single word hovered in the air. I had spoken her name. I breathed in, waiting. The silence was so still.

Natsumi turned, her brilliant brown eyes staring into my own blue ones. She smiled, but it was soft and sad. "A long time has passed since we first met," she said, her voice low and melodic, "but here we are. Such decisions, changing of the times, crossing and uncrossing, and they all lead here. So many ways it all could have gone—so many directions, some known and some unknown." She lingered on the last few words as though rolling them around her mouth.

Some know and some unknown. I blinked and took a single step closer. The roots were firm beneath my feet. "Natsumi, why are you here?"

"There are many different lives to be led, many that could be led, some that are, and some that aren't." Natsumi tilted her head and smiled. "My story is not to be told, not quite yet."

"Natsumi—"

She held up a hand. "No. We shall see each other again, but not here, and perhaps not for some time. Then you shall know my story, my life, who I am."

My lips parted as I searched for what to say. "I've never met anyone like you."

A smile creased the corners of Natsumi's eyes, a softer smile than I had ever seen on her face. "That may be."

"I have questions," I continued, sliding my damp hand down my tunic.

Natsumi smiled. "As does everyone, but we don't always receive the answers we seek. You will receive some of them in time." Natsumi looked up through the maze of roots stretching their fingers above our heads. "Juliet, there are things you can control, and there are things you cannot. Do not try to control that which is uncontrollable. People are broken down so that they may be built back up." She breathed in deeply.

"You're talking about me."

"Perhaps." Natsumi looked at me. "Do you think I am?"

"I don't know. I don't even know what you're talking about."

"You figured it out." She nodded, an approving smile curving her full lips. "Beware the pretender. Well done."

I reeled back. *Was that a test?* "Why didn't you ever tell Cruelon—" The words died in my mouth. *I wasn't the pretender. Tristan was.* The realization sent my heart pounding. I took another step forward. "It was Tristan."

Natsumi's eyes softened. "Yes."

"Why didn't you tell me if you knew?" I accused, waving a hand through the air. *Lives could have been saved.*

The smile left Natsumi's eyes. Her ivory skin lightened a shade. "It wasn't for me to tell."

She knew the day I arrived. She warned me. I shifted on the balls of my feet, feeling the scabbard of my katana bump against my thigh. "All you're giving me is more questions. I don't understand."

She laughed, a light, bell-like sound. "You will in time if you let yourself. Don't close yourself off, Juliet. Remember what I have said. And let Adnan help you, just as you have helped him."

"What do you mean?"

A breeze wove through the branches, bringing with it the familiar scent of warm bread and cinnamon. Natsumi's hair waved in the breeze. "Like I said, Juliet, no human is meant to have all the answers nor to know everything, but you shall have some answers, in time. Be patient." She backed away, still facing me.

"Wait—" I took a step forward and stumbled, reaching out as I tried to regain my balance. I saw the ground rushing up beneath me, and then my hand met a knobby root, suspending my downward motion for a brief second.

The ground opened beneath me—and I fell. Déjà vu, this time for real. I didn't scream. It was almost as though, in that moment, I had already accepted the inevitable. Time slowed.

I was going home.

Home.

But my limbs flailed, frenzied, as I was unable to fight the panic as I fell through the thick blackness. Cold air rushed across my face, hands, and body, and I blinked, but there was still nothing but darkness. Flashes of memory from the first time appeared before my eyes, but my brain didn't want to function. I couldn't remember how long it had seemed before it was all over—I didn't know.

Something touched me, and the pent-up scream ripped out of me, a shrill sound as it whipped away in the darkness. Flecks of dirt filled my open mouth. The air was thick with it.

A hand gripped me, this time keeping its hold. Someone was here with me. I couldn't hear anything, but I had the vague idea that someone had yelled something. I tried to slow my thrashing movements, reaching up to grab the unseen hand, then feeling arms encircle me. The rough material of a thick cloak blew against my face, almost suffocating me in its folds. But the smell, I knew that smell. Musty earth and rain.

Adnan—the Unknown.

There, below us, an iota of white light appeared. With every second, it grew larger and brighter, lightening the surrounding tunnel of earth. The light reached up to encircle us.

Home.

THE
STORY WILL
CONTINUE
IN
BOOK 3
OF THE
ROOTS
TRILOGY

Anne Elizabeth lives in the beautiful PNW with her husband and two children. Inspired by the grandeur of the world around her and the works of authors such as Tolkien and Lewis, Anne joyfully gifts her imagination and storytelling as she establishes her niche in familiar genres. Along with her literary pursuits, she enjoys adventures outside, a variety of arts and crafts, and is an avid board gamer.

Instagram: @anneelizabethwrites
Facebook: @AnneElizabethAuthor

www.ingramcontent.com/pod-product-compliance
Lightning Source LLC
Chambersburg PA
CBHW020247010826

48973CB00006B/1691